Laura's Story

by Julie Larade

 **FriesenPress**

Suite 300 – 990 Fort Street
Victoria, BC, Canada V8V 3K2
www.friesenpress.com

ISBN
978-1-4602-5273-4 (Hardcover)
978-1-4602-5274-1 (Paperback)
978-1-4602-5275-8 (eBook)

1. Fiction, Historical

Distributed to the trade by The Ingram Book Company

Dedication

To my parents, my baby sister Annette, Hélène LeBlanc, Margaret and Jérome Doucet and Luce Yvonne Larade.

And to Alexa, Alia and Lucie.

Table of Contents

Acknowledgements

I am forever grateful to all the friends, acquaintances and total strangers who so graciously helped me with the research of this book:

Margaret Ramard, Bernice Doucet-Pierce, Corinne Chiasson, Bernie L. Chiasson, Effie Dunn, Fraser Dunn, Lucille Mahoney, Amélia Roach, Sylvia and Albert Poirier, Diane Chiasson, Yvonne Poirier, Gladys LeLièvre, Janice Ferguson, David and Hilda Poirier, Germaine Fiset, Carol MacDonnell, Edith MacDonnell, Jean Naus, Aurea Gillis, Anne LeBlanc- Coady Thompkins Library, April Samson- NSCC Port Hawkesbury, Elaine MacLean- Reference Library St. Francis Xavier University, Maggie Neilson- Dalhousie University, James Rothwell- Sexton Design and Technology Library Dalhousie University, Nadine Frazer-Bate- Eastern Mainland Housing Authority, Writers' Federation of Nova Scotia and ALIS.

Marilyn Groves' cover illustration captures exactly everything I see in Laura. I am truly grateful for her talent and insight.

A sincere thank you to Jim St-Clair and to Pat O'Neil for their basic tips in book writing; to Marie AuCoin for her sound advice, especially for reminding me to "put meat on the bones"; to Marilyn Harrison and Hélèna Larade-AuCoin for their valuable feedback.

I am especially grateful to my mentor, the late Domithilde AuCoin, who always encouraged my efforts and shared my passion for writing, and to my editor, Jenna Kalinsky, for her probing questions, her expertise in the writing field, and her unfailing attentiveness and interest in my story. With Jenna's guidance, *Laura's Story* has indeed become the book I was inspired to write.

Un gros merci to Angele, Annette and Gilles for their love and confidence in me and to Alexa for prompting me to look deeper into my story with her persistent questions of what, where, why, when and how.

Lastly, to my devoted husband for believing in me, and for his encouragement and unwavering support throughout this project, merci du fond du coeur, my love.

Author's Note

My life has been deeply influenced by my parents, my step-grandmother and the Acadian history, culture and region. These are what have shaped me and my world, and as such, are what came to define the shape of this project.

My father was an avid storyteller who loved to embellish his tales while basking in our laughter. As he grew older I thought of recording these funny and sometimes sad anecdotes, but busy with a growing family, I put it off. When our nest was empty and I was retired, I woke up one morning with a powerful desire to put my pen to work.

While both my maternal and paternal grandparents passed on before I was born, my step-grandmother was an enormous inspiration to me. I cherished her enthusiasm for life and her determination to survive in the face of adversity. Her quiet and peaceful disposition along with her charm and wit were actually not that different from those of my father, one of her many step-sons. My step-grandmother was indeed the spark that brought this story to life.

Proud of my roots and fascinated by our ancestors' untold stories, I wanted to pay tribute to their efforts, to their bodies made muscular from hard labour, to their determination despite disappointment or hardship, to the land that has managed to survive amid weather and blight. These people were shaped by the land, by history, and by their daily toil, yet are still known and remembered for their good humour and feisty character, all of which makes me proud to be of such a legacy.

I am of this place: the land, the ocean, the people. It is my home and my heritage. This book celebrates all of this. Laura, a heroine in her own quiet right, embodies the strength and fortitude of my step-grandmother, and both continue to inspire me every day.

Laura's Story is a fictionalized account of a very real people and time. My wish is that you enjoy reading the book as much as I enjoyed writing it.

"I shall pass through this world but once. Any good therefore that I can do or any kindness that I can show to any human being, let me do it now. Let me not defer or neglect it, for I shall not pass this way again."

— Stephen Grellet

Chapter One
Early Days

It could have been fate, or an accident, but while climbing a ladder to wash her English employer's second story windows during the summer of 1938, Laura's mother, Joséphine Boudreau slipped and fell hard onto the ground, slipping quickly into delirium, then coma, and finally death.

Having first lost her father some years before and now her mother, Laura felt entirely alone in the world. Her sister had left three years before to marry and move to Antigonish, some 100 miles south of Inverness on the mainland, which as far as Laura was concerned was as far as the moon. Though Peggy and her husband George came as quickly as they could, by the time they arrived, the burial was long over.

Peggy convinced Laura that moving to Antigonish would be the best thing. "We'll be together again," she said. Laura had to admit she yearned to be with her sister again. Growing up, though they had looked so different as to not seem related with Peggy being so tall and angular with long unruly black hair, crooked teeth, and freckles, and Laura being shorter and rounder with chocolate curls and dimples, they had been inseparable. When Peggy left, Laura had cried until her eyes felt boiled. She'd felt insecure as if she'd lost a part of herself.

Though Laura didn't particularly want to start over in a new place where she wouldn't know anyone but her sister, with no skills or prospects for taking care of herself, she saw it was for the best. She packed her meager belongings and the few things her mother had cherished: her rosary and cross, the silver butter dish her father had given her on their first anniversary, her wedding dress, and her mother's wool, knitting needles and sewing kit into a bundle, and put the satchel into George's red wagon. As George pulled away, she felt an awful, crushing ache come over her. She steadied herself in the back of the wagon, waiting for her cold sweat to subside then turned for one last look at her home. In a flash, she remembered her young childhood in the little fishing village of Chéticamp, in Cape Breton, Nova Scotia, their carefree life there living in her grandparents' tiny but cozy home. Then after her father took a mining job in the Scottish town of Inverness and rented a Company house, she remembered the warmth and love she had felt there from her parents. Even after her father was killed and her mother had chosen to remain in Inverness, working as housekeeper, the small and rustic cabin they moved into had also been home.

As she turned around and they clacked off into the unknown, she felt more alone than any one of the cold stars in the sky above. Tears streamed down her face as her heart emptied itself of everything it longed for. By the time they reached the ferry to cross the Strait of Canso at Port Hastings, despite the humps and bumps of the rugged road, Laura had put her head down and fallen into troubled sleep, not awakening until George maneuvered the horse into the line-up where people were talking and laughing together.

Peggy must have covered her with a blanket, for she was warm beneath a chilly night sky awash with yet more stars and a full, bright moon. "Oh, you're awake, Laura. You'll get to see the ferry coming across. It operates around the clock now, so the wait is not as long. When we got married, we had to wait twenty hours in line." Peggy looked down at her kindly. "We're lucky tonight. The wind has died down, no strong currents. I think we'll have a safe crossing."

"What happens in the winter?"

"Dangerous crossings, longer waits, I imagine. George says there's talk about building a bridge of some sort. Time will tell."

Laura shivered. "Thanks for the blanket."

Peggy smiled sadly. "Did you get any sleep?"

"A bit," Laura nodded and shivered again.

Peggy held out her arm. "I'm sad too," she said quietly. She tucked the blanket tighter around her sister. "Are you still cold?"

"No." She looked at her sister whose eyes were dark against the night sky. "But to be truthful, I am a bit scared."

"Of what?" Peggy waved her hand. "What can we do but look forward? You'll be fine. And once I get pregnant, you'll help me take care of the babies. Anyhow," she continued, "soon, you'll probably find a man of your own." She looked Laura up and down. "Eighteen and grown downright pretty since I last saw you. You'll find someone in no time."

Laura smiled. Her sister had always had an answer for everything. Then Laura thought of Johnny, the charming young farmhand who came seasonally to help the Englishman with the harvest or haying. Her throat swelled as she realized she would never see him again. They didn't even get to say goodbye. "You know, Peggy, I would indeed like to find a man. Then I wouldn't be a burden to anyone." Her voice sounded hollow to her own ears.

"What makes you say that, my dear sister? You're not a burden. And I know you'll end up marrying the man of your dreams and living happily ever after!"

Laura nodded over to Peggy's husband who was patting the horse's neck. His tall, broad-shouldered physique was more commanding than she'd imagined, and his stern brow made him seem serious, but he had already shown himself to be kind and graceful and considerate. "George doesn't talk much, does he?"

"No. But he's a good man. Takes after his father."

"What's it like living with his parents?"

Peggy put on a remorsefully false cheer. "Really, they're very kind. They've done a lot for us. Patrick, that's his father, he doesn't say much like George. Goes to bed very early and rises with the sun. His mother-" Peggy paused, then sighed. "She does like to talk. I think she forgets to breathe when she's making up for what Patrick doesn't say." Peggy leaned forward and whispered. "She could talk for hours about the weather! Also you'll see, she really likes her own cooking. But between us, it's not very good!" Peggy rolled her eyes.

"Do you ever get a chance to cook?"

"Well, you know, a kitchen is not made for two women." Peggy raised an eyebrow. "She's very proud of her cooking, so she put me in charge of the cleaning and washing." Her face went sour. "What can I do; it's her house. She probably knows my biscuits would run circles around hers. She already has a job in store for you, I'm sure."

Laura's stomach rumbled. She suddenly craved her mother's Acadian dishes of fricot and meat pie. Their whole lives were gone now, their quiet childhood afternoons skating on the pond or fishing in Chéticamp, the tang of the sea air. Nights knitting by the fire in Inverness singing Acadian songs and lullabies, all gone.

The ferry began to approach the dock. Children raced back and the men stubbed out their cigarettes. Soon George geared up the horse and wagon onto the ferry's platform and away they sailed across the strait. It took some forty minutes to cross; they reached the house in the wee hours of the morning. Laura was exhausted and her heart heavy, but she realized she'd actually enjoyed the journey, all the new sights and smells. And a new beginning; she was starting to think it could be exciting.

She looked in her satchel and brought out the goodbye gift the Englishman's children had gotten her: a notebook with a pencil so she could record her travels. Laura felt a thrill of energy run through her; maybe this was her chance. Her chance to start anew. She fingered the little pencil and the rough paper of the lovely leather-bound book and practiced holding the pencil like she would if she were writing something down. Someday, she told herself. Someday.

George's house was a small modest two-bedroom home on the out-skirts of the town of Antigonish. George's mother had left a pillow and blankets on the sofa. After a few hours of sleep, Laura woke up to the aroma of fresh strawberries simmering on the stove.

A big friendly-faced woman called over from the kitchen where she was returning to the table with a saucer. "Come, Laura, have some breakfast. You must be starved. I'm George's mother, Sadie Mae, and this is Patrick," she said as she pointed to her snow haired husband who was already licking his plate. The old man nodded to Laura and briefly smiled. She smiled back. Only true love would make a man lick his plate if his wife were a bad cook.

"How was the ride?" the old man asked.

"Fine, thank you," said Laura. She felt her heart drop again at the reminder that her mother was dead.

He smiled and turned to his wife. "Is George up yet?"

Sadie Mae shook her head and winked. "That Peggy of ours must just tucker him out nights."

Patrick ignored her. "Tell him to meet me in the field behind the barn. We have to turn the hay. Don't mind me, ladies, I've got work to do." Patrick stood and disappeared through the doorway.

"Here, Laura, have some breakfast. You must be tired after that long ride." She paused. "I'm sorry about your dear mother," she said. She took Laura's hand in hers and cleared her throat. "Now, don't be shy. I want you to make yourself at home. Your bed is the sofa as we only have two bedrooms. Patrick always said he would build an addition but when we realized we would only have one child, he never talked about it again. Now imagine, the house is full!" Sadie Mae dropped her voice to a whisper, "Maybe some grandchildren on the way, you never know."

George came in neatening his hair with his hand. "Morning, Ma. What are you going on about? Don't scare off Laura with all your talk. What's for breakfast?"

This was the most Laura had heard George say in two days. "I'll fetch you a plate," Sadie Mae said, going to the cupboard. Her genial chatter continued, not missing a beat, as she sat down and took up the butter knife, "...do you know, our neighbour, Esther, God bless her soul, she is such a kind woman, but she throws everything away! Yes, she does!" Sadie Mae was waving the knife around as she talked.

"What do you mean?" yawned Peggy as she appeared in the kitchen.

"Ah, good morning, Peggy. Yes, well, she throws away whatever food is left on the table after each meal. She doesn't keep leftovers for the next day, not even the butter. She empties the dish in a pail with the rest of the food and feeds it to the cats. Those lucky animals eat better than we do. And I sometimes think leftovers are tastier than the real thing," she added.

Peggy winked at Laura. Sadie Mae was busying herself idly gathering some crumbs with her fingers, so Peggy "climbed on her forty-five" as Laura always said when Peggy was so focused on being efficient, and swept through to gather up breakfast: fresh bread, strawberries and whipped cream. It looked marvelous and Laura thought perhaps Peggy was exaggerating about Sadie Mae's abilities in the kitchen.

They sat down together and ate and then everyone got to work. George had picked up some supplies, so Laura and Peggy went to unload the wagon outside. While they were walking out, Peggy whispered, "What did you think of the bread?"

Laura swallowed. She still felt a globule of dough stuck in her throat. "Fine?"

"Laura! Stop being so nice...How was the bread?"

"Terrible?" Laura smiled. "But really, Peg, we can't all be as good as you." She laughed and looked around the yard, then chuckled to herself at her sister's smug expression. "I like the house, Peggy, all painted white."

Peggy glanced at the house then whispered, "Most people in the village assume that George's parents are rich because he always has the house painted. But it's a trick. Patrick mixes a quart of paint with God knows what and that gives him enough to paint the whole house. He's proud of his possessions; you should see his tools in the barn, all lined up, a place for each one and each one in its place. He also knows how to mend his own socks, sits by the fire at night on occasion, darning away, Sadie Mae going on about something or other." She sighed. "We would so like our own place. But we're grateful for this arrangement anyway. It's better than nothing, right?

Anyway, it forces us to do things out of the house. We've actually started going to some meetings. People from the town's university want to create a cooperative movement and organize adult education, actually, two priests, Coady and Thompkins, Reverend Coady is originally from Margaree, not too far from Inverness, you know-"

"Oh?" Laura was nodding, but she'd lost interest. She'd forgotten how Peggy liked to ramble on sometimes. It seemed her sister was more like her mother-in-law than she'd care to know.

"Yes, anyway, next time we go to one of these meetings, come with us. It's a fine way to get together with the people in the village. Lord knows, maybe you'll meet the man of your dreams!"

Laura nodded but a man was not on her mind at the very moment. She wasn't clear on what sort of meetings these were, but adult education sounded like a disease of some sort. Having to repeat Grade 3 three times had cured her of ever wanting to go back to school. She'd have to come up with an excuse to get out of going along.

As the weeks passed, Laura began to feel uncomfortable. She didn't like imposing on George's parents and the novelty of sleeping on a sofa had worn off. Patrick went to bed almost every night around seven, so Laura spent her evenings outside with Sadie Mae, who slowly got to know every aspect of Laura's life. Truth be told, she actually liked the older woman and found her talk a nice accompaniment.

Laura came up with several reasons she couldn't tag along to Peggy's meetings, and after a time, Peggy stopped asking her to join. Once winter came, there wasn't anything else to do but go to bed early too. The wind was as howling and fierce in Antigonish as it had been in Inverness; one particularly bad night, Laura remembered the time when her grandparents passed away. The Englishman, who had always seemed so imposing, insisted he drive her and her mother back to Chéticamp himself. They departed in the middle of a raging storm, snow streaming sideways from icy winds. He went as far as he could, but when they could no longer see the road, he regretfully turned his team around. Though she didn't get to say goodbye to her grandparents, she felt a new-found kinship with the man who had tried to give her that special gift. Any time after that, the worst winter storms instilled in her a feeling of warmth and generosity of spirit.

Any time Laura let her guard down and thought about her childhood, her parents, or the fact that she had only the future stretching before her without a thought as to what she'd do with it, her eyes misted up. She felt lost and alone. It was wonderful to be back together with Peggy, but her sister had her own life with her husband and her in-laws, so Peggy wasn't really hers anymore. In the evenings, as she looked out the window before settling down for the night on the sofa, she often heard whispers from George and Peggy's room and felt pangs of envy. Maybe she did need to start thinking about meeting a man. She would never feel so alone with a fine man like George by her side.

The full dimpled cheeks of her youth had leaned out and soft-ened, and her gentle face with her big blue eyes looked less cheru-bic and more womanly. She didn't imagine she was good looking, however, and though she knew she ought to, she didn't feel any heartfelt interest in meeting any of the local men. Her mother had been her most intimate companion all these last years, and she missed her quiet, solid company more than anything. Laura clung to her memories to keep herself warm.

One day in the following summer of '39, as she was returning to the house with a pail filled with blueberries, she was so busy daydreaming, she didn't notice a horse and buggy coming along. There was a shout and a scuffle of hooves, then suddenly the horse veered toward her and struck her down. She fell onto her face right into the pail of berries and scuffed her knee on the gravel.

"Miss, you'd best watch where you're going," the driver scolded her, clicking his tongue at his horse to right him.

Laura turned her head to retort that he should better keep a reign on his animal when she realized it was Johnny, the handsome young man who had worked for the English family in Inverness. Her heart sped up. She tried vainly to brush off the fruit from her face and think of something witty to say, but nothing came. She looked down at her dust-coated hands and dress. What on earth was he doing here? she wondered.

"I'm sorry; are you hurt?" He halted his horse and got down to look at her. "Wait a minute, I remember you. You're from the farm in Inverness."

Laura surprised herself by getting hot in the eyes. She was used to hearing Peggy say the name of the town where she had spent her childhood and teenage years, but when she heard it from him, his face alight with sympathy and familiarity, her eyes filled.

Breathless, he caught her by the arm and held her hands. "Are you all right?"

She nodded as he continued.

"You gave me a scare! I'm sorry about your blueberries."

This time, Laura smiled and knelt down on the grass, her whole body shaking. She tried to wipe her face but her attempts only caused the blueberries to spread even more.

He laughed. "You're a fine mess, I have to say." He moved her curls back from her cheeks with a soft strong hand. "There's a stream just beyond that hillock; come on."

He pulled Laura to her feet and they kneeled down together by the water. He dipped in his white and blue checkered handkerchief and washed her face, easily as if she were a child. She still hadn't spoken and knew if she were to try, her tongue would stick to the roof of her mouth.

He surveyed her by holding her chin. "That's better. At least the berries match your eyes."

Laura blushed and looked down.

"So what brings you to this part of the world now? Do you live around here?"

Laura took a breath and was shocked her voice still sounded as it always did. She told him a bit about her situation. As she talked, she realized it was nice, finally speaking to Johnny, as easily as she'd always imagined in her daydreams. Easy, peasy, squeezie, she laughed to herself.

He grinned back at her. "Laura, may I take you home?"

Quietly, they walked to the road where he helped her get into the buggy. She was thankful that her rescuer concentrated on the road ahead and left her alone with her thoughts. But Laura couldn't focus. A wonderful feeling stirred inside of her rather like the breeze that combed through the trees and wild flowers on the roadside.

When they arrived at George's parents' house, he helped her down and took a moment to gaze into her eyes.

"May I see you again?"

"Yes." She was smiling broadly but couldn't help it.

"Tomorrow?"

"Yes."

He smiled.

"I'd like to come 'round in the evening if that's alright."

Laura nodded. He whistled as he climbed up onto his rig, turned the buggy around and departed. Peggy dashed out of the house to her sister. She looked down at the empty bucket and Laura's disheveled hair, then at the young man some ways down the road.

"What happened to you and who was that man?" she asked in a rush.

Laura told Peggy all about her adventure.

Peggy grinned and draped her arms around her sister's shoulders. As they walked up to the house, Laura stopped and watched the buggy until it was just a dot in the distance.

After the blueberry incident, Laura and Johnny became inseparable. When he proposed, they set the date exactly two months from the day they met, for the second time.

Laura loved Johnny with all her heart and soul and to top it all, his home was just up the hill from Peggy and George. His parents had died the year before leaving him their small farm. Though the farm was humble, its upkeep was dear, so Johnny would occasionally leave to earn a bit extra. That was how he had come to be in Inverness periodically.

His house stood on a little hill with the barn and chicken coop nearby. It was a small, unpainted two-story house, somewhat shabby and grey, but not much different from any other. On the main floor were the kitchen and a bedroom. A big wood stove stood in the middle of the kitchen. There were two pails of water on the counter for convenience but no water pump, a luxury Laura had enjoyed at the English house and George's. The dishes were stacked on a shelf and food was stored inside a cupboard. The bedroom was small, with no clothes closet, but Laura didn't mind because her wardrobe was quite limited anyway. She tried to match her feelings of elation for having found this wonderful man with the simple dwelling that would now be her home and tried not to feel ungrateful when she caught herself wondering why he didn't repair some of the issues the house suffered from. He probably worked his fingers to the bone at his jobs and these home tasks had to fall by the wayside.

On the bed was a patchwork quilt; it had seen the years but was well made. He saw her looking at it. "My mother stitched that," he said proudly. "When I was a baby."

"It's lovely," Laura smiled at him.

She turned and climbed the ladder to check the upper floor. It was one big room where she was able to stand tall only in the middle, for the roof slanted sharply on both sides. She noticed the cracks in the ceiling where the rays of the sun pierced through and produced a rainbow of dust. Buckets decorated the wooden floor ready to catch drops from the falling rain. Her grandparents' tiny house on the main path of the harbour where she had grown up and her rustic Inverness cabin where she had lived with her mother had indeed both been in better shape than this old farm-house. Her mama used to pick up leftover furniture from the main house and provide them with a cozy, decent place to live. Laura realized she could do the same, thinking already back to one of her berry picking outings when she saw a huge hole filled with all kinds of discarded materials. Surely there would be some treasures to unearth.

Johnny waited nervously for her reaction to his humble domain. "Is it alright?"

Laura reached for him and kissed him softly. "That's all I needed to hear," he said with her mouth pressed against his.

The day of their wedding dawned bright and clear. It was Monday October 2, 1939. Peggy was Laura's maid-of-honour and George was Johnny's best man. Laura wore her mother's white bridal dress with a long veil and carried a small handmade bouquet. Peggy wore a beige ankle-length dress that she had borrowed from George's mother with a matching heart-shaped hat. When Peggy came into the bedroom and saw her sister in their mother's gown, they were both silent, tears in their eyes. Peggy took Laura's hands and they sat together for a few moments.

"Mama would be so proud to see you today," said Peggy.

"Thanks, Peggy. She'd be proud of you too." Laura bit her lip remembering how she and her mother had stood, watching Peggy go off to Antigonish with George, and her mother said, "Good, one less mouth to feed." Laura had been so hurt by those words; it stung even to remember the words. Yet now, all these years later, she understood her mother's loneliness and isolation. She was young but had to toil alone to make a life for herself and her two daughters after Laura's father was killed. How tired she must have been, how it aged her spirit. Laura closed her eyes and said a prayer for her mother. How grateful she was able to feel for her now.

Just then George and Johnny pulled up looking dapper in their three-piece suits, top hats and polished shoes. A few days prior, Johnny had washed and scrubbed his old buggy, but his neighbour had to borrow it the day before the wedding and still hadn't returned it. He had no choice but to take George's buggy, which was nicer than his but covered in mud. When Laura came outside, her heart fell a bit at the looks of it, but seeing Johnny beaming from the driver's seat melted her. She scolded herself for being so superficial. I'm marrying Johnny, not the buggy, she thought.

They made it to the parish church for 8:00 a.m. mass. Their closest neighbour, Esther, served breakfast for the wedding party and George's parents. Sadie Mae made sure to help her clear the table after the meal and packed up all the leftovers. Then they loaded up and travelled to town for a picture session and lunch at the local restaurant.

"Oh, Johnny! I'm so excited! My first time in a fancy restaurant!"

Johnny smiled and said softly, "Your first time for many things to come, Laura." Then he added, "It's just a pity the menu is somewhat limited due to the rations." He stood at the table and raised a toast to the soldiers away at war and to his new bride. Laura beamed at his sympathetic nature and everyone clinked glasses.

By mid-afternoon, they returned to the house. Sadie Mae had prepared the evening meal, some of which was recognizable from breakfast, and had invited a few guests. Sadie Mae had broken down at Peggy's insistence that she be allowed to bake some desserts for her own sister's wedding party. Her pies were the talk of the night where people hardly touched Sadie Mae's dishes.

Laura made sure to take a slice of Sadie Mae's crumble. She felt warm at the sight of the portly woman with the rosy cheeks standing alone by the desserts. She had tried so hard to put together a wonderful day. "Thank you for everything, Sadie Mae. You're a wonderful woman, taking me in when Mama died. How can I ever repay you?"

Sadie Mae's eyes filled and she hugged Laura. She looked over Laura's shoulder at Peggy, her young daughter-in-law, busy accepting people's congratulations on her pies, and bit her lip. "You would have made anyone a fine bride, but Johnny is a lucky man."

The couple lived three gentle, loving years together, but by the spring of their third year, it became a sore spot that there weren't any children yet. Peggy had had three miscarriages herself, and Laura worried that infertility ran in family lines. Not helping matters was that finally, after several years of war, Johnny and George's names appeared on the recruiting list posted in the village's Co-operative store.

When the time came for the men's departure, both sisters pretended to be brave and smiled through their tears. Yet not long after he left, Johnny returned home. On his way, he tried to remember the doctor's explanations, but it was all just a swirl of medical jargon. The only thing he remembered was the doctor's admonition that Johnny go see his family doctor for tests and medication.

Not having any money for extras, and accustomed to the occasional pains in his chest, Johnny figured it was the kind of thing he could put off until he had enough of a nest egg for a doctor's visit.

When Laura first caught sight of him, she broke into a run and threw her arms around his neck. "You didn't go! Is the war over? I'm so glad you're home! Is George back too? Won't Peggy be surprised!"

As Johnny embraced his tearful wife, he took a deep breath. He wasn't used to lying, but he didn't have the courage to tell her that he had failed his physical exam. "Believe it or not, they have enough men, so they sent me back. Maybe later if the war continues..." he paused. "But they did take George."

Laura stepped back and lovingly cupped her husband's face in her hands. "Oh well, at least for now you're safe. But poor Peggy. This will be hard for her." She stopped then looked again at her husband. "At least she's going to be very busy being a wonderful aunt," she said coyly.

Johnny just blinked for a moment. "Wait a second, you don't mean-"

Laura laughed.

Joseph Simon was born on January 25, 1943. There was no money for a doctor so Peggy and the elderly village midwife came. With their help, Laura gave birth to a healthy baby boy. Laura instantly forgot the pains of childbirth when she laid eyes on her brand new son. Johnny too was as proud as could be, although an underlying uneasy feeling surfaced now and then. His pains had been appearing more and more and he was having to lie to his wife to keep her from finding out.

Even while Laura dealt with the newborn and all the baby's accompanying challenges and beautiful fulfilling moments, she was able to see something was amiss with Johnny. He was clearly hiding something, but because he was putting on a normal front, she figured it was something he wanted to deal with on his own, so she didn't pry. The few times she did bring it up, Johnny told her she was imagining things. This made her fears grow even larger.

In early fall, when Laura conceived a second time, Peggy began acting more distant, then as if out of guilt, doubled her efforts to be kind and involved. On May 8, 1944, Laura birthed a second son, whom they named Joseph Thomas. The birth was difficult and long, and after the baby was tucked in beside Laura, Peggy sat on the side of the bed, unable to look her sister in the eye. "You know, Laura, Joe and Tom are very close in age. Maybe, well, with you in such a condition, taking care of a newborn and an infant could be just too much for you. You need to get your strength back." She turned her back to Laura and busied herself with some cloth diapers. "I did have an idea. What if I were to bring the baby to live with me for a few months, to give you a chance to get back on your feet?"

Laura realized something in this offer felt wrong. She was not too weak to notice her sister's curious expression or hear the peculiar tremor in her tone. Still, her mind wasn't clear. "But Peggy, you're taking care of George's parents. Remember Sadie Mae's last asthma attack? And without George home to help you-"

Peggy waved her hand in the air. "Nothing I can't handle. Listen, Laura, you lost a lot of blood. You need your rest."

Laura did what she could to hold on to her baby, but her eyes were already fluttering closed.

Peggy felt a wave of regret and also the thrill of possibility wash through her. Laura was just so weak. "Rest now. We'll talk about it later." Peggy paused at the door and crossed her arms over her chest. Laura and baby Thomas slept peacefully, nestled in against each other. She frowned. Having miscarried three times already, it seemed unlikely she would bear any children of her own, especially now with her husband off to war for who knew how long. It'd be fair, plus she was family, and it'd help Laura out, she thought. But she knew she was protesting too much; to envy someone for her good fortune, especially her sister; it was wrong. Besides, she didn't have the slightest idea how she would nurse the little one.

Peggy sighed and walked into the kitchen. "She's sleeping, so is the baby," she told Johnny.

Little Joe tugged at her dress. "Come, Peg."

"What is it, Joe?"

"Peg, play."

Johnny glanced outside. "Would you keep an eye on him for a while? I have to feed the animals."

"Sure, Johnny. Take your time."

Peggy squatted on the old rug and played with the little boy. As they built a tower out of stones and sticks, Joe giggling and falling backward over and over, Peg came to a solution that made her feel much lighter. It was reasonable, the right thing to do.

By the time Johnny returned to the house, Peggy and Joe were fixing dinner and humming silly rhymes.

"Listen, Johnny, I have an idea," said Peggy as she put a glass of water down before him. "Laura needs a lot of rest. And now that I look at you, you don't look so fit yourself. You're so grey in the face! So, let me help; I'd like to take little Joe home with me, just for a few months, so Laura can get her strength back. We'll come visit every day and you will be able to tend to your chores without worrying about a little fifteen month old ball of energy running underfoot. What do you say?"

"Did you talk about this with Laura?"

"Sort of."

"What did she say?"

"She fell asleep."

"Oh, well, we'll see." Peggy made it sound so easy, but Johnny felt a bit numb. "Maybe you're right." His head was buzzing and he felt faint.

When Johnny felt fit enough to stand, he went to the bedroom and talked it over with Laura. He didn't want to think about this idea, but when he did, he realized it might be for the best. And it wouldn't be forever, just until they both got on their feet. Laura was too weak to protest much, and that made the decision all the easier.

Later that afternoon, as he watched Peggy and his son Joe walk hand in hand down the path, Johnny gripped the windowsill, feeling waves of cold and sweat wash over him. He prayed his wife would soon be well enough to take care of both boys. He prayed that they would all be fine, that this too would pass.

Luckily Peggy kept her word and every day brought Joe around to visit. From her seat at the side of the bed, she peppered her stories to Laura with, "Guess what Joe did," and "Joe told me the funniest thing," or "I just love it when Joe...." She could see her stories were wearing on Laura, digging away at her, making her feel insecure, but she couldn't help herself. She reminded herself that she was helping her sister in need, and she was proud to do it.

Laura tried regularly to assert herself. "I feel better today, Peggy. I think you can leave Joe with us now."

But Peggy would tuck her sister's coverlet tighter into her bed or smooth her hair. "Nonsense! You still need plenty of rest and you know how Joe is so active. Don't you think it's best I keep him for a while yet? You do look quite exhausted, Laura."

Laura would look at her son. Seeing him thriving and well showed her how she needed to be stronger to care for him, to match his energy. "Well...I suppose so," she would concede.

Once summer came, Peggy stopped coming every day, saying it was better for Joe to be outdoors than at his mother's sickbed.

One day in late July, Laura walked on unsteady legs but with a voice as sure as iron, out to the kitchen where Johnny was preparing some fixings for dinner. "Johnny, why don't you hitch up the wagon and we'll go see Joe. It's been a while since Peggy came round with him. She's probably very busy with the garden and all."

"Sure, Laura. Are you sure you're up to it?"

"Yes, I'll be fine."

When they arrived at the farm, they found little Joe playing in the yard. A rope was looped around his waist with the other end tied to a post. Peggy was close by, cutting string beans. She quickly rose from her chair, untied little Joe so he could race to his parents, and walked up to greet them.

"What a surprise! Glad to see you! How's my baby nephew?" Peggy said as she unwrapped the baby and softly squeezed his cheeks.

"We're fine, Peg. You haven't been around much." Laura looked off to where Joe had been tethered. She was fuming that her son would be tied up like a dog.

Johnny led his horse to a post off to the side of the house. "I'll see if I can find Patrick and leave you ladies alone for a bit."

"I think he's in the field, turning the hay to dry."

Johnny nodded and soon found the old man doing work far better suited to a younger man. Johnny felt a weight of grief enter his heart as he wondered how George was faring overseas. "Here, Patrick. Let me give you a hand."

"Thank you, Johnny. You're a fine fellow. The bones just aren't as fit as they used to be," he said wiping the sweat off his forehead.

Johnny wanted to ask whether they'd heard from George, but Patrick didn't offer any information, which Johnny took to mean he hadn't heard from him. The men continued to work silently in the field, while the sisters tried to find their old common ground again amid entertaining the two little boys. Soon Laura tired and rested on the sofa. "You'll be ready to have Joe home in no time," Peggy said, ruffling the boy's hair.

Laura smiled. She felt weary, but beneath that, she could also feel her body healing. She knew it wouldn't be much longer. "I suppose you're right; today isn't the time."

"Oh, heaven's no. You've got a good deal of healing left to do. But soon," Peggy said, pressing her hand on Laura's forearm. She looked so assured and full of life, Laura didn't disagree. She saw how Joe bounced with health around her. Peg was good for him. But she was his mother and she would be back soon.

When Laura and Johnny walked around to get the horse, Peggy hugged little Joe close and waved goodbye. Peggy could see Laura was getting stronger. She knew. Laura would return very soon.

In early September, Laura, Johnny, and baby Thomas arrived at the MacDonald's house. When Peggy saw them coming up the drive, her heart raced. Without a word, holding onto Joe's hand, she slowly walked to the wagon. As soon as he recognized his parents, he wrenched himself free and ran up to them as if Peggy had never been.

"Father! Mother!"

"Hello, Joe! Come, climb into the wagon with us!"

Peggy looked at her sister, tears streaming down her face.

"Thank you, Peggy, for taking care of Joe. We really appreciate your kindness."

"Laura... I... I'm glad you're well. Little Joe's been a blessing." She looked down at her hands. "Would it be alright if I visited?"

"What are you saying? Of course you may visit, anytime," smiled Laura.

Johnny turned the wagon around as Peggy waved goodbye to Joe.

"I shall miss you," she muttered under her breath. She thought her heart might break into pieces. Peggy stood still for a long time, even after she was alone on the dusty road. She turned and looked at her life, then went inside to write another letter to George.

Laura suddenly found herself very busy taking care of her young ones and helping with the barn chores. She'd hoped that after Joe was home with her, the awkward tension between her and Peggy would disappear, but it remained, and Peggy, likely noticing it too, began staying away for longer and longer periods until she hadn't been by in so long, Laura couldn't say how long it had been.

In that absence, she realized how badly she missed her sister: the funny girl who was always so supportive and positive, who could talk her way in or out of anything, the one who used to play the piano with her head thrown back like a movie star. She suspected that the real Peggy was still there, inside; she just needed to be drawn out.

Johnny noticed his wife's sadness. "Why don't you go visit her? I'm sure she would love to see the boys."

"Maybe I will," Laura said. "I could make a nice lunch and bring it by." She furrowed her brow. "Though I'm sure Peggy will scold me and say she could've made the food."

"Doesn't matter," he said. "Just go."

The next day, Johnny drove her down in the horse-drawn wagon to see her sister, whose drawn face instantly perked up upon their arrival. Laura instantly felt a wash of love and familiarity. Any uncomfortable feelings didn't matter anymore. They needed each other; that much she knew.

"Any news?" she asked.

Peggy shook her head and swallowed hard.

"Have faith, Peggy. Shall we begin a novena?" Laura asked, bowing her head. She was grateful then to her mother who had given them the gift of faith.

Peggy nodded. "I've received a note that a barrel of clothing from George's relatives in the States is arriving soon. Could you give me a hand? I'm sure there'll be something for the boys. If the clothes don't fit, we can always make some alterations. And Sadie Mae is very helpful when it comes to sewing."

Laura tried not to let on how happy that news made her feel. "That would be wonderful. And good timing; the boys are in desperate need of warm winter jackets and new pants. As it is, I don't believe they own one decent pair, even for Sundays," she blushed. Making light of their finances wasn't easy. They'd been receiving a bit of money from the government for their children, which initially was a nice extra, but they'd come to rely on it and nowadays it was spent before the cheque arrived.

"Do you have any ration coupons left? I can spare some if you wish, you know, for tea and sugar, little things-"

"Thank you, Peggy. You're very kind. Are you still receiving those pay envelopes from the military?"

"Yes, but frankly, I would just rather have my husband back." Peggy bit off a fingernail. Laura had noticed that since George's deployment, her sister's hands looked ragged; Peggy had always prided herself on her neat fingernails and grooming.

Laura's heart pulled for her. "Peggy, what if Joe spent one day a week with you? He could even sleep over. Like old times."

"You mean it?" Peggy's eyes lifted and sparkled.

"Yes, but on one condition: no spoiling!" she leaned into Peggy, knowing that was an impossible request. If Joe wanted the moon, Peggy would try to get it for him.

"Oh, Laura! I would be thrilled, and I'm sure Sadie and Patrick will love it. I promise to bring him straight home the very next day."

Laura smiled for she had already planned on leaving Joe with Peggy. "He can stay today then. I just happen to have some spare diapers and a change of clothes."

Peggy glowed with joy and soon a pot of garden soup was simmering on the stove. After Laura left, Peggy and Joe played and enjoyed a piece of candy bar. "Don't tell Mama about this," said Peggy, pressing her sticky finger against her nephew's lips. Everything was calm until bedtime when he began to howl for his pacifier.

Sadie Mae had an idea and began bustling around looking for things. Peggy rocked the toddler and sang him French lullabies while she watched her mother-in-law remove the cap of a bottle of glue and boil it. She dried it off then stuffed the inside with a clean rag.

At first, Joe threw it on the floor, but little by little, he took to sucking on it as if it were the real thing.

"I never would have thought of that, Sadie Mae. You saved the night for us all."

"My pleasure," smiled the old lady.

Peggy looked at her mother-in-law. She and Peggy were both strong and sometimes clashed, but Peggy realized in that moment how much she respected her. "You know, Sadie Mae, you remind me of Mama," she said softly.

Sadie Mae looked startled. Peggy wasn't one for sentimentality. "Your mother? How so?"

"She was inventive, too. She worked for an English lady, and when the lady cast off an old coat, Mama repurposed it for me. She spent many evenings sewing by the light of the lamp. It was a pretty coat, navy with white trim. It was lovely, simply lovely. I felt so proud when I wore that coat."

Joe had fallen asleep in Peggy's arms. She touched his cheek. "The English family ran a large outfit: many cattle heads, a huge garden. The farm's produce travelled by train to the market. Mama used to say the train ride was so bumpy, by the time the cream reached Antigonish, it turned into butter!"

Sadie Mae covered her mouth with her hand to laugh. "We still receive products from the Inverness farms as well as wool, coal, passengers, even soldie-" she quickly switched topics, "the wool is transported to Truro where beautiful blankets are made! On your bed, the red woolen one with the white stripes is one of them."

Sadie Mae paused and let silence fill the kitchen. "It must have been hard for your mother, being widowed so soon after relocating the family to Inverness," she said quietly. "Did she speak any English?"

"A little, but she always spoke with a distinct accent."

"Can you still speak French?"

Peggy smiled. "Oué, Madame. Je parle Français, voilà." She laughed. "Though I'm sure it's pretty rusty by now. I was eight years old when we moved to Inverness. That's when I changed my name to Peggy from Marie Margaret-Anne."

Sadie Mae smiled. "What about Laura?"

"Laura was five when we left Chéticamp, but she seems to have lost the language, or perhaps it's just buried in there so deeply she can't get to it."

"Didn't your mother speak to her in French?"

"She did at first, then after a while, well, it was an English world we lived in." She paused and said sadly, "I remember one time I mistakenly spoke French in the English home where my mother worked. The look she gave me!" Peggy chuckled. "It could've frozen fire."

Sadie Mae took Peggy's hand in hers, the first time they'd shared such a touch in all their years. "Peggy, I'm glad to have had this time with you," she said, looking her in the eyes. "Tell me more about your childhood?"

That evening, Peggy rocked baby Joe and chatted easily with Sadie Mae, telling her about the little fishing village where she'd been born. She talked of the mountains on one side and the salt water of the Gulf of St. Lawrence on the other, the poor Acadian families selling their fish, the majestic church in the village's centre. As she talked, both of them felt for the first time grateful to George for bringing them together. Now all they needed was him to come home and complete the circle.

Joe's weekly sleepovers gave Peggy new life. This time, she didn't dare upset things by not returning him on time, fearing her sister would change her mind about letting her care for him. One day, however, they woke up to the sound of pounding rain. She knew it wouldn't be safe to bring Joe out into such weather. Anxiously she stared out the window at the dark grey sky.

The wind was thrashing violently as Peggy gathered Joe's things. "Laura wouldn't want you two out in this," said Sadie Mae as Peggy buttoned Joe into his coat. "Be reasonable."

Peggy's voice was tearful. "I don't have a choice; I told her I would bring him back." She set out, holding Joe. Blinded by the wind and rain, she often stopped to rest while comforting the little one, who was weeping from the crackling lightning. Their going was slow and slippery.

Fortunately as they were staggering up the path, Johnny happened to look out the window. He grabbed his coat, ran to her and took the lad in his arms to run him into the house. Peggy refused to come in, giving a poor excuse about having stew on the stove.

"Why would she come in such poor weather, Johnny, and then not stay?"

Johnny had seen a look of desperation on Peggy's face he'd never seen before. "Your sister loves Joe like he's her own. I think it means a lot to her to uphold the deal. She might not want to jeopardize that." Johnny didn't tell Laura about the tears pouring down Peggy's face that he knew weren't rain. "It can't be easy with George gone so long." Johnny kissed his wife's hair. "Maybe you should visit more often? Keep her spirits up?"

Laura loved her husband that much more in that moment. He was so loving, so open to others' experiences. "Of course you're right. I'll go tomorrow."

Laura didn't know that just that morning, when Johnny had been in their barn, sweeping the horse stall, he had inexplicably broken down into tears for George and all the other soldiers. He'd heard more reports of how Hitler's insanity had spread, how he'd murdered so many innocent people, and how many men were dying on the front lines. Johnny had leaned on his broom, tears falling quietly into the hay beneath him and stayed that way until his heartbeat felt normal again.

* * * * * *

April 1945

The war was finally over. George's last letter said he would soon be coming home. When the day arrived and he loped his way slowly into the yard, old Patrick and Sadie Mae knelt and fervently thanked the Lord for answering their prayers. Peggy ran to her husband and threw her arms around him. He was firm beneath his uniform, and his hands, rough and scarred, held her tenderly for a long time. When they finally let go of their embrace, and Peggy saw his face, she nearly gasped. His eyes were pulled down at the corners, exhausted and haunted. His tenuous smile looked like it belonged to someone else, someone who had been broken.

He stayed home and rested for a few months, eating well and playing cards with his family. Peggy watched how much he now enjoyed malt beer in the evening, something he hadn't done before, and quite a lot of it. The more he drank, the more he seemed to become unhinged, voicing opinions about the government, banging on the table or abruptly rushing outside for no apparent reason. But even during these episodes, he never spoke of his time overseas, and Peggy didn't dare ask. In the bedroom, he took her brusquely or tenderly in turns, often curling up in her arms without a word to find sleep.

One day, the two brothers-in-law were sitting in the barn having a smoke. Johnny coughed and held his chest a couple of times before stubbing his cigarette out. George was quiet a long time. Then he asked, "Why were you rejected exactly?"

Johnny looked at the ground and touched a smudge on his boot. "My heart's no good," he said clearly, looking then into George's eyes. "I don't know the particulars. But," he rubbed his face. "Don't you even think of telling Laura or Peggy. No sense in worrying them."

George took a long drag on his cigarette. He exhaled and nodded into the stream of smoke. "No use worrying them." Johnny shook his head and clenched his jaw. He thumped vigorously on his chest and stood. "We'd best be heading back. Getting on dinner time."

Chapter Two
Starting Over

It was December 1947 and Laura was in labour with her third child.

"Is she going to be all right?" Johnny asked Peggy. He'd heard his wife in labour before. This was different.

"She's going to be fine. Take the boys to the barn. Better yet, take them over to the house. George will care for them. Come back right away in case we need you, and check the fire in the stove before you leave," Peggy ordered. "And don't forget to dress the little ones in their woolens," she called out.

Johnny was relieved to have the busywork. As soon as the fire was going and the boys were snugly seated in the sleigh, they were on their way. The sky was inky blue and full of stars.

"Father, look, look, the first fall of snow! Isn't it grand?" exclaimed Tom. He stuck out his tongue to catch the flakes.

"That it is," answered Johnny glancing at his son, always so surprisingly articulate at only three and a half-years-old. Johnny marveled at how serene the world seemed: the moon shining behind the hills while the soft snow fell, his perfect sons beside him, while back at their run-down home, his wife was struggling with the pain of childbirth.

He frowned when he thought about the life he'd given her. Laura made the best of things, salvaging what she could from the dumps, and had given their house a charming, lively look. An area rug, though worn and faded, was spread on the kitchen floor and kept their feet warm. The boys played and wrestled on it so splinters were almost a thing of the past. Laura had even gathered old chipped saucers and cups, and over time, they learned to drink from the opposite sides of the flaws. The buckets were still standing upstairs as they had been when Laura had first inspected the house over eight years ago.

As the sleigh continued on its way, Johnny cringed further beneath his jacket. Laura was right to be upset when they tipped the buckets over. He hadn't put up a new roof, giving her excuse after excuse. He knew he couldn't afford to pay someone else to do it, but he also knew enough about the increasing pains in his chest that if he exerted himself too much, he'd be in trouble. Even his daily tasks often left him nauseous, gasping. He knew she wondered why he didn't make the fixes the house so needed and knew he was letting her down, but he simply couldn't be honest with her. He vowed to try harder; for now he only wanted her to make it through this birth. He would take care of everything, somehow.

By the time they arrived at Peggy and George's house, the boys had fallen asleep. George came outside and met them. "Stay long enough to warm up?" George asked, taking Tom into his arms.

"Thanks, George, but I'll be going back now."

George looked at Johnny's face. It was pale and there were dark circles beneath his eyes. "Are you OK, Johnny? You don't look yourself."

"I'm fine, don't you think anything of it." Johnny turned the sleigh around and raced home. From the yard, he could hear his wife's screams. The whole night, he paced between the house and the barn chain-smoking, periodically ducking into the house to check the fire in the stove. At one point, he became so lightheaded he sat right down in the snow. A moment later, he was fine again.

At long last, in the wee hours of the morning, like music to his ears, he heard it. The most beautiful sound ever: the first cry of his newborn.

He raced into the house. Peggy was in the kitchen washing some rags off in the sink with a bucket. "How's the baby? How is she? Is she going to be all right?"

"Why don't you ask her yourself?" answered Peggy. Her lips were tight as she wrung the rags then slapped them on the sideboard, but Johnny didn't care what mood she was in. He walked slowly into the tiny bedroom and paused in the doorway. Laura smiled at her husband from the bed, their new baby in her arms. She seemed alive and serene and even had color in her cheeks.

"You OK, Laura?"

"I'm fine," she whispered, adjusting the baby's blanket. "Look, another boy. Isn't he simply amazing?"

"Yes," whispered Johnny. "So are you. But would you have liked a girl?"

"Our little boy is perfect. A new brother for Joe and Tom. What shall we call him?"

"I'm not sure. Why don't we ask Peggy?" Johnny said mischievously.

"Johnny, you're being naughty! You know darn well she probably had a name chosen the minute I conceived!"

Peggy came to the door. "I hear you need a name?" she laughed, her earlier taut air gone as she laid eyes on the newborn. "What do you think of Benjamin Joseph? But because that's an awfully long name for such a tiny creature, we can call him Ben."

"It's a beautiful name, Peggy," said Laura. "Hi, Ben," she said to the baby and cuddled him.

A proud and happy Peggy returned home after the sun was high in the sky, shining brilliantly on the fresh snow. Not a few hours later, she returned with the boys and George. On the walk over, George noticed his wife was unusually drawn. "You must be tired," he said.

"No, no, I'm fine. I'll be fine," she said as she pulled the collar of her coat around her neck, "just a bit cold."

George had long since known in his heart that he and Peggy would never have their own children, and he knew that she knew this too, and seeing her sister have one after the other broke her spirit into pieces.

Joe and Tom ran ahead, shouting, "Hi, baby!" "Hey, baby!" "Yoo hoo, baby!" and occasionally stopped to throw snowballs. George suddenly laughed. He grabbed Peggy's hand, something he wasn't prone to do, and held it tight. She squeezed back. The squeeze was full of sorrow but also full of love. They would be alright.

* * * * * *

1950

Spring arrived overnight, with a few robins and random dandelions bursting through the wintered earth. Laura gathered as many of these wild yellow blooms as possible and made nosegays that she placed all throughout the house. She recalled how the old man at the English farm used to crawl around on his hands and knees to dig out each individual dandelion. "Pests," he called them, sweating through most mornings in his determination. Laura had a different view of the little flowers, for when they first appeared, it meant spring had arrived in Inverness. And with the new season, so would Johnny McPherson soon arrive too.

She chuckled at herself for spending such time daydreaming when there was so much to do on the farm. The cow had birthed a calf while four lambs had announced their arrival. With the sound of a steady soft rain upon the barn's roof, Johnny had begun the task of shearing the sheep.

Laura leaned against the fence surrounding the lambs' pen and watched her boys. As laughter and giggles reached her ears, she touched her chin to the top of the fence and sighed. Joe was already seven years old and growing like a weed. With his wavy hair and blue eyes, tall and somewhat skinny for his age, and a persistence that made him seem wiser than his years, Laura watched him strain all his muscles, his face deeply serious as he and his brother Tom, who laughed the whole time, held on to the frightened sheep.

But it was Tom whose now panicked voice broke into her reverie. "Mother! Come quickly!"

Joe had gotten his hand in the way of the shearer. Between his thumb and index finger, was a small gash that flowed blood onto the wool, turning it reddish pink. His father gathered him in his arms and rushed to the house with Tom and Laura trailing behind. Laura checked the kettle for hot water but only a small amount remained. Johnny started a fire in the stove as he told Tom to get more firewood.

His mother kept her hand on the wound while placing a damp cloth on Joe's forehead. The water was soon boiling so Laura cleaned the cut and applied a homemade bandage around it.

All the commotion woke two and a half-year-old Ben from his afternoon nap. He cried out and Tom ran into his parents' bedroom. Ben's legs were stuck in between the railings of his brown metallic crib. His older brother carefully released him and climbed into the crib with him. He played and laughed with his baby brother for a while to keep him busy.

Johnny returned to the barn. While Laura warmed up some beans for the evening's supper, she shook her head as she sliced the bread. It was ironic this had happened to Joe as he was so cautious, whereas Tom, with his round face, pert nose and innocent wide brown eyes was the adventurous free spirit more prone to accidents.

Laura went to the barn to fetch Johnny for supper. A cool breeze met her as she stepped outside and a light drizzle was still falling.

"Johnny, are you still here? Johnny?"

"Here, Laura."

Her husband was sitting on a stool slowly milking the cow. "Thought I'd do the milking before supper. It will give us a head start in cleaning the wool." He paused. "I was thinking. Maybe I should go look for a job at the mill. Just three, four days a week to begin. Until the boys are old enough to help more on the farm. A little more money could come in handy, you know, with repairs and things." His face darkened. "How would we have paid for a doctor this afternoon if Joe's accident had been more serious? We can only sell so many eggs and wool. It's barely enough to get by..."

Laura was surprised by this sudden burst of energy from Johnny, but she felt heavy at his suggestion. If he took a job at the mill, most of the farm labor would fall to her. She knew how well meaning he was, but she also saw he simply didn't have the energy of other men his age.

Johnny continued. "Soon Joe will be old enough to quit school and take care of the farm-"

Laura jumped up as if she had been stung. Every single day she regretted not being able to read. Hated that she couldn't write. Not even her own name. She thought often about the journal she'd carried from her home in Inverness and kept in a box on a shelf as if it were a precious, sad secret. Sometimes she had the feeling that without being able to make her name known in print, it was as if she didn't exist.

Her stool tumbled under the fat belly of the cow. She pointed her finger at her husband and looked him in the eye. "No son of mine is going to quit school before his time to work on a farm. Never. They are all getting an education, a good education, even if I have to do all the work on this farm by myself, do you hear me?" She surprised even herself to find there were tears in her eyes.

Johnny resumed the milking and smiled at his wife's passion. She adjusted her dress, picked up the stool and sat down calmly. "So," she said, "can I help?"

They sat in silence until the milking was done. Then effortlessly and delicately, Johnny lifted the bucket, put his arm around her shoulders and the two of them made their way outside. As it was still raining, Laura placed her sweater on top of her load so the wool wouldn't get too wet. From behind, Johnny admired his wife's figure and lustrous hair and noted her old housedress she wore day in and day out except for Sundays. He decided if he got the job at the mill, he'd get her something really nice for her 30th birthday. Though Laura would probably be equally as happy with a bouquet of wildflowers. He shook his head and felt the fullness of a man blessed.

As Johnny picked up the pails of milk again to climb the short slope that led to their humble house, he felt a sharp pain in his chest. This was a new one that had been coming on lately. He thought maybe he should go back to the English house in Inverness to earn a few extra dollars so he could go see a doctor. But he hated to leave Laura and the boys behind.

The month of May melted into June and life was very busy at the farm especially with Johnny now working at the mill. One warm evening as the sun sank slowly in the purple sky, Laura shaped the final biscuit for the oven while the last of the deer stew and dumplings simmered on the stove. She chuckled. Johnny always said, 'Laura, you make the best darn biscuits in the village!' Such a flatterer. Everyone knew Peggy was the queen of biscuits. When the hour grew long, she drew little Ben into her lap and rocked him, singing "Bonne nuit, cher enfant" over and over the way her mother had sung it to her. Joe and Tom were outside attempting to fix an old wagon in which they planned to carry bait, tackle and trout on their next fishing trip with their dad. The wagon would also serve as an extra carrier for the wool that remained to be washed in the river.

As Ben fell asleep in his mother's arms, she kissed his forehead and bent her head to study his lovely face. He was quite chubby with a fair complexion like his father. Laura settled in her rocking chair, vaguely listening to the boys' chatter through the open window. Some nights alone with the boys, she felt untethered, irritable, or just fatigued. She began singing to chase her blues away. It would have been easy to feel overwhelmed by the demands of her life; she managed all the housework and most of the farm chores. But she tossed her head. Best not to think about such things. She focused on Johnny, though by the time her husband returned home from work, he was exhausted and just stretched out on the old sofa. He'd always had low energy, but nowadays even the boys noticed that their father wasn't as much fun as he used to be.

Where is he? she wondered, before falling into a light sleep. Soon she was awakened by screams. Laura's body tensed as she tried to figure out whether they were real or dreamed. She heard them again, leapt from her chair and ran to the window. Joe was running up the steps.

"What on earth is wrong?"

"It's Father! He…he fell and he's not moving."

Laura quickly placed baby Ben in his crib and dashed out the door. Johnny was lying on the ground. Tom was crouched beside him crying and pounding on his chest, but Johnny didn't respond. Laura's legs gave out as she too knelt beside her husband. She tried desperately to find a pulse but panicked, and started shaking him. Still, there was no reaction.

"Tom, get Aunt Peggy! Hurry!"

Laura checked her husband's pulse again. Bursts of anger waved over her. He must have fainted from pure exhaustion; why was he so frail? She tried to lift him to carry him inside but he was far too heavy. "Johnny!" she yelled, shaking his shoulders, tears falling down her face. She looked up to see if George was coming, but the road was empty.

"Get some water, Joe! We'll splash some on his face. Maybe that will wake him up!"

Joe scurried inside to fetch a pot of water and a towel. By the time he reached his mother, he had spilled half the water on the ground. Laura soaked the towel and spread it on Johnny's forehead.

"Sorry, Mother," he began to weep.

She continued pressing the cold towel on her husband's face. "No matter, Joe. You're a good boy."

Then Tom, Peggy and George were running up to them. George jammed his fingers into Johnny's throat to get his pulse. He waited. And waited. "Laura," he said, his voice low and queer. "Laura." He took his hand away.

Laura lived a last moment in the space between her life and the reality before her. "No. He's just exhausted, too much work." Her voice didn't sound like hers. "He was going to repair the roof. He said so this morning. You're wrong, George. How dare you."

"Laura, stop. It's done." George put his hand on Johnny's chest a moment before he looked down and raked his hands through his hair. "He didn't ever tell you." George stood and yelled, "The coward never told you! He didn't say what kept him out of the war, why he was so tired all of the time, he didn't tell you?"

"What? What are you saying? He never said anything to me!"

"His heart wasn't right, that's what he told me. He didn't want to worry you."

"That's not possible. He was fine, just fine," Laura wrapped her arms around her husband's body and held him. Behind her, the boys were crying, but she was lost to her grief. Peggy held them close, then brought them into the house where she collected Ben, who had been wailing for being left alone so long.

George let Laura be, but after a long time, he lifted her weak form away from her husband's body. She made no sound, but as the minutes ahead began stacking up before her, she grew a look that was more and more stony, as if it were her only defense against what her life would now mean.

June 22, 1950 would be engraved in Laura's memory forever. Johnny's wooden coffin was placed in front of the window where Laura's rocking chair normally stood and was left there for two days so friends and colleagues could pay their respects. Laura knew that Johnny had been well-liked in the community, but she was surprised by the outpouring of sympathy that came. Laura accepted the hugs and handshakes though she didn't feel a thing.

After the first hour of the wake, she grew faint, so Peggy took her to the bedroom. Laura whispered, "Peggy, how will I do this alone? Please, please tell all these people, tell them to go away. I don't want them in my house."

"We can only hope that God will help you in your time of need."

"What kind of God would take my husband away?"

Peggy took Laura's hands and looked her firmly in the eyes. "You must have faith, Laura. That's what you told me when George was overseas. It's all I clung to."

"But that was different. George came back. Johnny is never coming back." Laura sobbed into the old quilt on their bed. Peggy knew no words would console her sister and left her there to fall asleep.

Out in the main room, she noticed how restless and uncomfortable the boys were and motioned to George to take them out. He rounded them up and they headed to the side of the barn to throw a ball around. George ran back to the house for his old baseball gloves. In no time, the boys were laughing and having fun, for a brief moment not thinking about how their hearts were hurting. Ben roamed around his brothers, happy to be out in the sunshine.

Realizing there was a circle of men in the barn, the boys slowly entered. They hid in one of the stalls while listening to the older men tell jokes and share some homemade brew. "Keep it down, boys," whispered George, glancing at the door for signs of Peggy. With the coast clear, the funny stories resumed. It seemed like a contest of who could tell the best story.

One man tipped his head back and drank deeply from the jug in his hand. He wiped his face with his sleeve and chuckled. "I remember one day when Johnny arrived at the mill, walked straight to this fellow and gave him a piece of his mind! This man had a car and had sped right by Johnny while going to work, never stopping to give him a lift, and it was pouring rain! The next day, Johnny got a ride but then the other fellow started going to work early. Ah, Johnny was a good lad, a fine fellow, full of life."

George knew the boys were close by, so he quickly added his own funny story. "After I had my kidney stones removed, Dooly here picked me up, so on our way home, when we stopped for a piss, I picked up a handful of pebbles, put them in a jar and took them home to show Peggy. I said to her, 'See, Peggy, this Mason jar half full of stones all came from my insides!' Without missing a beat, she said, 'You should go back to the hospital, pick up enough to fill in those big holes in the driveway!'"

After the laughter subsided, Dooly took his turn. He was a fairly tall man with broad shoulders, blue eyes, and a soft smile. "One time my uncle Bernie came to visit. He was quite a handsome man who loved beautiful women and gourmet food, in that order. My father asked him, 'Bernie, which girl would you choose, a beautiful, gorgeous woman who couldn't cook or an ugly, homely woman who was a terrific cook?' Uncle Bernie stood still, thinking, everyone anticipating an answer. Then he said, 'I would choose the beautiful one and eat at the restaurant!'" Everyone had a good laugh, even the boys from their hiding place.

The men continued to drink and were so busy with their story telling, they forgot the time. Soon Peggy arrived at the barn door and looked at her husband. "Will you find the boys, George. They need to come inside."

As soon as they heard their aunt's stern tone, Joe and Tom appeared, looking disheveled. They went and found Ben who had walked through cow manure. George helped bring them inside so Peggy could clean them up for supper then returned to the barn. As he approached, he overheard one of the men from the mill he didn't know very well. "Peggy and Laura sure are quite different in character, aren't they?" the man snickered. "That Peggy is very stiff; George can't pass too much by her, but Laura, now she is a sweet and soft thing. She would make someone a good wife."

He laughed but was stopped by Robert O'Brien, the town's lawyer and an upstanding fellow, who quickly retorted. "You talk too much. Johnny is not even cold and you're already thinking such nonsense. Anyway, who in his right mind would want to marry you, unshaven, dressed in rags, you look like a vagabond."

"Ah, I was only-" the man tried to apologize but he didn't get very far. George stormed over to him and knocked him off his feet with one quick punch. He reared back for a second, his biceps protruding through his shirt, his body stiff. In a quiet and slow voice, he said, "No one talks about my wife that way. And if any one of you ever touches Laura, even for a second, you'll answer to me!"

His eyes met O'Brien's and he nodded in thanks. Then he turned around and went back to the barn. The men dispersed and went home. Dooly followed George. While sipping on what was left of the brew, the two men quietly chatted away. "What happened to Johnny? How did he die?"

"Several years back, not long after I got home from overseas, he told me he was sick. I half believed him, I guess. He could talk his way through anything so I just assumed he had faked a condition to avoid going off to war." George slugged back some drink.

"Mmm. What will happen to Laura and the kids, now that he's gone?"

George sat quietly for a moment. "I don't know," he finally said.

Peggy had arranged a schedule for volunteers to sit up during the night with Laura so by late evening when everything was quiet, she was able to slip out and check on her husband. He was drunk, passed out in the hay. During the war, she knew the soldiers had slept outside beneath the stars most nights, and even now that he was home, it seemed George found it easier in some ways to rest among the animals in the barn. Sometimes she thought he preferred it. She found an old blanket and covered him. Angry and sad, Peggy walked home alone.

The next morning, she woke up early to the aroma of breakfast. She looked in the kitchen to see her husband shaving, while the teapot whistled and bacon sizzled in the frying pan. She prayed that this last day of the wake would be uneventful. As if hearing her thoughts, George wiped his face and turned around.

"I'm sorry about yesterday. I promise to behave today."

Secretly Peggy wanted to kiss him, but instead, she swiftly took up a cup and poured out some tea. "Good. After we eat, we'll go to the house. I hope Laura and the boys slept." She looked at him, her eyes softer. "Did you find someone to dig the grave?"

George nodded. They didn't speak of it explicitly, but he had had more than his share of this gruesome task during the war and couldn't bring himself to do it again, and especially not for his brother-in-law. To his great relief, Dooly stepped up.

That second day was very long and quiet. Around three o'clock, George got a fire going in the wood stove to make tea and prepare supper. He took the boys outside again but the glance he threw over to his wife conveyed he would behave. Laura resumed her place next to Johnny's coffin and robotically thanked the visitors one by one.

That night, she insisted on staying alone. "I'll be all right, Peggy. Please go home."

"Well, OK, but if you need anything, send the boys."

Laura breathed a sigh of relief. Finally she was alone with her sons and her husband. Even though Johnny was no longer of this life, he was still in their house and strangely enough, it was some comfort.

After the boys fell asleep, Laura stayed by her husband's side. She gazed at his white face and talked to him through her tears as if he were listening. She tried to say and think kind thoughts, but at the same time, she felt powerless and frustrated. There was nothing, no security for the future.

In the wee hours of the morning, she grabbed a pail of water and scrubbed the floor, putting all the energy she could muster into the task. By the time the sun rose, she was exhausted and ready for bed.

Peggy arrived early, prepared breakfast and tended to the boys. She then knocked on the bedroom door. It was time. A pale, disoriented Laura stared at her sister.

"What, what are you doing here so early?"

As she spoke, reality shifted and stared her straight in the face. Without a word, Peggy helped her dress in a black suit and matching hat, adorned with a veil. The outfit had belonged to George's mother. Now it was Laura's. It hung on her thin frame, but she didn't care. Peggy, Laura and the boys stayed in the bedroom while George and a few men from the village removed the coffin from its temporary resting place. Joe and Tom whimpered while baby Ben sat quietly on his mother's lap, knowing things were wrong.

Suddenly Laura blurted out, "Peggy, how am I going to pay for his funeral? I don't have a penny to my name!"

"Don't worry, Laura. George will think of something."

Soon someone rapped softly on the door. Slowly and silently, the family followed George and got into the wagon that would carry them down the long road. At church, Laura sat quietly, not moving a finger, not hearing the hymns, the prayers, or the sermon.

After the funeral, she remained in her room for five days, sleeping and staring into space. On the sixth day, she dressed and prepared a big breakfast for the boys. She was touched to see that the people in the village had brought enough food to last them for weeks. Laura normally hummed or sang as she prepared meals; she was silent now, and as if they were seeing a foreigner in their kitchen, the children stared wide-eyed at their mother. Peggy was at least pleased to see her up and about but frowned worriedly at her drawn, pale face. She watched sadly as Laura hugged her children, tears on her cheeks.

Laura looked around at her home with different eyes now. She'd done what she could to make it comfortable, but it was far from sound, and she and Johnny knew that all along. In the last few days, she began to see how Johnny's laziness or procrastinations were just the cover of a sick man. She was livid that he hadn't been straightforward with her. That he'd left her like this, completely unprepared.

During the following weeks, Laura went through the motions of living, fed her children, cleaned the house, helped the boys carry wood inside, milked the cow. It seemed now obvious to Laura how she'd lived in a make-believe world with her husband and children. Laughing and singing as she did her chores, lying in the grass with her boys watching the clouds drift in the sky and playing word games: good day, rainy day, happy day, cloudy day, funny day. These joyful moments were now things of the past. Even the fullness of the trees, the daisies and rich clover that surrounded the house had lost their charm. Laura felt no appreciation for any of it, blind to life's beauty.

Over the next weeks, Laura looked differently at her sister too, at her strength despite all her hardship of being unable to conceive, her husband gone to war for three years, her never knowing if he would return, taking charge of the farm, then caring for her sick in-laws alone. Peggy's strength and might were still evident as she helped Laura clean the house, wash the dishes, and sew patches on the boys' pants. She never ran out of things to say or positive enthusiasm for the daily act of living, even whistling as she left to go shopping or to the Credit Union to cash Laura's baby bonus cheques. Laura thought of her sister's energy as limitless, like a pail with no bottom. In fact, sometimes she wished Peggy would live a little more quietly, to let the air breathe a bit. She did go on, and in her high, bright voice, it could sometimes grate. But Laura tried to banish such thoughts.

One day in mid-September as Laura and Peggy were preparing supper, Peggy continued to relate the latest gossip and brag about her last round of biscuits as the best in the village. As usual, Laura rocked, tuned out her sister and drifted into a world of her own. There had been some rain of late, and the roof was a mess. She hated being dependent on her sister; it made her feel weak and small. Suddenly, weary of the sound of chatter, she cried out, "Who cares about so and so's problem? I have enough of my own."

Peggy put down her paring knife. "What is it, Laura?"

Laura began to cry; it was like a dam burst, the first time since the wake. Peggy leaned in and held her close until Laura's tears were spent and she could speak. "What am I going to do, Peggy? Fall will soon be upon us, then winter. There's no money, little food, this broken-down shack of a house. This year's crop was not plentiful, not at all. How can I provide for my family?"

"We'll help you."

"That's very kind, but I can't depend for our livelihood on you and George. It wouldn't be right. But I don't see how I can do it, not with Ben still being so young." Laura shuddered as she thought of families who had gotten separated after a similar tragedy, never to find their loved ones again. "What if they take my children away?" she whispered.

"Go put on a clean dress, wash your eyes and fix your hair. Joe and Tom will be coming in soon for supper. I'll trim your hair after you wash." Peggy rested on the easy assurances of the little efforts that made up a day. She didn't have any answers for Laura. Not any.

"Hello, Aunt Peggy! Boy, it sure smells good!" yelled Joe and Tom as they walked into the house.

"Perfect timing, boys! Just added some fresh string beans to the 'chiard', our mother's specialty. It just occurred to me that if someone planted a lot of seeds, beans would grow everywhere, might even be too much for a family of four, might have to sell some at the village even–"

Laura and the boys looked at Peggy in that same instant. A twinkle of a smile emerged on Laura's face. "Full moon, full of beans..."

Tom joined in, "…full of mischief, full of the devil, full of shit…"

"Hold your tongue, Thomas Joseph McPherson!"

Tom shrugged and bowed his head.

"How come Tom has the same name as I do?" asked Joe.

"Joseph, you mean? It refers to St. Joseph, the Virgin Mary's husband."

"He was a carpenter, wasn't he?"

"That's what the bible says."

"Well, I want to be a carpenter too when I grow up!"

Laura smiled at her eldest son. "I'll bet you're hungry; let's eat."

Everyone helped set the table and afterwards cleared it off. Then they went out to feed the cow, the sheep, the chickens and clean the pens. Homework was the last task of the evening, and Laura was relieved that the boys could help each other for she had no clue as to how to be useful. Johnny had always been the one to help with their studies.

After Peggy left, Laura put Ben in his crib then climbed up to the boys' room.

"I'm sorry I haven't been here for you during all of this," her voice trembled. "It's been a sad time for us all. But I'm here now, and I'm going to come up with a plan to keep us safe." The boys looked tentatively at her. She put a hand on each of theirs. "We're going to be fine."

For the first time since their father's death, over two months past already, Laura tucked them in and wished them goodnight. As she climbed down the ladder, Joe and Tom looked up at the ceiling and watched the stars dance in the sky through the cracks in the roof. They remembered the previous year's cold winter months when the walls were lined in white frost producing a soft, glimmering effect. Fortunately blankets were plentiful to keep them warm; at times, they could hardly move under their weight. On colder nights, Joe and Tom would tiptoe downstairs to join their parents. This had been a treat for the covers were always nice and warm. Now the bed would be bigger without their father.

Chapter Three
Away From Home

A few hard months after Johnny's death, on this first day of October, Laura finally allowed herself to enjoy a "lazy-day", Johnny's word for Sundays when the family could relax. After church and a quiet lunch, Joe and Tom played outside while Ben napped in his crib. Even Laura dozed off in her rocking chair.

She was jostled awake by Tom's happy cries, "Mother, Mother, wake up! Come and see!" The boys ran inside and dragged her to the door. "Look!"

George and a group of men were gathering in the yard. They carried lumber and shingles, buckets of tar, ladders, and all sorts of tools. Laura grabbed a sweater and ran outside. She was overwhelmed and yet somewhat scared. George, seeing her dismay and guessing why, hurried up to her.

"No need to worry, Laura. The local hardware store and a few generous people from town donated the materials. It's a chance to get together with the boys, show off our muscles and have some fun. And you *do* need a roof, right? Joe and Tom, come; you can help."

Without waiting for her reply, he returned to his crew, whistling. Laura was awash in gratitude. George had changed so much since returning home, drinking, speaking even less, acting erratically, but these episodes were few and Peggy was so lucky to have him. He was above all, a very good hearted person who was full of love. Laura started dancing with the boys as they used to.

By late afternoon, Peggy and several other women from the village arrived carrying baskets of food. The work was completed by then, as Laura's was but a small house, and everyone descended on the food.

"Thank you, thank you so very much...I...we really appreciate your kindness, thank you-" Laura said to the crowd assembling the meal.

"It's OK, Laura. They get the message," said Peggy, smiling at her sister.

"Yes, but they are so kind; this is enough food for a week!" Laura turned to Peggy, her hands on her hips, eyes flashing. "Was this your idea?"

Peggy smiled. Laura realized that though her sister could be many things: manipulative, loud, or overbearing, there was no denying, she was the best sister ever.

The night soon grew cool, a sure sign fall was upon them. When Laura tucked the boys in, she started to sing, "C'est la Poulette Grise." The boys did not understand a word.

"You hardly sing anymore, Mother. Where did you learn these songs?"

"My mother used to sing them. Both my parents were Acadians, you know. My mother's last name was Chiasson and my father was a Boudreau."

"Daddy in heaven?" asked little Ben.

Caught by surprise, Laura held Ben close to her and smiled sadly. "Yes, honey. I think so."

Tom chuckled. "Maybe he's the one who ordered this new roof!"

Joe chimed in. "Dad probably has connections up there. I just bet he's watching over us!"

Laura looked at her eldest son with awe. Joe was so young yet held such deep convictions. Laura took her boys' hands and thanked the Lord for his blessings, especially the new roof. She felt a little ambivalent in her prayer, part of her still feeling the anger of the betrayed, and the other part, comforted in His blessings.

Once the stove was checked for the night, Laura sat in her rocking chair looking out the window. Full moon again tonight...

full moon, full of beans, full of people, full of love. She chuckled at herself. She blew out the lamp and slowly climbed into bed.

The week went by quickly. Before she knew it, it was Sunday again. This one would not be a day of rest; in fact, she decided to forego church because there was too much to do. The Lord could've provided all he wanted, but she knew if they didn't harvest, there'd be nothing to eat that winter.

"Get up, boys. Time to take care of the crop before winter sets in."

The boys gathered the carrots and the remainder of the potatoes. Joe and Tom worked hard, but their hands were still quite small and it took several hours. Laura did most of the digging, and as she went through the rows and saw how poor the crop was, she felt her heart dropping further and further. She started to whistle tunelessly to keep her thoughts away.

As the afternoon wore off, Aunt Peggy came strutting up the path with more of her goodies. She looked so put together in a jaunty hat and smart coat, her full lips rouged. Laura knew she was covered in dirt and smelled like a potato herself. She forced a smile. "Good of you to come, Peg. Come inside. What do you have there?"

"Oh, just whipped these things up and thought you might like some." Peg paused and set the basket by an old crooked fence post. She didn't look at Laura. "So, I was talking to the priest the other day. He mentioned that you might be of service as a housekeeper, you know, something to help you make ends meet."

Laura wondered why Peg was acting so strangely. This was good news. She certainly knew how to keep a house.

"That's a good idea. When do I start?"

"The thing is," she dusted off the back of her hand, "the job is in a convent in Montreal."

"In Montreal? It's a bit far to move all of us there, Peg." Laura pulled her bun down which was scraggly and tried to re-pin it while she thought. "I mean, it could be nice, but it's awfully far from you-"

"Actually," interrupted Peggy, "You would go alone, or with Ben, and leave the boys. But we'll take good care of them until you're back."

Laura felt like she'd been slapped in the face. She'd come around and trusted her sister completely and yet here she was plotting to take her family away from her again. She finally spoke. "But it's so far; I couldn't possibly…"

"It's no problem; you'd take the train. The priest will pay the fare for both you and Ben."

Laura's first instinct was to gather her children in her arms, despite the elder ones being far too large for such things, run into the house and lock the door against Peggy. But her blood calmed in a minute when she realized whether Peggy's gesture was kind or manipulative, Laura really had no choice. There were hardly enough vegetables for autumn alone. "To leave Joe and Tom," Laura shook her head. This was exactly what she'd feared she would face, and here her sister was suggesting it as if it were a natural thing for a mother to do, to leave her children behind.

"Think about it, Laura." Peggy's eyes looked too kind, almost syrupy. "How will you manage this winter?" She looked sympathetically at the withered vegetables in the baskets. Neither of them spoke.

Laura raced to run through a mental list of how she in fact would manage and could tell Peggy thanks but no thanks and go away with her stupid idea: wood, enough to last the winter since George cut some logs, which he and the boys stacked in the barn. Food, the crop- Laura frowned. The rations would be very small. She stopped and felt tears coming. She'd spent most of the summer mourning rather than taking care of her family's garden. Milk, maybe, but they lacked fresh hay and oats for the cow. At least they had a new roof for the house, but the rest of it- she paused again.

Laura's stomach churned and her legs grew weak. It all had to add up; she had to see the light at the end of this dark, frightening tunnel. Heavily, she turned and looked out at the horizon, the small farms dotting the distance. There before her, her eyes fell on the barn, which was in worse shape than the house. Her mind raced; what if the boys grew so attached to Peggy they didn't want to return to her, and what of Ben, what if he forgot he even had brothers.

Aware of Peggy's heavy eyes on her, Laura suddenly felt so angry as if she would explode. Johnny put her into this situation from his selfishness. She thought he'd loved her, his family, but he obviously feared the truth more than he loved her.

She clenched her fingers tightly as her blood pressure rose again. "Thanks for the-" Laura didn't even know what Peggy had brought and didn't care. "I have to go in now."

Peggy bent down and handed over the basket. "Yes, I have to be going as well. George and I are going to Dooly's for supper. You know how his wife-"

"Goodbye, Peggy." Laura wrapped her sweater tightly over her chest and began to walk to the house. She didn't wait to see her sister off, but went inside and shut the door.

Not a few moments later, someone knocked. "Jésus, Marie, Joseph, what now," murmured Laura. She hadn't moved from the front window where she'd been looking out, seeing nothing. She figured it was one of the boys, though it did occur to her that they wouldn't have knocked.

When she opened it, a neighbouring farmer stood with his natty hat in his hands, his bristly face marred by evident scorn. "I didn't think anyone would ever answer this door. Are you Laura McPherson? Just widowed?"

"Yes-"

"Can I come in?" he asked.

"I suppose."

"Fine day," he said as he looked around. "Yes, well, it looks like Johnny didn't leave you in good standing."

"I don't see how that concerns you," Laura said dryly.

He spat on the floor. "Listen, I've come to ask your hand in marriage, seeing you're by yourself with the young ones. I'm widowed myself, just last week, got many little ones to care for. Seeing I need a wife and you need a husband, this might just be the solution to both our problems. Ten little ones I have, yes, my mother too. Even my older brother, he's sick, you know." He took a breath and smiled at her, his teeth foul from rot and nicotine. "But you will be boss in the kitchen. Yes, I guarantee that. The house is not big but we'll make do. I eat my breakfast at five o'clock every morning so you'll have to rise early. And then there are the barn chores. How old did you say your sons were?"

Laura didn't know whether to laugh or shout, but there was something so horrible, so wonderful happening inside her that was making her feel like exploding, she didn't mind. "I didn't."

The old farmer leaned forward. He smelled like manure and dirt. "How's that? What did you say?"

"I said I didn't say how old my sons are. Goodbye," she said abruptly and opened the door for him to leave. The old farmer looked at her before slowly turning around. Before he left, he leaned over and spat again, slowly, on her floor. As soon as his two feet were on the step, Laura slammed the door. She slid her back against the panel, her legs too weak to support her. She took a deep breath and heard him sputter, "Young women of today, they don't appreciate a good service when they see one."

After he left, she considered briefly whether she'd done the right thing, but she shuddered at the very thought of that horrible person ever being near her. With ten children of his own, his elderly mother and an ailing bachelor brother, all living under the same roof; where did he intend to put the boys, in the barn?

Laura looked around her home. It was shabby and ailing. She had little to no food, no money, no skills, and winter was coming. What would become of her and her children? Looking outside to make sure she was still alone, Laura let herself cry, which she did as if her heart were breaking. Johnny, she thought, how could you leave us in such a way? How could you? Please, God, I need a sign to show me that we're going to be OK. I need to know, please.

Laura pressed her eyes closed and when she looked up, all she saw through her tears was a spider crawling across the floor.

When the boys came inside, Laura's heart was beating in her chest in a way that made her feel like she couldn't catch her breath. It was all up to her now; there would be no divine intervention. Those childish dreams were over. And it would only be temporary, she told herself. "Boys, sit down."

She presented the facts shakily. Their faces grew more confused as she spoke. "But, Mother, it's too far. Will you at least be home for Christmas?"

None of the details had occurred to her. She looked at Joe's serious little upturned face. "I will do everything I can to be here for Christmas. But," she touched his cheek, "for certain I'll be home by spring. We'll buy seeds to plant the garden again and I might have enough money to paint the house. Wouldn't white be nice?"

Joe and Tom were both looking at the floor and didn't answer.

"I might even have enough money saved to buy some ice cream once in a while. How about that?"

"Will you write to us, Mother?" asked Joe.

"I'll try. I will. I will do my very best," replied Laura, a dagger piercing her heart. After all these years, she would now have to find a way to stay in touch with her boys. She would spend all her free time learning to read and write. It hadn't ever been much of an issue; Johnny helped with homework and signed papers. But now her life depended on it. "I will," she repeated. "I will."

A week later, George boarded up the house and herded the animals to his barn for the winter. Laura packed clothes for her and Ben in two small valises and Joe and Tom's things in a trunk and sadly walked behind the animals to George and Peggy's house. Outside it was cold and pouring rain, the weather matching the weather inside her soul. Laura had been left behind again and again, her father, her mother, her sister, her husband, but now leaving her boys gave her a feeling of loss in her belly greater than anything she'd ever known.

The final arrangements were completed for their dreaded journey to Montreal. Peggy was ever at the ready to help Laura seal things up and organize. She even took care of having the children's baby bonus cheque transferred into her name as their "guardian" so 'Laura didn't have to worry herself over that small detail.' This was just another thing in a bundle of things happening to her that made her feel like the floor was being dissolved beneath her feet, bit by bit by bit.

When the day came, Joe and Tom accompanied Ben and Laura to the train station and waved good-by until the train was out of the station. Laura knew the boys would be fine, well fed, loved, and would get everything they needed, but she still felt like they were being stolen from her. It wasn't rational, she knew, but the feeling was causing her head to throb with unshed tears.

Once they got underway, like any energetic three-year-old, Ben kept running up and down the aisle. As the train rocked back and forth and gradually picked up speed, Laura grew hot and pale, and became so weak that she thought she might pass out. She had to ask their seat neighbors to watch Ben several times so she could run with her hand over her mouth to the washroom. After a few hours of this, she was even too feeble to ask for help anymore and hoped they would just mind her son, which fortunately they did. She kept saying to herself, this must be a bad dream. How did we ever end up like this?

Finally, Ben got tired, settled in his seat and fell asleep, and Laura felt a little better and dozed off. She woke up when they arrived in Truro and had to transfer to another train. Laura couldn't read any of the signs, so she numbly held Ben as tightly as she could and followed everyone else. A woman off to their side caught Laura's eye. "Where are you two going?" she asked kindly. Laura told her, and the woman pointed to the right track. Laura looked over, and when she turned to give her thanks, the woman was gone.

Once they were settled on the next train, Laura searched in her bag for the care package Peggy had put there and came up with some sandwiches. Laura felt the lump in her throat grow larger; her sister did care so much. But still Laura couldn't help feeling like it was one last kindness before taking over as her children's mother, before getting what she had always coveted. Laura ground her teeth and forced herself to eat, knowing it would make her feel better. A fellow traveler offered Ben some milk and hot tea to her, which she sipped slowly, trying to settle her stomach. Soon, she and Ben fell asleep again, his head in her lap.

Upon their arrival in Montreal the next day, they disembarked to see a sister from the convent awaiting them. She came up to Laura and nodded, frowning. She inspected them from head to toe and looked at Ben with disdain, then motioned them to follow. Laura was glad she had packed only two small bags to carry their meager possessions: two housedresses and a Sunday dress, a few personal items for herself and some clothes for Ben. It was a strenuous walk and they sweated beneath their winter jackets. She hustled along, hoisting the bags in her hands periodically, calling to Ben to hurry. The nun stopped impatiently a few times, looking behind her to see if they were coming.

The convent was not too far from the train station, but by the time they arrived, Laura and Ben were exhausted.

"Enfin. Arrivée." Lady Superior greeted her with a face cold as stone. Laura didn't know how to respond, and simply waited for the nun to continue. Surely the sisters must speak some English, she thought. But the nun turned and wordlessly led Laura and Ben down a corridor and up three flights of stairs to a secluded corner in the attic of the convent. Laura was overcome with dizziness, not just from her exhaustion but also at the first sight of the room, which was the size of a large closet and stank of mothballs. Laura held Ben close and looked about. At least there was a window. She put their bags down and hoped the nun would indicate something about dinner, a glass of water, some gesture of humanity. "Vite, au travail. Descends à la cuisine, dès maintenant."

"Pardon me?"

The nun sighed with brittle annoyance. "You must come to work at once. Bring 'im wit' you," she sneered, looking at Ben.

Ben began to cry when they arrived in the kitchen; Laura realized they needed to eat immediately. When Mother Superior rounded the corner ahead of them, Laura grabbed some bread sitting out on a tray and put it into the pockets of her apron. She was shown the sink, and for the next several hours, she bent over to wash dishes and pots. Ben understood it wasn't time to act out and gingerly put bread in his mouth while playing quietly with some wooden spoons on the floor. When they were let go, they both fell asleep within seconds of falling into bed.

Though they'd arrived in mid-November, Laura's first day off was Christmas day. On Christmas morning, from the top of the stairs, she and her son could hear the nuns praying and singing holiday hymns. Their voices haunted the cold stone walls. Laura had always thought of Christ as welcoming, of religion as a kind of home, had believed it all throughout her life without question, but after all that had been taken from her and now having to live in this place, little more than a prison, she felt nothing.

Ben's hands were wrapped around her calf; she looked down at him, her heart filling instantly with love. The familiar melody of a Christmas hymn reached her ears, and for Ben's sake, she hummed along.

"Is your eye OK, Mama?"

"I'm fine, sweetheart." She swept the tear off her face with her hand and smiled.

They stayed like that, holding one another in the darkened staircase, until the little caretaker with the kind face, the one bright spot in the convent, happened by. "Laura, I've been looking for you. The misses has prepared a Christmas feast. You must join us." He pulled on his suspenders, an endearing habit of his.

She was overjoyed and quite moved he would seek her out. "Oh," she demurred. "We wouldn't want to impose, Monsieur Bergeron."

"Nonsense," he clucked. "And you must call me Pierre. Now, go get your coats. It's mighty cold out!"

Laura ran to grab their coats. She coughed from the exertion as she was doing more and more lately, tiny spots of blood appearing in her handkerchief. She came down and the three quietly disappeared into the evening fog down the street to Pierre's house. His wife, Emma, who greeted them effusively, was a tall, angular woman, but her children were just as short and stout as their father. The lot of them greeted the trio at the door with shouts of French good cheer. Laura laughed and more tears came, which she brushed away before anyone could see. The caretaker's sons were healthy and red-cheeked and made her long for Joe and Tom.

There wasn't time to think about that, though, because when Laura was ushered in and saw the generous spread on the table, she was stricken. She hadn't seen this much food in months: turkey, dressing, mashed potatoes, vegetables and apple pie for dessert. They encouraged Laura and Ben to eat their fill, which they did gladly. At the meal's end, Laura took her plate and stood. Emma grabbed her arm. "Laura, you guest today. Tomorrow we do dishes. Now, we sing!"

Laura laughed as Laurent, the middle son, led her into the living area where an old organ occupied most of the space. The lady of the house sat on the stool and began to play. The family sang peaceful French Christmas hymns and lively songs. Laura didn't understand the words but she felt their love permeate the whole room. Ben's color seemed much better and he looked so at home. Love truly is universal, she thought.

But soon, Ben was more than tired, and it was time to return to the convent. There were kisses for everyone and many words of thanks in both languages before they stole back into the night.

The dark days and months of winter melted together for Laura in a blur of fatigue and chill. Between caring for her son who tried to behave but often got into mischief and the backbreaking labour of her job, working from before dawn until long after dark, all without not having seen even a single penny, she was quite relieved to learn that in the new year, she would be given every Sunday off. When she told Pierre, he insisted she and Ben come to his house each week to spend it with him and his family. He truly was a godsend; apart from some gentle soul at the convent who nightly left Laura and Ben a plate of biscuits and two glasses of milk in the corner by their door where the food wouldn't be seen, Pierre and his family were their only friends in the world, their only other link to kindness. And when she found out he could read and write in English as well as speak it, the kind caretaker became her only link to home as well.

"You have a new letter for me to read, chérie?" he would ask each time he saw her.

After some weeks, she finally worked up the courage to ask him for help. "No, but I have a favour to ask. It's time I learn to read these letters for myself. And I want to write one in return." Laura looked him in the eye. "Will you help me?"

"Yes, next Sunday. You tell me what to write, and we do it."

Laura pondered a long time about what she would say in the letter. First, it had to be brief, because she didn't want to over-burden Pierre who was good enough to help. Second, she didn't want to give her sister or her sons cause to worry. However, she had never been a liar, and she knew it would be hard to stretch the truth as far as she needed to without breaking it.

The next week, Laura sat at the Bergeron kitchen table, ready.

Pierre hesitated. "I apologize, but my spelling is not-"

Laura chuckled. "Don't worry. They're going to be so happy to hear from us, you could misspell every word."

And for the next half hour, Laura dictated, and Pierre wrote painstakingly.

> Dear Peggie and George,
>
> How are you. Tanks again for taking care of my suns. Hope there not too much trouble.
>
> We miss you all a lot. We are doing just fine.
>
> Joe, Tom, Please behave and remember that we both love you very much.
>
> Your mother.

As Laura spent her days on her knees, scrubbing floors, or bent over a mop, she began to see how her dream of spending her off hours learning to read and write were the dream of a foolish woman. She felt she had aged so much, not only from the work, which had turned her hands into those of an old woman, but from the outright meanness of the nuns, who took pains to turn their backs on her. It was baffling; she'd arrived at this place to do a job, yet any time she spoke to Mother Superior, she was met with her contemptuous face and some harsh sounding words in French, if the woman deigned to speak to her at all. It must have been because she wasn't French herself. She was an outsider. Christ had led these holy women wrong, she thought bitterly.

By now, she was in desperate need of a new dress. The two she'd brought had become worn and ragged. By chance, while she was cleaning the closets, she found some printed fabric, enough to make herself a dress and a new shirt for Ben. She gathered up her courage and took the bolt to Mother Superior. "I found this beautiful material in one of the closets. It seems to have been there for a while...maybe if no one is using it, I could make a shirt for my son and a dress for myself. As you can see, mine is quite old and worn."

Mother Superior raised one eyebrow and shuffled some papers on her desk. Laura tried again, simplifying her words yet further, but the elder woman cut her off. "Je n'ai rien compris," she said and waved her hand at Laura to leave.

Laura stood still a moment, contemplating just taking the fabric. Not like there was much else they could do to punish her. The nun looked up at Laura like she was an idiot. "I have one dress. I wear it in the day. I wash it at night. Go now," she said in thickly-accented English.

Fuming, Laura walked out without another word. She was not surprised, but with each contact, she was continually amazed at their level of meanness. She returned to work and tried to think nothing of the whole episode. Two wrongs didn't make a right, she figured. She would do her job competently and not complain.

Yet her worn clothes and spirit aside, Laura began to wonder whether something larger were amiss. She didn't know what the priest had established with the nuns as far as her pay. When they didn't pay her after her first week, then not after two weeks, she reasoned they would pay her monthly; when that passed, she then assumed bimonthly, after that, quarterly. Once the end of February came, however, and she still hadn't seen a cent, a chill crept into her soul. Laura's mind went to the extremes: perhaps they thought that not only could they mistreat her as a maid, but because she couldn't speak their language, they didn't have to pay her either or perhaps the plates of biscuits and milk left behind were their way of paying her? She and Ben looked forward to this treat each day dearly, but if this was to be her pay, she would gladly give it up.

She finally asked Pierre to help her sort this out, knowing Mother Superior would not speak to her. He came back to Laura not long after he left, his head bent low. Apparently, he said, in exchange for Laura's duties as housekeeper, she was to receive free room and board, nothing more. Pierre spat out, "And she said to say you should be grateful for this generosity, the evil crone."

"No. No, there must be some mistake. This is not the arrangement we made!" Laura said loudly then broke down and sobbed. "I had planned to fix the house and buy seeds to plant. Now it's nearly too late for this year! I can't write to get myself out of this mess, and I don't like to impose on you." She blew her nose and hugged Ben, whose frightened eyes were wide. She thought for a moment about that horrible farmer. If she'd taken him up on his proposal at least she wouldn't have had to leave her sons. Tears dropped off her face. "Please," she said, feeling undone, her hair rough and tangled from that day's work, from fatigue, from all the weight she and her baby son had lost, "I'm sorry, but please help me write another letter? We must write to the parish priest in Antigonish. Tell him I must go home. Beg him for my return fare. I must get out of here."

Pierre set to writing the letter at once, and after several weeks, he got a response and some money for Laura's return fare. When he came to her in the hall, she made a small exclamation, then quietly leaned her mop against the stone wall, went to the kitchen where she found Ben coloring by the stove with some coal, took him up to their nasty closet room, threw everything in her suitcases and left, not bothering to shut the door on the way out.

As she was coming down the stairs with a bag in her right hand, Ben in her left hand, and the second bag tucked beneath her arm, she overheard Mother Superior and a few nuns laughing about something in the corridor. Laura stared at them, her face going hot and cold in turns, until they noticed her and their chatter died out. "Where are you going?" asked the head nun icily.

"We're leaving." Laura turned and wrenched Ben by the arm out the door.

Perhaps realizing how they were being left in the lurch, they all began uttering half-hearted apologies, imploring her to stay, all of them suddenly and quite conveniently speaking in broken English. She didn't even turn around as Pierre put her bags into his old pickup.

When they arrived at the train station, Laura grabbed his arm with one hand and clutched the letter Peggy had slipped in along with the Priest's letter with her other. "Wait. Before we go in, please read me my sister's letter once again."

He chuckled. "You want to make sure you're not dreaming, eh?"

Laura stared ahead in blank space, weighing every word: 'the boys miss you, they're so glad you and Ben are coming home, I'm preparing a feast for your arrival.' Tears of joy rolled down Laura's cheeks.

"Do you hear that, Ben? Aunt Peggy can't wait to see us!" Then, after Laura was certain little Ben was preoccupied, she whispered, "and Pierre, would you also read me the note the priest wrote to Peggy?"

······· **March 1, 1951** ·······

Peggy,

Please be at the train station on April 14 at three o'clock in the afternoon to meet your sister whom I am pulling away from an abominable situation. Clearly there was some kind of misunderstanding, and according to the convent's caretaker, Laura was only given an unsanitary closet-like apartment in an attic and was made to work as a slave with room and board, not a cent of pay for the whole time she's been there.

"You really told him!"

"Actually, my son helped me, with the spelling too! I hope you don't mind, but I had to. It's the truth."

Laura felt her face grow warm. She should have taken better care to understand this situation before walking into it. She'd trusted her sister blindly, and as a result, she'd given away her boys and lost months of their lives. She was so relieved to be leaving she didn't even care about any of that.

Pierre held the truck door open for her, but Laura paused. She opened her purse and found a stamp Peggy had sent. "I want you to have this."

He frowned. "But stamps are too expensive!"

Laura shrugged. "It's one of the few possessions I own that's worth anything, and it would mean so much to me if you would take it." She kissed Pierre on both cheeks.

He swallowed and nodded. "Life will not be the same at the convent without you and Ben around." He straightened up and said loudly, "We will miss you very much, Madame Laura." Then he bowed. They laughed and walked inside the train station.

Pierre stood with Laura and Ben in line to buy their tickets, counting out the bills she held from the priest at the cashier's window. While the three of them were waiting for the boarding call, Laura began to steam. She then turned to her friend and murmured, "If it hadn't been for you and your family, I think I would have died in that place." Her once soft, round face was hard around the jaw; she felt the tension in her temples. Her bones ached. "I cannot understand why the nuns were so mean. I thought their purpose in life was to help and serve others."

"Aie, me too. But they are quick to judge and forget to be human sometimes. A woman in your situation deserves our sympathy, not our scorn." He shook his head and sneered. "I'm sure they think by shunning you, they were forcing you to repent for your ways."

Laura raised one eyebrow. "What ways? Wait a minute, what did they think about me?"

Pierre looked at Laura carefully and paused. "You are not married, but you have Ben, non?" He pulled awkwardly at his suspenders.

Laura's jaw tightened again. "I'm a widow! My husband died last year leaving me with the family and no money! I don't understand. Surely the priest would have explained my situation." She took a deep breath. "If this is how they treat someone in need, I'd hate to see how they'd have treated me if they knew I had two other boys at home with no father at their side." She asked, "How can you work for them?"

Pierre's face was beet red. "I had no idea about your situation, but I feel so horrible, so sick in my heart. To treat anyone like they treated you... I stay because jobs are scarce. I do my chores and don't bother much with them. I get paid. They seem to be satisfied and I leave it at that. But," he leaned in and grinned, "if they knew my son and his girl are staying together, whooo..." He shook his hand and made a comic face.

The cloud above Laura lifted and the two of them roared with laughter until they were wiping tears away and Laura was bent over in a coughing fit. Ben was busy with a piece of string making cat's cradle and didn't notice the bitterness in his mother's laugh. Or the fact that it went on quite long and she had to wipe away her now usual traces of blood with her handkerchief. "Your son and his girl are living together?" echoed Laura as soon as she could talk. "Such a thing would be scandalous in Antigonish."

"Ach," he shook his head, "we love her like a daughter."

Here was a man comfortable in his life, thought Laura. She envied his easiness with the world.

Just then, the train whistle blew. Laura and Ben got on the train and waved goodbye to Monsieur Bergeron. "When will we see him again?" asked Ben as they found their seats.

They waved out the window some more. "I don't know, Ben. Perhaps never, but perhaps sooner than that." She smiled and roughed up his hair. Just then, she noticed a small, perfect spider's web in the sun-drenched corner of the window. It fluttered delicately in the breeze. She paused a moment, staring at it, the feat of it almost impossible to imagine. "Look, Ben how it glimmers in the sunlight. Isn't it the most beautiful thing?"

Laura felt this was a wonderful sign: spiders were good luck. And at long last, they were free. She smiled and hugged Ben tightly. She wanted to run and kick in the thin chilly sunshine like a colt after a long winter. The train puffed and chugged and left the station. She bought sandwiches and juice from the porter with the remainder of her money sent by the priest. Later when they got hungry again, they snacked on the bread and fruits Emma Bergeron had sent with her husband to give to Laura for the journey. Ben fell asleep as soon as darkness fell. Laura gazed out the window at the starlit sky for a while feeling finally at peace, as if Johnny had found them and would keep them safe. She too finally fell into a deep sleep.

The next morning Laura woke up slowly. She took a moment to realize where she was. When she sat up, she saw Ben's seat was empty. Panic overcame her. She stood abruptly, becoming a bit dizzy, and raced up the aisle looking for him. He wasn't in their car, so she went into the next, her cough kicking up loudly. She could feel people staring at her, shrinking back in their seats as if she were contagious.

She let out a small shriek when she finally spotted his shoes; he was sitting beside another passenger, recounting little stories as if they were old friends. "And then, we go to the house, and we play in the grass, so funny," he laughed. The gentleman he was with laughed as well.

"Benjamin, Come here now. I'm sorry if he troubled you. He must have wandered off while I was sleeping." Laura avoided Ben's new friend's eyes, picked the boy up brusquely and quickly returned to her seat. After scolding him for misbehaving, she calmed down a bit. Later on, the man found them and apologized for having caused her any anguish. He was finely dressed in a woolen coat and shiny leather shoes. Laura pulled her old coat around herself, her dress by now nearly falling apart. She coughed into her fist and tried to breathe normally.

"Please rest assured, Madame, I would not cause any harm to your little one. I thought I would keep him occupied while you rested. But I must ask, that cough sounds aggravated. Are you feeling well?"

Laura simply nodded but said nothing. She wanted this nicely dressed man with the sympathetic blue eyes to leave. He waited a few seconds, smiled and looked a bit confused, then turned to go back to his seat.

Once he turned, Laura realized she didn't want him to go after all. "Thank you for your concern. We're fine now, and I'm just overtired."

He smiled kindly at her and sat down in a vacant seat across from theirs. "Your little boy told me you're from Antigonish?"

"Yes."

"I'm from Antigonish myself, was away on business."

"From home; how lovely. Perhaps we know people in common."

Soon Laura felt quite comfortable with this man; he was generous with Ben, letting him play with his pocket watch, and laughed at his silly jokes. Laura watched his hands. He wore a wedding band. He saw her eyes on his hands, and offered one to her. "How awful of me. Where are my manners," he smiled. "Samuel O'Brien. I'm the town's Superintendent of works. We live on the outskirts."

"I recognize that name. Is your father a lawyer by any chance?"

"Yes. He's retired, now."

"I believe we live not too far from your father, a mile or so."

The train rambled on as they continued chatting. By the time they reached Truro, Laura had had several coughing fits. "Laura, why don't I take you to see a friend of mine? He's a doctor who can check you out, make sure nothing is wrong. He doesn't live far from the station. Actually, he's expecting me. We'll have plenty of time to catch the next train."

Laura panicked at the mention of a doctor. She had no way to pay him. And she'd heard about men who lured women off with their sweet words and feigned kindness, but Laura examined Sam. He seemed genuine, his hands nervously adjusting his tie, pulling at his ear. "I'll make sure we're back in time for our next train. It'd be my honour," he said and offered her his hand.

There was something so innocent and hopeful in this otherwise worldly man. Laura felt her heart twist slightly and rise in her chest. "Yes, we'd be glad to come with you."

Sam led them out of the station adeptly and stepped to the curb where he hailed a horse-drawn carriage. It brought them straight to the doctor's house, a beautiful mansion. A servant greeted them and behind him came the sweet odour of pinecones and simmering cranberry. Laura hadn't smelled anything but her mothball-infused attic space and bleach for so long, she felt hypnotized. The house was lavishly decorated with plush couches, large paintings on the walls, thick Persian carpets. Then she heard the soft strains of classical music- it was pure sound, not at all crackly like from a phonograph. The doctor saw her straining toward the sound. "That's our new radio. I must say, it's a fine invention. Such a pleasure to have the music on without having to crank!" he chuckled.

The doctor took her into his immaculate white office and listened to her chest. "You've been in the damp?" he asked, concerned.

Laura didn't want to confess to her conditions of the last several months, as if somehow they showcased how unfit she was not only as a mother but as someone who couldn't take care of herself. He gave her a bottle of cough elixir and cautioned her to rest.

His kindness, and the medicine, helped measurably and she enjoyed the rest of their visit, even giggling when she used the indoor bathroom and the pipes gurgled, causing her to yelp in surprise. The doctor's wife had prepared a light lunch of cheeses, bread and fruit that was brought by a servant and the three weary travelers ate and chatted easily. Laura felt peace come over her as if everything would be alright. As they were leaving, she didn't mention that in the opulent bathroom scented of lavender soap she'd coughed so much she brought up blood all over their beautiful tile floor.

The remainder of the journey was peaceful. She promised herself she would take better care, gain the weight she'd lost and bask in the love of her family. That would put all the color into her cheeks she needed. Ben fell asleep next to his mother before they pulled out of the station, and she stared out the window, feeling the greatest sense of home she'd ever had at the familiar land formations. Even the crows seemed to welcome her home as they flew and danced close by. It being a Saturday, they would have two whole days with the boys home from school. Just knowing she would soon be able to touch them sent a rush of excitement through her whole body.

When the train pulled in, she spotted them. Waving, crying and laughing simultaneously, she grabbed Ben's hand and quickly climbed down the steps. Laura was so busy with her sons, she forgot her luggage. Fortunately Mr. O'Brien noticed the bags and carried them down for her. When he saw her hugging and kissing her two boys, he wondered what would have pulled her away from them for so long. He lingered a moment to say a final goodbye, but the two boys were jabbering at the same time, and rough housing with Ben, and knowing he couldn't compete with such a loving reunion, Samuel smiled faintly, sadly, picked up his attaché and walked away.

Chapter Four
Blessings and Hardships

With her nose in her sons' hair and their voices in her ears, Laura's heart swelled to double. She tried not to weep but to laugh instead with joy. All of them were leaping onto each other's sentences trying to catch up on all the last months at once. Little Ben at first held back, but within a few minutes, he put one hand into each of his brother's warm palms. They exited the station and Laura climbed up behind them into the wagon.

George scratched his head and gestured to beside him. "Aren't you sitting in front?"

Laura's eyes were shining. "I'd like to sit with my boys if it's not improper," she said smiling. "Where's Peggy?"

"Oh, she's home, keeping the house warm and preparing a feast for your arrival. Are you sure you're comfortable back there? The floor of the wagon is mighty hard."

Laura looked down and the tears she'd worked so hard to hold back began to flock her skirt. "Very comfortable."

"I told you she'd cry," Tom elbowed Joe.

Laura playfully slapped his arm. "I deserve a few tears, don't I?"

"You go right ahead, Mother. Tom won't own up to it, but he cried the whole way here."

"I did not!" Tom laughed. "Only part of the way."

Everyone laughed. On the way to her sister's house, Laura sat between Joe and Tom with Ben on her lap and ached from finally having all of her sons' bodies so close to hers. She wrapped an arm around each of her two oldest boys against the chill wind brushing their faces. Looking at the rolling hills and scrub trees, she found it hard to imagine that she had been gone for almost five months, and now here it was, the middle of April 1951. Spring was almost on them. The group had fallen quiet, and the gentle rhythm of the carriage's bells kept time with the horses' hooves on the ground.

Then Laura said, "I almost forgot. I have a surprise for you. Here." Laura slowly opened the paper bag the doctor's wife had given her, and when she began to pull candies from it, the boys' eyes grew as big as marbles.

"Candy! Wow! They look just like the ones they had at the store at Christmas time, in the big glass jars!"

Laura smiled. "It does feel like Christmas, doesn't it? Why don't we each have one and save the rest for tonight's dessert." She was surprised by her familiar motherly tone, one she hadn't used with her boys in a long time.

Joe and Tom schemed as they whispered among themselves. "Let's keep this a secret. Won't Aunt Peggy be surprised," grinned Joe.

Ignoring a twinge of dark feelings, Laura smiled as she poked her nose into the bag. "Isn't the smell just superb? Ok, choose yours."

Joe took a chocolate with soft yellow cream inside while Tom picked a hard ribbon-like candy. Ben and his mother each picked a soft colour cream. Silently and happily they savoured their precious treats, wanting to make them last as long as possible.

"So tell me, Joe, tell me everything. School, life, your friends. Oh, I'm so pleased to be back!" exclaimed Laura as she kissed both Joe and Tom on their foreheads.

"These are so good, Mother! Could we please have just one more?"

There was no way she was going to resist anything the boys asked her. Not now. And the way she was feeling, not ever. A late spring snow began to flutter down, and all three boys settled into their mother's soothing embrace. Putting out their tongues to catch the little flakes, Tom and Ben giggled and laughed. Joe didn't join in. His face had fallen as if he had remembered something awful.

Finally, he blurted out, "Why didn't you come home for Christmas? You said you would try."

"I know, Joe. I know. And you have to know it isn't what I wanted. Let's just say things didn't turn out as I had planned. But I'm home now and we're going to be all right." Laura leaned over and squeezed his hand tight and tried to look into his eyes. He was clearly feeling betrayed though he seemed to be holding back beside himself. "Honey? We're going to be alright. I promise." He looked at her skeptically, and she saw his fear melt when she gave him her word.

They arrived not long after and all hopped out and rubbed their chilled behinds. Peggy was standing in the window; when they pulled up she burst out the front door. "Laura, Ben, welcome home! It's so good to see you again. Come, boys, take your mother's bags up to the house."

Laura was awash with emotion; anger, resentment, gratitude and love all pulsed in her throat.

"Come on in. I've made fresh biscuits and have potatoes and roast beef waiting, even homemade soup and meat pies like mother used to make. You must be famished."

Laura stared at her sister's back as she looped her arm around Ben and took on the stride of the boys. Was she over compensating for what she'd done to Laura, or was everything she'd done, all she was, unthinking, as if she had no idea, and this was how she showed her affection? Laura wondered. Regardless, when she heard just the mention of all those foods, tears sprang to her eyes. She looked at thin little Ben and began to cry. She hung back and let the tears fall silently.

As they walked up toward the house, George began doling out the chores. "Tom, you set the table then come outside to help Joe and me with the horses." He clicked his tongue and led the team off with Joe while Laura and Peg went into the house to get supper ready.

Laura came into the fragrant living room and slowly took off her coat, aware of her tattered dress against Peg's pert fresh one. The room was so still, she was aware of the clock ticking. "How are Patrick and Sadie Mae? Aren't they here?" she called out to Peg who was already in the kitchen.

Peg came out drying her hands on a dishtowel and sat down. "Laura, George's parents passed away just after Christmas."

"Oh, my. Why didn't you tell me in your letters?"

"I figured you had enough to deal with."

"What happened?"

"It was the strangest thing, really; they both ran a high fever for several days and died two days apart."

"No doctor, no medicine?"

Peggy shook her head and wiped a tear away. Laura was a bit surprised but touched. "The doctor did come, but it was too late."

Laura stared wide-eyed. "I feel terrible for George. Imagine dying two days apart like that. They were such nice folks."

Peggy sadly smiled. "I really came to know a new side of Sadie Mae after a spell. Dare say she became something like a friend. Don't get me wrong," she guffawed loudly, "she still drove me crazy at times, but I stopped wanting to poke her with a fork for it."

Both sisters fell quiet until Peggy spoke again, her voice cheery. "George has been working on the new highway. Hopefully he'll be able to make his stamps, but the weather is mighty unpredictable lately for April."

"What do you mean by stamps?"

"It's a kind of relief money the government pays when there's no work, but you have to work for so many weeks in order to collect. It's called unemployment insurance. Some people call it pogey. It sure would have helped early in the winter."

Laura narrowed her eyes, trying to put two and two together. Either Peg was lying or putting on a show. A fine dinner was nearly on the table; her sons looked well fed; and Peg's dress fabric was bright as if it hadn't been much washed. "Then it was a hardship taking care of the boys?"

"No, no, we were fine. And if we'd known just how sick they were, we'd have found the money for medicine." She wiped a tear away. "I, we never realized it was that serious. And then they were gone."

As if now released from a dreadful discomfort, Peggy took a deep breath, rose and said brightly, "Now, how about something to eat!"

"Let's do. I'm starved."

"So, how was your trip on the train?" Peggy smiled.

Laura didn't want to get into her adventures, and was relieved that just as she started in on an abridged version, the boys burst in from the barn, Ben's smile taking up half his face.

After dinner, over a cup of tea Laura mentioned returning to their own house. Peggy put her hand up. "Laura, there is no reason for you all to go back to a cold, empty house. You must stay with us until it gets warmer. Then we'll get the house ready together and you can move in time to plant your garden. You must wait for the right moon in order to plant. I think it's after June the eighth. Old Patrick knew. I should have listened better when he talked about such things. We'll buy some seeds..."

The boys who had gone off to play came running back into the room. "Mother, come see. Uncle George has built us bunk beds so we can all sleep in the same room! What do you think?"

Laura looked up at George who stood quietly with his cap in his hands, looking at Laura with a haunted, knowing expression. She could tell he knew the pain and trial she'd been through. She started to say thank you, but the words didn't come out. She opened her mouth then began to weep. The boys looked worried, and Tom held out his hand for Peggy so she could reassure him. "Oh, silly me," said Laura, blowing her nose. "I'm just being an old silly. Everything's just fine, boys. I promise." She held off the tears as best as she could for them, even though all she wanted to do was let them fall until she was empty. She hugged her children and wiped her tears on their shirts, looking over their rumpled heads to mouth 'thank you' to Peggy and George. Laura didn't care anymore what had happened or even what her sister's motives had been for sending her to the convent; she was home where she belonged and that's all she cared about.

After receiving word from the priest that this convent experience was a complete failure and there had been a gross miscommunication, Peggy realized some small, mean part of her she was not proud of had rejoiced in sending Laura away. But still she wouldn't have wanted Laura's time there to be so unbearable and inhumane. She felt terrible, then, guilt wrapping itself around her stomach. She ached to know what had happened there and wanted to ask about it, but George, knowing his wife as he did, pre-emptively made her promise she'd keep still until the boys were back in school. Laura's first weekend home belonged to her sons, he insisted. Peggy did hold her tongue, so much, in fact, Laura began to worry something was wrong or her sister was regretting her hospitality seeing how extra mouths would burden the family.

Monday morning arrived, and once the boys were off to school, Peggy neglected her usual chores and instead brewed fresh tea and asked Laura to sit. Ben romped around the living room and played with some empty spools of thread.

Peg bit her lip. "Laura, I have to know; was it really true, what the priest wrote in his note?"

Laura ringed her finger around the lip of the cup. "Yes, I mean, I might not have phrased it so bluntly, but it's all true. I was quite taken aback at how strongly the priest spoke on my behalf. And also quite touched."

Peg's voice was shaking. "Why didn't you tell me about those horrible conditions?"

"I couldn't, I...I didn't want to worry you. Please don't tell anyone."

"When I worked at the Mabou convent, taking piano lessons, do you remember that, the year I was away when we were children? The sisters were very kind. I can't understand why these, why they would be so horrible to you."

Laura bit her lip. She remembered that long, lonely year like it was yesterday. She'd missed her sister so much during that time. She stared at Peggy. She seemed authentically distraught, as if she had no idea why things had gone so sour. Laura's heart opened then, to the sister she'd always loved so dearly and trusted. There must have just been a terrible miscommunication after all. Peg wouldn't have told them a falsehood. After a moment of silence, Peggy bowed her head. "Can you ever forgive me?"

"Forgive you? For what?"

"For shipping you to Montreal-"

"Shipping me to Montreal? What are you saying?"

"Stop repeating every word I say! It's very annoying!"

Laura had never seen her sister act so strangely. Peggy rattled on. "It's my fault. Never should I have suggested you go away!"

"But it isn't your fault the nuns treated me in such a way, and actually it's not as if everything were bad; after all, I met the caretaker and his family, who were very kind. Oh, and on our way home, I talked with a man from Antigonish." Deep down, she realized she'd enjoyed Sam's company quite a bit and hoped she'd see him again. Laura wished she could tell Peggy about this, but even though Laura had decided to give her sister the benefit of the doubt, and had new feelings of love for her, Peggy was nonetheless an incurable gossip and Laura did not want her feelings for this man made public.

She looked at her sister, whose forehead was pursed. She saw how troubled Peggy was, how she was pulled into two directions by her feelings and her loyalty for her sister. Peg might not have always operated with honorable intentions, but she was still someone who tried to be a good person.

Just then, George walked inside, banging the door behind him. "George, for the love of God, fix that darn door. It makes so much noise, one of these days, it's going to wake the dead." Peggy glanced remorsefully at Laura, but Laura was lost in thought.

Then Laura turned around, "Peggy, how are Esther and her husband?"

"As nosy as ever. Why? Is she at the window?" Peggy walked over to look out.

"No, I don't see her."

George chuckled. "You soon will. Wait and see." George got up and opened and shut the door again. "Did it work this time?"

"Did what work?" George and Peggy were laughing now and Laura began to giggle without knowing what was happening.

"Is Esther at the window?"

Laura turned. "She is now. What's going on?"

George slapped his hands together. "I just have to bang that door and Esther appears in the window. Like magic."

"If she's not already there," said Peggy ruefully.

Laura shook her head. "Well, it feels good to be home, Esther or no Esther."

"Did I mention, Peggy, that Father MacKay is making his yearly visit?" said George. "He should be coming by next week."

"Oh?"

"And I have a good mind to tell him off. Sending Laura off to that God forsaken place-"

"Please don't talk badly about a man of the Lord, George."

"Man of the Lord? He's an ordinary person like you and me."

"Laura," said Peggy widening her eyes, her tone chirpy, "Let's tidy up, just in case he comes sooner than expected. I'm going to scrub the teapot."

George mumbled something under his breath and stormed out, slamming the door behind him.

Peggy and Laura ran to the window. "Like magic," they said in unison and laughed. "But Peggy, why is George so upset with Father MacKay? He's a good priest, isn't he?"

"That he is. And George knows it." She shook her head. "He just doesn't take too highly to priests. If it were up to him, there wouldn't be any money in the Sunday envelope."

"Yet George is such a generous man," said Laura.

Peggy shrugged, but Laura understood. She understood completely.

Gradually things fell into a routine. Mondays they washed. This was a challenging job especially since they had to carry the water from the well. Fortunately the well wasn't too far from the house. "At least we don't have to walk up a hill to get water," Peggy liked to say. Drying the clothes in such a chilly spring that seemed to rain endlessly was another matter. They would hang the clothes inside the house by the stove or simply wait for a peek of sun on another day to do the wash. Invariably, though, the rain would come and they would have to dash about plucking clothes from the line and bringing them in to dry by the stove anyway. Playing tag among the pants and shirts became the boys' favourite game. Tuesdays were for bread and pastry making. Peggy did most of this work while Laura ironed the clothes. Sometimes there was mending to do. On Wednesdays, the sisters sewed. They needed more blankets now that Laura and Ben were home and the warm weather simply refused to come. Saturday was cleaning day as the house had to be spick and span for Sunday, their day of rest. There was always something to do, and time passed by quickly.

On a late rainy afternoon by the end of the month, Father MacKay showed up at the door.

Peggy was flushed, her smile broad. "What a surprise, Father. Do come in."

He entered and took a look at the clothes hanging everywhere on their makeshift lines. "This must be a bad time for you?"

"We were actually expecting your visit a few weeks ago."

"Yes, well, I've been busy with several funerals and a visit from the bishop." He looked around and noticed Laura between a nightgown and undershirt. His tone became distinctly less official and softer. "Good afternoon, Laura."

"Hello, Father."

"Sorry for the mess," said Peggy as she grabbed some of the clothes off the line. "We always do the wash on Mondays, but when it started to rain after lunch, we took everything in."

The Father chuckled. "I know what it's like. My mother always did the wash on Mondays, come heck or high water!" he said with twinkling eyes.

Peggy held out a chair at the table, and he made his way over, slouching under the lines. He chuckled again. "My brothers and I used to play hide and seek on washdays." When he noticed Ben sitting on his mother's lap, he grinned. "Hello, there. Ben, is it?"

"You have a good memory, Father," smiled Laura as she looked down at Ben.

"Would you care for a cup of tea?" asked Peggy.

"No, thank you. I just have a minute."

Peggy glanced out the window. "But I thought you were making your annual visit."

"No, now that spring is finally here and it's a busy time for most of my parishioners, I'll resume my visits this fall." Then turning to Laura, he said, "How are you, Laura?"

"I'm fine. I want to thank-"

"Are you sure about that cup of tea? And biscuits, made fresh this morning?" interrupted Peggy.

"No, no, I just have a bit of business with Laura."

Peggy panicked. "Does she owe you money? For her trip back home from the convent? Well, she can't pay you; her pockets are empty."

The priest smiled politely and continued. "Actually, I'm looking for a housekeeper for the Glebe house. I'm here to offer you the position, Laura."

"Housekeeper? Well, I don't know," she paused, her heart sinking. "When-"

"As soon as you can. It's a paying job, of course." He looked intently at her. "I must say, I feel terrible about what happened. It was a dreadful miscommunication. I do say it's time I brush up on my French since obviously something didn't get communicated to the Sisters in my letter. You still look tired from your ordeal."

Laura lowered her head.

"But I hope I can make it up to you with this job."

Laura's voice felt stuck in her throat. "What about the boys?"

"Yes, well, I suppose you could take them with you, or maybe Peggy can care for them." He cleared his throat.

"I'd like to think it over if it's alright with you."

"Absolutely. Take your time."

"Thank you, Father. And thank you for the return fare." She wanted to say more, but she began to shake.

"Think nothing of it." He rose from the table and smiled gently at her. "Goodbye, Laura."

Peggy held the lines high so he didn't have to bend so much. When he stepped outside, he took a deep breath and looked about. "Looks like the sun is coming out after all. Another beautiful day."

Peggy smiled and nodded. "Good-bye, Father. So nice of you to come visit us," she said loudly. "Come again any time." Peggy remained on the steps. As she watched him leave, she frowned and muttered, "What a waste. Such a nice man. Would actually make a good husband for Laura." She shrugged and slowly turned around. "But he is a kind man, no matter what George says."

"That he is," swallowed Laura.

Peggy cleared her throat. "But clearly you shouldn't take the job, I mean you alone with the boys. Look at you; Father MacKay is right, you're still not rested up from the convent. And it would be so much work. Unless, I mean, like Father said, we could keep the boys, and you would stay with us on your day off, of course."

Laura's heart and mind began to race. She realized no matter how generous Peg was, no matter that they were family, Laura was entirely at the whim of her sister, who was housing them without asking for a nickel. And Peggy seemed quite aware she wielded such a power.

Peggy seemed suddenly cheerful as a songbird. "Why don't we go see George. He's probably fidgeting in the barn."

Laura dressed little Ben warmly without a word and off they went to seek George's opinion.

"Oh, good," he said, corralling Ben to his side. "Here, give me a hand. Peggy, turn the handle and Laura, spill a bit of this water on the wheel. I want to sharpen my axe but I need three sets of hands. Fancy, you comin' just in time." He smiled at Ben who hugged his broad leg. "What did Father MacKay want?"

"Laura, why don't you get the kitchen knives from the house? We'll get George to sharpen them. I'll watch Ben."

"Sure, Peggy." Laura's voice fell to a whisper. As she made her way to the house, her breathing became irregular. She already knew what was happening: Peggy was positioning the priest's offer to George as the best possible thing that could happen to them all. Laura went and got the knives, but before she could leave the house, she sank into a chair at the kitchen table and cried.

After a few minutes, she rose, wiped her eyes, and held her head high. She was grateful to her sister and brother-in-law and would do anything for them, anything to repay their kindness. But there was no way she would leave her sons again. Ever.

In the barn, George and Peggy were having a discussion in strained tones. When Peggy saw Laura enter, she closed her mouth and turned her head away. George's voice was even and calm in the quiet barn. "It's settled. I will not let you go through such an ordeal again, Laura. You need to get your strength back before you move into your house, so you will stay with us until the boys are done with school and can help out. We have enough to eat and wood to burn. Besides, I got news that a barrel of material is soon to arrive from the States. You girls will be busy up until we thaw out. And we also have a bit of money saved from what we received of the boys' baby bonus. It's not much, but it will help you get settled when you move back home." He returned to his ax, inspecting it from every angle. "And we don't want to get our hopes up yet until I can look into this a bit more, but my friend Dooly thought there might be a way you could get some money from the government, because you're a widow and all."

Laura was already shaking her head, imagining the worst. "But if I apply, could I lose my children? No, no, it's not worth it."

George chuckled. "Nothing like that. I honestly think it's just money to help you out, is all. We just have to fill in some forms-"

Laura shook her head again.

"Dooly knows about it, so we'll take care of it. How does that sound?"

Laura didn't know how to feel, but a faint light of hope grew in her. Did she dare dream that she could receive this extra money which would help her keep her family together, and survive without being a burden to anyone? Was what she'd said to Joe going to end up being true?

"Wonderful. It's settled, then." Peggy picked her skirt up and neatened it around her legs before standing. Laura didn't acknowledge how quick Peg was to want to ship her out again. Laura looked at her sister's fallen face and rather than feel angry, she was surprised to note how her heart opened. Clearly Peggy just wanted children so badly, was so hungry to be a mother, she simply wasn't able to be rational when it came to possibly getting to keep the boys, at whatever the cost. Laura looked at the circles beneath her sister's eyes, how she made the best of the hand dealt to her and also said nothing. All this emotion made her feel windblown, but things were going to be fine. Wind did tend to clean the air in the best way.

By the end of May, Laura and her three sons returned to their old house. Pushing the cobwebs aside, they slowly walked in. No one spoke as the boys fanned out and went to inspect the corners.

"Mother, we are going to be all right," said Joe when he saw the tears on her face. She knew he was worried and felt the burden of being the eldest, the man of the house not even nine-years-old.

She reached into her sleeve for her handkerchief and blew her nose. "Joe," she said looking straight into his eyes, which were tight with concern, "you are quite right. We are indeed going to be just fine. I feel it in my bones. What's more, we're about to start receiving another kind of money from the government, a pension, George called it. They just need to come by and visit us, then that's it- free money!" She smiled assuredly and clasped her hands over his. "When this money comes, we'll buy seeds and lots of food. Now, why don't we put our things away, clean up the place a bit and then see to the garden. What do you say?"

"Yes, Mother." he replied sadly. He turned and joined his brothers who had already made their way outside. Soon the three were running about and laughing. They were home.

A few days later after the boys had gone to school, a government inspector came by the house. By the time Peggy dropped in, Laura was still shaking. "They sure don't waste any time. You just moved back in," frowned Peggy. "What did he want?"

"I'm not sure. He didn't talk much. He inspected the house from top to bottom, even checked inside the cupboard and under the bed. I think he was looking for gold."

"Try to relax. I'll make you a cup of tea. These government people, they think they own the world! I brought you some seeds.

Maybe after school, we can plant with the children. There's no time to waste getting your garden up and growing. Good thing George got the soil ready for planting."

Laura looked at her sister and felt so grateful then for her. "Peggy?"

"Hmm?" Peggy was busy counting packets of seeds, her tongue in the corner of her mouth. Laura hugged her tight. "What's that for?"

"For being so kind. Both of you."

Then one warm June afternoon, Joe excitedly arrived home, waving an envelope in his hand. "Mother! Mother! It's from the government, see? Open it right away!"

Laura was shaking. She opened the envelope with trembling fingers. She handed the cheque to Joe. "I'm too nervous, Joe. What does it say?" His eyes went over the lines and his face registered disappointment. "What is it?"

"Gee, Mother, it isn't a lot."

Laura smiled reassuringly. "Oh, it's alright. Anything is better than nothing. With the baby bonus and this cheque, I'd say we're rich!"

"Actually, I was thinking...I saw a wanted ad at the garage the other day."

Laura ruffled his hair. "Joe, you're not even ten; I don't think it's time to begin work just yet. Now," she said, picking up the cheque, "would you like to come with me to the Credit Union?"

"Yes, Mother. First, it says here you have to sign your name on the back. I'll get a pen."

"My name?" Laura held the pen Joe had given her and looked at it.

"What's the matter?"

Laura pressed her lips together, then smiled at her son. "Joe, you know how Mother has trouble with reading? Well, writing is something I can't do either. This is what happens when you leave school early, and this is why I am very determined for you to stay in school. School is your job. And I need you to do very well, so you can grow up to teach me all you know."

He smiled his crooked-toothed smile. "That's ok; how about if I teach you how to write your name, right now?"

Laura's eyes opened as big and round as marbles. "No," she said, "Really? You think I could learn?"

"I don't see why not, Mother. It's just lines on a page, really. See, now watch me, then you do it."

After several tries, Laura concentrating on holding the pencil and looping it around the "u" and "a", she smiled at the paper. She put the pencil down, cupped Joe's face with her hands and kissed him on the forehead. "I can write my name, my own name. How about that? See, Joe, that was good thinking, teaching me. You're already so smart," she announced proudly. She broke into a dance and waltzed around the room. Joe laughed then joined her.

The following day after school, Laura met Joe in front of the Credit Union. She nervously clung to her son's arm and had broken into a healthy sweat by the time they reached the window. Yet the transaction was very easy: she handed over the cheque, signed another small piece of paper, and in return, the man handed her money. Laura was elated. This meant she would be able to take over her own money, not be dependent on anyone- her sister, soon not her children- just rely on herself. She looped her arm in her son's and smiled. "Since we're here, let's go get a few things at the Co-op," she said. A cloud darkened her thoughts as she imagined her sister's face when she'd tell her she wanted to have the baby bonus cheques transferred back into her name. After all, she was here to stay. But she pushed those thoughts from her mind. Peggy had no choice but to understand. And Laura wasn't about to live her whole life waiting for her sister to walk on over with the money each month. She could sign her own name. Manage her own home. It was time. She hugged Joe's arm tighter and giggled.

From behind, someone put a warm hand on Laura's shoulder. "Hello, Laura."

She turned around and came face to face with Samuel O'Brien.

"Hello, Sam. Fancy seeing you here!"

Sam smiled. "Tell me, how are you doing?"

Laura recognized how easily she was able to chat with him, and he her. Over near the linens, two women whispered, but not at all quietly. "Did you hear?" said one. "She called him Sam! For God's sake, and he's married! The nerve of her!"

"Sounds like an opportunist to me. I'd bet she's still playing the lonely widow card while she's cozying up to that family."

Sam and Laura overheard and paused their talk. Sam gently slid Laura over to the door and offered his arm. Laura shrank back horrified by what the women had said. But Sam just smiled. "I'm on my way home. Would you two like a ride?"

Laura nearly laughed out loud. "That sounds lovely, Sam; come, Joe." Laura couldn't resist looking back at the two women and smiling just a bit.

When they arrived, Sam slowed down. "Is this your home?" he asked.

Laura didn't answer. Joe piped up, "Sure is. This is my daddy's farm. Suits us just fine."

"Joe!"

Joe had already grabbed their bag from the back and hopped out. Laura opened the door. "Thank you so much for the ride."

"Any time, any time," he said. He waited until they were inside before driving slowly back down the lane.

Laura hummed while they walked in. "That was quite an adventure, but now it's time for your schoolwork," she said. She looked sadly at Joe as he settled his books on the kitchen table and felt silly that she'd needed him to go to the Credit Union. After all, the whole ordeal had been so simple. He was growing up too fast as it was. No need to put extra responsibilities on his shoulders. She vowed to make it up to him by taking over some of his chores on the weekend so he could study for his upcoming exams and maybe even teach her more about writing and reading after school was finished for the year. She decided to give him a small allowance. She chuckled. They could afford it now that the money was rolling in.

Laura and the boys were so busy, it was easy to push aside her vow to continue to work with Joe. She didn't quite feel physically herself yet, but she nonetheless worked morning to night keeping her home warm and clean and her boys healthy and fed. She went to see Peggy about getting the cheques back into her name now that she could cash them herself, but Peggy was out at the church, so George was happy to help her. She had to admit it was easier to deal with him than the little glare and quick smile she'd have gotten from her sister.

Once the next baby bonus installment came, finally in her name, with it and the widow's pension, she was able to buy a few hens for eggs and got a deal on a cow with a bad leg from a farmer nearby. She was a sweet thing with big brown eyes and gave creamy milk; Laura and the boys doted on her like she was a pet. In the summer, carrots, tomatoes, beans and cucumbers grew in abundance, and in the autumn, they were blessed with a big crop of turnips and cabbages; in fact, so many, Laura was able to sell a few at the market. At night, Laura watched the boys do their homework and packed their lunch cans for the next day, and they counted their blessings that they were together.

One sunny Monday morning the following spring of '52, Peggy stopped around for some tea. "By the way," she said, barely out of her coat, "did you know that the O'Briens down the road need a housekeeper? Yes, the last one quit, just like that!" Peggy snapped her fingers.

Laura remained quiet. O'Brien. That name had etched itself into her mind though she didn't dare dream anything of it, especially since it was so long ago. Just a name. A nice man, some kind conversation. Nothing else. Yet she thought, how utterly normal: just a job. Close to home. Helping a nice family, probably pays just fine. I've had enough of housekeeping jobs to last me a lifetime, she thought, but still, she had to be practical about taking care of her family, government money or not. The last year had been a challenge, working from so few resources. This might free her up a bit, be enough money to buy more sugar and flour and let the boys have ice cream once in a while. She drifted off into thoughts of the paper box with stripes of vanilla, chocolate and strawberry.

The boys would be in heaven. She smiled and stood, went to the counter and hugged her sister.

"Thank you."

The next day after Joe and Tom left for school, Laura washed her long hair and curled it with paper pieces. She fumbled with the paper as she'd never done this before; up until her time at the convent, her hair had had its own natural curl, but since then, it had grown limp and hadn't recovered. She then placed the small cast iron on the stove to iron her Sunday dress and took Ben outside to play in the sun and let her hair dry. After an early lunch, once she was ready and tidy, she put little Ben into the boys' wagon and off they went. She recalled that Robert O'Brien lived about a mile away. With her head high and back straight, she whistled a happy tune trying to muster up the courage to ask about the job.

It was a longer walk than she'd thought, though, and by the time she arrived, she was tired and perspiring. Her confidence had fallen and her heart was beating a mile a minute. When they reached the majestic white house, she stopped. It was similar to the doctor's house in Truro, large and stately, full of grace and opulence. She knew she didn't belong in such a fine place.

She was just about to turn around when she noticed an elderly man with a cane in hand, limping up the lane to greet her. With a pleasant smile on his lips, his white hair showing from under his cap, and eyes blue as the sky with a twinkle in each, Laura felt immediately at ease, as if he were familiar to her. He did look quite like his son. Close up, she recognized him and remembered he'd come to Johnny's wake, which touched her as well.

The old man smiled and motioned for her to sit a while on a nearby wooden bench. After catching his breath, he extended his hand. "Robert O'Brien. And you are?"

Laura sat down as Ben ran about, chasing butterflies. To her surprise, she felt quite at ease with this elderly gentleman and found the words easily. "On the train, I met a man whose name was Samuel O'Brien."

"Sam's my son. He and his wife Abby live here with me," he replied as he sadly gazed at the house.

"Any children?"

"No, no. Well, they had a little girl, but she died at birth." He smiled again. "I think she would now be about the same age as your little one."

"I'm so sorry."

"What's his name?"

"Ben," she called over, "come meet Mr. O'Brien." As he approached, Laura continued her story, "It was a real pleasure getting to talk to someone from home on the train ride back from Montreal."

"Sam is always on the road for meetings. I hardly see him these days." He clapped his hands down onto his thighs and stood. "What would you say to a glass of lemonade for your young man and a cup of tea for you?"

They walked into the house; Laura took one step into the kitchen and paused. It was huge. A long wooden table surrounded by cupboards was at one end. The whole room was perfumed by sprigs of rosemary drying on the window sill and was warm from the stove. There was a narrow stairway in one corner, an odd spot for stairs, she thought. "What a lovely home," she murmured, sitting in the chair Mr. O'Brien held out for her. She continued to look around while he fixed their drinks and in turns marveled at the space and furnishings and balked, wondering whether she'd be able to take care of it all.

She had to admit that chatting with Mr. O'Brien, similar as it had been with his son, was like talking to someone she'd known a long time. "Laura, I'm sure I'm supposed to ask you for references or make sure your polishing skills are up to snuff, but frankly I don't want to bother with any of that. We'd be very happy if you would work for us." He offered her his hand.

"I'd be delighted." She stood and collected their dishes. "I think I'll begin with these."

Just then, a petite lady in a fine dress entered the kitchen and stopped short when she saw Laura moving to the sink holding cups and saucers. Her gaze then panned over to Ben, who was racing several wooden spoons over the floor in the corner. Laura turned and hunted for a dishcloth so she could dry her hands. The lady slowly flipped her long blond hair over one shoulder and pursed her perfectly rouged lips. Laura looked down from the woman's cold gaze and noticed her hands. They were soft, her nails painted red, her skin flawless and creamy. Laura's own hands were dry, the skin flaking, and she realized there was a whole world out there full of elegance and refinement that she would never be a part of. When Laura met the woman's narrowed eyes, she shivered and instinctively moved towards Ben.

Mr. O'Brien stood, whistling, and came over to make introductions. "What is this, Robert?" Abby asked without taking her piercing eyes off Laura.

"Meet our new housekeeper, Laura, and this is her son Ben. Laura, this is my son's wife, Abby."

"Pleased to meet you, Miss Abby," muttered Laura. She wiped her hands on her skirt and made to offer one, but Abby just shrugged and left the room, leaving an air of arrogance behind her. Laura slumped into the nearest chair, her knees shaking. It was just too like the nuns.

"Did I-" she began to ask.

"No, no, don't worry, Laura. She'll come around." He came to the sink and quickly rinsed the soapy dishes. "How about if we call it a day? Will you come tomorrow around eight?"

It crossed Laura's mind to say she'd reconsidered, but she knew there wasn't any other job for her at the moment. As if he understood, Mr. O'Brien put the last cup into the drainer and held out his hand. "Come, I have something to show you."

She and Ben followed their new friend to the side of the house and entered an old greenhouse. The air was heavy and warm, and the profusion of color swarmed her thoughts. Baskets of marigolds, peonies and sweet peas hung from the corners while rows of violet, white and blue pansies looked on with their little faces. Mums and Sweet Williams lined the perimeters. Mr. O'Brien introduced her to the flowers as if they were his children, and before long, Laura forgot all about the tight feeling in her chest and just breathed in the heady scent of the blooms. She did notice the building was a bit ramshackle and thought perhaps she could bring George by to have a look.

Ben had his little hands cupped around a hardy mum. "Look, Mother, yellow-purple-red." He seemed to be transported, his little face in thrall.

Robert stared at the two of them, his wrinkled face alight with joy. "You like it in here, son?"

Ben grinned at him. "Yesyesyes!"

Robert laughed. "I don't have many people to share this place with; Sam is so busy and Abby's interests lie elsewhere." He frowned just a bit. "You know, my gardener is quite lazy and frankly I think his attentions lie elsewhere as well," he paused, "but perhaps little Ben here would like to help me make this greenhouse and my garden come to life." He turned to Ben, "What do you say, Ben, how'd you like a job?"

Laura chuckled. "He might be a bit too young to work, don't you think? Would you even want a four and a half-year-old employee?"

"We'll take our time and I'll show him what needs to be done, even if it's just fetching things now and then. My legs are not as strong as they used to be. What do you say, Ben?"

Ben stared wide-eyed and tugged on his mother's dress. Laura smiled.

"Thank you, Mr. O'Brien. I, we really appreciate your kindness."

"Call me Robert. See you tomorrow. You too, young man." He tousled Ben's hair.

"Yes, Mr. O'Brien. Robert. Thank you, and have a pleasant evening."

He smiled and waved good-bye.

As Laura walked home, pulling Ben in the wagon, she reviewed the day's events. They were bittersweet; certainly Robert was a lovely person, but as for Abby, Laura would just have to either ignore her or hope she warm up. She checked on Ben and noticed tucked in beside him was a bag full of bread, ham and fruits. What a lovely person this man was. She smiled; he'd already paid her with exactly what she needed and all she'd done that day was drink tea and wash a few saucers.

They made their way down the narrow trail to her house and paused to pick some buttercups and admire the poplars waving their leaves by the stream. Laura caught herself humming and realized she felt more at peace than she had in a long time. "Ben, do you want to hold the flowers?" she asked. He didn't answer, so she turned to see what he was up to. He'd been by her side, but he was gone. "Ben! Ben! Where are you?"

She threw the flowers down and looked frantically in all directions. Her legs were weak and wobbly. This was an unfortunate repeat of what had happened on the train. "Ben!" she called out again. Her head lightened and she felt faint. She steeled herself and recalled the St. Anthony's prayer, the patron Saint of lost things and missing persons.

"Please, St. Anthony, help me find my son," she thought.

Laura picked a direction and walked a little ways along the creek. There, blissfully wiggling his toes in the bubbles of the stream, was Ben, getting soaked and enjoying his newfound freedom. She grabbed him and held him tightly.

"Promise me you'll never wander off like that again!"

"No, Mama," he promised, pulling on her hair. She picked him up and carried him like a sack of flour back to the wagon. They bounced their way home.

As soon as the boys arrived home from school, Laura shared her good news. The boys were happy but Laura could see in their faces they were unsure. "Boys, this is a regular, normal job. I will be home every night for supper. Now run to Aunt Peggy's; tell her about my new job and ask her if you can stop by her place after school from now on. Tell her I'm starting tomorrow!"

"But mother, summer vacation is in four weeks."

"Oh, yes, that's true," she sighed. "Well, I'll walk over and have a talk with her after supper. I'm sure she won't mind keeping an eye on you for the summer months. Actually, I'm sure she'll be thrilled. Now, do your chores and finish your homework." In saying all of this, Laura actually began to feel quite grateful for her sister's love and interest in her children. It was finally going to work in her favour in a very big way.

The following morning, when Laura arrived at the O'Brien house, Robert had the fire going and the water boiling. He met her at the door.

"Good morning, Laura. Hello, Ben. Come on in."

"Thank you, Robert. Now, where shall I begin?"

"How about a cup of tea first? Have you eaten breakfast yet? How about some toast?"

Laura bowed her head. She hadn't left herself enough time to eat anything. "That's very kind of you, but I couldn't-"

Robert ignored her and plunked down a plate with thickly cut toast and jam. "There you go. Abby said she left you a list of things to do." He got the paper off the counter and skimmed through the list. "Whew, she's not wasting any time; she's starting you off with a complete house cleaning from top to bottom."

Laura pretended to skim it and nodded. "I guess I'll start with the dishes, then work my way around." It was a very long list. Laura had to wonder whether Abby were just terribly lonely; perhaps that's why she was so unfriendly, her soul left unattended. Robert had mentioned how Sam was rarely around, leaving early in the morning and often not returning home until long past supper time. And he travelled more than he was in town.

"I'm sure you'll do a fine job. I'll be in the greenhouse if you need me. Coming, Ben?"

It wasn't long before Laura understood why Robert was so keen to get himself a new gardening helper. The hired gardener had far more interest in roving his eye around the women of the house than on the flowers. The way he looked at her gave her the shivers, and she scuttled out of his way whenever he came near. Eventually he left her alone and reserved his sly gazes for Miss Abby, who didn't seem to mind being leered at one bit. Yet not long after Laura had begun, Robert let him go, saying he'd found someone else. She chuckled when he relayed this to her, wondering whether Robert had revealed that the someone else was a four year old.

Spring swiftly melted into summer, but the days were hardly lazy for Laura. The span of the house gave her quite a bit of exercise just trying to keep up. Six large rooms made up the first level, with a kitchen, a dining room, a spacious living area, a library next to the parlour and the master bedroom. A long spiral staircase enhanced the main entrance. The stairs led to a wide hallway and three large bedrooms and a bath. She looked at the gleaming white tub, sighed, then smiled. How she envied their indoor plumbing, but how lovely to be able to use it while here, she thought.

Old Mr. O'Brien had had this house built in his younger days when he first married. He and his wife had dreamt of filling the spacious rooms with children. But Samuel ended up being their only child. When Mrs. O'Brien died some years ago, Sam and his new wife Abby moved in, reinvigorating Robert's hope that the rooms would be filled with the sounds of children's voices. But it was not to be, and the couple remained childless.

Though the extravagant house initially excited Laura, eventually she felt her energy waning, particularly when Miss Abby was around, casting her withering glances over the surfaces Laura had just scrubbed. Her sour face was a constant reminder of the nuns at the convent. Laura began to wonder if the woman even had teeth, for she'd never seen her smile. Plus her lists grew longer by the day.

Finally after a few weeks, Miss Abby cornered Laura in the kitchen. She swept in, her delicate chiffon blouse rustling, and picked up the paper she'd left that Laura hadn't touched. "Listen, Laura! Why is it you ignore the things I write down? It's a list. I want you to do the things on the list."

"Yes, of course. I keep forgetting my glasses. I'm sorry, Madam."

"Remember to bring them with you. It's not my fault you're too daft to remember them."

"Yes, Madam."

Abby turned on her cream coloured heels and clicked away, muttering beneath her breath. Laura sat down heavily at the table and lifted the paper. The words on it might as well have been written in Greek.

Ben ran in from the hall. "Mama, Mama! I heard that lady whisper a bad word."

"I know, Ben. I know."

"Come see the flowers, Mama."

"Not now, Ben. I have too much work to do."

"Mama, please. I want you to see the flowers!" insisted Ben as he pulled the hem of her dress.

"Well, OK, but not for long."

Laura took Ben's hand and slipped the list inside her apron pocket. The greenhouse was indeed a great diversion. Eventually, she took out the paper and examined it again. Perhaps she could make out a letter or two.

"What do you have there, Laura?" Robert came up the row, wiping his hands on a towel. She hadn't heard him approach and it was too late to hide the paper. "Oh, it's just Miss Abby's list."

"Let me see. What does she have in store for you today? Ah, the windows. The rains do dirty them up quite a bit."

Laura pursued her lie. "Would you do me a favour; I've forgotten my glasses yet again, so could you please read me the other items?"

He frowned as he looked it over. "Seems you're in for a big day. My daughter-in-law is certainly ambitious. There is only so much a body can do. Take it easy; tomorrow is another day!"

Laura was relieved for the time being. Still, she had the impression that no matter how clean the house were to become, Abby more enjoyed toying with Laura than anything. "Do this! Do that! Not that way! This way!"

There was nothing to do about that but bite her lips raw and wish Sam would come home, or the gardener, she didn't care who it was, and pay this woman some attention so she'd leave her alone.

Her interest in Laura went beyond household interest and seemed to become a sport for her. One day, while Abby was entertaining a group of friends for lunch, Laura was serving them tea, and one of the ladies mentioned how delicious the tea biscuits were. Laura smiled and took a breath to say thank you when Abby chimed in, "Well, how nice of you to say. I made them myself this morning!" Laura closed her mouth and widened her eyes, then hurried into the kitchen before she said something she oughtn't, the vision of Abby's smug round face with her red apple cheeks burning into her eyes.

Laura thought she could beat this woman at her own game the following week at her next hosted luncheon. When it came time for the dessert, she presented a plate of scrawny looking biscuits, hard and tasteless. She knew she shouldn't have done that but the temptation was too great.

Abby stared in disbelief at the plate of biscuits and quickly scoffed in a loud voice, "Oh, my, I see Laura baked the biscuits this morning." She grinned with all her teeth showing. It was shocking to see them, they were neat in a row like a barracuda's. "Pity you're not such a good cook, are you, dear? Take them away!" The ladies murmured about how hard it was to get good help nowadays. "Oh, that's alright; listen, Laura, don't you worry; when I have a moment, I'd be happy to show you how to make real biscuits that will even put your sister Peggy's to shame!"

Laura, fuming, hurried to the kitchen and flipped the nasty biscuits into the sink. She could hear the laughter from the other room. It was bad enough to insult her in front of everyone, but to put down her sister, who was a superior cook to this woman any day, was going too far. Abby probably couldn't even boil water.

Laura punched her fist into her thigh; where did this arrogant, two-faced fake, who was too busy living off of her husband's hard work, getting her nails done or her hair styled, meeting this person or that at the diner, get off picking on me, she steamed. I'm the hardest working person in this house, working all the live long day, 'I've been working on the railroad-' Laura laughed as the lyrics of the song coursed through her head, 'just to pass the time away.' Why on earth were railroads in her head at a time like this? Oh, Abby O'Brien, go on with yourself, she thought. I'm the hardest working woman in this house, and proud of it. She smoothed her hands over her hair, took a breath, smiled, and hummed the tune again, this time out loud.

Laura resolved to simply view Abby as a silly woman, nothing more. Laura had bigger issues to worry over: making sure she had enough energy for her boys at night, for one. And keeping her health. She simply didn't have it in her to tangle with this person emotionally. Abby's sourpuss attitude is her problem. No wonder the last housekeeper quit. Good thing I am not a quitter. Good thing, thought Laura, grinding her teeth.

But something about Laura clearly piqued an emotional response in Abby, and after the biscuit episode, she became even more pinched and meaner. One morning, while Laura was sweeping the floor, Abby hurried downstairs, in a foul temper. "Clean the parlour rug! All of it! At once! It's filthy!"

"Yes, Madam."

Laura dragged the big rug outside, hung it over the white picket fence and pounced on it with a piece of wood to get the dust out. All the while, getting hotter and hotter in the summer sun, sweat pouring from her, she was fuming: how could such a rich person be so full of dirt, full of herself, full of shit! Laura stopped and looked around as she brought her hand to her mouth. Thank goodness no one could hear what she was thinking, she smirked.

She returned to beating the rug but had to stop several times to cough. It wasn't just the dust; the coughing spells had been coming on more frequently of late and the doctor's medicine was long gone. Laura reminded herself to talk to Peggy, then decided better of it. No point in worrying her. She looked down at her handkerchief dismayed that blood had smeared the beautiful embroidery. Her mother had toiled over this fancy work. Now she would have to wash it carefully and put it in a pot to boil. Another thing to do.

Sam was at home for a change, tying his tie in the upstairs bedroom, and at the sound of Laura's cough, he moved to the window to watch her outside attack the rug like a tiger. There was a hot wind that blew the rug from the fence. Laura fetched it, rolled it over the railing again and continued beating it. He marveled at her energy but at the same time he knew her aggravated cough was something in her that shouldn't have been. He closed his eyes briefly and hoped it wasn't tuberculosis. It was going around, such a devastating disease.

He made a mental note to discuss this with his father. But then he looked at his watch and hurried to finish dressing so he could catch his train. He hoped she'd be alright, he thought. Maybe it was just the dust.

Laura didn't have time to dwell on her health, instead focusing on the fact that her family was settled into a good routine. School started, the boys were happy with their classes and friends, and she felt so relieved at having a weekly salary with which to buy food for her family, plus a few extras like molasses, sugar, flour, tea, some meat and once in a while ice cream as a treat. She held her head high, and felt pride balloon up in her chest when the shopkeeper at the Co-op commented on how she'd heard Laura had gotten a good job. "Why yes, it is wonderful to be employed by such a lovely family," she said before hurrying out, her smile as broad as daylight.

Then one afternoon in December, Laura came home before the boys and saw she'd received a letter from the government. She quickly hid it before Joe came in and could see it. She knew it wasn't her monthly cheque, and it looked serious. It shamed her to depend on him and made her feel so small. She didn't know what to do about it and tried to act as if everything were perfectly fine until the boys went to bed and she was alone with her heart, which felt like a stone.

The following morning she went to work at Robert's, her feelings still pulling on her heavily. When he came into the kitchen in the afternoon, he looked at her and paused. "Something is wrong," he said. "I can read it in your face. Perhaps you need a raise? Abby does work you very hard."

Robert was such a kind man, so intelligent and curious about life. Laura began to tear up, but then she realized she could tell him the truth. He wouldn't judge her. She knew that much.

Taking a deep breath, she said, "I can't read and I can't write. My son taught me how to sign my name, but that's as far as we got." She sighed. "This letter came from the government. It could say anything on it, and I wouldn't have any idea."

Robert looked at the ground and shook his head. "Of course," he said kindly. "Those damn lists of my daughter-in-law's. I'll tell you, it's probably a good thing you can't read or you'd have quit long ago."

Laura laughed.

"How about this. If you teach me how to make your sister's famous biscuits, I'll teach you how to read and write."

"Oh, I couldn't-" she started to say. Then she burst into a smile. "I'd love to. If you think I'd be able to keep up."

Robert leaned in. "I wouldn't take you on as a student if I didn't think you couldn't do it." He grinned, "One's never too old to learn something new. But for now," he reached for the paper, "let's deal with this letter." Robert skimmed it and frowned. "Well, it's bad news, I'm afraid. It says you're to lose your pension because you're working." Robert shook his head. "It seems someone failed to mind his own business and told the government about your job here." He frowned, scanning the letter again. "I'd hoped to avoid this."

Laura sat down, her legs weak. "Am I in trouble?" `

"No, not at all. But it does say you'll need to pay back whatever you've received while you were employed."

Laura began to tremble and a sob burst from her. It was everything she feared, being poor again. "They can't expect such a thing; I don't have that kind of money saved up. What am I going to do?"

Robert sat beside Laura and put his hand on hers. "Why don't you let me look into this. I used to be a pretty darn good lawyer, you know. Maybe I can get them to waive your penalty. Use the old O'Brien charm." He smiled warmly. "I will say this, though; we need you here. So if you're be willing to stay, I'll gladly raise your present salary to match your monthly pension and a bit extra plus give you enough to compensate for having to repay the government. Does that seem fair to you?"

Laura looked up, her eyes still wet. "You would do that?"

Robert smiled and nodded.

She was filled with every emotion: gratitude for Robert's generosity and kindness, and shame from the government man's fingers touching all her cupboards, looking at her like she was a criminal. She would gladly work forever to avoid ever seeing him again. "Thank you so much," she whispered.

That evening, Laura brought the boys to Peggy's after supper and brushed up on her biscuit technique. From the next afternoon on, when Laura's work at the O'Brien house was nearly done and Ben was having his nap, she and Robert would sit at the kitchen table surrounded by books, paper and pencils. To be safe from Abby's wrath, though, she always kept a tea towel, a big dish of apples and pie plates nearby. Fortunately she only needed the apples once, for of late, Abby seemed unusually preoccupied. In fact, one morning Robert surprised Laura at the door. "Let's hit the books; Abby forgot to leave a list, and the house hasn't had a chance to get dirty since yesterday."

"To be honest, I'm enjoying learning from her lists. And she does have impeccable handwriting," Laura laughed. They sat with some tea Robert had brewing on the stove and pored over the materials he'd brought out: the day's newspaper, a few recipes, and two children's books. That day he also paid her and used the money to demonstrate the value.

On her next pay day, he paid her with a cheque. "Is that alright?" asked Robert. "I didn't manage to get any cash." Then he chuckled. "The Credit Union will probably be in awe of how beautiful your signature has become."

Laura felt proud then of her accomplishment. "I'm looking forward to my first solo trip. Thank you."

That afternoon she walked through the delicate snowfall into the Credit Union on her own feeling assured and competent. Everything looked so magical dusted in white. She waited in line and smiled when she handed her cheque over. But rather than handing her the money, the teller turned it over, frowned, cross checked it with the signature they had on file, and handed Robert's cheque back to her. "Ma'am, it doesn't appear to be your usual signature. Please wait here while I speak with the manager."

Laura's knees grew numb and her body went cold. Without waiting for the teller to come back, she ran out of the building.

She told Joe about it later that evening, but when he got his worried old man face, she instantly regretted burdening him. She touched the wrinkles and said, "You don't pay any mind to this. I'll straighten it all out." She stood. "Want a snack before bed? I baked some cookies today at work and snuck a few home."

When she told Robert about the incident, he shook his head at the irony of the situation. "I'll take care of it, don't you worry."

Laura was relieved. She didn't want to admit it to anyone but after a long day at work, going into town and dealing with the Credit Union then doing her shopping afterward, was taking up more energy than it seemed she had. Lately her body felt even more sluggish and heavy. The boys were busy being boys, playing and exploring. She was glad they didn't notice she had less patience and fell asleep before she could tell them stories. Even reciting the rosary at night had become a chore. She'd kept up with her faith because it was familiar to her, but her heart wasn't in it. Sometimes she'd fall asleep in the middle of a Hail Mary.

As the weeks and months flew by, she wondered if the extra dollars were worth remaining under Abby's whip. She wondered whether she might be better off staying at home and receiving her widow's pension, however meager. There wouldn't be money for extras, yet she doubted she would be this fatigued.

Though Robert and Sam were extremely kind, two years of housekeeping for Abby O'Brien had begun showing more and more in her body. She made it through her days, sometimes nearly numb with exhaustion, and at night, it took all her strength to get the boys through their homework and dinner and into bed, then to sterilize her handkerchiefs and make sure the house was somewhat tidy. On weekends, she made sure to smile a lot and put on a show that all was normal. She knew she needed to see a doctor, but she didn't know when she'd find the time. Besides, she reasoned, she was still functioning; she just needed more sleep. It took the strength of giants to get through the winter of '54, then spring, through the summer heat and the boys' boundless energy. By the time fall was in full swing, Laura knew something would soon give in her. She could feel it in her cells, and she was afraid.

One mid-November afternoon, Miss Abby, who was famous for her last minute decisions, barged into the kitchen, barking demands. "Laura, I'm having a dinner party tonight. I want the house spotless from top to bottom. Here's a list of duties and the menu for the dinner. Get cracking. Oh, and if Sam gets home before I do, tell him about the party. He was up and gone before I was able to tell him about it this morning. And try to follow the list this time."

Laura couldn't believe her ears. Not only less than a day's notice, but a go-between for Abby and Sam. Was she out of her mind? Laura looked down at her apron and worn shoes and laughed. She and Cinderella had more in common than she'd thought. Cin-der-el-la...Lau-ra-el-la? I guess that's me, she laughed sadly.

She didn't have time to stand around and feel upset. She caught herself wishing she still couldn't read so at least the list wouldn't make her feel so depleted, and that was even before she'd done the first task.

She rushed throughout the day trying to get as much done as she could, but everything seemed to go wrong. Frustrated and exhausted, but at least with dinner underway, she sat down for a minute at the kitchen table. She was awakened by Robert rushing into the kitchen. "What's burning?" he cried running to the stove.

Startled, Laura roused from her slumber. "Oh, no! I must have fallen asleep!"

Robert was already reaching for the oven mitts and fanning away the smoke. He took the pan from the oven; the roast was crinkled and burnt into a black crisp.

"What am I going to do? The dinner is in two hours. I don't have time to cook another roast, the pies are not finished; I still have to make the meringue and prepare the soup. Miss Abby will fire me. But, I mean, really, look at this list; not even Hercules could do it all," said Laura, shaking the paper as if it itself were to blame.

"I see someone's been studying her Greek history, Laura. At least you're achieving at something," he laughed. "Better that than some dinner party." Robert rolled up his sleeves and opened the window above the sink. "You know in my younger days, not only was I handsome, but I was also a pretty darn good cook!"

Abandoning all propriety, Laura threw her arms around old Mr. O'Brien. He warmly hugged her back. Just then Sam barged in, his hand over his nose. "What's going on? What's that smell?"

Laura lowered her head in embarrassment. She didn't want him to know how badly she'd bungled his wife's dinner. His voice was tender. "You know, I've never liked roast." She looked at him. He kept his gaze on hers for a long moment before she broke away.

Robert threw his son a dish towel. "No need to panic; the O'Brien boys to the rescue. By the way, Sam, your wife is having a dinner party. We all just found out." He winked at Laura. "Now that the roast is out of the way, let's get dinner started."

Sam smiled and raised his eyebrows. "My father is hard to say no to," he said, taking off his tie. Soon between the three of them, a feast of salads, seafood and desserts was lined up on the big kitchen table, along with a cornucopia spilling miniature pumpkins and gourds of yellow, orange and red, ready to go out to the dining room.

Robert paused before filling the tea kettle. "Do you suppose Hilary's coming?" he asked Sam, his nose wrinkling slightly.

"Abby still isn't speaking to her mother for some reason," he shrugged. "She won't tell me the particulars." He laughed ruefully. "At least we won't have to listen to her talk about 'society' this and 'society' that."

"A small blessing," agreed Robert.

Sam went upstairs to change and when the kettle whistled, Robert sat at the table with Laura and a cup of tea. "You know, Laura, before you came, this was a much lonelier house." He lowered his voice. "I don't want to speak ill of my daughter-in-law, but we don't have much in common, and as you know, Sam works very hard. I have my gardening and interests, but," he put a hand warmly on hers, "let's just say it's nice to have your company. And," he looked around to make sure they were alone, "my son seems to be enjoying your care of the house as well. I haven't seen him home this much in…" he paused, "well, in a long time, let's put it that way." A fatherly concern flickered over his eyes. "I just hope this isn't all too much for you. Perhaps we need to make sure you're enjoying your own cooking a bit more."

Laura smiled wanly. "I'm fine, don't you worry." She looked at the clock and stood slowly. "I'd best be getting home. Dinner to prepare for the boys." She turned and coughed into her hands, then took up her purse from the chair in the corner.

The next day, Robert was gone the whole day, but when Laura was getting ready to go home, a beautiful horse and buggy were waiting for her. In the carriage, she slumped to the side and dozed with her head in her hands. If she had been herself, she probably would have thought of herself as riding in Cinderella's pumpkin, recently changed to Laura-ella's carriage, or at least enjoyed the fall foliage passing by, but she hardly cared about the luxury or the scenery. Even when she got home, she only barely noticed how the boys had already lit the fire and put supper on the stove. She kissed each on the head and went straight to bed.

In the morning, her body just wouldn't move. Tom ran to fetch Aunt Peggy. By the time she arrived, Laura was ghostly pale, coughing much blood and running a high fever.

"Is Mother going to be all right?" asked the frightened boys.

Peggy was baffled; it seemed so sudden. Laura had always seemed fine. Tired, but more or less fine. "I don't know. I don't know what's wrong with her," she answered.

Laura stayed in bed for several weeks, but even with all that time, her condition hardly improved. George got an advance on a job with the Department of Highways to pay for the doctor. When he came, he gently asked Laura, "Have you been coughing for a while?"

"Yes…"

"When did you first notice blood in your phlegm?"

"At the convent…almost three years ago…"

96

"And you must be very tired," he said, checking her pulse again.

"Yes," she whispered. It was such a relief to say it aloud. To have someone understand. She let tears fall back onto her pillow.

The doctor patted her wrist and came out to the kitchen to speak with Peggy and George. "I won't mince words. Your sister is very sick. She needs hospital care."

George set his lips into a thin line and looked at Peggy. She didn't say a word, only nodded. They bundled Laura up and got her to the wagon, then into the hospital. A quick exam revealed it was tuberculosis after all.

The doctor in the hospital took Peggy and George aside. "She's an advanced case. And also quite contagious. It's a miracle neither her employers nor her family has contracted it. We'll be transferring her to the sanatorium in Kentville-"

"Kentville? In Annapolis Valley? But that's miles from here," said Peggy. She began to cry.

"It's the only place where we can hope to give her any promise of a future. I hope you can make arrangements for her children?"

Peggy looked at the floor; the tiles beneath her feet were cracked down the centre.

Chapter Five
More of the Same

"It's not fair that my sister should have to be separated from her boys again. It's as if fate were conspiring against her. Her, of all people." Peggy blew her nose loudly as George wordlessly tucked Laura's blankets around her limp body in the back seat of Robert's 1950 Mercury. He shut the door, gave Peggy a quick kiss, and got into the passenger seat, shaking the rain from his shoulders. Sam's hands were tight around the steering wheel, and without another word, he sped off. Peggy waved until the car was gone. She'd wanted to come, but of course she had to stay with the boys, to make sure life felt as normal as possible.

After a few minutes on the road, Sam said, "There are some sandwiches and a thermos of tea under your seat. My father packed enough for a whole crowd of people." He managed a small smile. "We should get comfortable. It's a long ride. And I spoke to a friend of mine this morning and he says some of the roads are washed out."

George turned around every so often to check on Laura, but she slept the whole trip. Neither man ate more than a bite or two and they didn't speak much. It took seven hours to get to Kentville, and when they pulled up to the hospital, Laura was immediately rushed into surgery. George came up with her, then sat in the waiting room and smoked one cigarette after another. When Sam came upstairs after parking the car, a nurse entered and told them it would be a long time before Laura would be out.

Just after dawn, a young nun greeted them with freshly brewed tea, bread and apple jelly. While they were eating, the doctor appeared in the doorway. He looked tired and was in no mood for conversation. "Laura has survived the operation. We removed her right lung-"

"Is she going to be all right?" interrupted George.

The doctor rubbed his neck. "I don't know. Time will tell."

"May we see her?"

"I'm afraid not. She is too weak and will be in isolation for a while yet. It's best you go home."

They cleaned up the breakfast, got their things together, put on their windbreakers and caps and went outside. On their way out, Sam said, "From one minute to the next she was fine, and now her life is uncertain." He paused. "At least there's hope. Doctors don't say that unless it's true, right?"

"Yeah, sure," said George. He looked quizzically at Sam while he rolled his cigarette. "Didn't occur to me to ask earlier, but does your wife know you're here?"

Sam raised an eyebrow and shrugged. "I left her a note. She keeps a busy social calendar." George offered Sam a cigarette, but he held up his hand. "No, thanks." He nodded at the stately buildings. "Nice place, at least."

George chuckled. "I'm sure Laura would like it. She has a thing for white buildings."

It was a beautiful spot. The two men took a seat on a bench to admire it while George smoked. The buildings topped a small hill, some overlooking the river. The main building was four stories adorned by two gables with a third one in the attic and two towers on either side. A row of trees separated the sanatorium from the river.

Out of habit, George carefully put the ashes of his lit cigarette in the cuff of his trouser leg. He sighed and clapped his hands on his thighs as he stood. "We'd better go. Long drive ahead."

Laura remained in isolation for several months. Her room was small, nearly as small as it had been at the convent, but it was warm and well lighted from the window that overlooked the river. She didn't have the strength to get out of bed, though, to enjoy the view. And for those who came to visit, they wore white masks, so for that time, she mostly only saw white suits and eyes. As she gradually normalized in body temperature and her coughing spells decreased, she started to look forward to the eye visits. Some were blue, others hazel, dark brown, light brown or greenish blue. She liked to imagine the faces to match the eyes by listening to the sound of the people's voices, feeling the touch of their hands, inspecting their demeanors.

One nurse in particular had bright blue eyes; within each of them was a yellow circle that reminded Laura of a halo. Her name was Louise. She had a soft voice and there were deep creases beside her eyes when she smiled, which was often. She visited Laura most evenings. Unlike the other nurses, she always had time for a conversation and made sure Laura was as comfortable as could be expected before leaving for the night. Laura opened up to her and talked about her husband and children, as if talking about them kept them with her.

A nurse's aid who came in as relief wasn't as compassionate; one night when Laura had been looking forward to her evening back rub, the new woman entered and made a face. "The air is way too stale and hot in this room! No wonder you're not making much progress!" She threw open the window, dropped an extra blanket on the radiator and left the room without another word. Laura was disappointed but tried at least to enjoy the fresh air. After a while, though, the air turned on her and the room became quite chilly. Laura was too weak to fetch the blanket, and by morning, she was shaking and feverish, nearly unable to respond to the day nurse, who grew alarmed and called for help. She slammed the window closed and grabbed a blanket from a cabinet and wrapped it around Laura; another nurse rushed in with some soup, and they spoon fed it to her until she slept.

Louise's return was a comfort to Laura, and so was the trainee's transfer to the laundry department, "where she couldn't inadvertently kill any towels or sheets with her love of fresh air," laughed

Louise ruefully. She would also read the letters Laura's family sent and answer them to the hesitant pace of Laura's dictation. Peggy's letters were loving and funny, never complaining, full of vivid stories about the boys. And she always made sure to send paper, envelopes and stamps, which touched Laura as these things cost a dear penny.

Little by little, Laura regained her strength and felt a new respect for God, whom, she knew, would give her her life back. Nurse Louise's faith was inspiring as well. Every night before she left, Louise held Laura's hand for a brief prayer. "God will look out for you," she said so convincingly, Laura knew, even after all she'd endured, she was right.

Once spring of 1955 came around, Laura was able to sit up in a chair by the window, look out at the river, and watch the birds in the trees while absorbing the warmth of the sun. When the window curtain brushed against her cheek, she felt as though God were in the room with her. That she was being watched over, guided, and healed. She thought about George and Peggy, who time and again had saved her from ruin, who kept her children alive and flourishing. She brushed aside feelings of guilt; she wasn't earning any money to help pay for the boys' keep, but at least they were receiving her baby bonus and her pension, which Robert had had the foresight to have instantly reinstated once she went into the hospital and organized with the Credit Union to be directed back to Peggy. She had to shake her head at the irony of things, but practically this was the only solution and the best one. Still, she was determined to get well so she could repay them for everything and right everything for the last time. She paused and thought about how fortunate she was to have her sister and brother-in-law. How wonderful they were. Thinking about how dedicated they were to helping her family, her heart felt like it would burst at the seams from gratitude.

She held the latest letter from Joe in her lap and looked at it again.

Dear Mother,

School is good. We had a snowstorm and couldn't go so we helped uncle George in the barn. It's a lot of work but still fun, especially when Uncle George gives a sip of rum or wiskey! He says it's good medicine for the heart.

Aunt Peggy's meals are as always delicious! She says it sure keeps her busy feeding four grown men. Uncle George has been busy and his friend Dooly has been by a lot to help and we now have electricity in the house and a new washing machine! It looks like a big round tub with a ringer that squeezes the water out of the clothes. Aunt Peggy says it's the best invention ever! The other day Ben knocked down the handle of the hose by mistake.and all the water from the machine poured on the floor! By the time aunt Peggy noticed, the kitchen was pretty well flooded! Now when she washes the clothes, we stay out of her way! Especially Ben!! But the floor was mighty clean after that! Did you notice that we are reviewing exclamation marks at school!!!!!

I almost forgot!! Big News!! Uncle George fixed a roof for a family in town and they gave him their old upright piano for Aunt Peggy! Also Uncle George got laid off for a while so he's busy cutting wood in the hills behind the house. Tom spends a lot of time with him. I help him too when I don't work at the garage. It's a lot more fun than pumping gas!! And another Big NEWS!! good and bad! Uncle George got a set of false teeth! The other day, in the woods, he put them on a stump to eat his lunch and then he forgot to put them back in his mouth! We've been looking for them

*ever since. He doesn't seem to be too worried and ant
Peggy says they will probably show up in the spring
when the snow melts!!*

*We hope your feeling better and you come
home soon!!!*

Your loving sons,

Joe, Tom, and Ben (I love you mama)

*PS. Please excuse my spelling mistakes!! Grade 6 is
no peace of cake!*

My word, things are happening there, thought Laura. Never a dull
moment. Yet every time Laura read this joyful letter, she felt a
sense of calm come over her. So much was happening without her,
but she was alive, and soon, she'd be holding her sons even tighter
than she held this letter. She knew their love for her was as ardent
as ever.

One morning, Laura woke up to a change in the air. She sat up
in bed and blinked. The sun shone on her face, and a soft warm
breeze moved the curtains. The birds were chirping and in the hall,
people were talking.

"What's happening?" she asked the attending nurse sleepily. The
woman leaned over Laura's bed and smiled. "Isolation time is over.
You've been in this room almost eight months. You are now being
officially transferred to a ward in the new pavilion."

Laura nearly gasped. "You have a face, lips, a nose! So, I'm being
transferred to a ward with other people? That means I'm better,
doesn't it. When can I go home?"

The nurse patted her arm and stood. "Oh, my dear, it will be
a while for that yet. You are no longer contagious, but still you
need plenty of rest, sunshine and proper medical attention." She
turned to the window. "What a beautiful day, it is! You will finally
be allowed visitors, you know," there was a sly tone to her voice.

"There have been many inquiries from a certain gentleman as to when that day would come."

Laura faintly smiled and waved her hand, though she was burning to ask who it was. Kind Robert, or Sam, whose gaze before she left had deeper emotion in it than she dared imagine possible. "Oh, I'm sure it's too far for them to travel," she laughed. "I'll have to be content with monthly letters."

The nurse brought in new bed linens and put them on the chair. Laura suddenly fully understood the situation. "Oh, my, a ward, doesn't that mean there will be many people all together?" Her heart pulsed. She'd grown accustomed to her solitary room, her only company the few eyes, Louise, and the fields, sky, birds, and even the rain and snow just outside her window. What if there's no window in this ward? What if someone snores or coughs and keeps me awake at night or gets sick and gives it to the rest of us? What if I don't fit in with the other women?

As though able to read her patient's mind, the nurse with the pale greenish eyes softly reassured her, "Don't worry, Laura. You'll be fine. New friends are often just what a person needs to feel better!"

Soon an orderly came to Laura's room, helped her pack her few things, and brought her to the new pavilion. When she finally reached her new bed, she was exhausted and slept the rest of the day. When she awoke toward evening, a woman was sitting beside her bed. Laura knew it was Louise the moment she saw her face, even before she spoke. She had a warm smile, and soft features that perfectly suited her rose-colored complexion. Her face showed a few wrinkles and her hair was black, tinged with grey.

"You look exactly the way I imagined."

Louise smiled. "How are you doing?"

Laura tried to sound nonchalant even though she was feeling terribly nervous. She looked around at her new surroundings. The huge room was separated into several cubicles with four beds to each section, three of which had women in them, and half walls separating each cubicle. "Oh, fine. You know, it's a big change."

Louise patted her hand as if she understood exactly. She stayed until Laura dozed off again.

The next day Laura decided she'd better make herself at home and get to know her roommates: a young woman named Anne, and an older woman they came to call "The Talker". Anne had a sweet smile and dimples over freckled cheeks. Her dark hair was as glossy as if it had been polished. Her gentle disposition seemed incongruous with the fact of her illness. "I've been here since I was nineteen. Well, on and off. Imagine, I'm thirty now." Anne smiled and shrugged. "I had dreams, you know, of normal things like getting married, having children, but I'm too old for any of that now." Anne's tone was so matter of fact, Laura had to shake her head to fully absorb the reality of Anne's life.

"I'm so sorry..." She paused, realizing the same could as easily have happened to her. She was getting off with a light sentence in comparison. She had her beautiful family to go home to.

Anne shook her head. "It's alright. I get to meet some very nice people anyway. What about you, Laura? What's your story?

It didn't take long before Laura adjusted to her new surroundings and befriended several people on her floor. She and Anne became instant friends and soon were sharing tears and laughs from the heart. Often members of the same family: parents, toddlers and teenagers were patients together at the "san", as everyone called it. She gravitated toward the children and would entertain several at a time, the group of them sitting on her bed as she read to them. The children came to calling her all sorts of pet names, and their affection made her miss her own boys more and more, as she was able to live with them only through their letters that she kept in a pretty linen-lined box by the bed.

And it was amusing to watch Anne and The Talker butt heads. Laura tuned The Talker out or learned to say "mmm," or "hmm" to keep up her end of the conversation, but when Anne finally lost her patience and threw a pillow at the woman, Laura had to laugh. "For Christ's sake," Anne rolled her eyes, "Don't you ever shut up?"

Her new living situation might have allowed for less time for her to be alone with her thoughts, but at least her days were far more interesting than they had been when she had been confined to her isolated quarters. She came to truly enjoy being able to leave her room to eat with all the other patients. The large cafeteria amazed her; it had dozens of steel tables and matching chairs aligned in perfect rows, and peach silk curtains adorning the large windows. The floor was also so clean and shiny that one could have eaten off of it. And best of all, it had electricity. At first, mealtime was stressful, for she wasn't used to the noise and rush of cafeteria life, and her homesickness made her long for her little kitchen with its faded rug and cast iron pots. But slowly and gradually, she warmed up to the fun of eating with friends and came to look forward to it.

When mealtimes were over, between getting to and from the dining hall and The Talker's incessant chatter, Laura mostly slept and dreamed. Since coming to the new ward, she dreamt often of Johnny coming home from the war. Most of them were nightmares, casting her into the pouring rain and cold, Laura standing on the train station platform, eagerly awaiting Johnny's return. But when his train arrived, his expressionless face shadowed in a window, the train would always chug right through the station, with the whistle trailing in the air behind it as it disappeared from view.

When Louise would come to visit in the evenings, more and more Laura tried to keep her by her bedside as long as she could. One night, her friend asked quietly, "What's wrong, Laura?"

Laura looked down at her bedclothes. "Nothing..."

"You're talking a mile a minute. Aren't you tired?" She winked and whispered close to Laura's ear, "Do you think The Talker's chatter is catching?"

Laura laughed, but soon grew serious again. "I have dreams," she whispered. "They're horrible." Instantly her body was shaking and tears were streaming down her face.

Louise smiled gently. "Do you ever pray for him? Maybe if you lit a candle, it might help."

"How? Or where?"

"Come with me."

Laura slowly climbed out of bed and followed Louise to a little chapel on the next floor. Upon entering the small and serene room, Laura's eyes fell on the big crucifix nailed to the wall. She felt immediately at peace. Off to the side was a small altar covered with a white cloth and adorned with two candles whose flames danced in their glass. Nurse Louise touched her shoulder and left her alone. Laura sank into one of the few pews and stared at the cross for a while, then lit a candle for Johnny. Louise returned and helped Laura back to her bed. She slept soundly that night, the first night in a very long while.

The days became routine and Laura stopped spending much time each day wondering how long she'd be in this life and instead just began living. Then came a warm summer day that was so pure, the sky so blue, Laura had to spend the afternoon outdoors. She was propped up on three pillows in her chair, wrapped in blankets, enjoying the ripples in the water and how the water tickled the rocks, when suddenly a man behind her said quietly, "Well, don't you look like a lady of luxury."

Laura nearly jumped from her chair. It was unmistakably Robert O'Brien. She reached around and sure enough, it was him and his gently wrinkled caring face smiling back at her. Her heart jumped when she saw Sam standing behind him with his hat in his hands, looking both hopeful and worried.

"What in the name..." sputtered Laura as she laughed. "How did you get here?" Her heart caught a bit in her chest.

"We missed our Laura-ella," Robert said with a twinkle in his eye.

Laura laughed, forgetting that so long ago, she'd mentioned this silly name to him. "Laura-ella...that seems like a hundred years in the past."

Feeling suddenly shy, she looked down. Robert was full of the genteel kindness and friendship he had always shown her. But Sam, he was different. He seemed nervous.

"How are you, Laura?" His voice broke a little bit.

She knew she was pale and frail; perhaps her sickness was making him uncomfortable. She smiled as brightly as she could.

"I'm just fine, now that you're here. And I am getting better and stronger every day. But tell me, what are you doing here?"

"I had a business meeting in Halifax, and my father came along. We're on our way home and thought we'd drop by to visit." He sat beside her. She could feel the heat and familiar soapy smell coming off of him and felt her heart beat faster. She took a breath. Her illness did strange things to her.

"I'm so pleased. Imagine my very first visitors in almost a year. How is everything back home, Miss Abby?"

Sam's face soured for a brief second before he smiled. "You know my wife, busy as usual. I haven't seen much of her lately. You look far better than the last time we saw you; is the food good?"

"Not bad, well, not as good as my sister Peggy's, of course!" she winked.

"When do you think you will be coming home?" Sam asked.

Laura lowered her head surprised at the sudden tears pouring down her cheeks. She wiped her nose. "I…I…don't know."

Sam put his hand on hers. He squeezed, just slightly, but she didn't dare look into his eyes. His touch was so warm. "Your old job is still waiting for you, if you want it back, that is."

Laura looked up. "You haven't replaced me?"

Sam smiled. "That would be impossible."

Laura made a face of mock disgust. "The dishes are probably piled a mile high by now."

Everyone laughed. Then Robert motioned to Sam that he should give her the bouquet of roses they'd brought. "What do you have there?" Laura teased.

"I hope you like them," he murmured, handing them to her.

She laid them in her lap. "They're beautiful. Such colours!"

"Father," Sam said quickly, "don't you have something for Laura, too?"

"Yes, yes. Here you go." He handed her a huge bag filled with books, newspapers, magazines, even a scrapbook, along with several notebooks and some pens and pencils.

Struggling not to cry again, Laura cleared her throat. "It feels like Christmas! I've never received so many gifts before. Thank you very much."

Laura wiped away some escaped tears and tried to hold her treasures close to her heart, but her arms were shaky, so she put the bag at her feet.

"Laura, you look tired; maybe I'll tour the grounds and you rest a while?" Sam waited for Robert, who sat down in Sam's place after he'd stood. "Father, are you going to join me?"

Robert leaned back and crossed his arms. "I'm feeling a bit tired myself, son. I think I'll stay here, keep our Laura company."

Sam raised his eyebrow slightly at Robert, but proceeded down the path, "Alright. I'll just be a minute, then."

Robert lifted his hand then leaned back once Sam was out of sight. "Laura? I am going to tell you something I should not."

She just looked at him.

"It's not my place to say…" he paused and looked down. "I just," he took a deep breath and smiled. "I just want you to know we're happy you're here. In our lives. Sam and I. You bring a breath of fresh air to the house, to Sam." He lifted his head and looked about furtively. "Do you know," he raised his voice, "I couldn't agree more, these clouds do look exactly like galloping steeds."

Laura wasn't quite sure what had just happened, but she had the feeling more was said in what Robert didn't say. She felt then a sense of joy. She believed she understood. There was a reason Sam had come to visit her.

Sam came back a few minutes later looking glum. "I asked about your release, Laura, and they said you're doing well, really well. Won't be long now, in fact."

Laura scrunched up her nose. "They didn't say that, did they, Samuel Roberts."

He shrugged and laughed a bit. "They did say we should have faith. That faith is what keeps us alive. I can do that if you can."

"I can." Laura didn't dare look at him. "I can."

Once they left, Laura felt her chest expand and grow, rather like a bloom opening. She whispered "faith, have faith" to herself, over and over, like a prayer. It never occurred to her during the entire time of the O'Briens' visit that Kentville was nowhere near on their way home.

On their drive back from the san, father and son remained quiet for the better part of the first hour. Suddenly Robert turned to Sam. "Do you want to tell me what's going on with Abby?"

Sam fumbled with the windshield wipers. "Uh, what?"

"You remember her, your wife?" Robert said. He raised his eyebrows.

Sam was quiet then he shook his head and sighed. "I thought I knew her better. She's like a spirit, some kind of ghost. I see her then I don't. Who knows, maybe she's having an affair." He smiled sadly. "I guess it's for the best we're not bringing up a child after all, not with her like this."

Robert touched his son's arm. "I suppose you're right." He thought for a minute. "Can it be she's still not coping? I've been finding empty bottles around the house. You're not home enough to drink that kind of alcohol."

Sam let out a laugh, short and terse. "I can't imagine her drinking like a sailor either. But then again, she's become someone I don't really know...." He drifted into silence.

Eventually, Robert fell asleep leaving Sam alone with his thoughts. It started to rain and he had to slow down for the roads were fast becoming muddy and treacherous. The miserable weather matched his mood. He kept thinking about Laura, wishing there were something he could do for her to help speed her healing and get her home. Somehow even though he knew he shouldn't feel this way, he knew he felt whole when he was with her.

When in the early days of 1956 Laura's health was steadily improving, the doctor recommended she undergo a series of treatments consisting of twenty-seven pills a day and two needles a week. This would speed her recovery, he said. "Hardly," she thought after yet another day of nausea and a sore bottom from all the shots. Yet each treatment brought the results of her X-rays and sputum tests closer to the healthy range. She felt the end of her time at this place had to be near. So full of warmth from the friendships she'd made and feeling such gratitude for the care she'd received, she had plenty of energy to fill her scrapbook with clippings from the newspapers and magazines Robert O'Brien sent her from time to time.

One evening during her usual visit, Louise asked, "Laura, are you still having those bad dreams?"

Laura smiled. "Sometimes, but when I light a candle, they usually go away for a while. Strange, isn't it?"

"Well, I had a thought; why don't you write in the notebooks your friend brought you? It might help, putting your thoughts down on paper."

"That's not a bad idea." She felt her old fear at not being able to write then realized that person was no longer her. Joy flooded her body. "Actually, it's a perfect idea!"

From that very night, Laura started keeping a journal. She wrote down brief thoughts, observations, questions, curiosities. When she was stuck for a word or the spelling of one, she asked her friends in the cubicle or a staff member for help. She soon began attending a daily one-hour class to upgrade her education, and whenever she could, she read.

But after about a month of such enthusiasm, she realized the headaches and fatigue she'd been experiencing were from her overdoing it. Not wanting to jeopardize her health, she pulled back just enough to look around herself at the things she hadn't been seeing. For example, she realized she hadn't seen much of Anne lately. She had also been spending every afternoon taking courses, but she seemed to always be gone far longer than the class time. "Where is Anne? I haven't seen her all day," she asked her nurse before dinner that evening.

The elderly woman touched her cotton-spun white hair and smiled secretively. "You'll have to ask her yourself," she said and left.

The next morning upon waking, Laura cornered her friend. Anne was sitting up, applying lipstick. "Lipstick? Alright, what are you up to?"

Anne leaned in and whispered. "Do you know, life is very strange. I came here to die. Now I'm healthy, soon to go home with a diploma in my hands, something I never dreamed to achieve!" She leaned in close. "And I met a man." Her cheeks were aglow. She sat back and sighed, "Imagine; but for TB, I never would have met him."

Laura was surprised that she was crying. "I'm so happy for you, Anne."

Anne took Laura's hand. "You will be going home soon, too, my friend. The treatment will work for you as it did for me, you'll see."

Within days, Anne was discharged. She and her François soon married; he continued to work at the san while Anne took a job at the local hospital. But she never forgot her friend and visited often, always happy to hear about Laura's boys' latest adventures.

Over the rest of that year, more patients came and went, most of whom were kind and genuine. A new patient from Laura's hometown of Chéticamp in Cape Breton took Anne's bed. The Chéticamp girl, as everyone called her until they learned her name was Sara, taught Laura how to follow a pattern and to crochet. Laura gladly took to the needlework and couldn't wait to show Peggy. Once Sara felt well enough to move around their ward, she introduced Laura to several other residents from her village. The longing in Laura's heart for home grew more and more every day until it felt like a mountain inside. Laura saw it as a sign that she was meant to return home very soon.

1957 arrived. Laura liked the symmetry of the numbers, all odd, so nicely spaced for herself and her three boys, and saw it as yet another sign. This time it was the right one. After two long years at the san, the day came when the doctor greeted Laura with a kind smile. "Today I'm going to give you some wonderful news. But also a decision to make," he said. Her heart leapt around inside her ribcage.

"You are well enough to go home. However," he said to her as she grinned, "if you take a last set of treatments, you're improving your chances of remaining well by a great percentage. I'll leave it up to you."

Laura didn't know what to make of this, and her body was perplexed as well, her throat seizing up and her stomach tight. She ached to see her children with her whole soul. She walked straight from the doctor's office to the little chapel. Over the next three days, she spent hour upon hour there, resting and praying, hoping to do the right thing.

On the third day when Louise came to visit, Laura took her wrinkled hands in her own slim ones. "I know a guarantee is unrealistic, yet what if I refuse the treatment and then have to come back? In my time here, I've seen too many patients excited about going home, only to return worse off and utterly heartbroken." Her voice was shaking but resolute. She knew she'd do the right thing. "Louise, I know this much; once I go home, it will be for good."

Chapter Six
Back Home Again

Peggy wrung out her dishcloth after tidying the kitchen and laughed at herself; going from a quiet, empty house to having three boys in a blink had turned out to be far more than she'd bargained for. From the first minute after Laura went into the hospital when Peggy scrubbed the boys with hot water and soap and cut their hair to the scalp, then got onto her knees with them to scrub their little house from top to bottom, life was nonstop mayhem. Yet she had to admit that it was wonderful to have such life bursting in the home. And eventually things calmed down a bit as they found their rhythm; after school and on Saturdays, while Joe worked at Dooly's garage in town, Tom followed his uncle around, tending to the chicken coop and cleaning the stable. Later when George got laid off from work for a spell, he worked in the woods cutting pulp, and Joe and Tom joined him whenever they could. In the evenings, in spite of everyone's exhaustion, they still took time to show off their muscles in arm-wrestling matches. George also took the boys under his wing showing them not just how to care for the farm but how to make a bit of extra income by trapping muskrat and beaver. They removed the skin, which they stretched and dried on shingles. Once the pelts were ready to sell, they sent them away. They celebrated when a cheque came in the mail, and Uncle George fairly doled out everyone's share of the meager profits.

Aunt Peggy also taught them some homemaking; over the summer, she took them into the fields to pick berries and apples then taught the boys how to preserve the fruits. Ben did his share of the picking, but he was a daydreamer like his mother and spent most of the time chasing after the insects flying about or picking new flowers for his collection. Tom, who was becoming quite the storyteller, kept his aunt amused with anecdotes and jokes while they worked.

Joe didn't care much for berry picking, but he joined in solidly and didn't mention his preferences; he knew to be grateful for all his aunt and uncle were doing for him and his brothers. At night, lying in his bunk bed with his brothers warmly breathing in their beds beneath him, even with all the work and chores they had to do, and the heaviness of missing his mother, he knew they were all going to end up being fine, and the knots in his shoulders were relaxing bit by bit.

Once summer peaked and gently slid into autumn, the boys returned to school, begrudgingly doing their homework with much nudging from their aunt, who threatened them with no dessert if they didn't make their grades. Each of the boys shot up in height, Joe looking more and more like his father with his reddish mop and freckles while Tom resembled his mother, shorter, a bit stocky with light brown curls like Ben's.

Peggy, who when taking care of Tom and Joe while Laura was at the convent had felt nervous about raising the boys and kept more of an iron hand in disciplining them, this time allowed herself to embrace the boys and their growth as people as fully as if they were her own flesh and blood, spoiling them here and there, relaxing a bit and having some fun with them. She was aware that her sister might be gone a long time, or even never return, and based on this, shaky though it made her feel, she let herself immerse and take the kind of pride in their busy lives only a parent could, thrilling at their successes and wearing heavily their disappointments. She told herself time and again that taking her sister's sons to heart was the right thing to do, that raising them not only with food and shelter but with her whole self was giving them the family, the home, they deserved. She couldn't keep her love on hold until Laura returned, for no one knew when, or even if, that would be.

Yet when Tom mentioned at supper one early winter evening that she hadn't brought up Laura in a while, she realized with chagrin that the absence wasn't entirely unintentional. A sharp guilt came into her stomach then, but she shooed it away like a wasp and stood to fetch more buns to feed *her* boys, she thought petulantly. And they were just as much hers as they were Laura's; she'd raised them for just as much of their lives as had her sister. She had a right to lay claim.

One night, close to Christmas, Laura still not in any shape to come home, Peggy was folding towels by the linen closet and heard muffled crying coming from the boys' room. She paused by their closed door and listened. It was Ben. Without hearing him say a word, she knew he ached for his mother. No matter how ardently Peggy loved them, she heard in his sobs that she was never going to be enough. The realization didn't shock her, though. Rather, it melted into her heart in the way fall gives way to winter, and the leaves dry away from the trees. It was simply the way it was. She touched the door lightly, her heart extending through the cracks in the wood to his little body, his gentle sobs, and felt helplessness, and love.

They had sporadic mail from Laura all that wet spring until one April day, Joe came bursting in from outside, his shoes caked in black mud. "Aunt Peggy! Look, a letter from Mother!"

Tom and Ben erupted from the kitchen. "Let me hold it! I want to read it! No, it's my turn!" they shouted as they scuffled for the envelope in Joe's hand.

"What's all this commotion?" demanded Aunt Peggy, as she wiped her hands on her apron and met the boys at the door.

Joe breathlessly answered, "It's a letter from Mother!"

"Oh my. I hope nothing's wrong. We received one not too long ago." She reached for it.

"But I want to read it!" Joe burst out, his usually sensible face quivering.

"You read last time. It's my turn!" retorted Tom.

"What about me?" cried Ben.

"Alright, what if Ben opens the letter and I read? Is that fair?" The boys nodded. "Ok, here goes!" Peggy smiled, wishing she understood why she was nervous, then feeling sick for knowing there was a part of her that might rejoice if it were less than positive news.

April 10, 1957

Dear Peggy, George, Joe, Tom and Ben,

"How come I'm always last?" moaned Ben.

"It's because mother loves you so. Now, go on, Aunt Peggy," ordered Tom.

"Ok...Dear Peggy-" "You already read that part!"

Peggy continued, "Great news, I am coming home! The doctor says my health has improved so much so that I am well, fit as a fiddle. I will receive my official release in six weeks. Can't wait to see you all! I'm thinking of hopping on the mail truck, then maybe connecting with the train. I will write later to confirm the time of my arrival. With all my love to you both and the boys, Laura."

The boys began chattering at once. "Take it slowly, boys. Your mom will still need plenty of rest, and lots of fresh air and sunshine," said Peggy quietly. She cleared her throat.

But as the day progressed, it was clear her words of caution had fallen on deaf ears. That night before going to sleep, they talked over each other, making plans.

"We should organize a big surprise for Mama. I wonder if she will look the same. I can't wait!" said Ben.

Joe sat up in his bed. "Wait, Aunt Peggy said she'll need lots of sun and rest. What if we build her a sunroom?"

"What's a sunroom?" asked Ben.

"It's a room made mostly of windows. We could build it on the southern side of the house where it will face the sun, make it nice and cozy."

"Great idea, Joe," said Tom sarcastically. "How are we going to build such a thing with no money?"

"I guess you're right. But let's talk to Uncle George about it anyway." He laid back down and crossed his arms beneath his head. The other two fell silent.

After a while, Tom whispered into the dark room, "You still awake?"

Both Joe and Ben said, "Yes."

The three of them tiptoed to their aunt and uncle's bedroom and softly rapped on the door.

"You boys should be in bed. But come on in." Peggy and George looked at each other and smiled as they sat up against their pillows. "They must be so excited," she whispered.

The boys sat at the foot of the bed, nudging each other's elbows. Finally Tom blurted out, "We've been talking. Joe has a plan." Then the three began speaking over each other.

Uncle George chuckled. "Slow down, boys. Tomorrow morning, I'll check in the barn, see what kind of wood I can spare."

"You mean, you'll help us? We can do it?" said Ben.

"Maybe. Now go to bed!"

The boys happily scurried to their bedroom and fell asleep as soon as their heads hit the pillows. Meanwhile, George turned to Peggy. "You know Dooly has an old empty barn. He's been after me for a while now to tear it down. I imagine we could use the wood to build a sunroom." He was smiling impishly.

Peggy lovingly hugged her husband. "You're something else, George MacDonald."

"Why not; it'd be good for them. Joe is already fourteen, Tom is trailing close behind. No reason they can't help. What do you think?"

Peggy smiled. "I think Laura is in for the surprise of her life!" Peggy laid down, surprised at the lightness in her belly.

The next morning, the boys woke up very early, for they didn't want to miss their uncle before he set out for the barn. The house was still a bit chilly. Covered in blankets and fingers crossed for good luck, they sat at the table, staring at George, who was completely absorbed in sprinkling brown sugar on his hot porridge. Then, he slowly smothered his bread with a big spoonful of raspberry jam. Patiently, they waited as he sipped his tea. Finally Peggy decided they'd been tortured enough. She set big bowls of porridge before the three. "You'd best eat a hearty breakfast. You're going to be very busy today and for the next few weeks."

They laughed with joy and ate voraciously. Then the two bigger boys hopped on the tractor with their uncle while Ben stayed behind, his chin quivering. Peggy put her arm around him. "I could really use your help. Maybe tomorrow, after church, we could all go to the old barn. I'll even bring a picnic basket. For now, let's gather the eggs and feed the chickens." Trailing behind his aunt in the yard, the boy wiped his nose on his sleeve between sniffles. Soon, he was busy and feeling like his old self again.

George, Joe and Tom spent every spare moment after school and on weekends, demolishing Dooly's old barn and transporting the wood up to the old shack. Even Sam and his father came around a few times to pitch in when they could. The boys and men alike worked hard, and in no time, where grass and rocks had once stood now was a completed sunroom. Painting the inside was a real treat, for the boys had proudly bought the needed materials with their own savings. While they painted, George and Sam, who had stopped by to see the finished product, chatted outside in the sunshine.

George knew about the O'Brien's finances. He was fiercely proud, but he also knew Laura would benefit from Sam knowing a few things about her humble life. He would be able to help her in a way that George and Peggy could not. George had always felt a soft spot for his sister-in-law, felt she'd been dealt some bad cards in life. The war had messed him up, and every day he felt rough, but his sister-in-law, she still had some purity in her, she still believed in hope. George envied that. "You know, Sam," he said, taking a long drag on his cigarette. "Laura doesn't have running water. Or electricity. No commodities at all."

"Aie," Sam said. George could see in Sam's face that he was surprised and also chagrined. "Well, that is going to be hard for her, especially now that she's so spoiled by all that indoor plumbing at the san," Sam winked. "Tell you what, if you will help me with the work, I think we can make life a bit more pleasant and convenient for her. What do you say?"

"I'll do whatever I can. Laura is a special gal, and those boys are like my own."

"Oh, by the way, in a few weeks, I have a meeting in Halifax." Sam paused. "I can pick up Laura on my way home, I mean, if it's all right with you and Peggy?"

George stared at Sam. He had the impression the gentleman was asking for more than permission to drive her home. "Well, that would be mighty kind of you, Sam, mighty kind. I'll tell Peggy, and she'll send Laura a note."

By the time Laura was ready to come home, the boys' dream had become a reality. The day before the long awaited arrival, they relaxed in the sunroom, enjoying the sun's warmth. While Ben put the finishing touches on his drawings that he would hang on the wall, his brothers were quiet. Joe finally broke the silence. "Let's promise to help Mother as much as we can from now on. Father's gone, it seems such a long time ago. Let's do our best to keep Mother."

"How about if we buy her a gift, like a radio?" said Tom.

"But we haven't any money," said Ben.

"Well, actually, we do," replied Joe. "Tom and I still have a bit of money left from our savings, you know, from our odd jobs, the sale of the pelts, our berries, and I've been collecting beer bottles. And if the radio costs more than that, maybe Uncle George will make up the difference, like a loan." Joe realized once he'd said all of this how ardently he didn't want to be poor anymore. He wanted to be comfortable, to make sure his family was comfortable, and not live by scraping and collecting a penny here and there. He made a silent vow to himself then to make it big in the world. To earn lots and lots of money so his mother and family would never go again without food, shelter or medications.

* * * * * *

After saying goodbye to her friends and to Louise, Laura sat by the door, ready for her journey home. When she spotted Sam, she excitedly ran to him, and threw her arms around him, only realizing after a moment how inappropriate that was. Her cheeks blazed and she stepped back. His smile showed no similar misgivings. "Here," he said, holding out a linen bag. "Peggy sent this."

Laura looked puzzled then opened it. "Oh," she whispered. It was a new dress, a coat with matching hat, and new shoes, socks and undergarments; her sister thought of everything. "Peggy must have received a barrel of clothing from the States again. To be honest, I haven't worn anything but pajamas in a few years. Are you in a hurry, Sam? Do I have time to change?" she asked excitedly.

"No, no hurry at all. I'll wait for you over there," he pointed to a bench just outside in the sunshine. As she walked away, slim and lovely as ever, Sam wished he had also brought her flowers or candies, something to show he cared. While she was dressing, he strolled into the little confectionery shop situated at the main entrance and bought her a large bouquet of purple lilies. When Laura returned in her new clothes, her good health shining in her cheeks, Sam had to admit she looked exquisite.

"You've changed, Laura—"

"I know, isn't Peggy something else, sending me this new wardrobe?"

Sam smiled. "Well, yes, the clothes, but that's not quite what I meant. There's something else. You seem," he smiled, unsure how to say what he wanted, "like you've grown into a stronger person. Not just physically."

On their way home, Sam kept his eyes on the road. Laura glanced sideways a few times, still in awe of his kindness. She felt a sudden attack of nerves and began chatting to cover the silence. "Have you seen the boys lately? I bet they've grown so much." She swallowed hard. "It's hard to imagine I've been away for over two and a half years. Thank goodness for Peggy and George. I wonder what the house will look like, being empty that long. And how is your father? I'll be glad to see him. I want to show him my journals. I know he'll be proud."

"Your journals?"

Sitting on the edge of her seat, Laura explained about the scrapbooks and her musings she'd been keeping. Eventually, the excitement of her return home tired her. Settling next to Sam, she dozed off for a short while. Upon waking, she turned her attention to the countryside.

"Isn't it strange that those round hills seem to follow the river, as if protecting the flow of the water from eroding the soil?"

Sam smiled. "That's such an intelligent observation, Laura. But do you mean the dykes? They were built by the Acadians long ago. And that's exactly what they're for, to prevent the water from eroding the rich fertile soil found in the valley."

"The Acadians?"

"Yes. They came from France in the early 1600's, built a new life, worked the soil-"

Laura laughed. "I'm Acadian!"

"You are? How so?"

"My maiden name is Boudreau. My parents were born in Chéticamp, and so were my sister and I. It's a small village in Cape Breton."

"I actually went to Chéticamp once. Lovely village and the people were very hospitable. But how-"

Laura recounted her childhood story.

"Your mother felt tremendous pressure to assimilate," he said sadly. "That's such a loss. For you and for the culture."

"As-si-mi-la-te? What does that mean?"

"To become absorbed into the dominant culture."

"You are such a walking dictionary," laughed Laura.

Sam chuckled and his cheeks reddened. "I do like to read, is all. I'm sure you've seen my father's library?"

"Yes, I dusted it more than a few times."

"Well, when you come back to work, you can read the books too."

Laura smiled, so pleased he wanted her back. "Yes, it is a shame. At first, Mother spoke only in French when we were inside our little cabin but eventually she dropped it altogether. My poor mother. She died too young." Laura sighed. "Being able to speak French would have served me well in Montreal," she said bitterly.

"Why did you go there? I recall you and Ben looked rather like you'd been through a great ordeal when we met on the train. You, mostly, you had this lost expression in your eyes. And you were both so thin."

"It's a long story. Maybe someday I'll tell you about it."

"Why don't you lay back for a while?"

Wrapped in the warm blanket she had found on the seat, Laura relaxed and eventually dozed off. Sam was feeling contented in the same way he imagined one felt after a satisfying meal. He felt so at home with Laura. Not like his wife with whom he'd shared about five words in the last month, all of them terse. Actually, that wasn't fair; her mood had seemed somewhat improved recently. Sam felt a small glimmer of his love for his wife, of late more in habit than real, but she was his wife, and he had committed to her. He just didn't know if she felt the same way.

As soon as the boys heard the sound of Sam's sedan late that afternoon, they dashed outside. Tears streaming down their faces, they hugged and kissed their mother the moment she stepped shyly from the car. Laura, holding the three of them with all her strength, looked up at Peggy and let the tears that had been in her chest the whole drive home flow. "I don't know what I would have done without you and George," she said when Peggy joined the huddle. "I am so glad you're my sister, my best friend in the whole world."

Looking up at the old house, she didn't even notice its fresh coat of grey paint and the new addition. She and the boys just began to catch up in fractured sentences, everyone's voices layering the other. Sam waved awkwardly and made for his car. "Sam, no, please stay for supper? I'm sure Peggy has more than enough," Laura called out.

"Another time," he said. "You get caught up first." He started up the car and drove off slowly.

Peggy gently hugged her sister again as if she couldn't believe she was finally touching her. "Dinner is ready," she said motioning everyone inside. The odor of chicken stew was tantalizing, but Ben grabbed Laura's hand and almost dragged her to the sunroom away from the dinner table.

She was stunned and at first the boys looked at one another, wondering whether she disapproved. "But how? I don't know what to say. Look at that," she walked to the farthest side and looked out. "This is the most special room I've ever seen." Her voice was almost a whisper. "And look, painted walls, and Ben's drawings, and how did you paint this lawn chair with bees and ladybugs?" Laura sank into the chair and closed her eyes.

"Here, Mama, use this warm blanket; Aunt Peggy made it just for you!" he proudly exclaimed.

Laura lovingly squeezed her youngest son's cheeks. "That's quite an exquisite pattern, Peg. One of your creations?" she looked up at her sister.

Peggy nodded. Laura cuddled in the chair. "It sure feels good to be home." The boys piled next to her and jabbered away, "We got the idea from Aunt Peggy. She said you needed lots of sunshine and rest; Joe engineered the whole project and Uncle George and Sam helped. It was a lot of fun, and we painted the walls in lavender, your favourite colour, Mother; we tore down Dooly's old barn and used the wood; I drew paintings of flowers and insects so you wouldn't be lonely when we're at school."

"This is one of the best gifts I've ever received," Laura said when they quieted down.

"Wait a second; then what's the best one?" asked Ben, pouting.

"That's easy. You, Tom and Joe. You three are top of the list."

Peggy erupted into goose bumps seeing the pure love over all their faces. "The boys also got you something else, Laura," she said handing a box over.

Laura unwrapped the newsprint slowly. She gasped. "A radio. Do you know, I've never had one," whispered Laura. "And this one is so pretty, like a blue box with knobs," she exclaimed.

"And the last surprise is Uncle George and Sam put in running water and a toilet," said Joe proudly.

"What? Oh my," said Laura her face pursing up with worry. "But electricity is so expensi-"

"Don't worry," Peggy held up her hand. "Sam is paying the first few months until you get back on your feet and you'll keep receiving your monthly pension until you get back to work. It'll be fine."

Laura burst out crying. Her sons were bewildered for they assumed she would be happy knowing they had electricity. "I'm sorry, so sorry, I'm just so happy," she wiped her eyes.

"Well, it's clear I'm not going to be able to move you from this room, so I'll have dinner come to you," laughed Peggy. She made several trips to the kitchen until all their plates were full of food. George joined them soon and the whole family sat in the gleam of the sunset, happily cocooned in love.

When Peggy stood to clear their plates, Laura looked at her over the tops of her sons' heads and mouthed, "I love you." Peg burst into great honking tears, and the two women began to laugh.

The following Monday, after the three boys were off to school, Laura sat at the kitchen table, staring at the cupboards and the blanket Peggy had hung around the toilet in the corner. Faced with her earlier life, one that seemed so long ago yet at the same time so immediate, she got to her knees to touch the old faded rug. Tears ran down her face and over her nose. Johnny was gone. He was never coming back. When she stood, she was determined to carry on with her usual chores, not let things slide. She climbed the ladder to straighten the beds; to her surprise, they were already made. Peggy had trained the boys well.

Out of habit, she looked out for the buckets of water but quickly remembered the roof was now sound. Just then someone rapped softly on the door. Laura welcomed the diversion and wiped her eyes. It was Peggy; she looked like she'd dressed hastily, her hair afloat in the breeze. "What a nice surprise! Want some tea? Thank you for everything. How can I ever repay you? You even put food in the house! I thought Monday was your most busy day with the wash and all?" Laura was surprised by how nervous she felt. Being thrust so fully back into her earlier life was like a shock of cold water.

"We have a lot of catching up to do," said Peggy without looking at Laura. She put down her purse and made for the cupboards to make the tea.

Laura smiled. "I can manage, Peg. Thank you. Why don't you sit for a minute?"

"Sorry. It's habit. So, how are you feeling?"

Laura smiled sadly. "It's so odd but so wonderful," she quickly brightened her voice, not wanting to complain, "and do I ever like having running water! It's a whole new world to not have to carry buckets anymore. And that dash outside in winter for the toilet..." Laura shuddered and laughed, "we certainly won't miss that." She sat and looked at her sister. "Is it really true that Sam O'Brien is taking care of my electric bill? And he paid for the installation as well?"

"Yes."

"Don't you find that strange, Peggy? I mean, I was just his housekeeper." Laura wanted someone to tell her that Sam was just looking after his investment; after all, she did keep a clean house. She wanted to hear that he was happily married, that he and Miss Abby were seen sharing a soda in town, anything to keep her from thinking what she'd been thinking. "I do miss Johnny," she said instead. It was true. She missed her husband dearly in this moment, more than in most moments.

Peggy searched Laura's face. "He's just being kind. I'm sure he'd do this for anyone."

"Yes. Of course."

"Now, come, let's sit in the sunroom."

They sipped their tea and listened to the birds. Then Peggy began asking Laura question after question about her life at the san. Laura took out her scrapbook and flipped through the pages, regaling her sister with stories. But Peggy's curiosity was tireless, which Laura admitted was both a blessing and a curse, and after a while, Laura felt fatigued. She rested while her sister slipped easily into caregiver mode and cleared the breakfast dishes, tidied up, and prepared the boys' supper. When Laura felt better, she joined Peggy in the kitchen and watched her cook, moving easily around Laura's table and pots as if it were second nature. "So when will I hear you play your new piano, Peggy?"

"Soon. I've been taking a few lessons from the lady down the road. George has awful headaches, though so I can't often practice..."

"What do you mean? Is he sick?"

"No, no, but now that the conservatives are in power, funding got cut all over and he lost his job," she smiled wanly. "He really took it hard that the Liberals lost. You know how devoted he is to that party!"

Laura smiled, "What's he going to do?"

"Well, pogey is better than nothing. And he keeps busy with the barn, hauling manure, preparing the ground for planting. Tom will be coming after school to help him." Peggy's face turned worried. "It's just..." she paused. "Well, I can't fault him for having a drink here and there, now can I? When he wakes up shouting, or for no reason has these tremors..." Peggy picked up a dishcloth, "I guess I can't fault him for taking the edge off of that. But then he gets bad headaches afterwards. Some of them lay him out flat."

Laura nodded. Peggy murmured, "I just wish it didn't have to come to that." She turned, her face bright. "But he really is so good to me, and has so much fun with the boys; did they tell you how on the eve of All Saints Day, the four of them sneaked out, caught a baby calf and dressed it up in overalls and a straw hat? The following day, the priest was saying mass outside in the cemetery, you know, to honour the dead, and there was the poor calf, all dressed up, running about among the tombstones. Can you imagine the priest and parishioners' reactions?"

In between giggles, Laura said, "Oh, I've missed so much; tell me more."

"Well..." Peggy thought. "Old Esther is up to new tricks. You remember her, of course. Lately she's been borrowing, just bread, for some reason, but she comes around all the time to borrow mine, and when she returns it, it's dense and dry, not fit even for the pigs. George and the boys refused to eat it. I have to come up with something to stop her," Peggy sighed.

"Why don't you just keep her bread so the next time she needs to borrow some, she can borrow her own?"

Peggy slapped the table and cackled with laughter. "Laura, you are a genius."

The boys enjoyed spoiling their mother; every day, Ben brought her fresh flowers; Joe had become a regular Mr. Fix-it; and Tom helped with the cooking and kept everyone amused with jokes. And hearing her sons' chatter was restorative beyond any needles or treatment she could ever have. Women regularly came by with food for the house; those still apprehensive of Laura's illness simply left baskets and others came in for a cup of tea. Peggy made it a regular practice to hang around the house during the day to take the edges off of Laura's work. "Peggy, you certainly do shoo every-one out quickly." Laura felt some regret at being inhospitable.

"You need your rest. End of story!"

Laura sighed. She remembered this well, having to change a subject so as to not speak her mind. She almost opened her mouth to ask whether they could please transfer her cheques back into her name, but she stopped herself. "Speaking of stories, the boys told me you got a washing machine?" she said instead.

"I completely forgot to tell you." Peggy sat down as if to prepare for a long tale. Laura wondered whether it counted as gossip if it were about oneself. "Every Tuesday and Friday night, George would disappear, saying he had somewhere to go. I didn't think much of it at first, but eventually I got quite suspicious. So one Friday night, Joe and I went on a search."

"Joe went with you?"

"Yes, George had repaired an old bicycle for the boys so I hopped on the bar while he pedaled. We checked all the bootleggers we could find, but there was no sign of him."

At this point, Laura giggled beside herself, as she pictured Joe and his aunt riding a bike on a starlit night. Her sister didn't notice and continued her story.

"Then I started to imagine the worst, that he might be cheating on me, or was so drunk he was lying in a ditch somewhere..."

Laura wondered how Peggy could sound so chipper about these things.

"I didn't think it was that, really; he'd been having a dry spell, was in a good mood, yet he would never reveal his whereabouts on Tuesday and Friday nights."

By this time, Laura was very curious. "Did you find out?"

"One evening, I walked, all by myself, and practically reached the town. Took me almost half the night. By chance, I happened to check the train station. Still don't know how I got there, but I did. And would you believe," she leaned forward, her wide face and big features alight, "there he was, unloading freight! I felt awful for doubting him. I returned home, lit the fire and baked him a fresh batch of biscuits."

"In the middle of the night?"

She nodded. "When he got home after dawn, imagine his surprise!" She clucked her tongue, "That man. To think he wanted it to be a surprise. He put electricity in the house and bought a washing machine, even installed a toilet like yours. Like you, I have no fondness for running to the outhouse on wintry mornings."

Johnny would have never done anything like this for Laura and she felt her stomach sour at the thought. She felt mean for feeling this way. If she'd known he'd had a heart condition, she wouldn't have spent those years wondering why he was so lazy. She just got used to thinking ill of his behaviour. Now when she slipped into the habitual resentful feelings, she felt dreadful, heavy as lead. "That's quite a story," she said.

Peggy looked long at Laura. "You're tired again. Go into the sunroom and I'll start dinner." Laura opened her mouth to protest, not wanting to be mothered, but she realized resting was for the greater good and more productive than arguing with her bull in a china shop sister. She went quietly into the room, still marveling at the engineering of it, how her little boy, a man of almost fifteen, made it happen with his own hands. Can't laze in here forever though, she thought. She wondered how the O'Briens were managing and felt a pull on her heart. What if she did go back to work for them, what if she put herself back in the hospital? Or died? And Sam, it wasn't right for her to work for him. It wasn't proper. She remembered the nasty old biddies in town from so long ago, how low she'd felt at their meanness.

Laura picked up the rosary beads on the side table and easily slid them between her fingers. She held them a long time then straightened out as much as her body would let her. She was thinking nonsense. It'd be good for her to get back to work. Her X-rays and sputum tests were all showing normal, and soon she would be her old self again. Or her new old self. She chuckled and felt full of gratitude then; the sun was in full afternoon bloom, the grasses blowing in a gentle breeze. Her children were well and healthy and good, and her sister, never matter her domineering nature, she was gold, truly.

Laura let a tear slide down her nose. Thank you, dear God. Thank you for all your blessings. If He had a plan for her, perhaps the bumps and detours were part of it. Quite a busy job, being God, she reasoned. He must have some help. Bet more jobs are available up there than down here. At that she laughed out loud.

"Mother!" yelled Ben running through the door and throwing down his schoolbag. "I have today's bouquet for you!"

Laura put down her beads and rose to greet her son. He had unflaggingly kept up his work in the O'Briens' greenhouse, lovingly tending to the flowers so that his efforts took up a good deal of the space. Each day he brought her a new arrangement, delighting in combining colours and textures, always explaining the names of each bloom and its origins or some little information about the flower. "Mother, remember how two people asked me on the way home yesterday if I would make them bouquets for special occasions? Well, I told Mr. O'Brien about it, and he says I should set up a business, a real one, and charge money! He wants to help too, and Tom is ready to get started."

"Oh, Ben, that sounds like an imposition on Mr. O'Brien-"

"He said you'd say that, so he said to tell you that it's not a problem and he wants to do it. Please, can we?"

Laura laughed. "If he says it's alright, I don't see why not."

That summer of '57 sped by for Laura and the boys. Thanks to Peggy's help and kindness and steady sunshine, Laura flourished. One Sunday at the end of September, the boys stayed home from their jobs and visits, and Sam and his father came around for dinner. Laura had invited them to thank them for all they'd done for her, but they insisted they bring dinner, saying they had more leftovers than they knew what to do with.

After they caught up, while Laura and Robert relaxed in the sunroom, Sam and the boys cut into firewood George had delivered. Sam came in for a glass of water, and his father rose and went outside to join the boys.

Laura and Sam sat awkwardly for a moment. "By the way, you didn't need to bring so much food; it'll last for days. And look," she leaned over to the side table. "Your father brought me a book on the Acadians. Did you tell him I came from an Acadian family?" she asked slyly.

"Yes. I've read this one; it's quite interesting."

Laura grinned and clasped the book to her chest as if she were holding a genuine treasure. Quietly they watched the action outside then she said, "I'm sorry Miss Abby couldn't join you today." She realized once she said it she didn't mean it. Not one bit.

If Sam noticed her insincerity, he didn't react to it. He just shook his head. "I'm afraid Abby isn't around much these days, and on Sundays, she's never home. When I ask her where she goes, she's very evasive." Sam looked Laura in the eyes. "I don't mind telling you that we lost our baby, years ago. Ever since then, she's become someone else."

"I'm so sorry, Sam."

Sam sat numbly in his chair, his shoulders slumped, then stood quickly. "Best I return to work before I get fired."

"Sam, you don't have to do this. George said he would come help the boys chop the wood-"

He waved his hand dismissively. "I know, but I want to. So does Father. But I'd meant to ask, coal is so much better than wood- it

131

doesn't burn as quickly and keeps the house warmer for longer-and we're planning on buying some. Would you like to share in a half-ton load? Also now that you have running water, keeping things consistently warm is important so the pipes don't freeze."

The familiar clench of fear came into her. "Oh, uh, I don't know. Maybe wood will be alright-"

"Listen, the train comes in every Tuesday and Friday bringing coal from Inverness. I'll just check to see what it costs and let you know. It's dirty, coal, but it would do wonders for keeping the house warm."

A few weeks later, Sam came to Laura with the good news that he had more coal than he could possibly use all by himself so he'd bring her the extra, which would last her a long time. His timing was perfect as the weather had begun to turn cool. One morning after the first frost, Laura carefully nailed a large blanket in the door entry to the sunroom so the warm kitchen air would not escape. When she finished, she stared at it with a heavy heart. She historically had always feared the long cold months that lay ahead, but then she realized her house would now be warmer than it had ever been. They had enough money, and they had each other. Life was definitely much improved. In most every way.

* * * * * *

Christmas was fast approaching, and the boys were excited. In early December, they cut a tree and placed it in the usual corner, but by the time Christmas drew near, almost all the needles had fallen off. Joe cut another one, though it wasn't as nice, so he added some extra branches to make it bushier. Snow fell continuously; even the road leading to the house became blocked. Three days before Christmas, Tom awoke complaining of a bellyache. He was running a high fever. On Christmas Eve, he was still very sick and slipped into a delirium.

Laura was angry at her resistance to get him help earlier; wasn't this exactly how she lost her husband? Her need to hold on to every penny could cost her her son's life. She grabbed Joe by the shoulders and told him to get to Peggy and George's house to call the doctor as quickly as possible.

The winds were gusting and by the time he arrived, he was white as a snowman. George prepared to go out to the main road to meet the doctor alone, but Joe said, "He's my brother and my responsibility," standing tall with his face tense and his shoulders hunched as before a fight. George steered him outside and said, "I don't have time to argue. Dry yourself a bit while I hitch up the horse to the sleigh. I'm sure the doctor won't be able to reach your place by car in this weather."

Waiting for the doctor and getting him to the house seemed to take a long time. Laura was pacing, biting her fingernails when they arrived. The doctor went up to the loft, his knees creaking. "He needs to get to the hospital right away," he said after he came back down and put his stethoscope in his bag. "I think his appendix might have ruptured."

Laura wrapped him in woolen blankets, and George carried him to the sleigh. Normally the sound of sleigh bells at this time of year was enchanting. Tonight, as George, the doctor and Tom sped off into the dark to the main road, they only sounded out everyone's worry.

The following day was not the relaxed Christmas day the family had hoped for. George and Peggy arrived early to pick up Laura, Joe and Ben. "I called Sam, and he said he has some work to do, but we can certainly borrow his car to go see Tom this afternoon," said George.

It was the most beautiful Christmas day, Laura's first Christmas home from the san. A light snow danced around the travelers, sleigh bells could be heard in the distance, and the air smelled sweetly of snow and wood smoke. Yet everyone's heart weighed heavily. Laura was frantic on the inside at the thought of her son possibly dying.

Robert met the quiet group at the door. "Come in! Merry Christmas! Brrr, mighty cold! Come by the fire and warm up a bit."

He put his arm around Ben and ushered him inside. "No need for any of you to worry about Tom. Sam telephoned the hospital, and they say he's going to be all right and they're taking good care of him." He rubbed his chin and smiled heartily. "You all go on ahead, but hurry back; now that Tom's out of the woods, I thought you all might like to be cheered up with some special Christmas supper. The turkey is already in the oven, and I'll make sure dinner is ready when you get back from the hospital."

Everyone began to celebrate, but Peggy's smile was tight. "You're sure you're up to it, Robert?" Laura, already standing at the door, thought she heard her sister's claws extend just a bit. Christmas dinner had always been her jurisdiction. But he just laughed, handed George the keys, and swept everyone out the door. Laura didn't care who made the dinner, or even whether they had dinner at all. All that mattered was that her son was alright.

By the time the family got there, Tom's fever was down and he was resting. Laura spent the whole time holding his hand and his brothers awkwardly told him to get better soon so they could build the biggest snowman there ever was. When they left, the family rode home in silence until Joe and Ben looked at each other, then excitedly leaned over the front seat and offered their gifts to their aunt and uncle.

Since George was driving, Peggy unwrapped George's gift and held it out so he could see. "A tie; just what I needed, boys! Thank you!" he smiled.

Then Aunt Peggy opened her gift and frowned when she saw the price tag dangling. "Four dollars! Oh, no. That storekeeper took advantage of you. First thing tomorrow, this goes back."

Joe's face turned crimson. "But Aunt Peggy! It's a statue of the Virgin Mary. It's, well, it's special. We can't take it back!"

"We thought it would look nice on top of your piano," added Ben. "We got the same for Mama and she didn't complain."

"You take them both back, and if she won't give you a refund, I'll see to it myself!"

"Peggy, the boys meant well," Laura said trying to keep her anger out of her voice. No one else spoke the rest of the way.

By the time they reached Sam's house, supper was ready. Robert must have used every pot and pan in the house. He came out, his face red and shiny beneath his white hair. "How's Tom?"

"He's weak, but the doctor says he's going to be fine. He's a lucky boy. If Joe hadn't run to George for help, God knows what might have happened." Laura didn't want to talk about it anymore. She felt her ineptitude, larger than her own body, about to overwhelm her. It had come so close. She didn't dare tell anyone how she was feeling or they'd see her as unfit, she thought. She shook her head and vowed to enjoy the day. Tom would be fine.

After everyone was seated at the table and said grace, Robert proudly announced, "Dig in!" Sam arrived in time to carve the turkey, and the famished group took generous helpings of creamy mashed potatoes, carrots, turnips, dressing and gravy. The mood was light and gay. Again Sam was alone. Laura didn't want to ask where Miss Abby was for fear of spoiling the good cheer. Peggy however barreled right in with the questions. "Where is your wife? Why isn't she with you on Christmas?"

There was a silence before Sam answered. "Abby is visiting relatives." There was a sharpness to his tone that must have told Peggy not to pursue more questions, because all she said to that was, "Oh, how nice." Robert made a joke, and soon everyone was joyful again.

Filled and satisfied, the family stood to go sit by the fireplace. "We have something for you," said Ben to Sam.

Laura motioned to Ben, who ran to fetch the gift for Sam and his father.

"For us? But we didn't expect anything," said Robert as he gracefully pulled off the paper and folded it into a neat square. He and Sam exclaimed over the huge basket filled with canned jelly, mustard pickles, chow, canned beets and homemade bread.

Laura smiled. "Actually, you can thank yourself for this gift; most of these items come from your garden. I just changed their presentation." Everyone had a good laugh.

When they arrived home, it was too early for bed, so Laura lit a fire in the stove and felt deeply grateful for the coal, which kept the stove going. No longer did they come home to a house deathly cold to the elements. Soon, their little shack was warm and cozy. While she rocked by the window, Joe and Ben sprawled on the old faded rug, quietly reading their new comic books. She remembered the excited look on their faces, just that same morning when they had first spotted their Christmas presents, each a comic book and an orange. She didn't have the money for extravagant gifts, but she had enough for these, and they were just enough. She wondered how much the hospital would cost and tried not to think about it. Peggy was still holding on to Laura's baby bonus and pension money and doled it out as she saw fit. The more time went on, the harder it got for Laura to ask. But Peggy would pay whatever it cost to make sure Tom was OK. That much Laura knew.

She listened to the soothing holiday music on the radio and marveled at the simple but perfect joy in being home. Well, almost perfect. She imagined Tom alone in his bed on Christmas. But this was the way it was, and he was a strong boy. They'd be together soon. Then her thoughts moved to others who were alone, particularly Sam and Robert; they didn't seem concerned over Miss Abby's absence. In fact, she wondered whether anyone would've mentioned her if Peggy hadn't. It was definitely puzzling. Laura looked at the clock. "Time for bed, boys."

"Mother, isn't it strange that Robert and Sam didn't put up a Christmas tree?" asked Ben.

Laura didn't respond but only hugged her boys close. She didn't have an answer.

* * * * * *

After two weeks in the hospital, Tom was finally well enough to come home. It was another three months of convalescing at home before he could return to school. When he did go back to school, for the first few weeks, he stayed at Aunt Peggy's since the bus route was closer to their place. George walked him to the bus stop every morning, carrying his schoolbag and lunch can. He hoped no one would see them, George doting on him like he was a little grandmother.

By mid-spring of 1958, Laura finally got the doctor's approval that she could work again. Yet she wondered if going back to work was a wise choice. By now she was used to her daily routine and wasn't sure her health would hold under Abby's usual treatment. But she thought of Robert and Sam and smiled. She knew Robert would pay her far more than her meager monthly pension. And her heart was telling her to go.

Like she had done her first day at the O'Brien's, she curled her hair and pressed her dress. She wanted to believe she was excited simply to be going back to her job, but she knew it wasn't that. Peggy had found out through the grapevine that Abby had been so absent because she'd been having an affair. And now, she'd left Sam.

On the way, Laura found herself whistling, caught in her thoughts, until she came to a grove of apple trees bedecked in white blossoms. She marveled at their beauty; it was as if the trees were covered with snow. Then after searching and eventually finding her favourite lilac bush, she picked a magnificent bouquet to bring with her.

Both men were coincidentally at home and answered the door together. "Welcome back, Laura! Sit down and rest a while. How about some tea? What lovely lilacs."

Laura looked past them into the living room; it was full of books and papers. She wouldn't know where to put a vase if she could even locate one. She laughed. "What a fine greeting! And I'm honoured that you'd wait four years for me to have your house cleaned," she said impishly, raising an eyebrow at the mess.

Robert hooted and Sam turned red. "Alright, we'll make it up to you. How about two days a week and a small raise?"

"I don't think two days a week will ever be enough to get this big house back in order."

"Father, why don't we pitch in and help our Laura-ella for a few days."

Laura looked at Sam skeptically. Something in him had changed. He seemed jocular, lighter. Could it be he was relieved his wife had left? Was that possible? Robert took Laura's elbow and steered her toward the kitchen. "I think it's a grand idea, son," he said as he poured the tea, "but don't you have work to go to?" He winked at Laura.

"With all the overtime I've been putting in, I'm sure no one will complain."

There was a gentle silence, three old friends pleased to be in one another's company. Laura finally said softly, "Sam, I'm very sorry to hear about Miss Abby."

Sam stood to fetch the milk. "Let's look toward the future." He returned and raised his cup. "To new beginnings."

They clinked glasses and enjoyed their tea. Finally Laura stood. "Time to get to work; do you have a list?" she asked Robert with wide open eyes and a big smile.

In the following weeks of spring, Laura slid easily into her new routine with some added perks. She easily and without fanfare told Peggy, not asked, that they transfer the baby bonus back to her name and Peggy surprised her yet again by complying without a blink. Robert began picking her up each morning. Occasionally he came with his car; other times, he sent his horse and buggy, for he knew she loved that most. The boys, picking up on their mother's new content, thrived; they did well in school and kept busy with their side jobs and friends. Her singing and whistling had returned and she allowed herself the indulgences of playing word games in her head and lifting off into daydreams, the fancy of a contented soul, she thought happily. And she took immense pride walking into the government office and telling them herself that she no longer needed her pension, thank you. The clerk had looked at her a bit open-mouthed but smiled warmly when Laura departed. "Best of luck, Mrs. McPherson," she'd said. As Laura pushed open the front door and went out into the fresh air, she realized she wasn't dependent on anyone anymore for help. She felt about 20 pounds lighter as she walked away.

Yet despite everything ticking along so well, one evening she was rocking by the window staring at the moon as usual, and she suddenly felt more acutely than ever the loss in her heart for Johnny. Her heart beat, regular and strong, as if in a song of loss. Tears rolled down her face. When she next glanced up at the sky, out of nowhere, a shooting star appeared and in a flash was gone. A peaceful feeling came over her and took up safe residence in her body. That night, rather than toss and turn in her bed alone, she fell easily asleep to the gentle sound of rain droplets on the roof. Come morning, rather than feeling stiff and fatigued as she often did the day after work, she woke up refreshed and thought what a pleasant feeling it was to be alive and well.

That morning, when Laura arrived at the O'Brien's, she had the caretaker drop her off at the road. She stood in the centre and admired the majestic white house with its impressive front pillars as if she were seeing it for the first time. She allowed herself the fleeting thought of what it would be like to come home to this place, to feel the pride of walking into this proud white house at the end of a lane lined with tall oak trees. She stood a moment longer before making her way to the front door. Streaks of sunlight filtered through the leaves and soothingly warmed her whole body. She stared at the beautiful flower garden, which adorned the curve of the driveway. Odd she hadn't noticed this lovely picture before. She knelt to touch the soft petals, the leaves still wet with morning dew. She then proudly realized she was actually admiring Ben's handiwork, clearly a labour of love.

No one was about the house; Sam was away on business and Robert was in town. She thought about sad Miss Abby and couldn't recall her ever breaking into an authentic smile, not once. What a shame, thought Laura. She'd had a wonderful husband, a dear father-in-law, a beautiful house, every reason to be happy, yet she never seemed to appreciate how fortunate she was. I hope she finds what she's looking for, thought Laura, going inside.

Summer passed lazily, kindly, everyone growing healthy and strong from the sun and outdoor play. Laura and the boys spent more time at the O'Brien house, enjoying evening picnics and tea after church, and Ben and Tom worked every day in the greenhouse.

Heightening the carefree days was some news Peggy gave Laura, though Laura didn't dare ask how her sister had received this private information. Apparently Sam had found his wife. But, and here was the part that made Laura's heart skip, knowing where she was, he chose not to go look for her. Amid the sun and floral scent in the air, from that day on, Laura found herself feeling giddy when she was near Sam, then chagrined for not taking higher ground. He was still married, after all.

Once September came, on the days Laura worked, Robert insisted she prepare supper for all of them. Sam began to make a point of joining the "family" meals, playing catch with the boys while dinner was being readied. Ben, who when he was younger seemed to have two left arms, improved quickly and boasted of his new skills to his older brother. "Sam bought me a bran' new glove. Look, Joe!"

During these happy family evenings, though, Joe tended to hang back. He didn't much care for the way Samuel O'Brien was starting to look at his mother. It wasn't the look an employer gave to an employee. Joe wasn't as much disturbed as he was frightened. He could see his mother looking back. The wound of his dead father wasn't yet healed enough for him to accept that this was happening. As the man of his house, she was his responsibility, he felt, and he was losing his grip on the family.

One Indian summer evening, as Laura brought a plate piled high with chicken outside to the O'Brien veranda and everyone ran in from the ball playing looking tanned and relaxed did Joe realize the sweet hum on the breeze was coming from his mother. She was looking right at Sam and he was looking at her. Joe saw that in this moment, no one else existed.

Chapter Seven
Rosalie

In April of 1959, Sam received the news that his drunken wife had fallen down a flight of stairs and broke her back. Immediately, he rushed to the room in the hospital where she lay in critical condition. Sam held her scrawny hand and looked upon her wasted face and remembered how lovely she used to be, recognizing nothing of the feelings he'd once had for her.

"Please forgive me," she whispered again and again as she drifted in and out of consciousness.

It was clear to Sam that his wife was going to die. He smoothed her hair. "There's nothing to forgive. I should have worked fewer hours so we could have spent more time together, we could have tried for another child. You once were my heart," he added softly.

Abby broke down and sobbed. She passed away later that day. Sam couldn't help but wonder if her injuries were only a part of her death. Her soul seemed missing, as if her heart were broken, beyond repair.

Days after Abby's funeral, Sam went through his wife's affairs. He noticed a monthly transfer of funds to a St. Anne's Orphanage, several miles away, on the other side of town. Strange that Abby never mentioned it. It was a fair amount of money; she must have been more charitable than he gave her credit for. But the longer he thought about it, the more something didn't sit right with him. This wasn't just a donation out of goodwill. The sum was too regular, and too large.

A week later, Sam stood in front of a large brown brick building with narrow windows that looked more like a prison than an orphanage. He trudged through dirty snow as he inspected the premises. At least the poor kids had a swing set and teeter-totters in the play area, and he hoped that the presence of flower boxes, empty now, meant there would be some flowers in them come warmer weather.

Inside was neat and orderly, with children's paintings on the walls. It was actually quite a lively place. The headmistress, who had been watching him through her office window, finally emerged and approached him.

"Hello, Mr. O'Brien," she said as she extended her hand. "I'm the headmistress. The children call me Miss Barbara."

Sam stiffened. "How do you know my name?"

She beckoned him into the main office. "Tea?"

He nodded numbly. "What-"

She sat down in the chair opposite him and leaned forward. "Mr. O'Brien," she began soberly, "we've been expecting you. Since Abby's untimely demise."

"I have to admit I don't understand what's happening."

Miss Barbara took a deep breath. Her brow creased. "Mr. O'Brien. I'm about to tell you some difficult things..." she paused. Sam stared at her. "About ten years ago, did you travel to the US for a work contract?"

"How would you know about that? That's," he thought a minute, "that's just before my wife lost our baby. So how does her miscarriage concern Abby's monthly payment to this orphanage?"

Miss Barbara smiled kindly. "Your wife carried a dark secret. The baby did not die. She was born. A little girl. She...she's here."

"What?!" whispered Sam. "I have a daughter??" His legs suddenly became weak and his breathing uneven. "But why? Why would Abby lie to me about our own daughter, our baby? It doesn't make sense. Are you sure?" Tears were in his eyes now, and he brusquely rubbed his thumb over them.

The headmistress stood and brought him all the documents she'd readied after she heard the news of Abby's death. She handed him the birth certificate. The baby was born on March 10, 1949, to Abigail and Samuel O'Brien.

"What about the doctor, the nurse, surely the nun would not allow such a thing to happen!"

"The doctor left shortly thereafter, moved to Ontario. As far as the nurse, she was sworn to secrecy, and apparently, the nun attending the doctor, was sent to fetch something or other, and by the time she returned, she was told the baby had died."

Sam stood. "I want to see her."

"Come with me. Just follow my cue."

Sam followed her to the auditorium where the children were practising for an Easter Sunday variety show. He looked at all the children trying to find the one who could be his. As they walked slowly down the aisle towards the group, his eyes searched for a resemblance of some kind in each of the children. By now, anger, excitement and fear stirred so violently his stomach he thought he might choke.

Miss Barbara stopped in front of a pudgy little girl with globed eyes and a shy smile. "Hello, Rosalie. How are you today? My friend's name is Sam."

The little girl looked at the stranger and extended her hand.

"Rosalie play drums!" she said cheerfully.

Sam smiled somewhat, fighting to keep himself under control, but as soon as they returned to the office, he unleashed a torrent of emotion.

"What kind of system are you running? I have a daughter who is ten years old, whom I didn't even know existed until now and... and she's..." he didn't dare say it aloud.

Miss Barbara shrank back; she had been dreading this encounter for a while. She sat down and examined the back of her hand. "Abby's mother was with her at the time of the delivery. It was a difficult birth, and Abby was very weak for several days afterward. The doctor feared she wouldn't pull through..." she paused. "That's all important but not right now. The fact is your daughter has something called Down's syndrome." She grimaced. "Your mother-in-law, as you probably well know, was an overly proud and arrogant woman, and her words, which I still remember to this day, were, 'I will not accept a less than perfect grandchild.'"

At this, Sam, who had sat down during this story, was now unable to stop his tears. He began to weep.

Barbara touched his arm. "Your mother-in-law had a lot of power, Mr. O'Brien. The doctor who delivered the baby owed her a big favour. So by the time we received your daughter, the news was out that Abby had had a miscarriage."

Sam looked at her, his eyes furious and confused. "How could Abby let this happen? To her own baby?"

"Abby was a sweet and soft-tempered young girl at the time. After she gave birth, she was exhausted. With you gone, she simply didn't have the strength to battle against her mother's domineering character. Hillary took advantage of her daughter's vulnerable condition. By the time Abby regained enough strength to realize what was happening, it was already a done deal. Gradually, her mother more or less convinced her that they had done the right thing."

Sam realized that this kind woman across from him was complicit in the whole affair. "Why did you agree to such a deceitful plan?" His voice was very loud.

She folded her hands together and brought them to her mouth. "It has bothered me since the day I agreed to keep quiet. But the fact is the orphanage was in bad need of repair. The board was about to close us down if we didn't meet their standards and they weren't wrong. The building had old wiring and some faulty windows that had been boarded up, was a terrible fire hazard, and there were no funds for restoration." She continued sadly, "I know keeping this a secret from you was wrong, but Abby's mother was powerful, and, Mr. O'Brien, in this case, it was the money that talked, to be frank. On the same day your daughter was born, we received much needed funds for the orphanage. And I'm sorry to say that's the fact of it."

Sam was shaking by now. He cupped his head in his hands as he bent forward in his chair.

The head mistress continued. "We called her Rosalie."

Sam looked up. "Abby didn't even give her a name?"

"No, by the time she woke up and was coherent, her baby was gone. Only when Rosalie was a year old, did Abby first come to visit her."

Sam remembered how distraught and weak Abby had been after losing their child. She never fully recovered physically or emotionally.

"After Rosalie's first birthday, Abby visited her every Sunday, bringing her pretty dresses and ribbons for her hair. She spent all her time with her, never letting on she was her mother. At first, Rosalie slept a lot so Abby simply stared at her. When she first started to walk at two and a half, Abby was there. Later, Rosalie loved the swings, so her mother bought us a beautiful new swing set. Every Sunday she pushed her on the swings, singing silly rhymes. She's a happy girl, very sociable and loves to play the drums." Miss Barbara cleared her throat. "As Rosalie grew and thrived, Abby gradually turned very bitter towards her mother. She also blamed herself for losing her precious child, so she started drinking. I only know this because she would often show up drunk, even in the mornings."

As Miss Barbara poured herself another cup of tea, Sam reflected on this sad situation. He'd known there was a wound festering in his wife's heart, and assumed that she simply wasn't capable of love any more once she lost the baby, turning over time into a bitter, resentful person and shutting out her mother, Sam, even herself. Yet this woman Barbara described, one who was so loving toward her daughter, this was the woman he'd married. He felt empty. She'd never confided in him. What kind of marriage did they have at all? She must not have felt she could come to him. He'd never felt so low in his life.

Miss Barbara said gently, "By the time Abby gathered enough courage to tell you the whole story, she thought it was too late. She was scared you would never forgive her, and might take Rosalie away and forbid her from ever seeing her child again. A few days before her accident, she came to see me, her secret too much to bear anymore. She was inconsolable, as if all those years of holding in her secret were emerging. 'What kind of mother gives her baby away," she cried. Eventually, Abby's mother's pride and vanity, I think, are what destroyed her."

"It's murder," murmured Sam. He wasn't sorry that he was glad Hilary had passed away just a month before from a stroke or else he'd want to confront her with a fury he'd never even imagined he was capable of. He regretted now that he had taken time out of his schedule to attend the funeral.

Abruptly, he rose from his chair. He had to get out, had to breathe, but he was compelled to see Rosalie again. He stared through the glass of the door. She was small for her age but well built, with a beautiful round face and dark brown eyes, a cute little button of a nose. She's pretty, very pretty, thought Sam. "I'll be back," he whispered before he turned and left.

By the time he arrived home, it was very late. Unable to contain his emotions, he rushed through the front door to immediately recheck Abby's journal. There it was: a visit to the orphanage every Sunday. It all made sense. The gardener must have driven her; how else would she go unless she took a taxi? How was it no one brought it to his attention seeing as how people loved to gossip so much?

He read the journal again, his wife's pain heaving through his body. She had written about Laura, how seeing her striving to keep her family together against many odds, how she was such a good mother tore at her. She wrote of her shame over the way she had treated Laura and hoped the food she put in her wagon would somehow make up for her mean behaviour. All along, Sam had thought his father was the one secretly placing the bags of food in Ben's wagon. The good heart she'd had when Sam married her was still in there. And now it was too late to save her.

Like a broken man, he slowly climbed up to bed but sleep would not come. After much tossing and turning, he finally made his way downstairs to the library. There, he frantically searched for as much as he could find on Down's syndrome. In the wee hours of the morning, spent, he returned to bed. By late afternoon, he woke up and walked into the kitchen for a cup of tea.

Laura was shocked to see him unshaved, pale as a ghost with bulging red eyes. She realized that Abby must have meant more to him than she had originally thought. She tried not to be bothered by this. After all, they shared a whole history, a home, a child who never came to be.

The next few days Sam acted uncharacteristically; he skipped work; locked himself in the library for hours on end; then he'd leave the house with no explanation. His father and Laura were getting worried.

Finally one afternoon, he sat down at the kitchen table for a cup of tea and began to talk. He told Laura and Robert everything.

"I've heard of Down's syndrome, but I don't know its particulars," said Robert.

Sam went into the library and brought back his notes and a few books. He flipped to a marked page. "Down's syndrome is due to a chromosomal defect," he read. "An extra chromosome adds additional genetic information, which upsets a person's 'normal' growth and development." Laura didn't look like she understood, and Robert just seemed overwhelmed, so Sam explained it again. "People with this condition are slower than normal. The head-mistress at the orphanage told me that Rosalie, my daughter," he paused, "it feels very odd to say that." He shook his head. "Anyway, she first raised her head at eight months and didn't walk until she was two and a half."

Sam's father held his head in his hands. After a quiet lapse of time, he finally asked, "How many chromosomes does a 'normal' person have?"

Sam searched his notes, "Here. It says we have forty-six while people with Down's syndrome have forty-seven."

"Where did you find out all this information?" asked Laura.

"I've been researching for the past several days in the library here and I also checked the town's university library and spoke to a few professors, even went to see the doctor. It's a miracle I found this book; it was just published a few months ago."

Laura and Robert looked at each other. Then they both asked in unison, "What can we do?"

Sam began to laugh and cry at the same time. Laura was so touched at his display of emotion, she put her hand on his. He looked at her gratefully and squeezed her hand in return. "What is she like?" quietly asked Robert smiling at the two.

Sam answered calmly. "Her name is Rosalie. She looks a bit like her mother but her eyes are the same colour as mine. They have an upward and outward slant. She may be different, but who isn't, right? And she's my child. You'll see when you meet her. She is very sociable and likes music, so the headmistress says."

"A granddaughter! When can we bring her home?"

"Anytime, I guess. I'm her father after all." Sam was grinning.

The three were laughing and talking all at once.

"I'll call the orphanage."

"I'll get the car."

"I'll prepare her room."

Sam suddenly stopped, turned around, and shook his head. "We can't do this now. It's too fast. I have to think about it, talk to the headmistress. I don't want to upset the little one."

He grabbed his jacket and went outside to the front veranda. Laura and Robert let him go. He laughed then held on to one of the wide pillars with both hands and began to cry. His knuckles turned white and his whole body shook.

Sam sat on the veranda for a long time. It was an unusually warm evening for April. Before Laura was about to return home, she came to the front door and watched him for a few moments. He looked like a lost soul. She opened the screen door and sat quietly beside him. He took her hand and held it tightly, without saying a word. To a passerby, they looked like two lovebirds sitting on a fence, but these two people were caught in their own private thoughts, just barely beginning to meet each other in the new way that can only be started by the touch of two hands. The moon was rising behind the rolling hills and the nighttime crickets were in full buzz chorus. Finally, Laura tried to take her hand back and began to stand. Sam held to her fast, "Don't go yet, Laura."

She sat down again, and with his eyes on the moon, he said, "You know, Laura, my first reaction was what did I do wrong?

Or what did Abby do wrong? She must have been in turmoil all these years, hiding our child." Then Sam smiled. "She's as cute as a button, pleasant and cheerful. I think we'll be alright. But..." he paused and looked into Laura's eyes. "Will you help me? Will you help me care for Rosalie? I'm sure she will need constant supervision." Sam sighed, looked away then brought his eyes back to hers. "I know you are the right person to care for her. I need you, Laura."

Laura felt in his eyes, in his words, he was asking her to embark on a different level of relationship with his family, but she needed to be sure. "I would be glad to. But with all the housework, I'm not sure I can keep an eye on her all the time." Laura looked him straight on. She ached to help Sam, to be needed by him, but she vowed that nothing would ever come between her and her children again. "Who's going to care for her when you're away on meetings? I can't leave the boys, I won't."

Sam bent down and slid his fingers through his hair. "My life has drastically changed in the past few days. Abby's gone forever, and now, I have a ten-year-old daughter." He straightened, rose from the bench and sat on the rail. Looking into the night, he continued as if thinking out loud. "Of course, I'll have to change my schedule. From now on, I'll try to be home every night." Laura lowered her head and smiled. He actually had been home almost every night for supper since Abby had left him. "As far as the housework, I'll hire another housekeeper so you can tend exclusively to Rosalie. And I will raise your wages."

Laura tried to process all this new information. She wanted this, hadn't realized or allowed herself to think about this, but here it was, and she realized she wanted this, very badly. But she thought about the details: what if the girl was difficult to manage? What if she overextended herself again? She had to think about her health. Even the extra money, which would be wonderful, would mean she'd be gone from the boys all week.

His back was to Laura but it was as if he'd read her every thought. Then slowly he turned around. "I hope Rosalie will think of the boys as her brothers. That will surely make her feel even more at home. And don't worry about overnight. If I do have to be away, I'll make other arrangements so you won't have to stay." He smiled softly at Laura.

She blushed, rose from her seat and fumbled with her dress. "I should be going."

He waited for her to meet his eyes. When she did, he smiled and held out his hand. "Come," he said softly, "I'll take you home."

* * * * * *

Sam and his father decided it'd be better for Rosalie if they could get acquainted first before uprooting her. They visited her often and she soon became very comfortable with them.

In early May, Sam brought Laura along. Having never been in one of these institutions, seeing all the children, she was subdued and grateful for all she had, for her boys, and for her sister and brother-in-law. It was a clean nice place, with the children's art on the walls, but she fought back tears trying to imagine her boys having to grow up here, without her.

In Miss Barbara's office, Laura pulled out a notebook and a pen to take notes. Sam beamed at how personally she was taking on his life. The headmistress painted a picture, a mixture of roses and thorns, of Rosalie's care. "Rosalie's food still has to be mashed, for her muscles are not quite yet under control. Leaving a few lumps will help strengthen these muscles. She eats with a special spoon," she smiled. "Actually it's just a regular spoon with a black handle, but for Rosalie no other utensil will do. I suggest you buy several of these spoons..." she smiled again, obviously remembering lost and found episodes with the spoon, then, continued, "Her speech and reading skills need individual attention. A one-on-one approach is preferable. Talking, for Rosalie, will probably be a lifelong challenge. She skips certain words and sometimes she might be hard to understand. But be patient with her. Always encourage her to speak in simple sentences. There's only so much she can do. She always tries her best and thrives on positive reinforcement, whether it be a treat or a special activity. I must say, she can be a handful at times, especially when things don't go her way; she often pouts, but these incidents usually don't last long. Remember to be firm when she acts up. She needs guidance and support as well as a lot of love. And make sure the doors are locked because she likes to venture out. Oh, one more thing, her favourite toy is a smooth piece of wood about the size of a ruler. She likes to rock back and forth and pass it through her fingers. She's also extremely fond of music." The headmistress looked at Laura. "Why don't you spend some time with her, get to know her routine?"

When Laura first met Rosalie, her head reeling from all Miss Barbara had said, she was hesitant, but they instantly liked each other and any shyness melted away. Proudly, Rosalie showed Laura her room where everything was in its place. "I love swim!"

"You love to swim?" asked Laura.

"Yes! You swim?"

"No, maybe you can teach me!"

Rosalie laughed.

The day finally arrived when Rosalie was ready to move into her father's house. She raced through the halls singing, "Daddy home, Daddy home!" as she kissed her friends and teachers goodbye.

While Sam was picking her up, Grandpa Robert, Laura and Peggy anxiously awaited their arrival at home. Rosalie got out of the car dressed in an outfit so new it still had creases in it, and went to the front door, clutching a colourful satchel in both hands, as if for dear life. Laura smiled for she reminded her of Anne of Green Gables.

As Rosalie made her way into the big house, she immediately set about looking in every corner and nodding her approval. Laura, with Peggy's help, had prepared her a most beautiful room next to her father's. Rosalie paused in the bedroom doorway before racing in, squealing in delight over the polka dot bedspread and matching curtains, then turned around and ran at Sam for a hug so hard she nearly knocked him over. Everyone laughed from joy and also relief- it was remarkable how enthusiastic she was for her new home.

When Rosalie went on to inspect another room, Laura approached Sam. "How did it go?" she murmured.

Sam shook his head in disgust. "The head mistress actually had the audacity to ask me if we could wait a few more weeks, obviously not wanting the truth to come out. Who knows; maybe she hadn't been able to speak to her lawyers. I told her I don't care, enough secrets. She's my daughter and I'm taking her home with me."

Laura was very proud of Sam; he was behaving like a true mother hen, or a true father hen. She had to admit it warmed her heart.

Laura had decided it was best not to say anything to the boys about Rosalie in case there were any problems bringing her home, but with her now safely at Sam's house, she was happy to sit down at dinner and break the news to them. They were very excited and bombarded her with questions. "What does she look like? Can she talk? Can she walk? When can we meet her?"

Laura smiled. "She's wonderful, a very sweet little thing. Sam invited us over for supper next Sunday. His father is cooking. Shall we go?"

They all agreed. That night, Laura slept well feeling like things were slowly becoming right with the world. Over at the O'Brien home, however, things were not as calm. Rosalie whimpered constantly in her new bed, and Sam had to go in to try and soothe her every few minutes. "What's the matter, Rosalie? Can't you sleep?"

"My room," she said between sniffles.

"I know, but try to sleep." Then he had an idea. "Maybe this week, we could visit Miss Barbara. Would you like that?"

She nodded and just before midnight finally fell asleep. When Sam eventually got to climb into his own bed, he realized that this father business wasn't as easy as it sounded.

The following Sunday, as soon as the McPhersons arrived, with her piece of wood in hand, Rosalie bounded over to the boys. Joe and Tom were slightly nervous initially, but Ben warmed to her straight away.

She pulled at their jackets, put them away, and showed them where to sit. "Come," she said proudly.

Ben touched her hair. "I like your name, Ros-a-lie, like a rose." He smiled at her as he offered her three beautiful yellow roses from the greenhouse.

"Ben. Beautiful!" she smiled broadly. "Miss Barbara say, I pretty like rose. I'm Rosalie!"

Sam put his hands on his daughter's shoulders. "Well, Ros-a-lie, shall we show our guests to the dinner table?"

Ben helped her arrange the flowers in a vase as he talked smoothly about different flowers, insects and birds. She listened intently, then stated, "Butterflies!" making Ben smile.

Dinner was quiet as the boys tried not to watch Rosalie smacking and dropping food from her mouth. Their mother's eyes firmly told them to behave. Finally, Sam, staring at the table, barked, "Rosalie, try to eat better!"

Instantly, the little one rose from her chair and hid behind the door between the dining room and kitchen. Ben pushed his chair to go to her, but Sam stopped him. "Let her be, Ben. She must learn. She's pouting, but she'll eventually come out. It's a big adjustment from the orphanage to here."

Laura added, "It's a big adjustment for us all, I think." Sam smiled gratefully, and soon Rosalie came out of hiding and took her place at the table. Conversation and good humour resumed as if nothing had happened, and Sam ruffled Rosalie's glossy hair and she hugged him. When dinner was over, Rosalie assigned a chore to each person: washing and drying the dishes, cleaning the stove, and sweeping the floor. Once everything was cleared to her satisfaction, she took Tom's hand and led them all into the living room.

"Come, see drums!"

Tom was amazed for it was the best set of drums he had ever seen. "Can you play?"

Rosalie replied shyly, "I...try..." Rosalie settled herself on a stool and played with her whole heart. It was intriguing to see her move the sticks from one hand to the next with so much ease. It was also more noise than music, but one couldn't help but appreciate her love for it. Rosalie beamed at their raucous applause.

Sam watched his daughter and wiped a tear off his cheek. This was the hand he'd been dealt, and in spite of who she was, or perhaps exactly because of who she was, he loved Rosalie dearly. Laura noticed and put a comforting arm across his back. Joe happened to look over and saw his mother holding Sam, and as soon as Rosalie was finished, he made an excuse that he was meeting friends. He departed, and Tom, Ben and Rosalie ventured into the library, or the "book room" as Rosalie called it, to search for butterfly pictures.

"Tomorrow, I'll bring my collection box to show you."

Rosalie looked upset. "Hurt wings?"

"No, no, they're not real. They are made of plastic. It was a gift from your father for Christmas."

"Christmas!" Rosalie relaxed and smiled.

The children, happy and content as they got to know one another, let Laura and Sam quietly go outside. They sat together on the porch, their hips lightly touching, and watched the night sky.

* * * * * *

Now that Rosalie was living with the O'Briens, Laura resumed her five days a week schedule. Sam hired a full time housekeeper, which allowed Laura to spend all of her time with Rosalie. Laura enjoyed the freedom from back and knee pain and also some additional time to herself during the otherwise busy day. During the little one's daily nap, Laura spent the time in Sam's library reading and finding books to bring home. During the evenings, while the boys finished their chores and homework, she read or dabbled in her journal. When she let go, her memories took over and she'd find herself dropping tears on the page, writing mostly about Johnny and the journey of her family. One time, Ben noticed and came to her, "What's wrong? Do you want a 'kerchief'?"

She swallowed hard and smiled, "Yes, Ben. That's kind of you."

He disappeared into the bedroom and returned with a long white blanket trailing behind him. He offered it to his mother and asked, with mischief in his eyes, "Is it big enough?"

She laughed so hard she was sure she'd wake the dead.

The following day, in the book room, Laura helped Rosalie practise her reading skills. Imagine, thought Laura, how fascinating it is to see how life comes full circle. Not long ago, I was learning to read, and now it's my turn to help someone else. Circle, full circle, circle of friends, circle of love... she laughed at herself then tickled Rosalie, who quickly joined in the fun. "Rosalie, repeat after me." Laura took the little one's arms and together they formed big circles. "Circle, full circle." As Laura prompted, Rosalie said the words over and over. "Good, Rosalie. Now try, circle of friends."

"Friends," said the little one. "Laura, my friend."

Laura grabbed the little one and held her close. This was what mothers did, she thought. They fell in love with their children, over and over, the room in their hearts infinite.

Sam had come home early from work that afternoon; when he came into the house, he followed the sound of happy giggles up to the library. He stood in the doorway and felt emotion expand in his chest so large he thought his heart would pop. "What about me?" he said, and dove in. When they paused to catch their breath, Rosalie said, "I read. Laura...good teacher... good friend."

Sam beamed. "You can read? Show me, Rosalie." The little one picked up a small paperback and showed off her limited skill. Sam smiled sadly but quickly remembered the headmistress' advice. "That's very good." As he hugged her, his eyes fell on Laura. "I agree with you wholeheartedly: Laura is a good teacher and a good friend." He then held the little one at arm's length and asked, "Can you say that?" The little one smiled and said, "Good friend."

Sam smiled and repeated Rosalie's words. Then he noticed a stack of books on the table. "What are these?" he asked as he picked one up. "They're all history books. Feeling patriotic?" he smiled at

Laura. "I remember this one. Did you read the one on the Acadians my father brought to you the day we visited you last summer?"

"Yes, it was most interesting and it made me even more curious to find something on my own native village of Chéticamp." She didn't mention that she'd always had unresolved feelings about her childhood home, like she'd been pulled away from fundamental things, things that had given her meaning, too soon. It made her feel as though she were unfinished in some way. She came to realize this when she met the Chéticamp girl at the san, heard her accent, knew the landmarks she'd spoken of. Yet when she was here, with Sam, she felt that sense of wholeness, and that didn't have anything to do with one's location.

"This is a good one too," he picked up the book and read the jacket copy. "The first section is on the early Acadians. There's another book that comes to mind I think you'd enjoy; it's at the library in town." He realized that now that he'd arrived home, Laura would probably leave for the day. He wanted to keep her with him, to prolong the inevitable, so he clapped his hands together. "Speaking of going into town, who wants to get an ice cream?"

"Yippee!" Rosalie clapped her hands too.

Sam was ushering Rosalie through the door when he noticed Laura holding back. "Laura, is it alright for you to come with us?"

"Oh, that's a wonderful idea; a trip to town would be lovely." Her boys were all busy that afternoon, and she wanted to stay with Sam. She didn't dare tell him about the feeling she was having in her chest, how pulled she was feeling. How desperately she wanted to give in to the depths in Sam's eyes. His smile. The warmth that came off his body when she stood beside him. Yet, she didn't dare, for she wasn't completely sure of how he felt about her. Already she cared so dearly for Rosalie. She would never be able to let her go if things didn't work out with him.

As if Sam understood, he said, "It's only an ice cream. We'll go slow." He held his hand out to her. She took it.

At the ice cream parlour, they decided to celebrate the nice day with cones rather than sundaes or floats. The three took their ice creams outside and sat on a bench, with Rosalie between the two adults. There was a sweet breeze in the air and the sunshine was warm. Rosalie set about eating her cone from the top but when it began to melt down the sides and she tried to lick the drips, her jaw wouldn't cooperate and the ice cream listed to the side. She cried out and threw it on the ground then began to sob.

"Spoon, Father!"

Laura and Sam desperately looked at each other, until Laura said brightly to Sam, "Well, I don't have a black spoon, but I do have this spoon here. I would so like to share my ice cream with both of you. It's a different spoon, but it's just as good as any other."

"Black spoon," the little girl said but stole a look at Laura who was taking a big bite out of her cone.

"Just try one bite," said Laura, popping some into Rosalie's open mouth. The girl squealed in delight and ate the rest of Laura's ice cream that way. On their way home, she fell asleep with her head resting on Laura's shoulder. Sam and Laura were quite content. "You know, Sam, the beauty of the countryside never ceases to amaze me. The swaying of the tall grass in the breeze, it looks like a velvet blanket protecting all the life that lies beneath."

Sam watched her from time to time, when she spoke or in their quiet moments. He then turned his eyes to the fields as they drove by, realizing he had never viewed his surroundings through such an articulate lens. Laura truly opened his eyes to the world in a way no one ever had. She was like the earth herself, rooted and strong, beautiful, with so much lying beneath. Bumping along in his old truck, which they'd had to take as he'd had to bring his sedan into the shop for repairs, the wind fluttering Rosalie's hair so it tickled the back of his bare forearm, a feeling of calm, of right, entered Sam. He looked at Laura, giggling at the bumps in the road. When she looked back over his new daughter's head at him, he knew that in his life as it was now, everything was as it should be.

His mind turned to the logistics of the rest of the family. Joe was aware of what was happening; the boy was bright and keen, this much Sam knew. Sam started to wonder just how to ingratiate himself to the boy when he hit a pothole and the truck backfired.

Rosalie, and Laura, who had fallen asleep as well, stirred but did not wake. He relaxed a bit and thought about how he couldn't wait to get rid of the old jalopy.

Suddenly, Sam realized, of course, what sixteen-year-old wouldn't like his very own wheels? The truck needed repairs, but why not give it to the boy? Then he realized it was actually a terrible plan. It would seem like a fairly transparent attempt to buy the boy's affection. He decided then he would offer to sell him the truck, at a low price, and Joe could pay for it once a month until it was paid off.

Sam drove Laura straight to her house. By chance, Joe was sitting on the steps, fiddling with a pocket knife. "Hello, Joe," she said as she got out of the car. "Did you light up the stove yet?"

Joe shook his head.

"Aren't Tom and Ben home?"

"They're still at Aunt Peggy's."

Laura turned around. "Thank you for the ride, Sam. Best I go in and start supper. Bye, Rosalie. See you tomorrow." Laura darted into the house.

Sam smiled, nodded and took a deep breath, which he let out slowly as he waited for her to get inside. He got out of the truck's cab and went over to Joe.

"What are you making, Joe?"

Joe didn't look up. "Nothing."

Sam looked around the old shack and frowned. "Uh, I was thinking, Joe. With your job after school at the garage and taking your mother for errands..." Sam stopped, looked around again as if he had heard a noise then cleared his throat.

"Yes, well, as I was saying...You do quite a lot of running around, Joe."

"My running around is none of your business."

"No, no, that's not what I mean," said Sam. He was taken aback by the boy's coldness. Joe had always been friendly toward him.

"Then, what do you mean?"

"Well, I was thinking, once my car gets out of the shop, I'd like to get rid of this truck. Maybe you'd like to buy it?" Sam turned around and examined the jalopy. "I'd have to get a few repairs done, of course. Wouldn't want to sell you a piece of junk, after all."

Raising his head, Joe took a big puff from his cigarette and smoke rings covered his face. "What's it to you if I have a set of wheels or not? Besides, how would I pay for it? I give most of my earnings to Mother; there's not much left for me."

"I'm sure we could come to some kind of agreement."

Joe straightened up and approached the old thing. He waved at Rosalie and winked. "It does need a few repairs. I could probably do it in my spare time at the garage. Couldn't pay for the parts, though."

"Why don't you get it in ship-shape and foot me the bill?"

"What's your price?" asked Joe.

"I don't know. Never sold a vehicle before."

"Mmm," he said, opening the hood and scanning his eyes over the engine. Rosalie was resting her chin on her crossed arms in the open window and watched Joe keenly. "I'd only be able to give you a few dollars a month. That's all I can spare." Sam could hear the boy trying to temper the excitement in his voice but didn't let on. Joe dropped to his back and scooted beneath the chassis. He thunked a few pipes before scooting out, a light smear of grease on his nose. He stood and brushed himself off.

"I think that sounds fair," Sam said casually. Joe ambled back to Sam. They shook hands and Joe finally cracked a smile.

After Sam left, Joe busied himself chopping wood and avoiding his mother until he knew how he'd tell her. By the time he mustered enough courage to talk to her about the deal, it was late in the evening.

"That's why you've been so chipper tonight. But you really can't afford it. We can't afford it. Why would Sam put such an idea into your head? And why didn't he discuss it with me first?"

"But Mother, having a truck will be great. I can drive you to work every morning on my way to school and take you to the Co-op on

Saturdays. And... and to see Aunt Peggy! Most times you're so tired from all that walking."

"Well, I suppose." She kept on rocking at full speed. "What about money for gas and the monthly payment? Surely you can't-"

"I'll put in extra shifts. You'll see. And I'll give you the same money I always do."

Laura's eyes softened. "Well, you can't neglect your school work. That comes first." She paused. "And make sure you don't miss a payment. Sam O'Brien is a kind man and I don't want to take advantage of his kindness."

"Yes, Mother," beamed Joe.

Alone that night outside with a cigarette, smoke wafting up to tickle the underside of the moon, Joe realized all things considered, Sam was actually pretty alright. Maybe he'd be good for his mother after all. Take care of her. He was a decent fellow.

* * * * * *

Once it was decided that Joe would buy Sam's truck, the following weekend, his sedan freshly out of the shop and in trade-in condition, Sam drove the whole crowd into town to pick up the new car he'd chosen: a 1959 Chevrolet Bel Air. The kids were all mad for it, climbing over the leather seats. Tom especially kept whistling in admiration as he checked beneath the hood, thumped the rims, huffed on then polished the shiny chrome bumpers with his sleeve. Afterwards to celebrate, they went to the ice cream parlour and got cones. As the children enjoyed chatting over theirs at a table outside, and Sam caught up with an old friend he'd run into, Laura decided to take a quick stroll, to look in some shops and enjoy the air. "Keep an eye on Rosalie, boys. I won't be long."

Laura was admiring a nicely arranged flowerbed when she overheard two old crones on a nearby porch. She didn't believe her ears at first, but as she listened more carefully, she realized they were in fact talking about her. And it seemed they wanted her to overhear; no one was that deaf. "Did you hear about that poor brazen widow trying to get herself a wealthy man and a big fancy house?" said one.

"Well, if you ask me, he's wasting his time. Samuel O'Brien could have the pick of the crop! Why he would waste his time on this Laura girl is beyond me. You know, my niece Eula would be a much better match for him."

"He probably just wants someone to take care of his retarded daughter," the one scoffed.

"Aie, yes, undoubtedly."

Shaken, Laura quickly ducked her head and retreated. Her eyes filled with tears and as she walked away, she bumped into a lamppost, dropping her ice cream cone. She hurried back to join the kids. When Sam noticed her, he knew instantly something was wrong. He quickly said goodbye to his friend and came to her side. "What happened? You have a bump on your forehead."

Without answering, she asked, "Are you ready to go?"

The kids looked at one another. It wasn't like their mother to sound so abrupt. During the short trip back, everyone was ill at ease: the boys bickered amongst themselves and Rosalie whined. Laura could hardly hide her tears. The joy of the new car was spoiled. By the time Sam reached Laura's house, Laura was sitting tall, her face stone hard.

Sam looked at her. "Rosalie, why don't you go inside with Tom and Ben. Father wants to talk to Laura."

Rosalie nodded.

Laura went to exit the car, but Sam grabbed her arm before she could get out. "What on earth is the matter?"

She shook her head, averting his gaze.

"Something must have happened outside the store. You're a terrible liar, Laura. You wear it in your face. What's wrong?"

She swallowed hard. "I can't talk about it now, Sam. Maybe tomorrow. I have to go." That said, she wrenched her arm away and went inside without looking back. Sam sat in the car a minute, utterly perplexed. Tom caught his eye and he shrugged. Ben brought Rosalie back to the car and they drove slowly off. Alone, the boys worriedly looked at one another then went inside to bed without a word.

The next morning, Sam stopped by on his way to work. Laura claimed stomach trouble and tried to shut the door on him, but he muscled his way in. "Listen, Laura, maybe taking care of Rosalie is too much for you. How about if you rest today? My father can easily look after her and I'll come home early." He knew this wasn't the problem, but he didn't know what else to say.

Laura shook her head. "It's not Rosalie."

Sam toyed with his hat. He had to ask. "What is it, then? Is it me? Did I do something to offend you?"

"No. No, it's not you," Laura replied softly. Tears pooled up in her eyes. "I just overheard something, something ugly, is all," she whispered. "It's nothing."

Sam's voice was hard. "What did you hear?"

She threw her hands into the air then she proceeded to relate the conversation she had overheard the day before.

Hardly able to contain his fury, Sam did his utmost to reassure her. "Don't pay any attention to those gossipmongers, Laura. I value your friendship. More than I can say. You are very special and have a heart of gold. And to be honest, I'm at my most happy when you're around." There was an anger in his throat despite the vulnerable admission. He looked into her eyes.

"What about Rosalie?" she asked.

Sam nodded. "It's true, she does need someone to tend to her needs when I'm not around. I can't imagine anyone else but you doing it. Rosalie adores you and...and..." He stopped, fearing he might say too much and scare her away. He motioned that they should sit. "Listen, tomorrow those ladies will be talking about someone else, and you and I will already be old news. We don't have any control over what people gossip about. If it happens to be a slow week, they invent a story. Please, don't allow it to bother you."

Laura had to smile. She socked him lightly in the thigh. "You sound just like your father."

Sam grinned, so relieved she was not taking it as hard. "Well, we are related!"

"Alright, then. I'll get my things and if you wouldn't mind dropping me at the house on your way to work-"

Sam insisted, "I meant what I said about your taking a day off. Maybe it's best if you relax. I'm sure it'll do Father and Rosalie some good to have a day on their own. How's your head?"

"I'm fine; it's just a little bump. No, I feel much better. Let's go." Sam raised his eyebrow at her stubbornness. It seemed he wasn't the only one who had developed such parental feelings for his daughter. Or felt close enough with him to sock him in the thigh, which actually still stung a bit. That made him smile.

The feelings he was having, feeling this fullness, of having everything he wanted just within reach, lasted the whole drive. Going to work was the last thing on his mind. When they reached the house, Sam turned off the engine and rested his arm on the seat behind Laura. "Why don't I play hooky and you and I take Rosalie for a ride, bring a picnic basket and enjoy the day? What do you say?"

Laura widened her eyes. "But don't you have important things to do at the office?"

A brief sadness flittered through Sam's eyes. He had missed so much by working the way he did. "You know, even just in the last couple of years, I've worked enough overtime for three people." He touched her cheek. "Sometimes, Laura, it's important to take a day off to do things that really matter. And maybe," he hesitated, then grinned, "we can really give those biddies something to talk about."

* * * * * *

Rosalie was flourishing in her new home with such loving attention from her new family and "extended" family, but some things remained from her days at the orphanage, things that no matter how much attention or care she got, remained a part of her. When her bangs began to hang in her eyes and her ends needed straightening, Laura casually mentioned a haircut. Rosalie heard the word "haircut" and instantly spun herself into a world class tantrum.

Peggy happened to be over to the house for a cup of tea. "It's no problem," she said matter of factly over the girl's wails, "you just bring her around and we'll get it done."

Laura was hesitant, but as the little girl was beginning to look unkempt, the next afternoon she brought her to Peggy's. Rosalie ran straight to the piano, and realizing pulling her away would cause everyone more distress, they set up a station of molasses cookies and milk, which she set to eating happily, and Peggy was then able to guide her into the spare room. Peggy chatted happily and Rosalie too, until the buzzing started and Rosalie began to shriek enough to bring the roof down.

Laura paced and bit her thumbnail, until finally Rosalie emerged sniveling and tear streaked, her neck red from the clipper, her hair shorter but awkwardly shorn. Peggy clunked in after her and waved her hand dismissively. "Her hair turned out fine, she'll be all right."

Laura bit down on the inside of her cheek and smiled. "Rosalie, you look beautiful. Do you want to go play outside with the flowers? Stay close to the house." The girl nodded solemnly and went out the door. Laura watched her from the window, fuming.

"I know, I know, I need new clippers," Peggy stared at Laura's back. "Listen, it's not such a big deal; she's a kid. It'll grow back."

Laura turned around. "Why are you like that? As if you don't care? Even the Christmas present from the boys. You were too severe with them when they meant well."

"Ah," Peggy waved her hand again. "The boys are too busy to care. You think they even remember that? They hardly pay me the time of day anymore with their after school jobs and Tom always helping George, never even coming in for more than a few minutes."

Laura stared at her sister, still angry. Then she saw the hurt in Peggy's face. Peggy had invested in the boys like a mother would, opened herself to true maternal feelings, but now the boys were taken up with their own lives. This brusqueness was her shield against feeling that way again, feeling that way toward Rosalie. Laura saw it all now. Of course that's why she wasn't softening toward the little girl; her sister simply didn't want to go through this again. Moreover, Laura had been so busy caring for Rosalie, she had neglected Peggy too. This favour was the first time in ages she'd been around. Of course her sister felt used.

After a few minutes of silence, Laura asked, "Do you still play the piano?"

"Yes, sometimes."

"And sewing?"

"Sometimes, too..."

Laura instantly felt terrible. These hobbies were but poor substitutions for mothering. "I'm sorry we don't see each other as much," she frowned. "Between working five days a week for Sam and taking care of the boys, I've hardly got a minute. But that's no good. Without family, we are nothing. Maybe I could come around for..." she smiled, "a fitting? Now that Sam has hired another housekeeper and she does the heavy work, I could use some lighter frocks, something even, pretty, for a change. Could you, by any chance..." Laura felt herself blushing furiously.

Peggy sighed. "Laura, say no more. It would be my pleasure," she said smiling wide. "I have some material tucked away in a box. I'm sure you could find something to your liking. Check in the catalogue and choose a style. I'll make it exactly the way you want."

"Thanks," Laura said, relieved, all traces of their earlier tense moment gone. Still, her insides churned when she thought of Rosalie.

"Peggy!" A woman with a voice shrill as a siren came stomping up the walk. "Your girl wandered off; you don't want her to do that, do you?" Esther was holding Rosalie by the hand, but not rudely. She touched the little one on the shoulder. "We wouldn't want for anything to happen to you, right sweetheart?"

Rosalie beamed at her, lurched forward and gave her a tight hug. The ladies all giggled. "All right there, honey, I have to go. You girls have yourselves a good night," said Esther. She turned around and waved behind herself as she left. Peggy just stared at Laura as if to say, "What on earth was that?" Then both ladies smiled. "Good old Esther," whispered Peggy. "Always full of surprises."

Their departure from Peggy's may have been upbeat, but the more Laura looked at Rosalie's butchered silky hair, the more she strengthened her resolve never to bring her to Peggy for a haircut again. Her vow was further reinforced that night; when Rosalie greeted Sam, she wailed about her long hair being gone. When she tried to demonstrate how she couldn't loop it through her fingers anymore, that set off a whole new avalanche of yelling until Laura finally calmed her down with promises of ice cream after dinner.

Rosalie's temper might have had its distinct flares, and some might have found them off-putting, and they could be plentiful and loud, but it seemed Sam and Laura were more and more touched by Rosalie's moods. It was as if she and her passionate tempera-ment were the grace of their blooming love: a few starts, a few stops, a pitfall or two. But she was generally a happy, contented little person, and above all, moods or not, she was becoming theirs, and that love gave birth to a patience neither knew he had, one that triumphed over all else.

Despite the trips to the lake with the boys, running after the white butterflies that fluttered in the late morning sun, and ice cold lemonade Laura made in the afternoons, Laura noticed that these days, Rosalie was not her usual happy self. She refused to eat, ran a constant fever, and developed a boil on the right side of her neck. One day while both Sam and his father were away, Rosalie's condition grew worse. Laura immediately called Peggy on the new machine: one long ring, followed by two small ones. Private lines hadn't gotten outside of town yet; miraculously no one else was chatting on the phone at that moment and her sister's voice came on the line.

Peggy and George dropped everything and came over. By the time they arrived at the house, the boil had ruptured, giving off an infectious stench. Unable to comprehend the situation, the little one panicked. She kicked and screamed while blood, water and puss trickled down her nightgown and onto the floor. Laura and Peggy cajoled, sang, and tickled the girl to the floor to calm and clean her simultaneously. Finally she did calm, her temperature came down a bit, and she fell asleep.

When Sam and his father arrived, Peggy met them at the door. "Hush, Rosalie and Laura are sleeping," she said loudly. From the bedroom, Laura heard the demanding way her sister greeted Sam and cringed. She extricated herself from Rosalie's leg which lay over hers and went into the kitchen.

Sam looked relieved to see her. "I'm so sorry I wasn't here. Are you all right? How is she?"

"She's going to be fine."

Peggy smiled. "We'll be going home now. Laura, do you want a ride?"

"I'll drive her home, Peggy. Thank you again." said Sam.

Peggy raised one penciled eyebrow but said nothing. "Well, alright then!" she said brightly.

Laura walked her to the door. "Thank you again. I could not have done this without you. I mean that, Peg."

"Laura," said Peggy, taking her younger sister by the shoulders. "I might be a lot of things, but just know that among them, I will always be here for you. Through thick or thin, through husbands or," she smiled impishly, "other certain people who happen to be men," she whispered.

Laura couldn't help herself and smiled.

"And that's all the answer I needed," cackled Peggy. "You know what George would say? He'd say, 'too bad he's a Conservative, but, darn him, it's probably the only fault he has.'" She turned around and walked into the wind to her husband who had started up their noisy tractor.

Laura turned around, feeling like her whole body must be crimson, and thanked her stars Sam had gone into the bedroom to check on Rosalie and hadn't heard a word.

The next day, Sam took the little one to see the doctor. As soon as they returned, Laura asked, "What did he say?"

Sam was rooting around in his briefcase for something. "The boil is usually a result of an infection, caused by a bacteria...a cluster of boils forms a carbuncle. Apparently it begins with a small red spot, so if we see another, I must take her to the doctor at once."

Laura was quiet. She hadn't understood a number of the words Sam had so easily used to describe Rosalie's condition. She felt her old shame run through her. "I have to go," Sam said, "but I'll see you later this afternoon."

Robert stepped forward to Laura who was standing at the open door. "I think we should look in my encyclopedia to see what Rosalie's condition was," he said gently. "I didn't understand half of that mumbo-jumbo my son just threw at us, carbuncle, carburetor, barnacle, who knows," he looped Laura's arm into his. "We haven't read together in a while, have we!"

Laura could've kissed him. Except that would have really complicated things, she thought. This made her giggle. How wonderful it was to be known by someone so well, he could read in her face what she was thinking. She also realized that with the events of the last few days, she was very, very tired.

Finally it was Sunday and Laura sat for what seemed to be the first time since she'd risen that morning to scrub the floor, apart from a quick cup of tea and sandwich at noon. The floor had needed doing for some time, and this day there was no getting around it. Joe pulled up in Sam's old jalopy and cut the *put-put* of the engine.

"Hello, Mother. Are the boys in bed already?" He pulled off his dirty boots. Laura tried not to think about the marks they were leaving. "I'm starved!"

Laura said quietly, "You know, you never used to work at the garage on Sundays. Usually Dooly's was closed on the day of the Lord."

"I know but it was an emergency. This fellow needed his car-"

"Who needed his car?" interrupted Tom in a strained whisper as he came down the ladder.

"Tom! Are you sure Ben is sleeping?"

"Yes, Mama," answered Tom in a sweet sing-song imitation of his younger brother. "I wish Ben would try to go to bed by himself. He's already eleven years old. Every time he wakes up and I'm not there, he gets so upset. How come he doesn't want to go to bed by himself? What is he scared of?"

Laura knew exactly why Ben was afraid to go to sleep alone at night. She hadn't told the other boys much about their time in the convent, but since those wretched days, Ben was fragile in some ways that she feared were permanent. "Let's just say when we were away, he and I, he was very young, and it was a very troubling experience. The room was cold, the nuns were unfriendly. We usually went to bed hungry. That kind of insecurity stays with a person, I suppose."

Tom bit his thumbnail. "We were so happy to have you home. It was worst for you, but we missed you, both of you, let's just say. I mean, Aunt Peggy was OK, but-"

"Alright, now, Peggy is quite wonderful and took excellent care of you. You know that. And to be honest, I was worried you'd prefer it with her. George's house is a good deal nicer than this old thing, after all!"

Joe lit a cigarette. "Mother? It's like they say in that Oz movie: There's no place like home."

After a few moments of silence, Laura sighed. "Speaking of home," she said, "I need to talk to you and George about repairing this one. I think before winter comes we might need new windows. And I noticed the other day when I was walking up the lane that a few of the shingles are rotten." She smiled. "And... while we're at it, what would you think of painting it white?"

The boys smiled back. It wasn't the first time their mother had mentioned wanting a white house. "You know," Joe waved his cigarette in the air, "one day, I'm going to have a house like Robert and Sam, huge with beautiful furniture, and painted white, of course. But I've been thinking. I want to quit school and find a job. Most do-"

"Nonsense!" Laura stood from her chair as if the conversation were finished. She turned. "If your friends jumped off a cliff, does it mean you have to follow?" Her face was hard, her eyes flashing. "When you graduate and then go on to Vocational school or better still, to the town's university, then you will find a great job."

Laura went into the kitchen and Joe followed her to the door, jammed his shoes on his feet and stepped outside. He looked up at the sky: pure black, not a single star. Joe wished in that moment for just one, so he could wish on it and talk to his dad, something he'd done since he was a child. He was upset, but wasn't sure why. Mother didn't have any idea what university cost, and why shouldn't he get a job if he wanted one? He was nearly grown enough to make up his mind. Such rebellious thoughts made him feel sad and heavy. He stubbed out his cigarette and went back inside to the kitchen.

"Mother?"

Laura was scrubbing an already clean pot.

"Mother, I'm sorry. I just want to do the right thing. Start pulling my weight more, you know?"

Laura rested the metal sponge on the counter. "You pull plenty. Your job is to become as educated as you can. You want to end up like me? Not even able to write my own name?" Her voice trembled. "We've been through this before. I've made my position very clear."

Joe absently traced his finger over the grain in the wood table. "I've studied at this table since I was small, you know? I can read, I can write. And so can you now too."

Laura's shoulders softened. "I'm sorry, Joe. You should do what pleases you." She looked down at her rough hands. "So should I, for that matter," she laughed quietly. "It's my only Sunday after all."

"Speaking of which, you have seemed more tired lately. I was thinking why don't you bring Rosalie here during the week for a day, let her play with Ben, and Tom could help you around the house when he's not with Uncle George, then you wouldn't have to do everything on Sunday."

She shook her head, "Oh, that's asking for too much..." but her voice suggested she liked the idea.

"Anyway, Mother, if you don't mind my saying, I think you could probably ask Sam for just about anything, and he'd say yes." Joe's eyes were shining, brazen, a little tentative. He wasn't sure how he wanted her to respond. This was the first time he'd mentioned to her that he knew what was happening between her and Sam O'Brien.

Tom came into the kitchen; he'd been checking up on Ben. "Sorry, Mother, no use pretending. We see how he looks at you."

Laura was speechless. She felt like crying: should she deny what was happening? Confide in her sons? She didn't even know what was happening.

Joe smiled. "We know you will always love Dad, but we like Sam. He's a good man."

That's all it took to open her heart. Tears slid down her face, and before she knew it, she began to laugh. She grabbed Joe by the arm and whirled him around, then grabbed Tom and caught him on the other arm. The three of them banged into the counter, the table, and amid holding their elbows and shins, they laughed and hugged each other close.

Chapter Eight
Tying the Knot

Even though her boys saw what Laura would've liked to deny, even though the old biddies in town saw it, even though she was sure the birds on the trees saw it, Sam and Laura never spoke of their growing feelings for each other. Laura thought perhaps everyone was just thinking wishfully, that the widow with three boys would be best off marrying someone like Sam, a hardworking, honest man with good means. She didn't want to rock any boats, and she also had been scarred by what she'd overheard in town. She wondered whether it was true, that maybe Sam did want her around to be a mother to Rosalie. She didn't suspect so, but just in case, she kept her guard up and continued to act as his hired help. This meant she had to yield to his decisions about Rosalie, even when she disagreed with them, like when he said he didn't want her going off to school in September. She knew Rosalie would thrive interacting with other children, but Sam was very protective of her and didn't want her left alone that long. Even though she certainly did well on her own and knew her own mind; she could amuse herself for hours playing with her special stick, keeping time to music on the radio, yet she wouldn't touch the expensive plush bear Sam had bought her.

When September did come, with the boys in school, Laura settled into a routine. Work during the day, play with Rosalie, and stave off her incessant questions about when Ben would come play with her. The boys scheduled their after school jobs and Laura had a bit more time to herself. She liked to use her nights to read and write or simply let her thoughts drift as she sat in her chair by the window.

One unusually stormy night, the wind picked up and rain began to dump down just as Joe came whistling in. "Where have you been until all hours?" she said sternly. "I kept your dinner warm until it cracked."

Joe kissed his mother on the forehead. "I'm sure it will still taste very good," he said and went cheerfully into the kitchen. He didn't feel he needed to tell his mother that he'd finally paid a visit to Sam, who had welcomed Joe enthusiastically and been immediately receptive to Joe's suggestion of Laura bringing Rosalie one day a week to her house, saying, "Yes, yes, of course, naturally," and nodding his head. In fact, a change occurred in Sam from the moment Joe appeared on his step until Joe made this suggestion, as if he were growing nervous. Joe wasn't sure what was wrong, but it seemed from how he tapped his foot and shifted his eyes around, that Sam had some things on his mind. Sam asked Joe some questions about Laura at home, frowning when Joe told him how hard she worked to maintain the house and keep the boys in line. Eventually he relaxed and he and Joe shared some cold cuts and cheese from the fridge and talked about sports teams and Joe's job at the garage. Joe hadn't been completely certain about his feelings toward Sam; after all, he held his father up on a pedestal, but he now saw how good of a man Sam was, and how much he cared about his mother. He had also seen how happy Laura was around Sam with his own eyes. He didn't say anything to Sam, but as he left the O'Brien house, he mentally gave his blessing to the two of them.

"Sleep tight, Mother," said Joe on his way upstairs, but she was comfortably in her chair, her head back, already asleep.

* * * * * *

The following Monday afternoon after school, Ben and Rosalie decided to go bird watching to see if they could spot one they hadn't already noted in Ben's book. They were so engrossed, they didn't notice thick charcoal clouds billow up and bluster in. The rain began and they sprinted to the veranda for cover, but arrived soaked anyway. The kids didn't care one bit, however, and didn't even accept the towels Laura brought out. Rosalie demonstrated the new rhythms she had practised on her drums, and the two kids laughed and had a great time. Laura sighed happily as she cherished this delightful sight from the window.

Sam had also left his office early and drove quickly to beat the storm home. But also because he wanted to see Laura. Enough days had passed since his talk with Joe, since his seeing what was in front of him all this time. Storms blew in and could blow things away that one loved. He didn't want to lose what he cared about. What he loved.

He quietly walked into the living room and stopped short when he saw the same scene Laura did standing at the window. He felt warm and dizzy. But also very sure.

"Laura," he said quietly.

She turned. She was wearing one of the new dresses Peggy had made for her. Peggy might have had a grating laugh or lacked a few graces, but there was no mistake in how talented with a needle and thread she was; pleats accentuated Laura's slender waist, puffed sleeves made her wrists look fine and delicate, and the blue and yellow floral pattern suited her eyes perfectly. "You're home early, Sam."

He strode toward her. "I have a plan."

Laura folded her arms over her chest and smiled. "Oh, you do?"

As he looked into her lovely eyes, for a moment, he forgot what he was about to say. He shook his head and cleared his throat, he repeated the words he had practised on his way home from work. He smoothed a lock of her hair behind her ear. "Maybe you don't need to go to your house anymore at the end of the day," he said.

She looked perplexed.

He cleared his throat again. "What I'm saying is maybe my home could be your home too. Yours and the boys."

A frown started on her brow. "What do you mean?"

Sam took a shallow breath. "I realized it so long ago, and yet... I haven't said a thing, not wanting to lose you, if you weren't ready-"

"What are you saying, Sam?" Her question came out in a whisper.

"I want you to marry me, Laura. I love you. And I think-"

"Sam, wait, I-" but he was already so close, his face beside hers. Then his mouth was on hers. She put her arms around his neck and was kissing him back, their bodies so close, before she realized what she was doing. She pulled away and looked down. "I... I can't. I'm sorry."

Sam waited. He cleared his throat again. "What's holding you back, Laura?" He smoothed her hair then ran his thumb over her lips.

She closed her eyes and sighed at his touch. "I'm... I'm just not sure. I don't know."

He took her chin and made her look him in the eyes. He knew she wanted to say yes. "You have been on your own and independent for a very long time. I know you're considering the boys, and that is one of the reasons I love you. Will you please think about it?"

Laura, her hand over her mouth, still warm and pulsing from the kiss, nodded before quickly leaving the room without looking at him.

When Joe arrived home from work that evening, Laura was in her chair in the moon room. He noticed Laura's pensive mood without even seeing her face. She barely greeted him as he came in, and he didn't smell any dinner cooking. He went to her side. "Mother? Is everything alright?"

She'd bitten a few of her nails down to the quick, he noticed. Maybe she had found out he'd gone to see Sam and was upset with him for intruding. When she finally smiled at him distractedly, he knew he wasn't in trouble. "Sit down, Joe. I need to talk with you," she said.

Even though her face suggested she was anything but ill- in fact, she looked rosy-cheeked and her eyes were luminous- immediately the same flash of fear he'd had so many years ago when she took sick raced through him. He sat on the chair across from her and waited. In silence, they watched the moon rise over the mountains. Some late birds cheeped their way across the horizon.

Finally Laura broke into the heavy silence. "Sam asked me to marry him today."

Joe looked down at his grease-stained hands surprised by how his stomach could suddenly go from fear to despair. Not days before, he had reconciled himself to their coupling, felt good about it, magnanimous even. But in the end, faced with the reality of it actually happening, there was simply no way for Joe to explain the complicated feelings he had about his mother taking up with another man. That even though he was 16 and couldn't do justice to all they needed, he was after all the man of his house and had been since his father died. This was his territory, and he felt trod on. Yet he also knew that no matter how many hours he worked, no matter how grease-stained or callused his hands, no matter how many cars he fixed, he would never be able to provide in the same way.

"Do you love him?" he asked, knowing the answer.

"I don't know." She looked at him. She was lying; he could see it in her eyes.

"Listen, Dooly asked me to work full time. I'm really serious about quitting school. I want to make money, lots of it, buy a fancy car, help you out." His voice turned indignantly youthful and bitter, "I'm sure I can't do near as well taking care of you and the boys as him, but-"

"Joe, it's not about that, and you know it," she touched his arm. "Besides, as we've discussed, you're not budging from that school until graduation day."

"Well, I'm sure you'll do the right thing," he said, and went up the ladder, wishing he could be more supportive. Once he got upstairs, it occurred to him that if she did marry Sam, everyone would win: she'd be happy and taken care of, he would be off the hook for worrying about the family's future, and maybe even Sam would foot the bill for university. Joe hadn't even considered that. He felt instantly guilty for thinking about the money, but knew for Sam it wouldn't be a hardship, and in fact, his getting educated was exactly what his mother wanted. That helped. And his heart lightened.

Meanwhile, in the moon room, Laura's thoughts were now on Joe. He had been wearing his father's shoes for so many years despite the fact that they were entirely too large and heavy for him. She was so touched at his wanting to care for the family, and what she wanted for him more than anything was for him to just be free, a teenager without such adult cares.

Head down, she whispered, "Please, give me a sign." At the exact moment she looked into the night sky, a shooting star trailed across the dark. It lasted only a few seconds, but it was just long enough. She knew what to do. Her brain raced: to-do, moon-tune, sky-pie… "Oh, no, not now," she laughed. She rose gently, as if to not disturb the night, and slept with peace in a way she hadn't in a very long time.

The next morning, Laura rose early to warm up the little house then prepared a nice breakfast of pancakes for the boys. She let her mind wander while they were bubbling in the pan, and they burned. She didn't mind; whistling, she threw them outside for the crows and set up another round. Didn't matter; life was smiling on her today. Then broom in hand, she started singing and dancing around the kitchen.

"What's going on, Mama?" asked a sleepy-eyed Ben. "You sure are in a good mood this morning!"

"Come dance with me, my son, come on…" Tom and Joe soon appeared, woken by all the noise downstairs, and came into the kitchen, their hair every which way. She piled up the pancakes and poured herself a cup of tea. Once the boys were seated, Laura put her arms out. "I have decided to take your advice, Joe. I'm going to marry Sam. This means we'll soon have a new home."

Tom leaned out of his chair and fell over. "Holy cow," he said, hopping up to hug her. "Congratulations! We're happy for you, Mother. And Sam is lucky to have you." He chuckled. "Anyway, we're there so much, we might as well move in permanently!"

Joe and Tom pretended to argue over which room would be theirs, when Ben, who hadn't spoken this whole time, began to tremble. A tear fell down his thick lashes onto the table. "I'm not moving." he said quietly.

"What's that, Benny?" asked Tom.

This time Ben shouted, "I'm not moving. I'm not going anywhere!" He fled from the table, grabbed his schoolbag, and ran out the front door for his bus, leaving Laura and his brothers at the table in perplexed silence.

"What, what was that about?" asked Joe.

"He's the last one I thought would object," declared Laura. She felt like weeping. He loved Sam and Robert, he was best friends with Rosalie. The greenhouse, the nice meals, the garden. She didn't know what to think; the boy had spent more time at the O'Brien house than his own from the time he was very young.

"I don't know," murmured Laura. They stood from the table, leaving their breakfast, mostly uneaten. No one had an appetite any more.

In the truck on their way to school, Joe said, "Tom, you need to talk to Ben, figure out what's bothering him and set him straight. Come hell or high water, we are moving into Sam O'Brien's house."

Tom looked at Joe, taken aback. "Take it easy, Joe. Anyway, it's mother's decision, not ours. Besides, you weren't too keen on him at first. What made you change your mind?"

Joe kept his face to the road and didn't answer.

Tom sucked in his breath. "Oh, now I remember; he bought you off. You took the bait, hook, line, and sinker. Now I get it, as soon as Sam sold you his truck, you-"

"This old piece of junk? You must be kidding."

"No, I get it now; Sam softened you up! Now all you care about is moving into that big mansion of his. How low can you get?"

Joe's knuckles were taut over the wheel. "Stop it, Tom." He jammed the brakes and pulled the truck off the road so abruptly, a cloud of dust escaped from the back. He looked at his brother, his blue eyes flashing. "It's not about me, you idiot. It's no secret the house is falling apart. What is she going to do when we're on our own? Who will take care of her then? Do you want her to be alone forever?"

Tom tried to interject, "Yes, but–"

"I mean, I can get a full time job anytime. My friend did, just took a job one morning, didn't like it then found another one the following day, just like that. Then I could buy the material to fix the house, make it nice and comfortable so she wouldn't have to work so hard. But be serious; do we expect her to have so much energy forever, with one lung, for God's sake?" Joe was blustering, not making sense, his inner conflict erupting.

To stop his brother, Tom punched the roof of the truck. "What the hell are you talking about? You're so mixed up, I can't keep up with you. One minute you want to quit school, find a job, build a house, get rich quick, and on the other hand, you told Mother to marry Sam. And if she does, obviously you're off the hook."

Joe's face fell and his body sank.

Tom felt like punching himself this time. What a heel he was. "Oh, Joe. I'm sorry. I'm really sorry. Listen, why should you have to take care of everything? Sam is great, and if you don't think Mother loves him, you're crazy. You've seen them together. They're like lovesick doves, those two." He brightened. "But you are right, you won't have to worry. You know that. Sam is the kind of man who would take care of us too, not just her. He's a good one, he is."

Joe smiled just barely but kept his head down.

"Let's say Mother and Sam do get married. Will you finish high school?"

Joe shrugged. "I think so. Besides if ever I want to go into architecture one day, I guess I'll need my Grade 12."

"Then, you know what to do," grinned Tom.

They looked at each other and laughed as Joe pulled into the school parking lot. "I guess you're right; things are about to get a lot easier," grinned Tom.

Suddenly Joe banged his fist on the steering wheel. "Damn, I forgot my report. Here, you get out, and I'll go back and get it."

As Tom opened the door, Joe said, "And talk to Ben, will you?"

Tom smiled. "Consider it already done."

With the house empty, Laura tried to put the difficulties of the morning behind her and focused on planning her day. She had been greatly relieved the day before that Robert wanted to take Rosalie on a picnic, leaving her alone on her "home" day to take care of things. And much was to be done: clothes to wash, house to clean, beans to cook. She was glad that the only vegetables in their crop that needed to be harvested were the carrots and turnips, and the boys were already committed to doing that after school the following day. Her thoughts on the garden, they naturally turned to Ben. His outburst, his anger; it just wasn't like him. Moving to the O'Briens' with the garden, the greenhouse, little Rosalie, she'd have thought he would leap at the chance.

Feeling a bit short of breath, she decided to take a break in her rocking chair by the window. She rested her eyes. After only a minute, though, the porch floorboards creaked long and slow. She stirred and looked out the window. She didn't see anything, but it did sound like someone was there. Laura rose from her chair, grabbed her sweater from the front hook and slowly ventured on to the porch. She shrugged; it was probably just the wind. As she turned to go back inside, there it was again, the creak of the wood and this time a low, sexy, and familiar drawl. "What's you doin'?"

Her heart ran cold; it was Miss Abby's gardener. The cold ran down her spine and weakened her legs. He had always looked at her with perverted, hungry eyes. She slowly backed away, her heart beating like a rabbit's. "What are you doing here?"

He didn't reply but took a step toward her. His tongue darted out to the corner of his mouth. Laura tried to remember where she kept the big stick in case of an intruder, but her mind was empty.

At that precise moment, Joe's pick-up turned into the driveway. The gardener suddenly stopped his approach and his smile vanished. Joe ran up, jumped over the rail and stood beside his mother. "What's going on?" he demanded, taking a threatening step toward the gardener.

"Joe, you remember the gardener. He was just leaving."

Without a word, the man turned around and stomped off.

Laura sank onto the old bench. "Thank God you're here," she whispered. Then she looked at him, suddenly stern. "But why are you here? What happened at school?"

He laughed. She was never going to let up about him not being in school, not even two minutes after some creep was going to rape her. "Don't worry; I just forgot a paper. In all the commotion this morning. Are you all right?"

"I'm OK. Thank you, Joe."

Her face and lips were quite pale. "I'll stay with you a while," he said. "I'll make some tea."

Laura nodded and they went in. While she sat in her chair, Joe inspected the house and yard just to be sure they were alone. He came back in and softly closed the door behind him. "I promise I'll go back to school tomorrow, but just for today, I think I'd like to stay home and help out with the chores."

She looked at him sternly, but relief was evident in her face. "And you don't have any exams or presentations today?"

"None." He knew his teacher would accept his paper late when he explained the situation. She was an understanding sort.

Laura had to admit she was very glad for his company. Plus they enjoyed chatting about things- they hadn't spent much time alone recently- and the chores went by quickly and kept her nerves at bay. Later in the afternoon, with supper simmering on the stove and bread baking in the oven, they sat in the kitchen with a cup of tea, Laura trying to put the morning out of her mind.

Just then, they both heard a strange noise. "What's that?" Laura whispered.

Joe stepped outside, taking the broad stick that Laura had specifically gone and unearthed with him. He was gone several minutes, and Laura bit down a few more nails. When he returned, he shrugged, "Nothing there, just the wind, I suppose." Nonetheless, he stayed until Tom and Ben came up the lane. He ran outside and explained to them what had happened during the day before he hopped into the truck. Luckily he'd only be a few minutes late getting to the garage.

Ben put his things on the front steps and marched around the back of the house to do "first patrol"; Joe beeped the horn over the rumble of the engine and hollered to Tom, "Did you speak to him?"

"He's OK. You'll see. And don't worry. I'll keep my ears and eyes open tonight."

Joe nodded. He put the old jalopy in gear and waved out the open window as he drove off. Tom looked back towards the house and saw Ben sitting on the steps, with his lunch can and school bag in hand, almost as if he were afraid of going inside. Tom sat down beside him and said quietly, "Ben, go on, go talk to her. I'm sure she's worried about you."

Ben didn't move. "How about if we fill the wood box? That will surely put her in a good mood." Without answering, Ben put down his things and slowly walked to the woodpile with Tom. When they returned to the shack, each carrying an armful of firewood, their mother met them at the door. She'd seen them arrive long before, but acted surprised to see them. "Hello, boys. Back from school already?"

Tom winked at his mother as he went out the front door again. "Ben, why don't you straighten the logs so we can put as much as we can in the box. I'll fetch another armful."

Alone with her youngest son, Laura softly asked, "How was your day at school, Ben?"

The young lad stopped fixing the logs and looked up at his mother. He played with a curl that escaped into his eyes and looked at the ground. "I'm sorry… about this morning." He looked up at her shyly. "I think Sam is great." He smiled at her. "When do we move?"

Laura felt her nose tingle with tears. "When did you change your mind?" she asked, smoothing his hair.

"Well, when Joe asked about having our own rooms…I don't want to sleep alone in a room, by myself, so Tom said we can share a bedroom, him and me, and then I thought it would be alright."

Laura smiled sadly. There was nothing she could do to turn back the clock, to take back their time in the convent. She knew his whole life would be marred by this fear. But he would be alright.

She hugged him and rather than squirm away, he melted in, her body his old comfort.

"Well, good news there because you have nothing to worry about. There are only four bedrooms in Sam's house, which means one for Rosalie, one for Robert, one for Sam and me...and one for you three boys, just like here. So you see," she said, the tears sparkling in her eyes, "you're always going to be surrounded by your family. And we'll always keep you safe."

Ben smiled, then his brow furrowed. "Yes, but what about the man outside?"

"That man outside is long gone. Don't you worry." In a few minutes when Tom came in, Laura looked over Ben's head and mouthed, "Well?" Tom held up his hands to show her all was clear. Then he widened his eyes and looked pointedly at Ben, and Laura smiled.

Later that night, Joe double-checked the windows and the door while Tom went out into the night with a lantern to inspect the parameters of their little shack. Everything seemed quiet.

The next morning after a difficult sleep, Laura was almost relieved to have something to tell Sam about that was so dramatic, it diverted his attention from the tension between the two of them. Sam was furious when she told him and left the house in a hurry.

Upon his return, he assured her that the episode with the gardener would never happen again. "You'll never have to worry about him again. He won't be returning to our village, ever."

Laura didn't ask after the particulars. She knew Sam had some powerful contacts in town, but just how powerful she hadn't realized until this moment. She was thankful the gardener wouldn't be able to stalk anyone else she cared about.

"I'll be out of town until the weekend," said Sam, his brow furrowed. "But I promise you'll be perfectly safe." He reached for Laura's face then let his hand drop. She was disappointed, realizing she craved his touch.

The following Sunday, after the chores were finished in the late morning, Joe and Tom hung around the house. Laura thought that odd as they always disappeared off to their jobs or friends, but assumed they had homework to finish or were still concerned about the lurking gardener. They even put together an early cold lunch of chicken and potato salad. Afterwards Tom said casually, "Mother, why don't you visit Aunt Peggy? You haven't seen her in a while."

"That's a great idea, Tom. It's exactly what I need to do." Laura hadn't wanted to visit Peggy in a while because she didn't want to get into having to talk about her relationship with Sam, but now at the suggestion, she felt a pang for the kind of home and familiarity Peggy gave her. Joe even offered to drive her in his truck. Laura sat back, enjoying how considerate her boys were being. The autumn leaves were in full colour, waving gently in the cool breeze.

Suddenly Joe stopped the truck. "What's wro..." began Laura before looking ahead. Crossing the road was a doe followed by her fawn, both of them trotting along at their own leisurely pace. The sun shone on their coats and they gleamed in the light. Laura brought both hands to her chest. "Have you ever seen anything quite as beautiful, Joe?" She bit her lip. "It's a sign, a good sign."

Joe smiled. His mother was always looking for signs to make sure she was doing the right thing. "It's just the sign you needed, Mother."

Peggy was delighted to see her sister and nephew. Joe chatted quickly then said he'd return in a few hours to pick up his mother. Laura and Peggy went inside to share some biscuits and tea. Peggy caught Laura up on all the latest gossip. When Peggy had spent her information, there was a lull in the conversation. Laura knew she had to bring up the big issue in her life before it hit the gossip mill and Peggy found out from someone else. Being in that sort of secondary position would about kill her sister.

"I suppose I have some news of my own. Sam has asked me to marry him."

For once, Peggy just looked at her without saying a word. Finally she asked, "And? You're going to say yes, right?"

Laura touched the embossed design on the tea cup. "Do you remember when Johnny and I got married? How excited we felt? Was it because we were young and naive, or I wonder whether my feelings for Sam are different." She frowned. "Has life gotten in the way of my heart? I mean, do I still have dreams at my age? Or are they finally coming true and I'm scared they won't last?" She looked at Peggy. "I mean, dare I still feel this way?"

"So you do feel that way."

Laura's voice caught in her throat. "Very much."

"Well, good Lord, Laura, do you love him or not?"

Laura laughed. "You sound like Joe!" Laura nudged Peggy's arm. "Must have learned it from his aunt." Laura wouldn't mention her nagging fear that Sam's love was based in need. She refused to entertain it. To give it voice.

With a twinkle in her eyes, Peggy asked excitedly, "May I be your maid-of-honour?"

Both sisters burst out laughing.

Laura didn't know that while she was visiting Peggy, the boys were undertaking a secret project back at home. With the help of Sam and some of George's friends, they fixed the front steps, replaced the rotten shingles and painted the outside of the house.

By late afternoon, while Joe drove to Peggy's to pick up his mother, Sam, Tom and Ben finished the job and gathered the tools while Robert and Rosalie prepared supper. When Joe returned with Laura and turned the truck into the yard, Laura gasped and said, "Joe, what on earth..." but she lost her words. She got cautiously out of the truck as if she couldn't believe they had driven to her own home. The boys ran out of the house excitedly to show her every last nail and screw. They took her on a tour of the repairs then Ben laced his slim fingers in hers and led her inside.

The mouth-watering aroma of supper met her nostrils even before she entered. On the table lay a feast of pork chops, baked potatoes, turnips and carrots steaming in their serving dishes. Ben had even picked a fresh bouquet of cattails.

Then, Laura saw Sam standing by the cupboards, waiting for her. Their eyes met and she felt enveloped by love, in its purest form. Her heart nearly exploded inside her body, she was so flooded with emotion. Finally Sam broke the spell and said, "Maybe we should all eat and do some celebrating." Everyone sat down and had a wonderful time chatting and enjoying the food. Robert and Rosalie grew quite warm from all the compliments, and Sam seemed completely at ease in the little house. The boys tried to treat him as a guest, but he wouldn't hear of it, he said, and he replenished the serving dishes and added wood in the fire to boil water for tea as if he'd always known his way around. Afterwards, the boys left to meet their friends. Sam, his father and Ben played cards while Laura and Rosalie washed the dishes. Soon Rosalie and her grandpa left, while Ben finished his homework. Laura felt as nervous as she did when she first felt the stirrings of emotion for Sam. "Shall we sit in the moon room?" she asked him. She picked up her sweater and they went alone into the quiet.

"It's been quite a day," she said. "How long have you been planning this?"

"Not too long. It was Joe's idea, and I thought it was a marvelous one."

Laura thought a minute. "It's strange how life unravels..."

"What do you mean?"

"Well, when Johnny passed away, at first, I thought I would die too. But the children kept me going and somehow, with time, the pain gradually diminished. I missed him, but now, my boys, they seem to love you as much as..." She stopped and looked at Sam.

"As much as?"

Laura's face burned. "As much as I do."

Sam turned to her fully and took her hands in his. "Will you marry me, Laura?"

Laura couldn't speak, but she nodded. Then she stood up and sat in his lap and kissed him. "I would be honoured to become your wife," she whispered into his mouth. He put his hand on the back of her neck and kissed her again.

"Wait a second," she said, pulling away. "I have to know something. If we're to be married, why did you paint this house? Why all the effort?"

He traced circles on the back of her hand. "Firstly, it gave me a chance to spend time with the boys. Secondly, this is your house and it will always be your house. Maybe at some point, one of the boys would like to live in it. And I know it's been a dream of yours to have a white house." He laughed. "I thought, if that's what makes her say yes, then I have to do it!" He grew serious. "Laura McPherson, you have made me a very happy man. What do you say if we put a date on our wedding right now?"

Laura ducked her head. "Well, don't laugh, but I've always liked October for weddings. That's when the earth is so peaceful, still warm, with such a crackle of life in the air."

Sam laughed uproariously. "That's just around the corner, but if you want an October wedding, then, my love, that is when we will be married."

* * * * * *

"Why on earth would you want to do such a thing?" demanded Sam when Robert sat him down and told him of his plans.

Robert smiled kindly. "It isn't every day a man gets a second chance at love, my son. I want you to enjoy this without my old bones rattling around." Sam opened his mouth to protest and Robert shushed him. "It's not as if I'm going far. I intend to be just as much a part of all your lives as I am now. Just a few feet away, is all. With a bit of fixing up, that guest house will be perfect for me. And besides, with Rosalie and the boys, the house will be full! Sometimes an old man needs some peace and quiet," he winked.

Sam had to admit, the boys really rose to such projects and this one would be no different. When he told the boys they'd have a chance not just to do some minor repairs, but a major renovation, Joe leapt at the chance to show off his ability as a skillful artisan, while Tom cheerfully declared he'd help in any way he could. Even Uncle George wanted to pitch in. In just under three weeks, with a few extra hired hands and fortunately favourable weather, the old rundown guesthouse was transformed into a beautiful little cottage. Laura and Peggy were thrilled when Robert asked them to lend a helping hand in decorating the interior: new curtains, matching table cloths, family pictures on the wall, while Ben and

Rosalie were called upon to complete the picture with their special floral arrangements.

It had been a labour of love for everyone. The project ended with a grand finale as Ben and Rosalie organized a ribbon cutting ceremony. They assigned the job of Master of Ceremonies to Tom, as he was a natural. He found himself a top hat at an antiques store in town and took to the front easily. "Welcome, ladies and gentlemen, to the official opening of Robert O'Brien's newly renovated cottage!"

Ben signaled Rosalie for a drum roll, and she grinned while she banged happily away on her drums.

"And now before we proceed with the cutting of the ribbon, let me share a few laughs with you all. Knock, knock…"

"Who's there?" everyone called out in unison.

"Mary."

"Mary who?"

"Mary me, Laura!"

Sam winked at his bride-to-be while George and Robert grinned. Rosalie followed Ben's cue and gave another drum roll, which made everyone burst into more laughter. "More! More!" cried Laura and Peggy.

"Well now," smiled Tom, "This priest and his servant were having an argument. The servant was saying he could recite the full rosary without thinking of anything else except his prayers, and the priest told him it could not be done as his mind was sure to wander. 'If you can do it without thinking of anything else, I'll give you my horse,' said the priest. The servant was very excited and started to repeat his Holy Marys. He was doing quite well, already in the third decade, when suddenly he stopped and asked the priest, 'Does the saddle come with it?'" Everyone laughed uproariously.

The afternoon continued with lunch and warm cider that Robert had simmering on a wood fire pit outside. By late in the day, everyone had put on scarves and the crowd looked like a warm, close knit family: inside and out.

Sam and Laura chose Monday, October 12, 1959 for their wedding date. Both of them agreed that getting married on Thanksgiving day was truly symbolic, a sign of not only being grateful for things past but also for things to come.

Given Sam's stature in the community, he thought it only natural that they be married in the town's cathedral. When he casually mentioned it to Laura, however, she burst into tears and ran out of the room. She didn't know where else to go but home, her refuge and safe place. Once she arrived, though, she looked around and felt horrible. She would soon be leaving it, this house that Johnny had grown up in and that she'd shared with him, given birth to her three sons in. She'd be leaving it, casting it, and all their memories, aside.

She sat, exhausted, in her rocking chair. Her first instinct was to look for a sign, but she shut her eyes. "No signs, not this time," she said, and set her mouth into a hard line.

Not long after, Sam arrived. She heard his car pull up and felt so happy he'd come for her, and so sad she'd let him down. "Laura?" He came in and sat down gently beside her. "What is it?"

She didn't want to tell him, but it was only fair. She looked at her fiancé with tears in her eyes. "This was my home with Johnny. We married in our parish church. And though God has been there for me in the past, and his guidance certainly helped me get through difficult times at the san, I don't feel like I wish to be married in a cathedral, and I just can't bear being married in the parish church where we had Johnny's funeral. Neither feels right, in my heart." She thought a minute. "Maybe it's just a case of too much too soon. Though to be honest," she smiled wanly, "I don't think I'd ever feel differently, even with all the time in the world."

"You tell me, then, where do you want to be married?"

Laura looked him in the eyes. "I don't know."

"Do you want to be married?" he asked sadly.

"Yes, yes." she answered and took his hands in hers.

"What should we do, then?"

Then she had an idea. This house was her refuge, but Sam's home had become her new place of safety and home, or at least home away from home, as she wasn't sure anymore where her roots ended and began. Forget his conveniences or the fact that his, or their, bedroom was practically as large as her whole house, it was where she had spent so many years cooking, tending, and falling in love again. "You know, Sam, I love your house-"

"Not my house, Laura, it's *our* house now."

She smiled and blurted out, "I wish we could get married right there, with our family and a small group of friends-"

Sam sat back and slapped his thighs. "Laura, that would be very nice, I agree, but how on earth would we ever persuade the priest?" he laughed.

Laura looked down again.

"Alright, leave it to me. I'll think of something."

Several days later, Sam spoke with the priest and it was agreed that Sam and Laura would marry in a small church in the neighbouring parish, one with Acadian roots, which was the best compromise he could think of. That made Laura feel odd; of course she knew she was Acadian, but she didn't know what that meant to her anymore. Still it was the best option they could come to, and she marveled at Sam's ability to get the priest to accommodate her. "But how did you ever manage to convince the priest?"

"Oh, I can be quite persuasive if the need arises." Sam smiled rather sadly remembering his conversation with the priest, especially the part where he offered him a cash envelope. Then he added, "The banns will be published for three Sundays before the wedding day."

Apart from that little hiccup, everything else went smoothly. Since the wedding reception was to be held at the house, which made Laura very happy, Sam and the boys prepared the yard and decorated the veranda to both sisters' liking. Increasingly Peggy had been taking on more sewing projects; she liked the detailed work and was given requests from friends in the community: costumes like the ladybug vest she'd made for Ben when he was small, items for special occasions, it didn't matter, and she took great pride in her work. When the wedding date was set, she decided she would take care of making all the bridal party outfits. She also wanted to be in charge of the cooking. Along with Robert's help, she volunteered to host the breakfast following the mass, plus she wanted to oversee the evening supper because some women from town were going to be taking care of that meal. If anyone went home without believing both weren't fantastic, she would never want to show her face again. When Laura laughed and said, "Climbing up on your forty-five again, Peg?" Peggy just shrugged and grinned at her.

Rosalie and Ben were the natural choices to design the flower arrangements, so Laura was left to do very little else, which felt odd and quite indulgent. "I could get used to being so spoiled," she told Sam.

Peggy bit her tongue when George said his contribution would be to take Sam out into town for his last night as a free man. Two nights before the wedding, sometime after midnight, Peggy woke up, George still not in bed. She worried that they were drunk, the car overturned, she could only imagine. Anger rose in her throat; Sam wasn't the kind of person to do this. George must have persuaded him, the charming lug.

Finally, she went to the window despite admonishing herself that 'a watched pot never boils' but was quite relieved to see Sam's car parked, albeit crookedly, in their front yard. They must have been in the barn, she figured. Peggy went down to make sure they weren't still drinking and found both of them sound asleep in the hay.

The following morning, she woke them up with a tray of strong tea and bread and fled before they could realize how serious their hangovers were. There was much to do to get ready for the wedding, and to add to her stress Peggy was worried over the men's state once they came in the house.

To make matters worse, Esther picked that morning to drop by. Peggy was sure, as she opened the door to Esther's expectant face, that the woman knew two men were asleep like sows in the barn. She probably watched everything that went on through the trees.

"Everything fine, Peggy?" Esther asked in her pinched sing-song.

"Yes, yes, what can I do for you; I'm rather busy today."

"Well, since you've asked, do you have an extra can of tomato soup? I ran out, and spaghetti with no tomato soup is like toast without butter or salt cod without pork scraps!" Esther paused to catch her breath, looked around the yard, eyed the barn door, then crossed her arms over her chest and continued. "Sure is a nice day. Say, is that Sam O'Brien's car in the yard? Isn't he getting married tomorrow? What's he doing-"

Peggy's blood began to simmer. "Yes, and we have so much to do. Let me get you that soup," she said, rushing to the cupboards.

"Oh, yes, of course!" Esther giggled. "It slipped my mind!"

Peggy handed it to her. "I'm so sorry I can't chat, I'm sure you understand."

Esther looked down at the soup as if she had no idea what it was and muttered, "Yes, of course...well...I'll be on my way..."

Peggy watched her neighbour walk slowly away and could have kicked herself; she'd done everything she could do to dissuade Esther from borrowing food in the past, even going so far as to give her hard dry biscuits or stale bread, but here she'd so easily given her what she wanted in order to just get rid of her. Now Esther would probably take that as a sign she should come by whenever she darn well felt like it to borrow everything.

Esther looked tired from behind, her pudgy shoulders seemed heavy. Peggy watched her for a moment and felt remorse. Of course, Esther was just lonely. She shouldn't be so hard on her. Peggy remembered her dear mother who would always say "do good against bad." She must be stirring in her grave, thought Peggy. She groaned and exhaled then lifted her skirt at the ankles and ran after her neighbour to personally make sure she knew she was welcome at the wedding. Peggy decided to go a step further. "I don't want to impose, but would you be willing to help out at the breakfast after mass?" Esther grinned like she'd won the prize of her life. Peggy felt much better as she ran to the barn to check on the men, still sleeping their night off.

By noon, Sam returned home with the worst headache of his life while George continued to sleep until two. Peggy had been counting on George's help in the kitchen and fumed all afternoon even though he tried to fumble through some menial tasks. At her house, Laura was oblivious to all of this. She cleaned all day Sunday in case people came by then prepared herself: she put her hair into rag curls, scrubbed her face and filed her fingernails.

At 9:00 a.m. sharp Thanksgiving Monday morning, Rosalie was the first to appear at the back of the little church. She stood for a second, beaming with pride and joy as she looked at all the guests. She wore a soft yellow printed dress with matching ribbons in her hair and nodded to everyone as she slowly walked down the aisle.

She kept time with the music, her face serious, until she spotted the headmistress of the orphanage. Rosalie scurried over and giddily gave her a hug. "How are you today, Miss Barbara?" she asked, then, without waiting for an answer, she trotted back to her place and continued walking down the aisle. When she finally reached her father, she gave him a resounding kiss and took her place beside him, oblivious to the emotional scene her actions had created. Everyone was touched; there was not one dry eye left among the guests, and the wedding hadn't even begun.

Peggy wore a soft purple silk dress enhanced by a bouquet of silk flowers she'd stitched with pearls and sequins bought at the fabric shop in town. She was so proud and so happy, yet still quite angry at her husband. As she made her way down the aisle with her chin high, she tried only to think of Laura, but her own rocky marriage crept in to her thoughts. Once she noticed George, standing in the back, waiting to walk Laura down the aisle, her heart softened. He caught her eye and smiled sadly. This brought tears to her eyes.

George had never been as proud of his wife as when she walked by, nor had he felt so much remorse for causing her such pain. Pain had become so familiar to him, it was often easier to try and dull it. But then he did this to those he loved, upset them in immeasurable ways. George clenched and unclenched his fist, vowing to himself to try harder. He knew deeper than that, though, that he would fail. But not today. Today was about love.

At the back of the church, Laura paused before taking her trip down the aisle and into the waiting arms of her new husband. Just minutes before, she'd stood outside behind the church with her three boys. "Well, this is it," she said. Her hair was curled into a halo around her dimpled cheeks, and her lips were rouged. She wore a simple beige shift that hugged her slim figure accompanied by a matching pillbox hat, gloves, purse and shoes. Joe and Ben complimented Laura on how pretty she looked until she blushed. Ben didn't comment, and only toed shapes into the dirt. Finally he spoke. "Will you still love us as much?" he asked, looking beseechingly into his mother's eyes.

Laura smiled as she realized that though nearly 12, Ben was indeed still her baby. She hugged her sons close. "As much and more. I don't think I would have survived without the three of you. You are very precious to me. And I don't want you to worry about me anymore." She looked directly into Joe's eyes then swallowed hard. "Look at you, all dressed up and very handsome. Three of a kind, the three musketeers, my three sons, the three-"

Tom put a hand on his mother's shoulder and smiled, "Not now, Mother." They all laughed.

Now, with George by Laura's side, she took a few steps before pausing to admire her sons. Joe had taken his place beside Sam, looking proud. She could see in the last few weeks how much lighter Joe was feeling. He acted younger, rough housing with Ben, whistling while he did his chores. Her heart pinged a bit when she realized how much he looked like Johnny. Her gaze left Joe and moved over to Sam. They locked eyes. In that magical instant, she murmured, "Good-bye; I love you," to her dear Johnny and gently tucked his memory into a special place in her heart. She took a deep breath. She was ready. Robert was beaming with pride. Laura felt overwhelmed with joy for entering into such a family.

The mass went by in a blink with the exchange of rings and the pronouncement that they were officially husband and wife. Laura wanted the whole world to know she was Sam O'Brien's wife and was so happy to be able to share this private moment with her friends and family. Everyone admired the organist's music that floated up into the air and out the front door as the guests filtered out to congratulate the newlyweds. The warm sun and cloudless sky proved to Laura that her prayers had been answered, and the rosary on the clothesline also clearly didn't hurt. She and Sam hopped into his car, which the boys had decorated in white tissue paper flowers immediately after mass, and the newlyweds drove to Peggy and George's for breakfast.

The family gathered around the food and started up lots of happy conversation along with congratulating the new couple, who held hands the entire time. Just before noon, the party dissipated, everyone went home for a rest and chores, and in the evening when the sun was lowering itself in the sky and the air crisping, they returned to the O'Brien house for the wedding party.

The house was transformed: Joe had built a large trellis and set it on the porch between the two pillars. Roses partially covered it and pots of flowers lined each side of the steps. It was a beautiful, almost magical scene to behold. Inside, Ben and Robert had decorated the tables with field flowers they'd prepared into bouquets in the greenhouse, and the food was set up in the dining room and on smaller tables in the living room: sliced turkey and bowls of dressing, mashed potatoes with gravy, carrots and turnips, plates of fresh tomatoes and cucumbers, and Peggy's biscuits piled high. Apple and raisin pies stood off to the side by the wedding cake, which was sliced and distributed to everyone in napkins embossed with Laura and Sam's names. And the wine flowed giving everyone extra warm good cheer. Laura was glowing, chatting with her family and meeting Sam's relatives who had come in for the event, a few of his work colleagues and old friends.

Once the meal was finished and the tables pushed to the side, to everyone's delight, a fiddle player and a guitar player launched into jaunty tunes. Everyone was enjoying the music and wine and conversation, Sam's arm wrapped around Laura's slender waist, when suddenly Laura noticed two women enter, who quickly blurred due to the tears in her eyes. She broke away from Sam and ran to them.

"Anne, Louise, but how…" The three old friends from the sanitorium all began to chatter at once, hugging and kissing.

"We're so sorry to be so late," said Anne. "Would you believe just as we arrived at Louise's, we noticed we had a flat! We had to wait for my husband to change it. Luckily we had a spare in the trunk, but it still took some time. We broke every speed limit there was to get here," she laughed.

Anne clutched Laura's arms. "Still, though, we were both terribly sorry to miss so much of your special day-" she started.

"But you're here now!" Laura was beaming, her whole face alight with joy. "I can't believe it's you!"

Anne proudly introduced her husband, François. Sam, who had secretly invited them, joined them and wrapped his arms around his wife's waist. "How do you like my surprise?" he asked.

Laura looked at him in amazement. "You sent them invitations… but how did you know where… I'm just so happy!"

Sam kissed his new wife on the forehead. "François, let's you and I get something to drink." The men left the friends alone to catch up.

"Laura, you wear good health very well, I must say," joked Louise.

"Thank you. I still can't believe you're here! Louise, you look so beautiful as well; it's strange to see you in normal clothes."

Louise shrugged and smiled, "Actually, I've quit the nunnery. In fact, not too long after you were released from the san."

"You're not serious! But why?"

"Do you remember what you told me about your time at the convent?" Louise narrowed her eyes slightly.

"Yes?"

"Do you recall receiving food at your door every night?"

The realization hit Laura like cold water. She didn't know what to say. "How do you know about…" she didn't finish her sentence before the tears came again. "That was you?" she whispered.

Louise straightened herself. "Very much so," she laughed. "And you never recognized me?"

Laura stammered, "Well, I always thought you looked famil-iar, but I didn't ever consider putting two and two together." She laughed uproariously. "Not only could I not read, but apparently I was also not very strong in math!"

They all laughed. "Well, when you told me what happened to you there, what your experience was like, and how it would undoubtedly leave its mark not only on you, physically and emotionally, but also on Ben, I was furious. Mother Superior had ordered us to ignore you, which to my mind was inhumane..."

Louise sighed. "But no one dared to question her authority. Anyway, as soon as you left the convent, I requested a leave of absence from the religious community and transferred to the sanatorium in Kentville. My skills as a nurse were needed and even though it was a dreary place, it was still heaven compared to the convent. Imagine my surprise when I saw you there," she frowned, "and grief, knowing you were likely already suffering or took sick during your time at the convent, no heating, not enough food, no care. When you were discharged from the san, I quit."

"What do you do now?"

"I work at the hospital in Halifax. I enjoy it and it gives me great comfort that I can be of service...with a smile!"

Anne, fascinated by the story, said, "It never occurred to me before, but how did you come to be in a French convent in Montreal?"

"I was actually born in France and my parents called me Marie Louise, but we moved around a lot because my father was in the army. I learned several languages, actually."

Just then, Peggy joined the group. Laura put her arm around her sister's shoulders. "Anne, Louise, this is my sister Peggy. You remember her letters? Peggy is my saviour in more ways than one!"

Peggy pumped each of their hands. "Well, I feel I know you already. Laura has spoken highly of you two. Come meet Laura's sons."

"You go ahead, Anne. We'll join you in a few minutes," said Laura. Laura was still intrigued by Louise's story. Her eye caught Robert's, and he waved.

"Who is that?" asked Louise.

"Sam's father, Robert." She sighed. "I owe him so much. Do you know, he's responsible for me being able to read and write. Single-handedly taught me himself when I first started working for him. He's a wonderful man." All of a sudden Laura did do some math, and realized that Robert and Louise, both single, were around the same age. "Come, you must meet him."

Laura grabbed Louise's hand and found her father-in-law now strolling along, enjoying all the excitement. "Robert?"

Robert held out his arms, "My daughter, how nice it is to say that." He noticed Louise, and smiled shyly. "And who is your lovely companion?"

"This is Louise, my guardian angel from the san."

"Oh, yes, yes. I remember you; you're the one who took us to Laura when we visited her."

Immediately sensing the connection between the two, Laura slowly retreated and left them alone. She then joined Sam and Rosalie on the dance floor for a square set and danced, feeling a joy she didn't remember feeling in a long time.

When the band stopped for a break, Laura saw Peggy and the boys sitting together, talking and laughing. It warmed her to see them enjoying their special bond. She slipped into a chair nearby and listened to them reminiscing.

"Do you remember the time Uncle George made beer and put it by the chimney, and it leaked on the floor, and it was so messy and sticky that by the time the beer was ready, there was hardly any left because Tom and Uncle George had drunk most of it!"

"Not just me, Joe! You too!"

"And then we made the beer ourselves and got sick as dogs, and we were so afraid you'd hear us throwing up outside the house," continued Joe.

Peggy nodded.

"We were so scared of you, but you didn't scold us that much."

Peggy shrugged. "I prayed that if you got sick enough, you'd remember it for a long time, learn your lesson and hopefully never try it again."

"And then there was the time Tom started smoking; he coughed and threw up for days. You were saying he had a bad touch of the flu, but did you know he had been smoking?"

"Yes, of course. I could smell it miles away."

Laura had always thought her sons were angels, but this proved it: they were entirely normal. She put her arms around her sister's shoulders, looked at her sons and smiled. "You really gave your aunt a hard time. And you, Peggy, telling me in your letters that everything was fine!"

Keeping her eyes on the boys, Peggy said softly. "I wouldn't have had it any other way. Besides, you had to concentrate on getting better. Plus there was no way I was going to squeal on my favourite nephews." Amid the laughter and stories, Peggy scanned the crowd for her husband. She was afraid he'd have dipped one too many times into the whiskey. When she spotted him, he was standing off to the side by himself wearing a lost look. She slipped away from Laura and the boys and came to him, took his hand and without a word, kissed him softly on the cheek. George smiled at her and held her close. They shared a wordless conversation then with their eyes, and without any warning, dashed to the dance floor and outdid everyone there, just like they used to when they were courting.

Later in the evening when the moon came out, full and bright, and conversations became quieter murmurs, Laura put on a shawl and sat down on the veranda. Peggy joined her. "Are you all right?"

"Yes, yes, I'm fine," answered Laura brightly. She rubbed her hands together. "Getting cool out," she said, biting her lower lip and shaking her leg.

"Alright, what's wrong? It's not that cold out, you know."

Laura let her smile fade as she looked into her sister's eyes. Instantly, Peggy smiled broadly. She took Laura's hands in hers, and whispered, "Don't worry; they say it's like riding a bicycle...once you learn, you never forget!" Laura looked at her surprised before they both burst out laughing.

Soon the musicians departed and their guests said goodbye. The boys went back to the old shack and Peggy tried to persuade

Rosalie to sleep over with her and George so the newlyweds could have a night alone. "It'll be fun, Rosalie. We'll drink hot chocolate and I have your favourite cookies. I'll even play you a song on the piano," she tried, but Rosalie wouldn't budge. When she had her mind set, it was hard to convince her otherwise.

"No, Aunt Peggy. My room...my bed...Rosalie's bed!"

Peggy knew no amount of sweets or begging would budge her, so she left, mouthing, "sorry" to Laura as she turned the sleepy girl over to her new mother.

They finished saying their goodbyes to those last to leave, then father and daughter went into the kitchen to eat their favourite snack of molasses cookies with a spot of jam in the middle while Laura went into the living room to relax by the fireplace. Fondly remembering the wonderful day, she slowly removed her shoes, the flowers from her hair and slid comfortably into the big chair. How I love to dance in Sam's arms. His touch is almost electric, she thought. Joe and Tom danced too, and so did Ben with Rosalie. Even Robert seemed to have a great time. It was a beautiful wedding.

Shaking her head, she smiled as she recalled her conversation with Peggy. She marveled how at times, her sister seemed to know her better than anyone, including herself. Sometimes, it's as if she saw with her heart. She laughed at herself. It was a wonderful day, and the night would be as well.

"What are you smiling about?" asked Sam as he appeared in the living room, holding his sleepy-eyed daughter over his shoulder. Laura looked up to see her husband and got lost in her train of thoughts as she let herself admire his strong body, his well-shaped biceps, his loving smile...

"Laura?"

She smiled, "Oh...I was just thinking about my sister."

"She really did a tremendous job! Everything went without a hitch."

"Did you notice how cold she was towards George when we arrived for the wedding, then, by the end of the evening, they both seemed very happy together."

"Mmm," said Sam distractedly. "I think love was in the air. Listen, when I come down, remind me. There's something I must tell you." He turned his head towards his daughter, "Say goodnight, Rosalie."

"Oh, my, no, the little one is already sleeping soundly in your arms," whispered Laura.

Sam climbed the stairs slowly. He wouldn't trade his daughter for the world, but he often dreaded her usual bedtime fuss when she was overtired, and tonight the most ever; yet as he laid her in her bed, strangely enough, she was out like a light. Sam lovingly looked at his daughter, then tiptoed out and took the stairs as gingerly as if they were hot coals.

"She didn't wake up?" asked Laura from the bottom of the stairs.

"No, she's sleeping like a baby." He took Laura's hand in his. He guided her to the bedroom, left the door ajar behind them but only a sliver, led her to beside the bed, and turned to face her. Sam put his arms around Laura's waist.

"What was it you wanted to tell me?" she asked.

"I love you, Mrs. O'Brien," he murmured into her neck.

"How I love the sound of those words," she whispered. She tenderly slid into his embrace and slowly pressed her body against his. "And I love you." She kissed him gently.

He began to unbutton her dress, and let his fingers linger on her back. As the moon crept higher into the sky and darkness fell over everything, Laura realized that love didn't have anything to do with bicycles or moons. It was just love. By the time she and Sam finally fell asleep, the moon had spent itself, and was soon to hand the night over to the sun.

Chapter Nine
Destination Honeymoon

A few days after the wedding, the boys moved into the house, kept on with school and merged gracefully, for the most part, into their new lives as McPherson-O'Briens. Ben delighted in being able to dart out of the house on the first frosty mornings to have some private moments of fresh air to admire the way nature was shutting itself up for the season, Joe relaxed his hours at Dooly's so he could study a bit more, and Tom spent ever more time with his uncle, helping out with the barn or helping him take the edge off his hurting soul, which despite his desire to heal and feel like his old self again, seemed with time, only to worsen and grow more hollow.

As for Laura, she tried to revel in being Sam's wife, but right after their wedding weekend, he was back at work on a new contract and was so busy, she didn't get the chance to see much of him. The wedding was beautiful, but the downside of their October nuptials was that Sam was already committed to this work that started after the Thanksgiving holiday. Their honeymoon, which he promised would be worth waiting for, would have to come when the contract ended in early July. In the meantime, during the initial days when Sam was so extremely busy, she was ever more grateful for the telephone as it was often the only way they were able to catch up during the day, though their calls were usually filled with her telling him about Rosalie. She tried not to mind this, telling herself it was only natural they'd want to talk about his daughter.

The winter was mild for the most part, and quite busy and filled with visits and school projects and keeping house, so the months flew by. Spring came in gently and Laura found true enjoyment in reading on the veranda, even learning new recipes from books. Since their wedding and her new life began in Sam's house, the niggling feeling of rootlessness began scratching away at her. She found some books on the Acadians, the history and customs, reading about them as if they were supposed to feel familiar but noting that they did not. She also began taking Rosalie to the orphanage twice a week to see her friends, and at home, she tutored the little one to help her with her studies. From time to time she dabbled in her journal but she only scratched out brief thoughts. She realized she didn't want to think about the past anymore; living in the present was busy, and fulfilling, enough.

Once the snow faded and the ground softened into spring, Ben was back into the gardening, up at dawn each day to work in the greenhouse. And Tom, who had taken on some inches over the winter months, had grown yet more handsome with his warm smile and curly hair. He was stocky where Joe was tall and thin, but he liked to joke that his being closer to the ground kept him humble.

Finally the July day of their departure for their honeymoon dawned bright and hot. Laura emerged from the house to greet Peggy who was just arriving down the dusty lane as Sam was packing the car.

Peggy approached, and she and Laura embraced. Laura pulled away and raised an eyebrow. "Did Sam happen to mention to you at least where he's taking me?"

"Nope, and it's staying a secret until you get there. I mean, even if I knew. Which I don't."

"Peggy! That's not fair."

Sam emerged from the house with a leather satchel under each arm. "Last load. What do you think, my bride; should we get going?"

Peggy pointed to her wrist. "Can't keep a new husband waiting; come on, I'll walk you over."

Though the day was yellow with summer sun, flowers waving in the breeze and leaves clapping lightly in the trees, at this dismissal and Peggy's seeming rush to get Laura off, Laura felt a sudden weight in her chest that she knew had nothing to do with her former disease. She took a shallow breath. It was nothing. Why all these years later would she still be worried that leaving her children would encourage them to think of Peggy as more of a mother than her? Laura felt her chest pulse with habitual hot, angry light. She looked at Peggy, who helped her at every turn, even planned her entire wedding, but who would nonetheless feel right at home playing mother to the boys yet another time. It wasn't Peggy's fault her body had let her down, and Laura needed to feel grateful. "In everything give thanks: for this is the will of God," she reminded herself.

Laura swallowed hard. "It's really nice of you to watch after the boys while I'm gone," she sighed, slipped her arm under Peggy's, then smiled brightly. Both women walked down the gravel walk.

"Oh, they hardly need to be watched anymore," said Peggy. "You concentrate on your new priority of being Sam's wife. It'll do you some good."

Laura didn't respond. This was her third time leaving her boys with Peggy, and the third time was the charm, she knew. Some charm, she laughed at herself. Here she was about to go on a holiday, a real honest to goodness holiday, and she was trudging toward the car as if it were the convent all over again.

As she walked, her sister just slightly more ahead, Laura tried to distinguish her footsteps from Peggy's, but for some reason, she couldn't hear her shoes make a sound, as if she were already not there.

Once in the car, as the house disappeared into the distance, Laura broke their silence. "Alright, Samuel O'Brien, I didn't spend almost three years in that sanitarium getting over tuberculosis only to die from curiosity in this car!"

Sam roared with laughter and took up Laura's hand in his. "Fair enough. We are on our way to..." he paused and looked at her, his face full of expectation, "Cape Breton. Your home. First stop, Inverness, then Chéticamp." He smiled. "What do you say about that?"

Her eyes misted up. "Really?" she whispered. She was surprised by feeling reticent, suddenly, somehow ill prepared. She wished she'd had time to think about this.

"Nothing like starting a new life with me by going back to your roots. Give our future a good foundation."

"Only you, Mr. Superintendent, would think in terms of building something." Laura slapped Sam on the arm and nestled her head into his shoulder chiding herself for being ridiculous. It was a truly wonderful gesture, and she would revel in the comfort of sharing her original home with her husband.

They rode in comfortable quiet until the familiar blanket of fatigue wrapped itself around her. Drifting off, she thought about her mother and the fateful day she died. Not once in her life did Laura ever believe she would have the chance to return to Inverness where she'd spent her childhood and teenage years, let alone her birth village of Chéticamp. Deep in her had always resided the feeling that she was missing something, something essential, something others took for granted. It was that innate given of having roots. Knowing where one stemmed from, his family, his heritage. Laura hadn't realized until this past winter how the unsettled feeling she'd always had, one that came and went in waves, had reared up and was now something she could consciously identify. She wasn't entirely sure she liked being so aware, that knowledge in this case didn't necessarily give her power. And now, ironically, she was going back. She wasn't at all sure how she felt about this yet.

After some forty miles of narrow, winding roads, they finally reached the toll booth in Aulds Cove, just before the causeway. The car came to a stop, and Laura sat upright. "I know exactly where we are; we crossed this same stretch of water on a ferry in 1938, Peggy, George and I, not long after mother passed away. But now look at this: a brand new road and railroad track. Isn't this grand? When did it open?"

205

"August 13, 1955 was the official opening. Believe it or not, I was here." Sam laughed. "I can't believe that was five years ago already." He looked at her warmly. "So much has happened since then."

"You were here? What was it like?"

"Oh, it was a big party; thousands of people, an inaugural address and the cutting of the ribbon, and then the famous march across the causeway led by some hundred pipers in kilts, followed by dignitaries and official guests, decorated boats in the water, marching bands, even air force jets flying above. The day ended with a ceilidh with food and entertainment," laughed Sam. "It was a wonderful event."

"I haven't heard the word 'ceilidh' before." Laura caressed Sam's palm.

"It's Gaelic for a frolic. A party with music and dance."

"It must have been quite something. And now people can cross whenever it suits them."

"Yes, but would you believe, there was a lot of controversy over creating the Causeway."

"What do you mean?"

"Well, some people feared that building it might interfere with the lobster industry, others worried that if there were another world war, the causeway would more or less open the road to coal and steel plants on the opposite side of the island. It's interesting how people are scared of change; I mean, this is progress! Port Hawkesbury boasts one of the deepest ice-free harbours on the Atlantic Seaboard, and it's sure to become a vibrant and prosperous city in the future."

Laura loved talking to Sam about feats of engineering. His whole body came alive. He was such a believer in progress. And faith. Two things she so needed in her life.

Taking Route 19, they arrived in Inverness around eight o'clock and parked at the hotel. She recognized the row of Company houses, the church and the beach as they drove in, its tangy sharp scent in the air so familiar, so fundamentally home, it actually hurt her heart. They had a late fish supper at the local restaurant and strolled back to their room by way of the shore. "Wasn't the moon lovely casting its reflection on the water? I could have stayed there all night. Do you think there are people on the moon?" Laura asked teasingly. Things were exactly the same but entirely different. She was trying not to think about the fact that she was home but it felt like it wasn't in any way hers.

"Well, I know of a cow that jumps over the moon, now and then." Sam looked at Laura. "Come here, my bride." He took her into his arms and kissed her softly.

"Ah, yes. I've heard that one too," she whispered. She let go of her worries, so happy to be in his arms. It was thrilling to know they'd have several days of just the two of them to catch up and be in love.

* * * * * *

The next morning, Laura was eager to show her husband where she had lived as a girl. Driving by the Company house, Laura could practically see her mother trudging up to mass as she did every morning. And on their way to the small rustic cabin, images of the Englishman's confident daughters snapping their chewing gum as they lay on the haystacks in the sun and of Johnny, his broad arms flexing as he forked hay or sheared a sheep went through her head. But when they reached the outskirts of town where the English house had once proudly stood, only an old shack remained. Even the cabin was in ruins. Laura felt empty, like her past had been erased.

The couple walked slowly up the old unkempt driveway and looked around. Tall grass was growing where apple and cherry trees were once cultivated. No one was around; Laura had so hoped to talk to someone who might remember her mother. As they were returning to the car, an older gentleman came from around back.

Laura related her story, and the old man smiled, nodding his head. "Yes, I remember. She had two lovely girls," he looked her up and down. "You must be one of them. You look like her."

Laura grinned and extended her hand.

"Yes," he said, "I worked for the English family too now and then. Fine people they were, kind and hospitable."

"What happened?"

"Well, they both died, oh, several years ago. As the children moved away to find work, the old homestead sort of slipped away into ruin."

"That's too bad."

"Yes, work is scarce around here. People migrate to the Boston States or to Ontario to find decent jobs. Sometimes whole families move away." He shrugged. "Who knows; maybe one of the children will come back and restore the old place someday."

As the old man spoke, he looked sadly at the rundown land. Touched by his forlorn words, the couple followed his gaze and remained silent for a moment. Finally Sam asked, "Do you live far from here? May we give you a lift?"

"Thanks, but got to get my exercise. Good-bye, folks. Have your-selves a good trip." They shook hands and parted ways.

By late afternoon Sam and Laura arrived at their final destination, an Inn overlooking the ocean. The Island Inn stood proudly on the southern tip of Chéticamp Island. At first sight, Laura felt uneasy for it reminded her of the sanitarium: big and majestic walled with windows. But soon after they entered, its beauty and charm filled her with a feeling of safety. The furniture was made of gleaming woods and plush upholstery, certainly nothing picked from dumps. She knelt to examine the rug that covered part of the floor.

"They're made of heavy fabric scraps, a blend of pattern and colour, very popular craft around these parts," said the innkeeper. Laura smiled and nodded.

By the front bay window were two rocking chairs. She sat in one and stared out at the endless ocean, the hills and mountains. She felt very small. It was an incredible thing, she marveled, that when things in her life were extinguished, systems like the sea existed to sweep up and enfold- rather like the tide. She smiled. Nature certainly had its ways of keeping a person in balance. That thought comforted her, and she nestled more deeply into her chair to gaze out at the water. When the innkeeper came around to the front desk, Laura stood from her chair and went to him. "I was wondering about my maternal grandparents' home, the house where my mother grew up. I might like to see it. Would you know the name Josephine Chiasson?"

"Aie," he said, smiling slowly. "You mean, Josephine who married William Boudreau? They were your parents? I went to primary school with your mother. Used to pull on her pinafore." He was grinning now. "Small world, isn't it." He examined Laura a moment and grew serious. "Your mother's home? You don't remember, right? Your grandparents died before you were even born, if I'm not mistaken." Laura swallowed hard. So much history was at her fingertips, she felt dizzy. "Here," he reached into his pocket and pulled out a scrap of paper and a nub of a pencil and proceeded to draw her a map.

"I can't thank you enough," whispered Laura. She held the paper in her hand but didn't look at it. When the innkeeper excused himself to go into the back, she folded it neatly and put it into her handbag.

Wordlessly, a servant came around and took their luggage, and after some time, Sam gently guided Laura to dinner. When they finished, he asked, "Shall we have a walk?"

Their walk to the cliff was short, but soon Laura began to shiver. The night air had brought a chill, and dark thunderclouds appeared overhead. Suddenly a flash of lightning lit up the sky and unleashed a torrent of wind and rain. "This way," shouted Sam over the wind. They raced back to the Inn, but a huge gust of wind picked up and knocked Laura over. Sam grabbed her and they made it back, soaked and chilled.

The old innkeeper held the door open with both hands for them then shut it tightly and locked it. Exhausted and breathless, the two just looked at each other.

"You're alright," the Innkeeper said. "You made it in time."

"What on earth..." Laura couldn't catch her breath.

"The southeast winds, we call them suêtes, sometimes they rage without any warning," he said calmly, going to the counter.

"No warnings?"

"Well, there are a few signs the locals know about. The day before a big southeast, the weather is calm, often a very nice day, and then a few hours beforehand the wind picks up, you can hear a noise growling in the mountains, and the smoke from chimneys rises straight up." He jerked his knotted thumb toward two kerosene lamps on the counter. "It's a good thing we won't be needing these tonight, eh?" he said. "At least so far," he chuckled. "I tell you, when we know of a southeast coming, especially in the wintertime, no one dares go out. All shutters are closed. Any loose thing around the house is gathered and stored away." He looked at the pair, dripping on the rug and clucked his tongue. "Yes, well, we probably should have warned you. Sorry if you got scared. Best you go change before you catch a cold."

"Now he tells us," whispered Sam. Laura was shivering violently and couldn't respond.

In the room, Laura put on a nightgown and slipped into bed. She thought about her children and hoped they were safe.

"You rest. I have some work I need to do, so I'll do it downstairs. I won't be long. Unless I get blown away."

Laura tried not to feel disappointed. "Your contract isn't over?"

"This is for another client. Nothing too intensive. I'll be up soon."

She blew him a kiss. Sam laughed. "That kind I can handle."

When Sam went downstairs, the older gentleman was resting in an easy chair with the day's paper. At Sam's footsteps, he looked up. "How's the misses?" He motioned to the other chair across from him.

Sam settled in. "She's fine, resting. We certainly got a good scare tonight. Any other hazards we should look out for during our stay?"

The old man smiled as he lit his pipe. "No, the southeast winds are the worst of it." He chuckled to himself. "I remember one time a farmer from St-Joseph-Du-Moine, the next village up the road, during one of our strongest southeast winds, the roof of his chicken coop flew off and landed in the opposite field." He chuckled again, but Sam just looked concerned.

Soon after, Sam climbed the stairs and joined his wife in bed, but he was unable to sleep until the wee hours of the morning when the wind finally stopped howling.

The next day, Sam took Laura's hand as they finished breakfast. "I'm so sorry to do this to you, but I have to go to town to meet with some men at the fish plant before we head to the national park later in the afternoon. It won't take long, though," he said.

They drove, each in his own thoughts, though once they entered the busy village, Laura became quite absorbed by the action and sat up high in her seat to take it all in. Lobster season had just finished; people were milling about, and fishermen were hauling in their traps at the water's edge.

The main street, with its church majestically in the middle, was flanked by harbour on one side and houses on the other, everything protected by the mountains behind. They drove past where she had lived with her grandparents. She remembered the exact spot when she and her mother had visited in 1934, two years before her grandparents passed away, but the tiny house was no longer there. Laura quietly wiped her eyes and shuddered at the emptiness that filled her.

While Sam went about his business, Laura decided to distract herself by looking in the shops. She entered a rustic shop overflowing with goods; she bought different coloured material in various patterns for Peggy and new shoes for Rosalie, plus some gifts for the boys. While she paid, she chatted with the cashier about the weather. Outside, she replaced her wallet in her handbag and with striking clarity recalled her early days after Johnny died when she didn't know the value of money and had to bring little Joe along to help her shop. She tightly held her bag, smiled broadly, and walked down the street in the warm sun until she saw a shop with hooked rugs in the window. She peered closer through the glass; each stitch was perfectly like the others, an extraordinary show of pride and workmanship. She instantly thought of her sister: her dedication, her pride. Her mouth watered imagining Peggy's consistently perfect biscuits and she laughed before entering the shop.

The couple met for a late lunch of fish and chips, a local favorite, then continued north, arriving at the national park by two o'clock.

Rather than drive straight to the park's office at the main entrance, however, Sam detoured in order to show Laura a bit of the park. He drove up the first big hill, which had a stunning overlook, and brought the car up to the edge. Laura put her hands in front of her face. "Turn back, Sam, I can't look," she said, "please."

"Laura," Sam said gently pulling her hands down. "Just look. Have you ever seen such a view?" He scanned the horizon and said softly, "We're on the edge of it, the vast, endless ocean. And there's the lighthouse at the tip of the island." He turned his head and pointed, "And look, Laura, look towards the southwest, the silhouette of the church. You have to see how beautiful it all is."

But Laura squeezed her eyes shut and gripped the dash. "I can't," she whispered. "Please go back down."

Without a word, Sam put the car into reverse and took them back down to the park's entry. They drove in silence until he parked. He looked at her, her face still pale. "It's alright now," he said gently. "And I won't be long. Don't wander off or you might meet up with a bear." He brushed the back of his finger against her cheek and walked off.

Laura slowly left the car and made her way to a bench. She sat, feeling very much alone, and tried her best to shoo away the flies. Tears sat heavily in her throat; this honeymoon was turning out to be a glorified business trip, and anything that might have been for pleasure she couldn't enjoy. She couldn't even force herself to admire a beautiful view. Mostly, she realized, she was upset that everything felt and looked different from what she might have remembered. Nothing felt as it should have.

She shook her head and decided to make the best of this gentle day. She looked about for something to do; off to the side of the park's entrance was a large field, tall grasses waving in the breeze. Figuring there wouldn't be any bears in the open, she wandered over and strolled down the rocky dirt road running down the centre of the field. The air smelled sweet and dusty. After a time, she came upon an old woman in a kerchief on her knees. She was filling containers with plump red strawberries. Wild berries; that would be nice, thought Laura. She and Sam could enjoy them after supper. Her brow furrowed. And if he's not there, the heck with him, she thought. I'll eat the whole lot myself.

Laura approached the woman. "Do you mind if I pick a few as well?" she asked.

The woman looked mildly confused, but smiled revealing strong white teeth with several gaps between. The skin on her face was thick and brown. Laura gestured to one of the buckets. "Ah, oué, oué," she said. The two women crawled side by side, filling their buckets, each speaking in her own language, conversing like old friends.

By the time they returned to the Inn, the couple was finally able to relax together over dinner. "How was your meeting at the park?" Laura asked.

Sam flicked his wine glass with a finger, making it sing. "Very satisfying!"

"I really don't even know what the purpose of a national park is; isn't that silly?"

"Not at all." Sam took Laura's hand across the table. "Well, to start, it provides magnificent scenery, a beautiful drive along the ocean, valleys and camping grounds."

"What about the Cabot Trail? I'd be scared." Laura recalled with perfect clarity the fear she'd felt when she and Sam were perched on the overlook.

Sam laughed. "The roads are much better now. Guardrails are placed along the most dangerous parts and paving should be completed by next summer. Here's an idea; why don't we plan to come back then and tour the trail? We could bring the children."

Laura considered it. "I suppose I could give it a try," she said with a small smile. "But tell me, I interrupted you; what else is there to know about the park?"

"I think I mentioned all the beautiful aspects," said Sam. He thought a moment. "I suppose there are also economic benefits to the local people. And it's a haven for animals and plants. A preservation area of sorts." Sam paused. "Though the creation of it caused a lot of bitterness. The government expropriated the people who lived there from the land-"

"Ex- sorry?"

"Expropriated. The Acadians who used to live in Cap Rouge on the Chéticamp side of the park had to move when the government took the land over in the 30s. These people were for the most part poor but they were strongly attached to their land. Relocating might have given some a better life, but it's never easy to leave what you love."

Sam watched his wife who had grown quiet. She was looking out the window, and he couldn't tell if she was taking this last thought to heart. He took her hand. "Laura?"

Her eyes were distant. "Hmm?"

"I admire you very much. Did you know that?"

"Admire me? Why on earth-"

"You are stronger than anyone I know. You've left your sons not once but twice, both times not knowing if you would return. You must have remarkable faith."

Laura said nothing. Then she whispered, "It really is a most beautiful place here, like heaven on earth." She didn't say much for the rest of the meal, blaming fatigue.

* * * * * *

On Saturday morning, the day they were to drive home, Laura rose early with Sam. Since he had unfinished business to attend to at the national park, she thought she would go for one last walk along the beach.

This early, the beach was still empty. She walked alone along where sand and sea continuously met, ever changing the landscape. Laura enjoyed seeing the previous day's remains in the sand, whether they were sandcastles, sculpted mermaids decorated with driftwood and bird feathers, name sketches or tracks of all kinds: dog, bicycle, adult and children's footprints. They were faded from the wind, but still identifiable.

Laura marveled at the sandpipers as they searched for food while jellyfish and squids lined the shore. Perched on the rocks, a flock of sea gulls patiently waited for her to continue her stroll so they could grab their prey. Completing this perfect picture, dry seaweed cushioned part of the dune and glittered in the still-fragile morning light.

An onlooker might have viewed this place as lonely, but Laura saw how it was bubbling with undercurrents and above-ground activity. A narrow stream trickled down a curved path, giving the impression of having been designed by hand. As its unsteady borders gradually eroded, the rippling water widened its course at the mouth where the two, stream and ocean, became one.

Laura stopped at the merging waters and listened. She felt lonely but whole at the same time. Nothing was perfect; there was a rock in the stream's path deviating it slightly, but the water just went around and carried on. Goose bumps flecked her arms.

She continued down the shore until she discovered a hidden cove. It reminded her of a time long ago, when her sons were small. She and Johnny often took them to a tiny beach, similar to this one. They built sandcastle after sandcastle. Laura remembered being surprised that both Joe and Tom, rambunctious, active boys, took such delicate care with the details and were devastated when a wave came and took one away.

Taking a deep breath, she opened her heart to admire the vast body of water that lay before her. So many droplets, too many to count like the grains of sand between her toes. She stood before the water and felt its power enter her. Suddenly, yet with a heavenly feeling of calm inside her, as if she had been called out to the sea, Laura walked toward the water and waded in. She took small steps to adjust to the cold but she didn't stop, continuing in until the water was up past her knees, then past her waist, then to her neck. Everything Laura had known, all she had endured. It was this easy; she felt then like she was the sea, beginning again, herself a new tide. Feeling nothing, no pain, nothing in her body at all but peace, Laura let herself slip beneath the water's surface. She stayed there, her single lung bursting.

* * * * * *

"What in the world," Sam was stammering when he saw Laura's still wet hair and different outfit. "How could you? You might have drowned! Why would you take such a risk? Do you have no regard for your health?!" He ducked into the car for a blanket to drape around her. "Look, you're still shivering."

Laura felt her earlier calm melt at her husband's worry; she'd never seen him angry like this before. Yet when she spoke, she surprised herself by how measured her voice came out. "I understand your concern," she paused for a few seconds then, her eyes lit up as she stared at the ocean. "But that was one of the most wonderful experiences I've ever had....aside from marrying you, of course." She took his warm hands in hers. "Sam, I want to live. I feel this is my chance to finally do it right. I want to live every moment. We never know how many there are going to be."

Sam held her close. Arm in arm, they leaned against the side of the car and took in one last view. He closed his eyes and whispered, "Being aware of how precious life is, living each moment, reflecting...seems two great minds think alike." He smiled at her.

Laura smiled back but looked at him quizzically. "What do you mean?"

He hefted himself off the car, opened the car door, and handed a bag to her. Inside she found several books, a beautiful journal with her name engraved on it and two thick black scribblers.

"When did you... but I thought you were working the whole time! Thank you so much," she murmured as she kissed him.

Sam touched the scribblers. "I got you these because I thought you might like to keep a record of the books you read, a dairy of sorts, with short summaries, similar to Ben's notebook on birds and flowers. Now that you read so beautifully, it's a gift to be able to remember it all. It *is* like a new beginning, a new life."

Laura smiled. "Two great minds is right. Thank you."

Sam looked lovingly into her eyes. "To our new beginning."

Laura touched the rough leather surface of the scribblers. She had so much she wanted to say, things that went far beyond birds and flowers. Her heart longed to let her give rise to it all. She thought about the little crumpled paper with the hand drawn map in her purse and how she hadn't used it. She hadn't sought out any extended family at all or visited the cemetery. Their trip was not the heartwarming homecoming she'd anticipated, and as they drove away, she felt rather hollow. Sam's intentions were kind, but her heart wanted more. "A new beginning," she murmured. Hearing her own voice echo these words aloud was a kind of confirmation. She could believe in them.

When they were almost home, Sam took a shortcut and passed the lane leading to Laura's old house. Panic gripped her after they were long past it and froze itself around her heart even as they kept on and soon pulled down Sam and Laura's long driveway, the oak trees majestically lining both sides of the path. Normally Laura took such comfort in the gentle swish of their branches, strolling with little Rosalie beneath their canopy. Today, however, they were cold and impervious.

She pulled abruptly away from Sam. What right did she have? Flitting around with another man after she'd pledged her love and life to Johnny, after she'd made a family with him. But, she also realized, he had betrayed her. He was a coward. And he was dead.

"What's wrong?" Sam put on the brake.

"I… it's still an adjustment, is all. Even after all this time," she looked down.

Sam brushed her lips with his fingers. "You just have to relax and let me dote on you. We're forever, you and I. You know that, don't you?"

Laura bit her lip. "I guess I'm just feeling a little vulnerable."

Sam laughed. "I must say, going from maid who couldn't read a grocery list to my wife who lets such fancy words drip off her tongue is a marvelous progression," he joked.

Laura waved her hand at him. "Alright, stop it now." Some tears were starting in her eyes. "I just hadn't thought about my house. I… I mean my old house. And the barn. When we drove past them, it all came flooding in."

Sam twisted one of her curls around his finger. "We'll keep them. Like I said, maybe down the road, one of the boys will settle there. I paid the taxes in full for the year, and now that we're married, it will be my pleasure to continue doing so, to keep the house in the family."

She was crying now, wordlessly.

"It'll all be wonderful. You'll see."

The couple kissed but was soon interrupted by Rosalie, who came running down the long path and crashed into the car with one arm. On the other was a cast. As she ran alongside the car, she explained, panting, "Went swimming... river...Rosalie fell...broke arm...Aunt Peggy... hospital...hurt a lot! Ride in Joe's truck...fun!! But...I cry."

Sam stopped so Rosalie could hop into the front seat. She told her story again while Sam put the car in gear and drove down the lane. Laura wiped her face and smiled at her daughter, relieved she was alright. When they parked, Rosalie leapt out and ran to the house, yelling to Peggy while Sam and Laura got their bags. "Aunt Peggy! Look! Father and Laura-mama... home!" She emerged seconds later holding Peggy's hand, almost dragging her outside.

Laura felt puzzlement and thrill flush over her that overshadowed her worry over Rosalie's arm and earlier upset. "What did she call me?" she asked Peggy.

Before she could answer, Rosalie exclaimed excitedly. "Peggy said... call you... Laura-mama." Without waiting for an answer, her eyes twinkling, she asked, "You like?"

Laura almost choked with love and didn't know whom to love more: Rosalie or Peggy. She hugged Rosalie again. "Yes, I like very much. May I sign your cast?"

The little one was ecstatic.

"Now, Rosalie, should we go find your brothers?"

The words were no sooner said than Rosalie turned and ran to the greenhouse yelling for Ben. Laura and Sam followed. Ben had clippers in his hand and looked serene in his element.

"Ben, am I glad to see you!"

"Mama, welcome home! Come see my new flowers."

Laura smiled. Robert soon also came to greet the couple. "Welcome back, you two! Did you have a pleasant trip?"

"Yes, very nice! I understand a lot happened while we were gone," said Sam.

Robert rolled his eyes, smiled and shrugged. "Fortunately, all's well that ends well," he said.

Everyone admired the blooms for a bit then they went into the house. Peggy was back at the stove, and on the table were jars full of strawberries. Laura laughed. "When did you pick these?"

Peggy wiped her hands on Laura's apron she was wearing. "This morning, with Rosalie and Ben. Aren't they lovely?"

"They sure are. Well, it seems there's a lot of this going around, the great minds thinking alike," laughed Laura, pulling out a jar of berries from her satchel.

Peggy had to laugh. "You went strawberry picking on your honeymoon?"

Laura looked away from her juice-stained apron over her sister's broad frame. "Where are Joe and Tom?"

"Joe's working at the garage and Tom is helping George mend a fence."

"Oh," said Laura. The house suddenly seemed large and empty, the bounty of berries taunting her. Peggy looked suddenly harried. "Speaking of George, I'm sure he's anxious to have me back. I'd better get home."

Laura wondered why Peggy's mood shifted so quickly. "But won't you please stay for supper?"

"No, no. I'll be on my way." She quickly undid the apron and hung it on a chair. "But welcome back, Laura! We'll catch up soon."

"Thank you for everything, Peggy. I owe you."

"You don't owe me a thing! What are sisters for?" she said over her shoulder. Peggy picked up her handbag and a small valise by the front door and dashed out.

"Wait, Sam will drive you home," called Laura, but Peggy was already down the lane, almost out of view. It had been a week away from her husband. She'd so wanted to spend that time with her nephews, fill that corner of her heart that always stood empty.

They were growing so quickly, so busy with their friends and jobs. She knew it was wise to put her attentions elsewhere. She thought about that same corner, the one that longed for the George she used to know. He did need her, and she hadn't been there for him. She wondered what state he'd be in on her return.

* * * * * *

As soon as Peggy arrived home, she went to the barn and found Tom and George. Tom had syrupy, red eyes, and was slumped over on a barrel with a cigarette in his hand, and George was passed out in the hay. Peggy fought her emotions, her throat tight.

"Tom," she worked to keep her voice even. "You are smoking above a pile of hay. There is dry hay all around. Animals, wood, our home, our livelihood, and you're smoking." Tears gutted her voice. She looked at George out of habit as if for back up. He was snoring softly into the hay, his clothes hanging on him. She hadn't noticed it earlier but from this distance, it was clear he'd lost more weight.

"Sorry, so sorry, Aunt Peggy, didn't mean anything by it," he said slowly and stubbed out his cigarette on the bottom of his boot. "It's just that it was so hot this afternoon. We only drank a bit."

"A bit? He's out cold! And you? You're not exactly sober, my young nephew." She went to George. He smelled like he hadn't bathed the whole time she was gone. "Help me get him into the house."

Even with some dropped pounds, George was still a big man. Peggy was at least grateful the barn was close to the house for it took all their combined strength to drag him in. Tom helped her undress him and remove his boots then he sank into the living room sofa himself.

Peggy was devastated. She knew Laura was disappointed her sons weren't home when she returned from her trip. Joe would come home after work, he always did, but Tom, he couldn't show up like this. Peggy went to the phone to make an excuse for him, but words failed her. She didn't know what she would say. She gently replaced the receiver in its cradle.

Chapter Ten
Summer Daze

The summer of 1960 had the feeling of change and newness to it. Laura and Sam were home from their honeymoon, school was out for the year, and the boys were enjoying their summer routines. There was a sense of freedom in everything: in the music, in the possibility of the age, and in the future. Over the last year, Joe had shot up, his body now strong and lean, and with his dimpled cheeks and reddish hair, he could pick from nearly any girl in his class. And he did, now that things were off his shoulders and he didn't have to worry about being home for chores or to watch over his brothers. He'd resisted staying in school earlier, believing work was more productive than a piece of paper, but now he was looking forward to entering Grade 12, earning his diploma, and going off to vocational school. He'd even heard of an architectural program in Halifax that sounded perfect for him, but he didn't say anything to his family as Halifax was quite far and there was no guarantee he'd get in anyway.

When he wasn't working, Joe took advantage of the sultry after-noons to go out with any number of girls while Tom's days were busy with odd jobs, telling jokes with his friends and generally having a good time, often with his uncle, doing things he knew he oughtn't but did anyway. He'd bought a bike off a friend, and it was fine except he knew he'd paid too much for it. It got him around, but now that he was sixteen, he was itching to get his driver's license. He began secretly plotting how he'd be able to afford a car of his own. Driving his uncle's tractor was fine for delivering his home-made brew from the house to the shack, but it wasn't something he could drive around town.

No one knew he'd been using the old house for a private bootleg-ging business. The house was secluded and his friends felt comfort-able coming around for a few smokes and a drink. He knew his mother and Aunt Peggy would be so disappointed if they found out, but he figured he wasn't doing anyone any harm, and besides, he reasoned, he was getting some independence. Anyway, his mother was busy with Sam and the younger kids, and Aunt Peggy had her own problems. Tom knew he shouldn't encourage his uncle's drink-ing, but drinking relaxed him and let him have some joy he couldn't get from life, not from anything else, at least when sober. He had nightmares from the war, waking up in sweats. And he tried to go without, staying dry for weeks at a time, but then he'd have one beer, and he'd drink until he passed out and was sick for days. Then he'd get right back up like nothing had happened, tend to the barn, and it'd start all over again. It hurt all of them to see him this way. But Tom and his uncle, when they were together, it was like they understood each other. Tom felt he had in him everything a boy could want in a father.

One warm Saturday afternoon Tom had a few friends by. They sat in the sunroom where they watched the squirrels play in the trees. "You started coming back to church, eh, Tom? Now that your mother married a rich guy, you don't have a choice, I suppose."

Tom scratched the back of his neck, ignoring the sarcasm in his friend's voice. "You know, once my father died, every single Sunday, Uncle George and Aunt Peggy picked us up in their wagon and trucked the whole lot of us off to church. My mother didn't like it, all those people staring at us with their sorry eyes, wondering how she was making out with no money and three boys..." Tom laughed ruefully. "Well, she showed them. Doing fine with Sam, alright. But the rub is now that she's with Sam, and he's so prominent in the community and all that, we all still have to go. I don't think my mother's heart is in it either, but she knows it's important."

"Well," said Leo, "at least you'll have something good to say at confession," he raised his bottle and laughed.

"Come on, nothing wrong with a drink on a Saturday afternoon, right, boys? Even Jesus enjoyed wine, right?" He clinked his bottle with each of his friends. "Cheers. Have another on me." The boys enjoyed until sundown, bought some more of Tom's homemade brew then said their goodbyes.

Tom's friend Bill hung back, not wanting to go. Tom was glad for the sale, mentally adding up his recent earnings and rejoicing his new situation of being able to keep the money rather than having to give it to his mother that he didn't notice Bill's demeanor change from amiable to melancholic.

Bill lit another cigarette. "None too keen to get back home, I guess."

Tom finally looked closely at his friend's face and now noticed how his brow was unnaturally heavy. "What do you mean?"

Bill shook his head. "Oh, you know. Just don't tell anyone at school I said anything, OK?" Bill ducked his head and he roughed up his hair a few times with one hand. "It's nothing much, just that my old man, he gets out of control is all. Beats my mom, my sister..." he let his sentence trail off.

Tom frowned. "And you too, I suppose?"

"He just doesn't know how to hold on, you know, when things are hard. Your uncle sounds about like that too."

Tom shook his head "Yeah, but the difference is my uncle wouldn't hurt a fly." Tom stared at Bill. "What can I do?"

"I have some money saved," Bill said, blowing smoke out into the growing dark. Neither boy moved to light a lamp. "I'll be alright. But you can't tell any of our friends."

Tom couldn't see the expression in his friend's eyes, but he knew there was fierce pride there. "I promise."

They sat quietly together for a while longer until Bill took up his things and left. Tom had made a promise, but he also didn't want to see what would happen to Bill and his family if he didn't help in some way. He felt torn in a terrible way.

* * * * * *

Summer was always exciting in Antigonish. There were concerts and the Highland Games, and Joe and Tom especially liked the outdoor dances. Joe twirled under the stars with the girls while Tom hung off to the sides sipping on pints, the air all around them smelling of freshly cut hay. More often than not, Joe had to drag a drunken Tom home and try to get him up to bed without waking the whole house. When the fair came to town bringing with it games, caramel apples, stuffed bears, daring rides and loud music, it was a terrific place for the boys to hang out with their friends. After Tom bought yet another round of tickets so he could win stuffed bears for this girl or that, Joe looked at his brother funny. "Where on earth are you getting all this money?" he demanded.

Tom grinned and looked sly. "I have my ways, brother. You have money too, you know, working all this time, why are you being such a cheapskate? Spend a bit, have some fun."

Joe realized he'd never felt comfortable spending money, not even on something he needed.

"Mother and Sam are doing fine, you know. You don't need to worry so much," said Tom kindly.

Joe looked at him a long moment. His brother, jokey, carefree Tom, with his very serious face, was totally right. He smiled.

On Sundays after their obligatory turn at church, Sam took to handing the boys some money so the four kids could go for a ride and get some burgers. It was a great treat for Joe and Tom to hop into Sam's Chevrolet Bel Air and cruise by their friends on Main Street. And Ben, though quite a bit taller than his step sister, was as doting and loving as if they saw eye to eye. Rosalie, now that her cast was off, was able to sit with her arms crossed in the open window, her freckled face squinting against the sunlight, the ribbons from her pigtails slapping the wind. After they ate and topped off their lunch with an ice cream sundae, the older boys loved running their fingers over the shiny new cars in the GM and Ford dealerships, fantasizing which cars they'd buy if they could.

On their way home each week, Rosalie and Ben liked to drum out the beat coming from the radio.

On the last day of the fair, while they were driving by, the fair's lights blazed and music tinnily blared. Rosalie gasped. "Fair, we go fair? Please, please, please?

Joe and Tom looked at one another, their expressions identical. They wanted to take her, but they were worried. She was unpredictable, and what if one of the other children made a fuss over how she was different? It would break her heart. But her "pleases" grew more impassioned, so they parked and Ben tucked her arm beneath his and held her tight. A mixture of terror and magic seemed to float from her eyes when she saw the Ferris wheel, the merry-go-round, and all the dizzying rides.

They headed straight for some little cars that drove in a circle. Ben got in with Rosalie, and Tom and Joe leaned against the low fence to watch and share a cigarette. "You know," said Tom, "look at Ben." The boys focused on their younger brother, who was laughing and holding tightly to Rosalie. "He's just as comfortable with Rosalie as he was when he wore his ladybug shirt to school. He's truly his own person. Not many people around are like that."

"And," added Joe, "she is in heaven. Look at her face."

The boys were quiet a moment. "You know, in some way, I envy them both." said Joe. "You know what I mean? They know how to live. No cares, no worries." He smiled. "Rosalie is a lot like Mother that way. And this guy," he said raising his voice as Ben and Rosalie came tripping off the ride to them, "he's all right. I think we'll keep him."

"Who, me? Gee, thanks, Joe," laughed Ben.

* * * * * *

In a blink, summer ended and school resumed. By the end of September, the mornings were already getting a light frost, so Ben regretfully closed up the greenhouse business for the year. Tom used to be around to help out, but lately he always seemed to be otherwise busy. Ben caught him by the arm one afternoon after school as Tom seemed to be wobbling off in the wrong direction. "I have a lot to do with shutting up the greenhouse. Robert's off somewhere. I thought you were going to help me."

"Sorry, pal, but I have other things to do. Maybe tomorrow, yeah, tomorrow I can give you a hand."

Ben felt like punching his brother. He smelled like beer and school had only let out a few minutes before. He didn't say anything as Tom kept on.

When Ben returned home, Laura was in the kitchen pulling a chocolate cake out of the oven. Seeing her, looking at peace and bent over the fragrant baking, he got a wave of homesickness for the way things once were. "Mama? Do you want to go for a walk down to the river?"

Laura looked pleasantly surprised then smiled. "I would love to, Benny. Let me get my sweater."

As the two walked in silence down the lane, Laura took her son's hand and squeezed it. "You've grown," she said. His curly head almost came up to her shoulder. She realized with a plunge in her stomach that there were a number of things she wasn't keeping up with. She'd let life with Sam take over her time and thoughts even though straight from their wedding he was busier with work than ever. Rather than think about it, not wanting to know the truth, she'd baked more, cleaned harder, persisted in her particular hearty brand of cheeriness that could make anything unpleasant seem just fine. She knew Tom had been drinking, she could see Peggy had grown quiet, she'd stopped writing.

But now that the boys were back in school, and Rosalie spending long periods painting or playing with her dolls, the house was still during those moments, just the ticking of the clock. In the quiet spaces, Laura was seeing that her world could use her again, the her that faced things head on.

She and Ben arrived to the banks and found a sandy spot where they could sit down. They watched the minnows dart in between the river grass and the late afternoon sparkle of the sun on the water. "Thanks for inviting me, Ben. I haven't been around much lately. This is just what I needed."

He slipped his lean fingers through hers. "Me, too, Mama."

Now that Laura had realized how much she'd been neglecting, she felt invigorated by the idea that she was going to be purposeful. There was so much to take care of but mostly a much needed and overdue visit to Peggy, whom, she realized, she hadn't seen in several weeks, an unheard amount of time for the two sisters.

She didn't even ring up; the next morning after washing the breakfast dishes, she left Rosalie with her Grandpa Robert and just walked on over. "Hello, stranger! I haven't seen you practically since we got back from our honeymoon. You're not in hiding, are you?" Laura chuckled as she walked inside past Peggy, whose face she noticed was pale and drawn.

"Come on in," said Peggy looking around the house's perimeter as if for something or someone before shutting the door behind Laura.

"Here, I brought you something. For taking care of the children while we were away. High time I came around with this gift."

Peggy wiped her hands on her apron. "Thank you," she looked at the package before putting it on the table. "So tell me about your trip. And how are Sam and Rosalie?"

"They're fine; go on, open it," said Laura, picking up the gift from the table and offering it again to her sister. Peg broke the paper open at the taped seams. When she saw what it was, she sat down on a kitchen chair and cried.

"What's the matter?"

"How did you know?"

"Know what?"

"Did Tom tell you? I told him not to say a word!"

"Tom?" Laura was confused. "What is going on, Peggy?"

Peggy looked at Laura and realized from her sister's confusion, she didn't have any idea what had been happening. "George, he's been drinking heavily, all summer, and still going strong. It's a good thing Tom was around because he did most of the work in the barn and in the fields."

Laura sat too. "But why? What's brought this on?"

"I don't know."

"And what about the sheets?"

Peggy made an ugly noise and tossed the package back onto the table. She stood and walked to the window. "When he's that drunk, he wets the bed. I can't reach him; it's like he's in another world."

"Why didn't you tell me before? Where is he now?"

Peg's face was awash in heat spots beneath her blazing freckles. "He's probably out in the barn, smoking. I give him hell for it, but it goes in one ear, out the other. Tom smokes with him, you know!" she looked accusatorily at Laura.

"Has he been able to work? What about the hay? That's a big job."

"Tom and Joe helped him and so did their friends."

"So how are you getting by then?"

"He works now and then at odd jobs around the village, and I sell eggs and butter to the Co-op store. I do some sewing, which is actually one of the only things I do that brings me pleasure these days. And he found buyers for the lambs and a few cattle heads. We're OK. He still needs to cut the firewood before the winter," Peggy paused, "if he can stay sober for that long."

Laura looked into her lap. Her other gift for Peggy seemed inconsequential now. But she handed it to her wordlessly anyway. Her sister's fingers were shaking, Laura noticed. This wasn't how she'd wanted things to turn out. No one did.

"Oh my, Laura, how beautiful," she murmured. Peggy pulled out a hooked rug, displaying intricate colourful details of a rough sea where the high waves lashed against imposingly large rocks and in the corner, a lighthouse meant to guide any lost ship.

The tears in her sister's eyes told Laura that this gift was anything but inconsequential; she'd clearly derived a very personal meaning from the scene given what was happening to her. Laura breathed out. "I bought it in Chéticamp. They have the most marvelous rugs and what's most intriguing is each stitch is made by hand. Sam and I talked to a few 'hookers,'" Laura giggled into her hand, "but really we were quite overwhelmed at how genuinely enthused they are about their work. A real labour of love."

Peggy smiled. "You certainly sound different these days. So scholarly." She looked down again, her fingers running over the rough stitches. "It must take forever to complete such a project with such tedious work."

"To talk to them, you'd have no idea the work was difficult. They take such a pride in it, rather like you with your sewing, Peg."

From the few simple minutes they spent together, Laura could see a change come over her sister, as if she were slowly releasing a long held in breath. Laura knew things were very hard, harder than she could imagine, but she was glad to be there for Peggy in some small way. And now that she had come to her senses and was reaching out, she would make herself helpful. It felt odd that she should be returning to her lovely, caring husband while Peg had to endure such hardship. Peggy, so capable, so selfless. So adept at keeping people afloat. She deserved better.

* * * * * *

With the onset of cooler weather, Tom knew his part time bootlegging enterprise needed to close down for the year. He had his friends over one crisp afternoon as a goodbye to the season. Again Bill hung back. "Has it gotten any better?" whispered Tom. "I've been wanting to know, but I didn't want to ask you at school."

Bill shook his head slowly and stared at the edge of his pocket knife he'd been absently playing with. "Nah, it's worse than ever. But listen, I've got to go." He saw Tom staring at his arms, which were spotted with bruises, and thrust his hands into his pockets before heading down the lane.

Tom had promised not to tell anyone at school, but he hadn't said anything about not telling his aunt and uncle. He couldn't stay silent anymore. He was afraid what would happen if he didn't get his friend some help.

Later after supper, he came over and told Peggy and George what was happening. As he talked, he could see his uncle reddening in the face. "No one treats his family like that, I don't care what kind of weak spirit he has. No one." He stood from the table.

"Where are you going at this hour?" Peggy asked.

"Settle this with Bill's father."

One look at George's face and Peggy knew not to say anything else. She and Tom watched him go down the lane. "Look at him, Tom. He looks like a soldier, a man of power, of steel." She was quiet a moment. "I feel quite lucky he's got a good soul in him."

"Will his visit do any good?"

"I certainly hope so. If anyone can convince your friend's father to treat his family better, it's George." She went into the kitchen. "Can't sit still now, so I may as well make some biscuits. You'll help eat them?" Tom smiled and followed her into the kitchen.

They weren't halfway through the first batch, when George returned, banging the door behind him. "What happened?"

"He was drunker than a skunk and told me to mind my own business. I tried to talk some sense into him, but-"

Tom couldn't help but burst out, "But Uncle George, the last time I saw Bill, he was black and blue. Can't you do something?"

His uncle sighed. "I'm sorry, Tom. That man is a nasty fellow needing some sense knocked into him." George walked to the window and stared out, his hands in his back pockets. "You tell your friend that he and his sister and his mother are welcome to stay here. And for as long as they need, right, Peggy?" he asked as he turned around.

"Yes, yes, tell your friend they're welcome. They'll be safe here."

George's eyebrow went up slightly at that, but he smiled at his nephew. "Tell him not to worry."

A few weeks later, Bill and his mother and sister unexpectedly appeared on their doorstep. Peggy was stunned; their haunted faces looked very similar to George's after he returned from the war.

"How about a cup of tea?" asked Peggy kindly as she took the woman by the elbow with one hand and put her hand on the little girl's back. She guided them gently inside.

"I can't thank you enough," whispered the woman. "George must have finally succeeded in talking some sense into him." Her face trembled, "My husband didn't say a word when we walked out."

"George? What do you mean?"

"He was over again this morning," said Bill's mother, smoothing the hair on her daughter.

Indeed, earlier that day, George had gone over in earnest. Something about this man and his broken spirit felt too familiar to him. George knew if he had more anger in him, he might also be someone who lashed out at those he loved. Seeing this man on the brink of losing his family, made him realize that he needed to change some things for himself before he lost Peggy for good. He decided as he left Bill's father's house, looking back at him slumped in a chair with his unwashed head in his hands, that he, George MacDonald, was going to become a new man. Someone Peggy and the whole family would be proud of.

Over the next days, Tom noticed his uncle's new demeanor almost instantly. He didn't say anything, though, just enjoyed seeing him and his aunt hold hands when they walked or share a kiss for no apparent reason. In the evenings, when Bill and his mother shared a tea with his aunt and uncle, the color in their faces was bright and promising. Though Tom was happy living with his mother and brothers at Sam's, he still spent a great deal of time with his aunt and uncle, feeling happy that as the first autumn leaves began to fall, he knew it was a magical time, full of the birth of good things, even as the world prepared itself to enter into slumber.

Chapter Eleven
Back To Reality

"Can't you just stay home this one weekend?" Laura asked, trying to keep her voice casual. Sam was leafing through a sheaf of papers he'd found on his desk after a long search in his files and nodded, though she couldn't be sure whether it was at what she'd said or at something that caught his eye on one of the pages.

"It would be nice to stay home, there's no question there. But this project is all deadlines, and the manager has said we have to stay on schedule or it will cost the firm thousands of dollars." He looked at Laura and sighed. He smiled sadly. "I'm sorry, you know."

"I know." She took her dust cloth and went back into the kitchen. Her chicken was nearly finished, but she knew Sam had to leave before he could eat with the family.

She'd nevertheless set his place at the table, and invited Agnes, their new housekeeper, a plump black woman with an ear-to-ear smile and upbeat look at life, to eat with them. She was a great appreciator of Laura's cooking and Laura truly enjoyed spending time with her.

She was grateful to have her help as well; she cared for the house beautifully, and with the boys in school, and Rosalie now going to the orphanage three days a week on her own by bus, Laura had far more time to herself. She napped, baked more, took longer walks, read in Robert's library for long stretches all sorts of books, and let herself sometimes just stare out at the changing landscape.

More and more she found herself walking to the man-made dumps. It wasn't as though she needed to forage for furniture any more, but Laura missed the feeling of being able to make something useful out of something old. When she found something she liked but that was too large to carry like a chair or sofa, she sent the boys there after school to pick it up.

One day, she found herself walking further and further, lost in thought. Soon, the landscape became familiar. She suddenly stopped short, realizing where she'd come. Up the lane stood the old farmhouse. She was flooded with emotion and felt tugged forward and backward. She spent what seemed like a very long time not going anywhere, just looking at her old home from far away, as if it were a painting. She stood so long, the air crisped up around her and the shadows grew long. She shivered. It had only been a year since she married Sam. I just need more time, she thought. She knew seeing the faded rug and the new roof would bring too much crashing down. She turned and righted her posture. Sam would come soon, she hoped, and Ben and Rosalie would surely be done with school by now. No, she would come back another time. Dried maple leaves skittered around her feet and she turned and walked away.

Laura continued to hunt for dumps but from that day forward, she made sure to head into other directions.

Sam noticed her new habit one evening after he came home and she was scrubbing the upholstery on a loveseat. He watched her and frowned. "Laura, if you want new chairs, we can go to the furniture store in town. I'm sure they have a very nice selection. Don't waste your time with this junk."

"Why should we spend your hard earned money when I can salvage a few things here and there?" she said, her tongue in the corner of her mouth. "Besides, I enjoy restoring these old pieces; they have character, don't you agree?"

Sam chuckled for her benefit. "I agree that you do good work. I do."

A few weeks went by and Laura realized if she didn't do something more productive than scrub old furniture, she would go mad.

She occasionally pulled out the scribblers that Sam had bought her in Cape Breton and made some half-hearted notes, but she didn't let herself sink into stories or details. Then one afternoon when she was picking Rosalie up from the bus, she realized she could be useful to the orphanage. Two days later, she accompanied Rosalie to school and surprised herself by assertively marching into the Director's office and announcing that she wanted to volunteer. They decided she would start with one day per week and Laura felt swelled up with pride.

One day, when she was reading and didn't meet the children at the bus stop as she usually did, Laura was surprised by the little one bursting into the house. "Laura-mama! Laura-mama! Where you are?"

"Rosalie? I'm in the library. And it's, 'where are you, not 'where-'"

"Here!"

"I know, Rosalie, but you must say, 'where are you and-"

"Laura-mama! I'm here, library!" The little one rolled her eyes, like she had seen Joe and Tom do then remembering the cause of her excitement, she said, "Miss Barbara 'tiring!"

Laura's laughter turned to puzzlement. "Do you mean she's tired?"

"No, no... 'tiring!"

This time Laura understood. "Re-tir-ing?"

"Yes...go away...not come back!"

Laura was surprised. She'd been working closely with everyone at the orphanage and hadn't heard anything about this. She kept her voice upbeat for Rosalie as they chatted further then got a snack, but that night, after Rosalie went to bed, she waited up for Sam and told him about it as he ate a late dinner.

"Won't be easy to find someone to replace her," he said. "She's definitely been good for the kids, exemplary, really." He finished eating then stood, kissing Laura on the forehead. "I've got to read over some briefs; why don't you go to bed, and I'll meet you there?" Laura walked away slowly. She didn't mind Sam's preoccupation this time, though. She was having ideas of her own.

Sam assisted in the hunt to find a replacement, using some of his contacts to cast a net for a new Miss Barbara. Laura decided whatever thoughts she was having were not to be, especially after Sam told her of a particular candidate's lofty educational background. He became the front-runner, and the board scheduled a meet-and-greet event.

That evening over tea and biscuits at the orphanage, it was easy to see that the applicant was an affable enough fellow. Laura watched him say the right one-liners to the right people, shaking hands, laughing in the perfect spots. It left her with an odd taste in her mouth. He acted like he owned the place already, she thought.

Laura and Rosalie stood off to the side as they watched the action. Laura had never felt comfortable in large crowds and gripped Rosalie's hand. So many people welcomed him warmly. She felt a sourness in her stomach. When she'd gone to the convent, what it would have meant to her to be so welcomed. Or at least not met with such disdain and silence, and only because of a misunderstanding. She let go of Rosalie's hand and removed her jacket, smiled and took up the girl's hand again. "Shall we get something to drink?" she asked.

Before they could go to the buffet table, Sam strode over to her with his arm outstretched and the man by his side. "Laura, meet our new chief of staff, Mr. Bernard Ray."

A subtle hush fell over Mr. Ray, the board members, the guests and even Sam as Mr. Ray took up Laura's hand and shook it. "I guess it's been decided, then," she said pleasantly. "Welcome." She was aware of everyone's eyes on her. Such a departure from the day she met Sam, drawn and pale in a worn grey coat with the ends trailing on the ground. She knew she looked the perfect wife: confident, groomed, slim in a soft green skirt and pillbox hat, the matching boxy jacket draped over an arm. Sam must have thought so too for he took her gently around her waist and yanked on one of Rosalie's ponytails, making her laugh.

Laura caught a glimpse of Mr. Ray amid all of this; she thought she noted a trace of indifference in his eyes, a skill in perceptivity she'd honed at the san. But she discounted her intuition. That was a long time ago, she thought. Sam wouldn't have chosen him unless he had a good feeling he'd do right by the children.

On their way home, Sam looked pleased with their selection. "I think Mr. Ray will make a good chief of staff. He seems to be intelligent and friendly, and he's certainly qualified."

Laura was quiet.

"Don't you think so, Laura?" He looked at her, but she kept her face forward. "What is it?"

"Tell me, how was he chosen?"

"Letters, all letters through the mail."

Laura smiled and tried to sound neutral. "I'm sure he'll be fine, but maybe just keep an eye on him."

It turned out the new chief of staff was just as pleasant as he'd been when they'd met him. Pleasant and trusting of that which had been established before his arrival, so much so, he didn't want to change a single thing. Twice a day, he'd walk the corridors complimenting his staff and residents alike, then return to his office. If anyone had an issue, he directed them to his secretary so she could handle it. He seemed to enjoy drinking tea more than anything else, and soon, people began ringing up Sam and the other members of the board because they couldn't get their issues attended to.

* * * * * *

True to his word, ever since visiting Bill's father that day, tea became George's drink of choice as well. He liked to keep a pot warm beneath Peggy's old knitted cozy all throughout the day for ready nips. With George back to what seemed to be his old self, Peggy's old spirit also returned. He and Peggy never talked about what provoked him so strongly to make such a drastic positive change in his life, but she suspected it had something to do with Bill's father. Bill and his mother were still boarding at their place, and they could see a change in them as well now that they weren't still living under the shadow of alcohol. Bill's mother liked to regale them with funny stories from her days as the priest's housekeeper, and they could see how it heartened her and made her feel proud to be able to pay their way with Peggy and George.

Peggy went back to burning up the phone lines to Laura. "Morning, Laura!"

Laura giggled. It wasn't even half past seven, yet here was Peggy, charged up and ready for her day like she used to be. She'd bet the day's biscuits were already in the oven as well. "Didn't you mention you bought loads of material while you were on your honeymoon?" Peggy asked.

"Yes, I bought a variety of colour patterns. How is George today; do you think you could leave him a few hours to come and see them?"

"Do you know, George is back to his old self, thank God, Dieu merci! He's working on the roads again. Did you hear the Trans-Canada Highway is going through Antigonish?"

"I did, actually. Sam says it's the first section of divided highway to be built in Canada!"

"Is that so? I hear the highway is going right through the homes of several black families."

Laura grew quiet. She had heard the same and hoped it wouldn't affect their housekeeper. Progress always had its negative side effects, she thought. She made a mental note to speak to Sam about this. Peggy didn't notice Laura's mood shift and kept on with her gossip, "Don't know, but George says it's creating quite a stir!" Peggy sighed. "Now, why don't we get together tonight. I can look at the material then we can sneak in a few games of cards?"

"Sounds good to me. I'm sure Sam will enjoy it, too." Laura said that as cheerfully as she could, knowing it was more than likely Sam would be nowhere close to coming home on time.

The fall of 1960 passed with the boys in school, the men working, Rosalie enjoying her special days at the orphanage, and the two sisters happy to enjoy their blossoming adult friendship on new, lighter terms, their old jealousies now little more than a shadow in their history.

The one night of fabric and cards turned into a twice-weekly event. George took to coming along, and Sam even made a point of getting home early enough to join in. Ben and Rosalie would sit with their homework and crayons, watching and laughing along, even when they didn't understand the jokes. When the women won, Peggy would leap up and dance around her chair. The noise often distracted Tom and Joe from their studies so they too joined in the fun. The parties would go until late, so Laura would often start getting out fresh bread, jam and cheeses along with some slices of cake to tie everyone over.

One Saturday night, Tom called into the kitchen, "Mother, why don't you make an Acadian chowder?"

"You mean a chicken fricot?"

"Yes!"

She laughed, "The only chicken I have is frozen; it would take all night to thaw it out!"

With a twinkle in her eye, Peggy quickly suggested, "George, go to the barn and butcher one."

"At this time of night? It's already ten o'clock," he chuckled.

The boys urged him on and he relented. "We're going with you!" they shouted.

"On the tractor?"

"We can take my old truck! Let's go!" said Joe.

"George," hollered Peggy as she rushed outside, "Get a young one. Hens take too long to cook."

"Ten-four, chief!" winked her husband as he saluted with his right hand.

Rosalie stationed herself by the window to wait for them to return, Peggy chopped the onions, and Laura peeled the potatoes, leaving them to soak in cold water. By the time the chicken fricot was ready, the little one had fallen asleep on the sofa but the card game behind her was still going strong.

* * * * * *

As fall deepened into early winter, the family started doing some intensive whispering about Robert, who was not at all his usual self. He was whistling more often, burned things in the kitchen, and sometimes was spotted just staring out the window. Laura and Sam wondered whether they should be worried until Tom discovered Robert's secret: one afternoon he spotted the elder man, cane in hand, strutting up the lane to the mailbox. He opened it, furtively looked about to see if anyone was around then pulled an envelope from the box and smelled it with his eyes closed. Tom took to spying on the postman and looking at the mail in the box before Robert could get there. It seemed he and Laura's ex-nun friend Louise had been corresponding, so much so that by Christmas, Louise decided to move to town to live near Robert.

In no time, she secured herself a nursing job at the hospital and spent the rest of her free time with Robert and the family. Laura was so happy her best friend from the san was now close by, almost family herself.

One day, while Robert was attending a town meeting, Louise came up to the house to visit Laura. They'd talked a bit about the convent at Laura's wedding, but here in this quieter moment, Louise wanted to know more about Laura's experience there. Laura briefly repeated the reason for her five-month stay, but Louise's curiosity was not satisfied. It seemed Louise wanted to know every last detail, from Laura's 4:30 a.m. daily wake up time to the vast floors she had to scrub on her knees, to how she fell asleep while praying at her bedside from sheer exhaustion. She'd been there, and Laura, a fellow woman, a woman with a young child, was being made to slave away under tortuous conditions. Louise had tried to smooth the edges by sneaking Laura food, but it haunted her that she had stood by while such ill treatment of a fellow human being and a baby went on and she had done nothing to stop it.

Louise swallowed hard, silent tears streaming down her cheeks. Laura held her friend's shoulder firmly. "Louise, but look at us now," she said, smiling gently then broader. "You're going to be my mother-in-law, aren't you?"

Louise's laugh could be heard all the way up the lane. "So I will," she whispered. "So I will."

And soon no one was surprised when Robert and Louise announced their engagement at a dinner they called at the cottage. Robert didn't let go of Louise's hand the whole evening except when she was serving dinner. "A February wedding," sighed Laura, taking Sam's hand in hers. "How romantic."

Sam laughed heartily. "My bride, I think you'd say that about a wedding in any month."

"I'll say this," said Robert standing at the table to make a toast. "I might have achieved a few simple things in my life: university graduate, a member of the Board of Trade, director of the newspaper, member of the Co-op movement-" Everyone chuckled. It was commonly known that Robert was one of the most respected members of their community. Whenever they went out with him, people approached him and showed genuine respect. "But let me tell you something," he continued, leaning down to kiss Louise's cheek, "none of that means anything without the love of this woman right here." Everyone clinked glasses and Peggy wiped her eyes with her napkin. "As long as there is love, there is hope," he said. Louise's face was pink and youthful as she gazed with joy at Robert.

The church wedding took place on a Friday evening, February 17, 1961. Peggy yet again ran the show and created some beautiful outfits for the bride and the maid of honour. Louise wore a long-sleeved pale blue suit with matching hat, shoes and purse that complemented her silver hair, and as her maid of honour, Laura wore a beige suit with matching hat, shoes and purse. Both of them carried handmade corsages. Snow fell softly, blanketing the world outside. After church, the group hurried to the parish hall for a light lunch and entertainment, which went on deep into the evening. Fiddle music and dancing broke out, and the boys took advantage of the free liquor, especially Tom, who downed one pint of beer after another.

Laura was enjoying visiting with people, but she kept her eye on her middle son. She wasn't able to count the number of drinks he'd had, she only noticed he was never without a beer bottle in his hand. At one point, she was chatting with Louise about the honeymoon when she heard a commotion outside. She soon realized that one of the shouting voices in the argument was Tom's. George lurched toward the door just as Laura broke from her conversation, but he was blind drunk and couldn't do much more than yell, "Tom, whatcherdoin, Tom?"

Sam came out and pulled Tom away from the other boy. Tom's face was streaked with tears. "What's happened?"

"He cheated me, this guy cheated me," Tom kept repeating, wiping his wet face on his suit jacket.

Inside, Laura stepped onto the dance floor and discretely pulled Joe aside. He nodded, took Tom by the shoulder and steered him toward the truck, without saying goodbye to anyone.

Laura looked around, the good mood spoiled. Peggy was trying to get George out, Rosalie had fallen asleep sprawled out on two chairs, and after helping tidy up, Laura and Sam carried her out to the car and drove home with her propped up between them in the front seat. Ben sat alone in the back. Laura wanted to ask him what he knew about Tom, but she didn't want to wake the girl. Or to hear the sound of her own voice asking about what was happening with her son.

After Rosalie was settled in bed, Sam and Laura checked on the boys, who were already fast asleep. Laura slowly climbed down the stairs and sat in the rocking chair by the window. In the sky, a beautiful half moon shone. The snow had tapered off and the moon's light lit up the yard. She noticed how lovely it all was but didn't feel comforted by it. She was deeply troubled from having seen her son so drunk. And she knew it wasn't his first time, not by a long shot.

Sam came in after her. "Laura, these things happen with boys, especially when there's liquor and ill feelings involved. Tomorrow, we'll laugh about it-"

Laura interrupted him. "What was the fight about?"

"Apparently, Tom felt his friend took advantage of him when he sold him that bike."

"He paid ten dollars for it, and that kind of money doesn't grow on trees," said Laura. "If the bike doesn't work properly, he's right to be upset." .

"It'll be alright, don't worry." He stroked her arm. "Father and Louise certainly seem to be very happy."

"Yes," Laura nodded absently. "A lovely couple." She wished the nice feeling of a wedding hadn't been so spoiled.

The next morning, Tom awoke with a splitting headache. Feeling ashamed of his behaviour, he sneaked out to visit his uncle, who was still in bed, sleeping off a most difficult night. In the afternoon, George finally rose. Before joining Tom in the barn to curry the horses, he gratefully took a cup of tea from Peggy, who wordlessly looked at him. "Peg," he said, meeting her worried eyes with his own swimming ones. "I am never going to touch another drop of liquor, as God is my witness."

Peggy smiled sadly. She hoped this time his promise would stick. She really did. The worst part was she knew he really wanted it. He was just powerless against its charms.

* * * * * *

Once the snow melted in the middle of the spring of '61, Laura resumed her long walks in the dandelion bedecked fields, smelling the wild flowers and marveling at all signs of life, the pussy willows and lilacs, the multi-coloured birds, and the soft velvet grass beneath her feet. The phone had rung that morning twice with complaints about Mr. Ray, but she firmly shook her head to rid herself of that problem now. Her daily walks, time in the library, rests: she'd earned these things and wanted for nothing else, truly.

Now that the weather was fine, Robert and Louise, newly retired, had taken over Ben's florist business. She liked to pop in to the greenhouse to help them fill orders.

At the end of June, Joe did it: he graduated from Grade 12. Laura couldn't stop the elated tears from filling her eyes as she squeezed her son and whispered in his ear, "You did it, Joe. You have made me so proud. And your father must be bursting, wherever he is."

All three boys were happy school was out for summer. But instead of long, lazy days stretching out before them, everyone seemed to launch into busy schedules straight away. Joe was still working at the garage and simply slipped into working full time hours. Tom, at his mother's urging, took on a job at a local restaurant rather than remain on the farm all summer to help out Uncle George. Laura's eyes had been opened, and she knew George's drinking was rubbing off on Tom. George was lost in a way that Tom was not, still young with his whole life ahead of him, but she could see how Tom romanticized all his uncle did and it frightened her. Ben, however, knew his own mind and was glad to try working on a farm for a change, so at least Laura was relieved her sister and George would still have the help they needed. And even Rosalie kept up her hours at the orphanage. To keep herself busy, Laura decided to commit to an extra day at the orphanage each week. She found she felt a strong sense of purpose helping the children.

One evening in late July, Sam came home early. Laura had been arranging blooms in a vase she'd found tucked in the back of a cupboard. She glanced at the clock. "It's only 3:30, Sam; is something wrong?"

Sam glanced at the flowers. His face tensed slightly. "I remember that vase," he said. "Wedding gift to Abby from someone. Never liked it much."

Laura looked down. Light refracted off the crystal making little rainbows on the polished table. "But never mind that," he said. "It seems you were right to have such reservations about our Mr. Ray at the orphanage. Things are really not working out."

Laura couldn't help but smile. "He's not a bad man; he's just a bit out to lunch, as they say." She neglected to say a blind person could've seen this coming.

"Well, he might be likeable but enrolment is declining..."

Laura felt suddenly nervous and at peace simultaneously. "Maybe it's time for a change."

"What do you mean?"

"I've been reading about Learning Centres for children who are physically and mentally handicapped. What if the orphanage were to branch out into this field?"

"Mmm, yes, but the province runs a Youth Training School in Truro. I don't see why we would want to duplicate those services."

"Think about it, Sam. If Rosalie is to continue to learn and thrive, she might have to go to the Training School. If the orphanage closes its doors, are you ready to send her there, and only see her on occasion?" She paused and watched as that information sank in. "What if we were to provide a place for the local children, a place for children like Rosalie, where they would come during the day, on a regular basis?"

Sam looked at Laura hard. She could see he was intrigued. "Explain." Laura rather liked Sam's brusqueness; it meant he was regarding her as he might a colleague, seriously, without all the gentle niceties. "As the kids are often considered non-trainable, an activity centre could well open doors to both handicapped children and parents alike."

Sam sat down and fanned himself with the day's newspaper from the side table. "Where on earth did you learn all of this?"

"Come into the library. I'll show you my research. It's not a new idea, just something new for this area."

"It sounds good so far. Maybe research it some more, give me something concrete, and I'll speak with the board members." He paused, "but what about Rosalie?"

"What do you think?"

"I suppose she could continue as she is presently doing. Actually the orphanage is already helping a lot of these children."

"Yes, imagine all the possibilities," Laura said, grinning.

"But how would we fund this operation? We have a hard enough time as it is."

Laura put her hands in the air. "Money and I are not as well acquainted in such matters, but maybe," she smiled a little smile, "your father could pull a few strings?"

Sam laughed. "Laura you are something else, you know that?"

She gave a small bow then said, "What's that...oh!" Laura ran out of the room to the kitchen where her pot of stew was starting to burn. She grabbed the handle and dropped the smoking mess in the sink. As she poured cold water over it, sizzling steam rising towards the ceiling, she leaned back against the counter. "You were saying?"

The two of them laughed for several minutes. "At least you are entirely predictable," said Sam, pulling his wife into a hug.

* * * * * *

After Mr. Ray was let go, a temporary administrator was chosen. He was actually a member of the staff who agreed to take this position while the board continued its search. The board seemed content that they'd found someone proactive this time, but still everyone kept his eye on him. The board members also began meeting bi-weekly to discuss their findings on turning the orphanage into an activity centre.

As time went on the administrator began feeling uncomfortable that so much weight was put on him after the failure of Mr. Ray, so he handed in his resignation.

Laura was sipping tea at the kitchen table, listening to the tick of the clock on the Tuesday morning after he'd decided to quit. She ringed the lip of the cup with her finger until the tea grew cool. The phone was on the other side of the room. She sat a bit longer. Then she stood and phoned Sam at work. She had nothing to lose. The worst anyone could say was no, she wasn't qualified, wasn't what they were looking for, didn't have the right color eyes, was too frail, etcetera etcetera. She hadn't said anything earlier and they'd chosen someone else. It was just her good luck that in the end, he didn't work out. "Alright," she heard herself say. "Please don't laugh. But I'd like to apply for the job."

Sam was talking to someone on the side. "Hold on a second, Laura. OK, what's that?"

She took a long breath. "I'm applying for the activity centre job."

"Oh," he said. "You got my attention that time." He was quiet a moment.

"Are you still there?

"I'm more than there, I'm thinking. Are you up to it?"

"Joe leaves in a few weeks for Halifax, Tom and Ben are pretty well grown up, Rosalie can come with me every day, the house-keeper is very efficient, and if it proves to be too much, we'll get an assistant or fire me."

Sam was quiet again, but Laura didn't interrupt. Finally he said, "My bride? This is the best idea I've heard all day. It'll have to pass a vote with the board, but as far as I'm concerned, you're hired."

* * * * * *

Ben loved his uncle dearly and tried to operate much as Tom did, but the reality was he was an altogether different person. Farm work didn't really suit his daydreaming, sensitive nature the way it did his brother. He often forgot to put the tools back in their exact spots or on his way to fetch something George had asked for, he would forget what it was.

Once Ben fetched the cow for milking, only when he returned, he'd brought the bull instead. "What the hell, Ben! Don't you know the difference between a cow and a bull?"

"Uh?"

"The cow, Ben. Go get the cow!"

"Ooops, sorry, Uncle George. But, can I eat my supper first? I'm mighty hungry."

George looked up and squarely stared Ben down. Not waiting to be told twice, Ben immediately turned and scurried down the field. While watching him disappear over the bend, George shook his head, took a long puff on his cigarette and muttered under his breath, "What will ever become of this young lad?" Once he saw Ben returning, his heart melted. "Dumb kid," he grinned. He ruffled Ben's hair hard when he came up to the barn and they both laughed.

Despite the hard work, Ben had to admit spending time with his uncle opened up a whole new adventure. He even tried to smoke, though it made him feel sick and he invariably fell into hacking and coughing, which made Uncle George laugh hard from the belly so loud he could surely be heard for miles. Aunt Peggy squawked at them about smoking in the barn every day, but Uncle George just nodded then lit up. He liked to keep a lit cigarette between his lips or behind an ear since he was always so busy with his hands.

One sultry day in August, George had been working in the stalls, and since they had plans to play cards later that evening, Peggy was having a nap. The smell of smoke finally became so thick it woke her from a deep dream. When she realized it was real, she leapt out of bed and ran outside. By then, the barn was filled with smoke. "George! George, where are you?" she screamed into the fire, but her voice was swallowed up by the noise and ash.

She ran to the barn and tried to enter, but the flames had already overtaken the barn floor and were reaching into the rafters. Desperately, she dashed back inside the house to call Laura, and when she came back out again, the barn was engulfed in flames.

Laura hung up and quickly called the fire department. Then she ran to the cottage, her chest bursting either from lack of oxygen or fear, she couldn't tell. Ben was working with George that day. Benny. His name caught in her throat.

Luckily, Louise and Robert were home. As she breathlessly explained, Robert grabbed the car keys and Louise immediately volunteered to watch the little one. As Robert sped to Peggy's, Laura gripped the dashboard, her head bent backwards looking at the sky, confused by an afternoon sunset, a stunning mixture of red, yellow and orange. She shivered and almost cried out when she realized the whole sky was turning dark from the fire.

When they arrived at the house, neighbours were carrying pails of water back and forth, desperately trying to control the fire, though it was clear these small buckets wouldn't do a bit of good. The entire barn was alight.

Amidst the confusion, Laura frantically searched for her sister, "Peggy! Where are you?"

"Laura," Peggy ran over to her and dryly cracked out, "George." She paused, her whole world in his name. "I don't know, where is he? Is he with Ben? Is he with you?" She turned and screamed out toward the flames, "George!"

Laura shook her head. "I haven't seen him, Peg. But Ben, where is Ben? Peggy, do you know where Ben is?"

"Ben didn't come today," said Peg, putting her hand on her sister's arm. Laura could barely feel her sister's weight, as if she weren't there. Peggy, awash in panic and tears, held Laura and prayed, and Laura, so filled with gratitude, bent over and burst into confused tears. She tried to think about George, but her thoughts were on her son. He was alright. He was alright. Her body convulsed with sobs of relief.

When Sam came with the boys, and Ben was there, looking well and fine if frightened and drawn, Laura rushed to her youngest son and held him close. Peggy moved in quickly and pulled Ben away from his mother. Her face was ragged, her voice scratchy. "Ben," she held his shoulders tightly, "what were George's plans for today? Was he going into town? He mentioned he might be, that's where he is, in town, probably having a beer or two, no..." she trailed off, lost in her thoughts, "no, he doesn't drink anymore, his damn cigarette, I told him not to smoke in the barn, George, where are you?" she cried, turning blindly to the blazing barn. Ben stood feebly under his aunt's hold and began to cry.

Laura gently took Peggy and gestured to Ben that he should stand with Sam. "He's probably out in the fields, fixing a broken fence, Peggy. Ben, watch for him. No doubt he will smell the smoke and come running."

When the fire department arrived, they hosed down the barn as well as the house. As the fire raged on, there was still no sign of George. At first, people said they had seen him here or there but eventually, the gossip died down to a whisper as everyone feared the worst. Esther arrived with jugs of drinking water. Peggy uttered her thanks and slumped to the ground. The family huddled together on the grass, frantically trying to think of anywhere George might be.

It soon became evident that the barn was beyond salvation for the hay had fuelled the fire with such rage, it took several hours for the flames to die down. By the end of the evening, only a grey smoking shell remained. The fire chief came up to Sam, motioning him to follow. "It's best you remove whatever you can from the house, just in case there's a flare-up during the night."

Without any hesitation, Sam turned to the boys, "Joe, Tom, come with me. Hurry! Ben, stay with your mother."

The men moved quickly, shoving pictures and other belongings into paper bags or into any other large containers they could find. Tom remembered his uncle's war medals and dashed into the bedroom. Soon most things were cleared out of the house. Laura tried to convince Peggy to go home with her and Robert, but she would not hear of it, not until she knew her husband was safe.

By this time, the family was completely silent. After the men were done inspecting the barn, the fire chief returned to speak with Sam. He started to tell him what he'd found, then paused and dug his fingers into his eyes. His voice was hoarse, but he started again, telling him that they were quite sure George had been in the barn, fallen, and his lit cigarette had ignited the hay. "He must have hit his head and passed out," he said.

Sam gripped the chief's hand then went to talk to Peggy. She listened to Sam then when he started to tell her his condolences, she shoved him. "You're wrong! George must have gone into the woods, maybe blueberry picking! Didn't you hear him say the other day how he wanted a blueberry pie, Laura? Don't look at me like that! He's coming back! I know. That damn cigarette! I kept telling him, one day, one day, but no, he wouldn't listen to me!"

Tears were rushing down Laura's face. "Hush, Peggy. Come, let's go to our house-"

"I'm not leaving, not without my husband."

As the neighbours quietly dispersed, Sam and Laura finally convinced Peggy to go with them. She was in no condition to stay by herself at the house. It smelled of smoke and death. The boys wore a gaunt look on their faces, unable to comprehend what had just happened. They loved their uncle like a father.

Peggy was in shock. Sam phoned the doctor who quickly came and administered a sedative. Gradually she settled down in the guest room. Laura held her like a baby, softly humming old Acadian lullabies, tears slowly streaming down their cheeks. She whispered, "You're not alone, Peggy. Sam and I, Rosalie and the boys, we're all here for you. Somehow we'll get through this."

But Peggy's face was numb and soon the medication took effect and she finally fell asleep. When Laura returned downstairs, she was exhausted and empty. "How are the boys, Sam?"

"They're sitting outside," he nodded.

Laura burst out crying and Sam held her tightly in his arms. "There's no body. What shall we do?"

"I'll talk to the funeral director in town and see the priest. Unfortunately they've probably experienced this before. In the meantime, try to rest. Louise told me she would take care of Rosalie for a while."

The smoke and ash were still hovering over the farm like a coming storm. Standing outside on Sam's veranda with his brothers seeing the gray sky and smelling the smoke, Tom felt a stone growing in his gut, getting larger and larger. Standing off to the side, with his curly hair and his sweet young face, Ben looked to him like an untouched lamb. Tom strode over to him and shoved him in the chest. His eyes were hot as if the fire raged inside them. "This is all your fault!"

"What? What's that supposed to mean?"

Joe stepped in between his two brothers. "Tom, you're acting crazy."

"Stay out of this, Joe," Tom warned without taking his eyes of Ben. "Uncle George was a neat freak, his tools in all the right places, never leaving anything lying around."

"It's not my fault he smoked."

"No, but it's your fault you're a scatterbrain. I bet he tripped on something you left lying around. He fell and was left unconscious. Picture the rest."

Ben's face quivered and he sank limply to the steps.

Joe said quietly, "That's not fair, Tom."

Tom's face was beaming with anger. "Not fair? Our little brother is accident prone. He lives in another world, with his trees and plants-"

Joe put his hand on his brother's chest. "We will never know what happened. Sometimes shit happens. But whatever, it's out of our hands." He fumbled for a cigarette, lit it, then changed his mind and squished it under his boot.

No one spoke for a long time. Tom couldn't bear to see his brother's face.

In the next few days, many people stopped by to bring food and offer their condolences. Peggy remained in bed, unable to face anyone, even her husband's best friend when he came by. He greeted the boys and the four of them sat outside with some iced lemonade, reminiscing about the years of the men's friendship. "You boys never knew this, but your uncle and I were on opposite ends of the spectrum; I'm a conservative, and your uncle was a firm Liberal."

"But you were best buddies," said Tom, astonished.

Dooly chuckled. "At the polls for one election, we accidentally met there and pretended to be total strangers." He grew quiet. "But we were fools; when the Liberals won, we didn't talk for about four months afterwards. What a waste of a good friendship." The boys were silent.

Then he slapped his knee and laughed, "I remember when old George called me over to show me his new pigs. Three of them, he said he had. I got to the sty, and there were two there, cute things. 'But where's the third,' I said. He pointed to a poster he'd tacked to the wall; there was the leader of the conservative party staring down at us. That was a good one." He swallowed hard and rubbed the back of his neck. "Old George. Stupid old George. Damn that guy."

Peggy had been listening from the open window, tears falling into her lap. Unable to stand it anymore, she muffled the sound of her sobs with the pillow.

After the remains of the barn had been cleared away and her belongings brought back into the house, Peggy decided to go home. Laura and Sam brought her up the lane. As soon as she looked up at the bare spot where the barn had once stood, her legs gave way.

"Peggy, please just stay with us, at least until next spring?"

"It's the end of August, Laura. That's my home, and I'm going to live there. Thank you, though. I'll be alright," she said quietly.

Laura, however, was not so sure. She visited Peggy as often as her sister would let her, at least every other day, bringing food, little treats, photographs, anything to help keep her sister's spirits up. She gratefully didn't have to ask the boys twice; they came along with her or visited on their own. Laura's heart swelled seeing her sons love their aunt as they did. There wasn't a trace of her old envy there; she felt full of blessings despite the terrible loss. But while Peggy received them all, it was clear from the film over her eyes she wanted them to leave, to mourn alone. She asked Sam to sell off their livestock, and she didn't light the stove once in the last weeks of summer. She said it was too hot to cook, but Laura could see from Peg's hollowing cheeks that she wasn't eating.

When summer of 1961 was nearly at its end, Joe was preparing to leave for Halifax, but he felt uneasy about leaving his aunt behind, hating the despair he saw in her eyes. On their last fishing trip to the river, Tom said he had a plan. "What if I move in with her, Joe, for a while, until she comes out of it? I could keep an eye on her and maybe help her regain some of her vitality-"

Joe laughed and cut his brother off, "Regain some of her vi-ta-li-ty? Who are you, *Shakespeare*?"

Tom sadly smiled. Not only would he miss his uncle, but he already felt lost at the thought of Joe being gone for a whole year.

"I'm sad too, you know," said Joe, looking at Tom. "But it's too late to reapply somewhere closer." He sighed. "I'd thought it would be such a grand adventure, and it was so generous of Sam to offer to support me, but now I don't want it."

Tom gripped Joe's arm. "You go and we'll be fine," he said. "Imagine how proud Mother will be."

Joe was struck by the ferocity in Tom's eyes, so similar to their mother's. He did feel proud then. Like he was meant to pursue his dream to be an architect and do the family right.

But a few days later, his departure was a far cry from the happy farewell scene he'd imagined. When he stepped onto the train and waved goodbye from his seat until he couldn't see his mother and Sam on the platform anymore, he knew the tears in their eyes were not of joy to see him go.

Chapter Twelve
Growing Up and Away

Even though Joe was plagued by deep sorrow for his uncle's passing, as he journeyed to his new life in Halifax, he began to feel surges of excitement. When he arrived in the city, he went downtown, and just stood still a moment, watching the buzz of activity on the street, feeling enlivened by all the people, the noise. Sam's cousin had offered to host him, and he and his wife were kind and generous, and soon he felt at home.

Once classes started at the Nova Scotia Technical College, Joe, steeped in theory, design, and all the hands-on training, let himself dream of owning his own architectural firm in the future. The coursework was intense from the first day, but he still went out and found a part time job on a construction site building a big hotel downtown. He was over committing himself, but he knew keeping occupied meant he wouldn't feel the loss of Uncle George or miss his family as much. His classmates began teasing him for being a workaholic. He even reserved his Saturday nights for writing letters home and reading those his mother had sent during the week rather than going out. And he liked to be alone when he read the letters; his mother did what she could to be upbeat, but the news was usually not very good. Aunt Peggy was still grieving terribly.

Back in Antigonish, Tom tried to concentrate on his studies, but more often than going to classes, he sat alone in the woods or walked in no particular direction, usually with a beer or bottle of whiskey in his hand. His uncle's death haunted him, and now with Joe gone, he felt entirely without the comfort of the two people closest to him. His mother was so busy he didn't like to bother her. And the more he let himself think it, the more he blamed Ben for his uncle's death. Tom didn't know if his earlier accusation was true; it might have been, though ultimately George could've been drunk or just not paying attention. But Ben should have been there that day; he should have prevented this from happening. Slowly, gently, he let himself drift into a world where no pain existed.

After the accident, he'd thought that staying with his aunt to help her out and protect her, much like his uncle would have done, was a good idea, but lately he was regretting this decision. Since the barn had burnt down, there was actually very little for him to do. Preparing supper and helping with the wash while his aunt mostly moped around the house kept them both in constant reminder that death hung over the farm. His aunt rarely bothered to dress, going around the house in an old robe and fuzzy slippers, mostly sitting by the window and staring out. Throughout the fall of '61 and winter of '62, Peggy's depression never lightened. In Laura's moments between work and her home life, she tried her best to bring her sister out of her gloom, yet nothing seemed to work.

Like Joe, Laura also occupied herself in order to lessen the pain. She threw her efforts into the orphanage, implementing her ideas until soon the facility became a full-fledged activity centre. Laura worked with the city councilor to secure some grants from the government so they were no longer dependent on private donations. She also hired a contractor and made some long-since needed adjustments to the space, knocking down a few walls and cheering things up with paint and pictures. In the spring of '62 with trumpeting tulips of all colors flanking the front doors, they re-opened the renovated facility as an "Activity Centre for Handicapped Children."

Several members of the board suggested the title should include Laura's name, but she firmly said no. The centre wasn't about her; she wanted it to be for and about the children. She also wasn't sure she could maintain the same pace and intensity at which she'd been working as the work tired her a great deal, but she didn't dare say anything to anyone, especially Sam. Instead, she put on an energetic smile and kept up the work, maintaining long hours, and catching up on paperwork over the weekends.

With this once tight knit family now unraveling, they nonetheless still came together for Sunday suppers. This was something Laura insisted on, though it taxed her energy that much more. She was often left sitting in a chair after everyone had gone their way. Not even Peggy remained to help out like she would have before George's passing. Laura wondered how she'd possibly wash dishes, put away food, even simply stand up, though somehow, each week, she managed to find the energy.

One Sunday during the long May weekend, after Peggy quietly excused herself the moment the meal was over, it became clear to the whole family that Peggy was becoming so thin, so withdrawn, she'd never be able to resurface if they didn't intervene in some way. "She'd always been so cheerful, so full of life," said Ben. He bit his thumbnail but everyone saw his chin quivering.

Tom glared at his brother across the table. He'd had a few slugs out of his bottle before supper and was feeling in fine form. He was conflicted remembering his little baby brother dancing in circles until he fell over and how they'd all laughed so hard; the flowers he liked to pluck and give to their mother; his round sweet eyes. How only Tom could get him to go to sleep every night. He squeezed his eyes closed to shut out these memories and snapped his fingers. "That's it!" he shouted a little too loudly. "She just needs a push. That would make her feel like herself again!"

Laura laughed at her son's enthusiasm. "Tom, that's a wonderful idea." She thought a minute. "Now that you bring it up, we need new curtains for the Activity Centre. The old ones are a shambles. That would be a perfect project for Peggy to keep her mind occupied. Besides, the centre has a budget for such things, so it'd help her make ends meet." Laura sighed. "I'm grateful in some ways she doesn't have a family to worry about. When your father died, I had nothing." Laura's eyes glazed over in an immediate and raw recollection of pain.

Ben quietly took her hand. "We survived, though, didn't we?"

Tom sneered and under the table, picked at a hangnail until it bled. Laura shook her head and smiled. "We did. And now look at us. I'll speak to her tomorrow. I can go in late." She paused and looked at her two boys. "We survived just fine. But Tom, your eyes don't look good. Why don't we make you an appointment with the doctor to check them?"

Tom laughed and slapped the table. He stood. "I'm right as rain, Mother. Don't you worry." He kissed her on the forehead and whistled his tuneless way to the door. "Thanks for supper," he called out. He felt little as he ventured out into the night air, but as he entered his aunt's dark and quiet house, he felt the weight of grief visit him, where it sat like an anvil on his heart.

Laura arrived at Peggy's early on Monday morning. Peggy was in her usual spot by the window. Because it was a holiday, Tom was still in bed. Laura went around and opened all the curtains. She made tea and brought her sister a cup. "Peggy, you must pull yourself together. This time will pass. You will never forget George and no one is asking you to. Sometimes you'll feel simply miserable, other times you'll feel better," she put her hand on Peggy's arm. It was warm and soft, the skin thin and full of blue veins, "but life goes on. Think of George; the last thing he'd want you to do is fritter your life away. God will provide."

Peggy suddenly turned around, and looked at Laura with a hard face. "Fritter? What kind of word is 'fritter'? And what do you know of this, that it will pass?" Streams of tears were suddenly running down her face. She put her face in her hands. "If he's such a good God, why doesn't he answer our prayers?" she exploded, her face red and puffy. She grabbed a tea towel. "I don't imagine he's in a hurry. Most of the time we drool and grovel before he even lifts a finger. Old man must be deaf or on vacation!"

Laura laid her hand on her sister's back. She felt her ribs through her nightgown. She said gently, "Maybe we should pray for other things, things that we can have a hand in ourselves. Like our happiness. For example," she grinned, "I know I will be happy if you bake us some biscuits."

Peggy stared at Laura, glowering. Then she threw back her head and laughed. Laura realized she could have just as easily cried. Or thrown a chair. Her sister would need to develop a skein over her raw emotional centre to survive. She knew then, in that release of a laugh, that Peggy would try to return to her old self, or become a new version of herself. That she would fight her way back.

"Peg, you're a butterfly, did you know that?" said Laura. "Remember what Mama used to say: Things will pass."

Peggy took a long, deep breath. "I remember." She stood and went to the cupboards. Laura joined Peggy and the two of them pulled out the ingredients and lit the oven. At the smell of baking biscuits, Tom shuffled into the kitchen, ruffling his hair and yawning, and soon Ben came and poked his head in the door. "I went up the lane looking for you and just had to follow my nose," he said timidly sticking his head through the front door as if it were the cage of a lion. Peggy and Laura looked at each other and smiled. Within no time, they were eating a fine lunch.

After they shared some more conversation and tears, Laura mentioned the sewing project to Peggy, who further surprised her by being instantly enthusiastic. It was as if she were simply waiting for a sign, something to break the glass she'd formed around herself to let her out. When Laura and Ben left, Peggy was running a hot bath, and had even pulled down her expensive bath salts George had given her for her birthday when they were first courting. She knew she was surrounded by love, and that the rest of her family would simply spread out to fill in the gap left by George.

They'd barely shut the front door when Tom came shooting down the front steps. "Mother, what did you say to Aunt Peggy that changed her so?"

She couldn't help but laugh, she was so relieved. Laura's eyes twinkled. "Fritter."

"What?" said Ben.

Their mother just laughed. "Actually it was something our mother used to say: 'It will pass.' It's such a simple phrase, and I guess that's what makes it so appropriate."

Tom and Ben looked at each other, shrugged their shoulders and grinned. "I like fritters," said Ben. Tom felt his skin prickle. Here he should have been happy to hear his aunt was finding a kind of healing, but inside he felt dark. Betrayed almost. As if his and his aunt's grief were a kind of solidarity. Now that she was feeling stirrings of life again, that left him alone. He walked apart from his brother and mother and felt more alone than he'd ever felt in his life.

The next day, Tom volunteered to take on more hours at the restaurant after school and on weekends, not wanting to spend any extra time around the house with his aunt or at Sam's, with everyone off doing what they did, busy and well adjusted. He didn't have to worry about giving his mother his earnings anymore, so he felt justified getting more and more alcohol either from Steve Mills, the local bootlegger, or from the social gatherings he went to. He didn't feel like reviving his beer making business now that he couldn't share a brew with his uncle, who had always been so complimentary of Tom's skills as a brewmeister.

He drank now before he left his bed in the mornings, carried a flask to work, and chewed gum to hide the smell. But one day his boss at the restaurant took him aside and fired him for drinking out back and showing up for work slurring his words. Tom didn't know where to go. He couldn't bear to go home. Eventually he did, but it didn't feel like he would ever feel at home anywhere anymore.

In June, right before the end of school, when his friend Bill mentioned he was finished with their town, and ready to move on, Tom didn't hesitate. They met on a rainy morning at the main road and with small satchels and no note left behind, they hitchhiked to the city.

* * * * * *

Hard at work at school, Joe knew none of what had happened at home. Laura was devastated at the disappearance of her son, but she didn't want to bother Joe with the news until his exams were finished for fear of upsetting his schooling.

Joe still maintained his reputation for one of the hardest working students in the program, but one late spring Saturday evening, feeling exams finally creeping out of his legs, he agreed to a night out with a friend. He dressed as did most young men of the time for a Saturday night: black pants, white shirt, tie, and shiny black shoes. They met downtown for a stroll. Charmed by the busy traffic and the night-lights he'd all but forgotten about, he shook his head. "Do you know, I feel like I'm seeing this place for the first time again," he said quietly. "I've had my head down the whole time with work and school. But look at all the restaurants, the different stores, construction, sailors. It's so busy."

Joe's friend Nick laughed. "You act like you just got released from prison."

Joe didn't respond to that, but he did smile broadly. "We definitely have to get something to eat," he exclaimed. "I'm starved."

"Actually, Joe, now that I see you like this, not so serious all the time, and looking pretty spiffy, I have to say," he laughed, "I think you and my cousin should meet. She's out tonight as well and mentioned we should try to run into one another."

Joe laughed. "This sounds like I'm being set up!" He realized however that he didn't mind, not at all. The warm air, the sky sparkling with blue and white along with patches of soft yellow and orange in the clouds above, these moments of beauty would be even finer with a girl at his side.

His friend didn't do his cousin justice when he briefly described her on their way over; as soon as Joe saw her, pretty as a movie star, with blond curly hair, rosy cheeks, and a radiant smile, he was hooked.

They strolled through the Public Gardens for a time. Nick had his arm looped around the other girl's waist and Joe and Delores leaned over a rail and talked. Joe realized she could say just about anything and he'd like her that much more. Her full skirt lifted a bit in the breeze and she had on a pale blue fluffy sweater that complemented her deep blue eyes.

"So, what do you do?" he asked, looking into her eyes. He ached to touch a lock of her hair that played over her cheek in the breeze but held himself back. He didn't want to scare her off.

"I'm training as an RN, a registered nurse."

"Do you like it?"

"Yes, very much. It's still my first year, and we don't get summers off like university students because it's a year-round program. It's so interesting but very intense." She paused, suddenly shy. Joe couldn't restrain himself any longer. He leaned in and put the pads of his calloused fingers to her cheek. It was the softest thing he'd ever felt.

The young couple chatted most of the evening and made plans to meet the next day. It didn't take long before they fell in love, but they were both also sturdily devoted to their burgeoning careers, and this made seeing one another steadily more difficult.

By the end of June, Joe finished his first year of college and decided to remain in Halifax for the summer. He liked the excitement of the city and its people, but mostly he wanted to spend more time with Delores. As he was writing his mother to tell her his decision, he felt regret; he couldn't recall the last time he'd written. The following week when he received her answer, he was stunned. He held the paper and re-read her letter several times without even seeing the words on the page. "I didn't want to burden you," it said.

Joe felt numb. But he was also angry. How could his brother have just walked away from the family and without a goodbye or even a note? He felt like a great gulf had opened up between him and the life he was leading now, and the family he'd left behind.

That divide made it easier for him to adjust his summer plans. Initially he'd thought he'd take it easy, spend some down time with Delores, but something pushed him to do more, take on more work, more responsibility. He enrolled in evening classes, which meant he worked days and studied weekends, leaving almost no time for his romance. When Delores realized Joe had cut all their plans to spend time together, not getting any summer holiday for herself, she knew his priorities were for his work and quietly let him go. He was hurt, probably more hurt than he let himself feel, but he stayed his course and upped his work hours, thinking only about the future and the business he wanted to own.

For two years he kept up such a pace, only keeping in the barest contact with home, only letting himself feel troubled by his brother's disappearance in brief spurts, until one afternoon in the spring of '64. He was walking briskly down the street, not looking up, not admiring the tulips sprouting from the thawing ground, when he suddenly did look up and caught a glimpse of himself in a store window. He was shocked by what he saw. His face had grown taut and around the eyes he looked like a much older man with worries. Like a man with no love. That realization hit Joe hard like a backhand to the jaw. He stood, stunned then sank onto a bench to sit in the sun a moment. He had family. He'd had a wonderful girl whom he'd wanted to marry. His need to succeed, to make money, to be secure, was stronger than his need for what mattered more than any of that. Rather than head home to make notes on the chapter in his blueprint course book, which was what he'd intended to do that afternoon, he let himself sit.

After a long time, so long his bones seemed to ache inside his body, he stood, walked a ways to the corner store and bought an ice cream. Just like the old days. He ate it and let himself enjoy every last bite.

From that day forward, Joe took every Sunday off to rest and slow down. He didn't want to end up dead or alone. He missed his family but most of all he missed his brother.

Joe rooted through the things he'd brought to Halifax and found a photo of Tom from Robert and Louise's wedding. In it, he was grinning madly, his arm draped over Ben, who was making a silly face at the camera. His mother still hadn't heard from Tom in all this time, and he thought, why not? He began carrying the photo around showing it to people he met. It wasn't inconceivable that

Tom could have come this way. Sure it was a huge world, and Tom could've gone to Timbuktu by then, but just the same, there was a tickle in his thoughts that made him start to show the picture to more, then even more, people.

One Sunday morning he stopped into a different corner store than his usual one for a paper and a pack of cigarettes. He pulled out the photo as he'd been doing so often, the edges were wearing down.

The clerk frowned and put on his glasses. "Mmm, yes, I think if you add long hair, he's your man. Reminds me of the kids playing in the rock and roll bands you see on the Ed Sullivan show," he chuckled.

Ignoring his comments, Joe's heart began to race. "Are you sure? Do you know where I can find him?"

"I somehow seem to think he rents a room not far from here. Was chatting with a fellow about it last time he was in."

Joe walked out trembling and smoked a cigarette, then another. He didn't feel the paper in his hand, the cool mist of the morning. So many emotions, relief, anxiety, anger, curiosity, all banged up against one another inside him so that he didn't feel any of them at all. He spent the rest of the morning showing Tom's photo to everyone in the neighborhood until someone pointed at a dilapidated three story building with crumbling stairs and a bleached front door.

He banged on the landlady's door and explained the situation. She looked dubious until he gave her ten dollars, after which he had the impression she'd have opened any door in the house. Once she ambled away, he tapped softly on Tom's door. There was some shuffling and sniffing before Tom opened. "Joe? Joe, it's you, isn't it?" He was swaying slightly. "Joe, I can't believe it."

They hugged each other hard, but Joe soon pulled away. "Why the heck didn't you call? We've been so worried. How could you just disappear for more than two years..." Joe couldn't help it; he was crying.

Tom looked at the floor and pulled at the back of his hair. Over the top of Tom's head, Joe saw an unmade single bed, one chair, some clothes lying on the floor and an ashtray overflowing with cigarette butts. "What's really going on, Tom?"

Tom stared at Joe for a long time. "How about you, Joe? Do you finally have your degree?"

Joe stiffened. "Not yet. I still have a few more years to go."

"You were always on a mission, Joe, the-get-things-done man. And old Benny, I'm sure he's just fine, right as rain."

Joe felt anger rise in his throat at the mockery in his brother's tone. And at how unkempt he was.

Tom ruffled the back of his long hair again. "Well, it was nice of you to come. Say hello to Mother for me," he turned around and waved dismissively in the air.

"Tom, here's at least my phone number. Call me sometime."

"Sure, Joe, sure," said Tom. He turned around and held the door open, waiting for his brother to leave.

Joe blindly stumbled down the stairs. This was hardly the reunion he could've hoped for. Yet what had he expected from someone who could abandon his family without a look back. After all, Tom always knew how to reach them but never once did.

Still, he'd found him.

Joe spent the rest of the day wondering how he should proceed, and whether to tell his mother. It was good news that he'd found Tom, but he was in terrible shape. Joe waited until the following morning before going to a pay phone to call his mother.

When Laura heard, "Do you accept a collect call from Joe McPherson?" on the phone line, her heart pounded loudly. In the moment before the operator connected the call, Laura stood and gently shut her office door. She could hear the children playing outside, laughing and shrieking. It was a peculiar mix of joy and fear in her chest as she sat back down. "What is it, Joe? What's happened?"

Joe's voice wavered. "I found Tom. And he's OK, or mostly OK. We're meeting again next week. He's not quite himself so I can't rush him. But I think I can get through to him."

Laura had a board meeting at 3:00 p.m. and Rosalie home with a cold being cared for by Agnes. Sam was away on a retreat. In that moment, none of that mattered. She blurted out, "I'll come. I'll get on the train and come." She'd been only half aware, half living, going through the motions, not knowing whether her son was even alive, or if he was, what would have driven him away. She was incomplete without her middle child, and here he was, alive, and in Halifax with Joe. She wanted to shout and dance and cry.

"Mother, he's not quite himself. Let me get through to him first. I don't think he's ready to see any of us, but I'll go slow and try to get him out of this, whatever he's going through. Why don't we talk in a week and I'll know better what's happening."

When Joe replaced the receiver on its hook, he felt terrible for lying to her, but he'd said what he'd wanted the truth to be, which in a way was a kind of attempt at repair. He knew he'd keep trying with Tom. He had to break through. Or else, something told him in his gut that Tom would eventually disappear forever or even die.

Laura carefully put down the phone, wishing Sam was back from the retreat. She went through the motions of her day, the paperwork, the meeting, visiting with the children, got home at five, quickly ate the chicken and vegetables Agnes had prepared without tasting a bite, bathed Rosalie and tucked her in then made sure Ben got to sleep without sneaking books and a flashlight under the covers, and then it was after 9:00 p.m. and she paused, exhausted. Even the thought of brewing a cup of tea was too much. She dragged herself into her rocking chair to look out at the sky. Joe's phone call made her realize she'd lost sight of what mattered; she'd put things other than her family first, important things, but she had always promised herself, especially after her time at the convent, that she would never let anything come between her and her family again. Yet here she was, putting other people before her own blood. And her own pleasures. She tried to remember the last time she'd written anything or read a stimulating book. Her hair had greyed, her patience lessened. There just wasn't enough time to do it all, she thought. Time, time to look at the moon, time, too much time, not enough time, time to go, what time is bed time... Laura sighed; even the word game wasn't fun anymore. She'd run away just like her son had. She knew then what she had to do.

Just before she dozed off, feeling calmer, she took one last look at the starlit sky. She hoped to see a sign, an omen, but nothing moved in that vast space. She let her eyes flutter down and did something she hadn't done in a long time: she prayed. Not by rote, not just to hear the words, but because it felt right in her soul, like she was coming back to a warm place, its light glowing at her through the dark.

The next morning was Tuesday, and Laura woke up in bed with Sam beside her. She smiled at her husband; he must have carried her to bed in the night.

He cracked an eye open. "A penny for your thoughts, my dear," a sleepy Sam whispered as he reached over to kiss her cheek.

Laura smiled. "Joe found Tom. And I'm quitting my job at the Centre."

Sam got to his elbows, his eyes open wide now. "What? Whe- I don't know what to ask you first."

"Joe found Tom in Halifax. I don't know how, but he did. He's not well, I think Joe is going to try and reason with him, see if he can get through to him. He asked me to be patient and not come just yet, which is the hardest thing anyone's ever asked me to do," she said, getting out of bed to see the rising sun. "And I think it's my fault he left, or even if it's not-" she held up a finger to shush a protesting Sam, "it's a reminder that I've been neglecting what's important. I want to stay home, spend time with Rosalie and Ben, be here when they get home from school, enjoy your company, write in my journal again..."

Sam joined her at the window. "I didn't want to say anything, but I agree with you. I think it's a wise decision," he kissed her neck.

She smiled happily. "Will you speak to the board for me?"

"Already done."

"And as soon as Joe says he thinks it's a good idea, will you come with me to Halifax?"

"Your wish is my command."

She hoped those weren't just idle words but that he meant it. She decided not to worry about that right then, turned and put her arms around his neck. "How was the retreat?"

"Not bad. We were a large group, several priests. I enjoyed it. But," he said, kissing her softly, "I'm glad to be home."

After Laura offered her resignation and brought possible candidates for her replacement to the board, she slept for the better part of two weeks. Gradually, her energy and good disposition returned. Mostly the weight of not knowing her son's whereabouts, whether he was even alive, lifted. She hadn't realized how much that hole in her heart was affecting her, making her hide in work. She picked up her journal again and it was like seeing an old friend the way the words burst from her onto the paper. Unlike earlier days when she happened into memory and shut herself off, this time she tread in, even if it hurt, the words validating her, a true kind of reward.

But as time passed, Joe was putting her off and putting her off, and she was starting to recognize from the little he told her that Tom was actually quite sick, far beyond an illness of the body. Her initial reaction of going to pick him up and bring him home was melting into a more mature knowledge that understood how this was far more complicated than that. Moving too quickly could put him off for good. At least he was talking to Joe. But though Laura was resuming her old easygoing self, there was still a hardened rock inside her heart, one that longed for everything to be right again. And that rock would weigh her down until it was smashed into pieces so small she could blow them away.

One afternoon when she visited her sister, Peggy showed her another barrel of fabric she had just received from George's aunt in the States. They riffled through the barrel exclaiming at a particular piece of fabric or bit of lace until Peggy unearthed a hat. It had large round borders and flowers on one side. Peggy tried it on and paraded around the kitchen. She looked tired and drawn, but it was clear she was trying very hard to regain her self and rejoin life.

"Quite charming," laughed Laura.

The hat brought out Peggy's old enthusiasm. "We should make some hats. Wouldn't it be fun? And we could make coats and dresses to match. I mean, look at all this material. I like sewing for the family and some friends, but I think there are women out there who'd like a nice hat here or there. Who knows, maybe it could be a business!"

"That's an excellent idea, Peg. Let's go to town this weekend to check out the fabric shop, stock up on thread and interfacing, whatever extra we need. Sam or Robert will drive us."

Peggy stopped and looked at her quietly. Peg hardly ever looked like that, so still. It unnerved Laura. "I have to say something; I can't go on pretending it's not on my mind. But I'm so desperate to know about Tom," she said. "Can you tell me anything?"

Laura felt ashamed; she'd been selfishly absorbing the problems of her family as her own. Or perhaps she'd used this as a chance to show Peggy her place, not let her tread on Laura's role as mother. She was ashamed for having thought this way. Peggy and Tom had always had an extremely close bond, just as he'd had with his uncle. Laura could see in Peggy's eyes that she was hurting too. Laura said in nearly a murmur, "He didn't leave with a financial fortune, my prodigal son, you know, but he did leave with a fortune."

Peggy raised her arms in exasperation. "What on earth are you saying?"

"You, I, his father, George, God rest his soul, together we raised Tom right. We taught him to love and respect others and other people's property, to be an honest person and have integrity. He's a good boy who just got mixed up. I know he will straighten out. I know he will." In saying it, somehow, she knew despite whatever she and Tom had already been through and whatever difficult times lay ahead, that it was true.

"Did Joe call? Did he meet with Tom again?"

"Yes and no. Joe is evasive. He's not revealing too much about Tom's whereabouts." How selfish she'd been, denying Peggy her right to know what was happening. She'd told herself Peggy needed to be protected from pain, her soul still fragile from George's death. "I wish I could tell you more," she said, and meant it. "Listen, soon we'll need to go to Halifax. At some point Joe will break through to Tom, and then I need to be there. Or perhaps sooner. Will you come?"

Peggy beamed. "It would be my pleasure."

From then on, with their new sewing project to occupy them and keep them close, most days the two sisters chatted, hummed, sang and sewed.

One afternoon, Laura was feeling more doubt than usual, her faith in how things would turn out well waning. It was all so much waiting, hoping, and so much prayer, but to what end, she wondered. "Do you believe in destiny, Peggy?" she asked.

Peggy was threading a needle with one eye closed. "Destiny? Mmm, I don't know. I suppose so."

"Like, do you think it was my destiny to go to the convent? What if I had received my pension after Johnny died instead of so much later?"

Peggy swallowed hard. "You didn't know about it. None of us knew anything about it. Dooly only just happened to mention it to George when he heard you were coming home from the convent. And, and, well, you did say you made friends with the caretaker and his family. That's something. And," Peggy brightened, "you met Sam on your way back. So though it was a terrible hardship, maybe it was your destiny!"

"True, but still..."

Peggy put the needle down and clenched her jaw. "Why are you asking about this anyway, Laura? Do you believe it was my destiny not to be able to have children of my own? Or that George went off to war and returned a shell of the man he used to be and he turned to booze to drown his sorrows, or...or that now, I'm all alone?"

Laura wiped a tear. "I... I was just thinking, is all. Don't get all fired up."

Peggy plucked some fabric lying off to her side and began to idly fold it. "You just do the best you can. God takes care of the rest."

"Do you truly believe that?"

Peggy stopped, stared in space and slowly nodded," Yes, I suppose so."

The two sisters remained silent, both concentrating on their work. Then Laura laid her fabric down and sighed. "Do you ask the Good Lord for his blessings?"

"Me? All the time. You know what the Bible says, 'Ask and it will be given.'"

"Does it happen? Do you get what you ask for?"

Peggy eyed her sister and shrugged. "Jésus, Marie, Joseph, you ask too many questions. How about a cup of tea?"

Laura rose and stretched her arms. She smiled. "Sure." While Peggy was getting the tea, Laura realized she was feeling annoyed and didn't want to pursue this conversation any more. "Tell me again the story about the tombstone. Was it the first time you visited the cemetery after George's death?"

"Yes," said Peggy quietly. "It was exactly a year to the day of his passing, August 21st, 1961." She paused. "Already three years ago. I can hardly believe it." She looked back at her needle. "That day, I was feeling lonelier than ever, so I went for a walk and ended up at the top of the hill, overlooking the ocean. So many thoughts raced through my mind as I begged God to answer my prayers." Peggy slipped into memory easily like a stone into water.

"George's horrible death was a nightmare. I talked to God, demanded to know, 'Isn't it written,' I said, 'knock and it'll be open; ask and you'll receive; seek and ye shall find?' Well, God, I've been knocking, asking and seeking for the past year, still no answer. I've been calling, but it would appear the line is always busy! What am I to do?"

Laura smiled; her sister had a great sense of humour even when she was being serious. Peggy stopped to catch her breath then continued, "I looked around to see if anyone was watching, but not a soul was about, so I lifted my arms into the air and said, 'I have no one to turn to, no one with whom to share my life, and my prayers are not answered. Or am I praying for the wrong thing? I had the right thing. He wasn't perfect, but he was mine. And now he's gone.'"

She continued. "All around me, wild flowers danced in the soft breeze. Patches of white daisies fluttered about, intermingling with dandelions and clover, the round, bushy package of bulgy lavender petals that taste like mint, you remember, Laura, we used to eat them when we were small."

Laura sadly smiled and nodded, but Peggy didn't seem to notice. "Then, I got up and slowly walked away, stopping from time to time to gaze at the water. I heard the distinct sound of birds chirping, singing, taking turns, like they were answering each other. Without thinking, I bent down to pick a flower, then another, and still another, until I had a beautiful bouquet of flowers in my hand. I stopped, looked around, and noticed that the water was far away now. An eagle flew above. It soared high in the sky, so free and majestic."

Laura was amazed at the vivid description she was hearing. She'd heard this story before, but had never heard Peggy tell it in such a beautiful way.

Peggy sighed. "Then, I slowly made my way through the field, and as if a force were pulling me in the direction of his grave, I mustered the meager courage I had and went into the quiet cemetery. It was completely still there. I remembered where to go from the funeral, so I walked slowly towards the grave. Before I got to it, I saw, Lord forbid, the tombstone was gone. Of course I became frantic, looking all around, sure I'd gone to the wrong spot, but no, it was the right one, and someone had removed the headstone. Who in his right mind would do such a thing? There was only a big dark hole. No wind could've done that; the stone was massive, maybe five feet or more, well embedded in the ground. So I returned home, very confused. That same afternoon, I decided to pay the neighbours a visit, you know, in case they might have heard of something, since Esther pretty well knows everything that goes on in the village," Peggy snickered. "I got there and the old man was fidgeting in his shed while Esther was tending to her flowers."

"Imagine my surprise when I saw the stone spread out in front of the shed. I instantly recognized it as George's gravestone; you know, it has a rounded top with wider sides. At first, Esther was furious that I would insinuate such a thing, but I told her, 'I've just come from the cemetery and George's headstone has been removed, and that, my dear neighbour, is it!' Finally I convinced the old man to turn the stone around and sure enough, there was George's name engraved in bold letters."

Laura wiped her tears from laughter and grief both, vividly visualizing her sister, handbag on her arm, demanding the stone be turned.

"I said, 'What nerve! What on earth possessed you to do such a thing?! Make sure you return my husband's tombstone to its proper place, now!' Poor Esther kept apologizing for the mishap; she really didn't seem to know what her husband had done. She'd just been so happy to see him come home with the perfect-sized step. Well, he took it out, reluctantly, a caught thief."

Even though Laura had heard this story probably a handful of times, she was freshly aghast. She shook her head. "And he didn't apologize."

"No, not a single word. He must have thought I would never visit the cemetery. I turned on my heels and headed home. Walking fast and steady. I was fuming. All of a sudden, my purse flew off my arm and landed in the ditch, and everything from in it shot out all over the road. Oh, did I curse as I tried to recover everything, and then I just started to cry. And, God help me, I thought for sure, I heard George's good wholehearted laugh!"

Once more, Laura wiped her eyes. Between giggles, she asked, "Did Esther's husband return the stone to its proper place?"

"Yes, I checked the next day. But not as sturdily as it should've been." She added sadly, "Imagine, Laura, George was born in 1912 and died in '61. Hardly an old man at 49. Not unlike Johnny..."

Laura didn't want to talk about that. "Quite a story, Peggy. You must remember to tell the boys, especially Tom when we see him. I can almost hear him laugh!"

"Ah, that boy," said Peggy. "You should march out to Halifax and drag him back by his scruff."

"Destiny, fate, prayer. I want these things to mean something, but I keep waiting. The old me would've believed that God takes care of all the little birds in the sky, so he'll take care of my Tom, but I don't believe that anymore. What about the birds that fly into a car's windshield, or are captured and devoured by cats, or perish from lack of food and cold."

Peggy smiled gently and took her sister's hand in hers. "I somehow remember your telling me not long ago that praying for happiness might just bring about what you need to feel stronger. What if we tried it now?"

Laura looked at her sister whose face had softened just by the mention of God's indulgence. She couldn't really understand how Peggy could feel so solid in her faith now. She'd been so shaken after George was so violently taken from her. It was as if she'd forgotten all about that.

All along Laura had tried to be the same, so level-headed, so patient about her son's illness and disappearance. She'd tried to hold on to her faith, tried ardently to believe even when she was being tested. But lately, it was as if she couldn't hold on any more. When she prayed, her voice didn't sound like hers, and rather than find solace, she felt heavy and brittle, like a rusted over knife.

* * * * * *

Tom kept Joe at an arm's length because he knew he was not strong enough to even begin to recuperate, to rejoin the healthy world. One weekend he drank so much he got himself arrested and spent the night in jail. Alone in his cell, painfully sobered up, he felt desperately empty. Joe was so solid, so driven; someday soon he'd have his own firm, a wife, a house. He knew where he was in the world and the world responded to him in kind; Ben had always known what he loved and would some day make a success of those passions. Yet for himself, Tom believed he had nothing. He'd joked and deflected and drank to hide that he didn't have direction. Drinking became his direction. All he'd had was his family, who loved him. And he didn't know how to repay them by showing how he'd fit into the world, so he left. Alone in his cell, tears dripped down his face onto his dirty pants. He'd failed everyone.

Upon his release the next morning, sunshine poured over his face. His throat was parched and his body ached for a drink. His first response was to check his pockets to see how much money he had for booze. When his fingers hit the warm metal, he paused. But rather than try to scrounge up the difference to buy whatever he could get, he pulled out the dime and turned to the nearest phone booth. He didn't know why, but the piece of paper Joe had written his phone number on was in his pocket too.

"Hello?" Tom hesitated. It was a woman. He considered hanging up. "Hello, is anyone there?"

"Sorry, is Joe at home?

The landlady sighed. "Hold on, I'll check." She leaned away from the receiver. "Joe! Call for you!"

He heard shoes pounding down the stairs. "Tom, is that you? I was just getting ready to leave. Where are you? How've you been?" His relieved voice turned angry. "Damn it, Tom, I've been lying to Mother telling her you're OK, but you could've been dead for all I knew."

Tom held the receiver and breathed into it. Joe said, "Tom, I'm sorry. Are you still there? Please?"

Tom's voice cracked. "Joe, I think I was dead. But I'm alive now. Can you pick me up?"

Within a few hours, the two brothers walked into Joe's boarding house. Joe brewed a fresh pot of tea, and they sat at the table, grateful no one else was home so they could have the kitchen to themselves.

Joe looked inquisitively at his brother but said nothing. The clock on the wall ticked.

Tom saw the state of his fingernails, how rough his hands were. He took them off the table. "It's a long story," he said. "It could take all day and night."

"I called into work and said I'm not coming. Take all the time you need." Joe laughed a little.

Tom sighed and stared at the scarred wood of the table. His body was hunched like a knot. "Do you remember how we enjoyed drinking Uncle George's homemade brew?"

"Of course. I know you really loved it. But I don't understand, I drank as well, and I didn't get hooked."

Tom nodded. "What you mean is you drank too but you didn't become a bum."

"That's not what I mean."

"It's true. Look at Mother, for instance. We all lived in the same house, ate the same food, drank the same milk, but we never contracted TB the way she did; so this is the same: I drank, you drank, and here you are, successful, a nice place to live, and here I am flat broke, no job, no place to stay." Tom frowned as he carefully put the ashes of his cigarette in the cuff of his trouser leg. He didn't want to say how he'd been kicked out of his room.

"Tom, you can stay with me, find a job, get back on your feet. I know my landlady won't mind so long as I pay my rent on time. Truth be told, I thought if I was lucky, you'd be staying with me, so I already got an extra cot from her and put it in my room."

Tom reddened, ashamed. "You know, we drank most of the time, you know, me and Uncle George. I had no idea what I wanted to do with the rest of my life. How is one supposed to know when you're sixteen, seventeen years old? Why did you know?" He threw up his hands and passed his fingers through his hair. Then he continued, bowing his head, "I hitchhiked my way to Halifax with Bill, stayed with some of his relatives for a while, got a job selling shoes and finally made enough to rent a room."

"I can't believe you were here the whole time and we never ran into each other," said Joe softly.

"But Joe, it was like I was being chased," said Tom, his eyes red and veined. They were wide open now, looking all over, but clearly not seeing anything.

"What do you mean?" Joe was having a hard time following Tom. He leaned forward.

"Well, you always had a vision, a dream, talking about one day building things, big, important things like buildings and bridges, and Ben was so in love with nature that half the time he was in his own world..." he paused. The old anger at his brother rose in his throat. He wanted to know and didn't want to know at the same time. "How is Ben doing?"

"He wants to be a plant science technician. He has applied at the Agricultural College in Truro."

"Mmm..." Tom drifted off.

"Tom?"

Tom began crying. "Sam let you borrow his car but never once offered it to me!"

"What?" Joe was trying to make sense out of his brother's roller-coaster conversation. "Why didn't you just ask him? That's what I did!"

"But I thought-"

"What?"

"I really missed you when you left, and..."

Joe sadly looked at his brother. "And Uncle George."

At the sound of his uncle's name, Tom let go and cried like a baby. Joe's lips quivered as he wiped away a few tears of his own. He checked his pockets for a handkerchief and finding none, he went to a drawer and brought out kitchen towels. He poured more tea and searched the cupboards for something to eat, coming up with a box of macaroons. The brothers snacked in silence.

After a while, Joe asked, "What was your dream as a boy?"

"I wanted my own car," said Tom numbly.

Together, they said, "Sleek-convertible-Thunderbird!"

Tom laughed so hard he dissolved into a coughing fit. The laughter in his body was rusty. And happy. In that instant, Joe suddenly realized how much he had missed his brother. His real brother, not this damaged mess of a person in front of him.

"Some dream," he said. "After the shoe job, I waited on tables in a bar, made some new friends and drank, drank all the time, loved it. But then I lost my job, started to help an old man in the shoeshine business. Earned enough to buy booze, a meal and rent a room."

Joe was shocked. "But why didn't you call me?"

Tom shook his head and whispered, "I spent last night in jail."

"Last night!"

"Yes. One good thing, no, two good things about jail: I got a hot wash and shave and a good meal. Got out this morning. And then there was the strangest thing..." Tom drifted off again.

"What do you mean?"

"Well, when I left the police station, I stopped just to breathe in some fresh air, when I noticed the shoeshine man standing next to a phone booth. He waved at me like he always did, smiling the way he always did with his big white teeth and twinkling eyes. So I rushed down the steps to meet him, but off to the side a flock of birds took flight, so I turned to see them rise into the sky," Tom was fluttering his hands in the air while he talked, lost in memory, "and when I arrived at the booth, he was gone...as if he had vanished into thin air...like the birds. I was baffled. Then, I found a dime in my pocket. Just one dime. And I called you."

"Maybe he was in a hurry to go somewhere?" Joe offered.

"He died last winter." Tom walked into the tiny living room and stood by the window, staring into space. When Joe joined him, he turned around to accept the cup he offered. "Did you miss Father, after he died?"

Joe nodded.

"I don't remember much," said Tom.

After a minute of silence, Joe asked gently, "Have you thought of AA?"

"What's that?" Joe knew from Tom's voice that he knew exactly what it was.

"Alcoholic's Anonymous, Tom."

Tom pretended not to hear and turned back to the window. "One morning when I arrived at our usual place, the bench was empty, which was strange since he was always there before me, as if he never went home. When I realized he wasn't coming, I went to his place. He'd died in the night." Tom placed his cup on the table beside him and slumped heavily into the sofa.

"It sounds like he was a good man."

"He was. I guess I loved him. With him, I felt like I could finally get on the right path. When he died I was all alone again."

"So what are you going to do now?"

Tom turned around. "I want to return home, but I can't bear to face Mother and Aunt Peggy..." He shuddered then continued. "I do want to make things right, get back on track. How is Rosalie? Is she still going to the orphanage?"

"It's an Activity Centre now, for the handicapped, a type of learning centre. Mother did that all herself. And Rosalie is happy there."

Tom frowned. "I remember Mother and Sam had really wanted to get that off the ground. Actually, that's all they talked about. Mother got so involved, she even seemed to forget about Aunt Peggy, and Aunt Peggy needed her."

"I guess we all have our ways of coping, Tom."

Tom didn't seem to hear him. "You know she even convinced me to volunteer at the Centre every Monday night with Ben."

"And you did it?"

"Yes, but I felt so sorry for those kids although they seemed to be happy, all the time singing bible songs. I was never comfortable there. And..." he paused, not wanting to talk about how he felt about his brother. He knew his feelings were not reasonable, that his blame was only grief looking for a home.

"Mother quit, finally. It was too much. And she realized she was neglecting things."

"Is she alright?"

"Yes, she's fine."

Joe rose from his chair. "How about if I call her, say you're alright?"

Tom nodded but said nothing. He sat numbly by while Joe phoned Laura. It being the end of the workday, some of the other boys who lived in the house began to filter in. Not yet ready to make conversation, when Joe hung up, Tom quietly asked if he could borrow some clothes. Joe took him to his room, and there, he laid down for a long solid sleep like he hadn't had in a very long time.

When he emerged and came slowly downstairs and into the kitchen, the sun was just setting. He saw Joe standing in the dim light, making sandwiches. "We missed dinner, but is this OK?"

asked Joe. Tom nodded, his heart nearly bursting open with gratitude. They ate and caught up, but Tom's head was pounding and
he returned to the bedroom to sleep again, this time fitfully. In the
middle of the night, he got up for some water. He came down to
the kitchen and automatically opened the fridge door. His eyes fell
on a bottle of beer. Breaking into a sweat, he stood there, staring
at the bottle. The light from the fridge penetrated his head, and
he slammed the door. One drink and it'd be all over. Quickly, he
swallowed the water from his glass and returned upstairs to bed, a
familiar melody humming in his head. He sat in the dark and took
several deep breaths, pleased when he felt dizzy and light. He had
controlled himself.

When Joe sat up in bed the next morning, Tom was already
awake, the bedding he'd used folded on top of his cot. "Tell me more
about this AA program, Joe."

Joe yawned. "Well, I'm not sure how it goes, but I've heard the
guys at work mention something. They probably have a group in
Antigonish; Sam would be able to find out, I'm sure."

Tom hardly heard a word his brother was saying. Instead, he
thought of his mother and said, "Bet she never expected to have an
alcoholic son." It was the first time he had referred to himself as an
alcoholic. He knew he had to say it to begin to fight against it.

Joe could see his brother was going to be in for a long, hard fight,
but it was clear Tom felt stronger just having Joe by his side. "What
do you say to us getting cleaned up and going to get you a job?"

Tom looked skeptical but his eyes had hope in them. "Really?"

"They're always looking for labourers on the construction sites.
Feel like hefting some weight?"

Tom laughed. He felt great. "I'm sure my muscles will go into
shock, but I'd love to."

On their way down, freshly washed and ready for whatever
life would bring next, they passed Ned and Brian, two of the five
guys who lived in the house, and Tom shook their hands. Then in
the kitchen the landlady was tidying up, and they greeted her so
warmly, asking her so graciously and with such flattery whether

Tom could stay a while, she had to laugh. "As long as there's no tomfoolery, Tom, you stay as long as you like."

Neither brother said it, but they both knew things were going to be OK.

* * * * * *

That evening, as Joe and Tom were making plans to come see their mother, Laura and Sam were relaxing in the living room. Sam had taken up the habit of smoking a pipe and Laura watched him as he carefully fiddled with it, turning it this way, that way, almost caressing it. She loved the smell on him, in his sweaters.

She stood and kissed him on the forehead. "We should pack. Rosalie already has her bag by the front door. The boys will understand. I just can't stay away any longer. There's having patience, and then there's the impossible."

"Laura, don't get your hopes up," he said, looking into her eyes. He knew she was now strong enough to handle many things, but seeing her son in bad condition, or worse, having him refuse her, could cause terrible harm. The phone rang and she broke away to answer it. "Yes, I accept," she said breathlessly. "Joe? Is that you?"

"I have good news, Mother! I talked to Tom, and actually, he's here, with me."

Laura sat down.

"Mother, are you there?"

"Yes, yes, I'm here," she whispered, gripping the receiver with one hand and resting the other against her chest. "May I speak with him?"

At the other end, Joe looked at Tom and pointed at the receiver, but Tom shook his head. "Uh, he's in the bathroom."

"Well, tell him we're coming up this weekend. We can't wait to see you both." When Laura returned to sit by Sam, she felt numb.

Sam looked at her, "You're pale. What's wrong?"

"It's Tom."

Sam put his pipe down. "Tom was calling?"

"No, it was Joe. Tom is staying with him. I told him we'll be there this weekend. Oh, I must call Peggy!" Laura ran back to the phone. Overjoyed, Peggy exclaimed, "Wonderful! Our prayers have been answered. What time do we leave?"

"After school, on Friday. But aren't you feeling well? Your voice sounds hoarse."

"It's nothing, I'm sure it's nothing. I'm just so excited!"

But when Friday came, Peggy phoned. She could barely move. She'd be fine alone, she assured Laura, but she shouldn't go to Halifax, expose them all to whatever she had. Through her cough, weak voice and sniffles, Laura heard how devastated her sister was.

"I'll report back, every moment," said Laura kindly. She hung up and quickly put together a basket for Peggy that Agnes would take over later. The family then packed up the car and Sam, Laura, Rosalie and Ben piled in and made the few hours' journey. Once they arrived in the big city, Sam stopped first to check in at the hotel then jumped back into the car to drive to Joe's boarding house.

Laura clutched Sam's hand. "It'll be fine, honey. Try to relax." He located the house and found a parking spot nearby. "Come on, Rosalie, let's go see Joe and Tom!"

Rosalie ran up the steps and pounded on the door. As soon as Joe opened it, she jumped into his arms, then twisted out of his embrace and threw herself into Tom. "Hello, step-brothers! Rosalie...happy!"

As Joe hugged the little one and ruffled Ben's hair, he said happily, "Hello, Mother, Sam. Come on in! What took you so long? Rosalie, did you drive?" he asked teasingly. Laura and Sam stood in the doorway. Laura was relieved to see Joe looked well, healthy, firm in the jaw like his father. She glanced away from him to her middle son. Her heart broke into pieces at the sight of him, with his long hair, so very thin, and looking as uncomfortable as at a job interview. She noticed Ben hung back and he didn't approach his brother, but she didn't mention it.

The little one chuckled. "Tom, when you home, you teach me! Rosalie wants to...drive."

"What have I started?" Joe rolled his eyes. Everyone laughed, the tension released, and Laura moved toward Tom. She didn't try to hug him or take his hand, but she stood close and let her body just be next to his, hopefully a comfort to them both.

The next morning, Joe proudly took his family to his work site. Tom hung back, still not quite sure how to react. Laura concentrated on asking Joe about his courses and his work and refrained from questioning Tom, nearly biting her tongue against saying anything that could sound like lecturing or scolding, though she was plenty angry and burning with questions. It seemed only Rosalie with her easy, childish innocence, could draw him out. She even got him to smile a few times.

By early afternoon, Sam, Laura and Rosalie decided to let the boys have some breathing room and visited Sam's cousin. On the way to the car, Laura murmured to Sam, "So what do you think?"

"Well, he's somewhat dull and quiet, which is understandable. I mean, we haven't seen him in a long time. I think he'll come around; just give him time," said Sam softly.

They decided to leave their cares for a while and had a very nice visit with Sam's cousin, who served them a full afternoon tea with little sandwiches, pots of cream and strawberries. Rosalie was in heaven with all the miniature food. That night, they went to the theatre. Laura marveled at the traffic and Sam laughed. "You get used to it," he said. By the time they reached their hotel room late that evening, Laura was spent. "Did Joe say there was a parade tomorrow?"

"Yes, so after mass, why don't you rest; I'll take Rosalie and the boys to the parade and afterwards, we'll go home."

"Thanks, Sam." Laura's head was already on her pillow. "Do you think Tom will come back with us?"

Sam knew without a doubt that Tom would not, but he didn't want to be so blunt. "Oh, well, maybe it's actually best he stay with Joe for a while, get his footing, and when he's ready to come home, we'll let him tell us. I don't think it'll be long. I could see in the way he was looking at all of us, mostly you and Rosalie, that he was homesick as anything." Laura smiled and closed her eyes.

"And I thought we could stop briefly in Truro on our way home, see an old friend of mine at the Agricultural College and speak to him about Ben. What do you say?"

"I say that's a wonderful idea. Our family is being tested, but in the end, we are all strong as giants. Did you see Rosalie's face when they brought out those tiny sandwiches? I wish I could have had a picture."

Sam smiled. "I have a story for you. I think it was 1958, the streets were lined with people from all over, and so many doctors."

"What was the occasion?"

"Princess Margaret was visiting the city."

"It must have been grand!" dreamed Laura.

"It was, but do you remember the doctor from Truro?"

"I'll never forget."

"He told me how a woman from a small village in Cape Breton had travelled all the way to Halifax with her six-month-old baby girl to see a doctor at the children's hospital. To get here, she boarded the mail truck to Inverness, then took the train."

"How brave!"

"Not unlike you," added Sam. "Anyway the little girl couldn't even hold her head up, such a tiny bundle. In any case, it was a hot day in July, and by the time they arrived in the city, the baby had developed a rash all over her body. A relative rushed them to the hospital where a young intern turned them away, fearing the baby might have the measles."

"That's ridiculous!"

"I know. Most of the doctors were watching the parade, trying to catch a glimpse of Princess Margaret. So, her relative telephoned his family doctor who stopped by that same evening. Turned out to be only a heat rash. He made an appointment with a pediatrician the very next day."

"And?"

Sam smiled, sorrow and joy in his face both. "The little baby girl had Down's syndrome like Rosalie. What was most amazing though, he said, was the mother's reaction. When he told her about her daughter's condition, she was happy, even excited that her beloved daughter would one day be able to walk, ride a tricycle and eventually be potty trained. She simply accepted the fact that her baby was different, slow in all areas. Full of hope, she left the doctor's office a happy woman."

Laura smiled and a tear slipped down her temple. What a sharp contrast from Rosalie's grandmother. She wondered what would have happened to her if that woman had accepted the little one as she was. How Sam and Abby's lives would have been forever altered. And hers.

* * * * * *

A few weeks later by the end of September, Tom called of his own volition. "Joe is driving me home after work, this coming Friday. We'll be there for a late supper," he paused. "Is that alright with you?"

"Tom, it's far more than alright. I'll count the minutes until then."

In the days that followed, Laura dropped her usual relaxed pace, and prepared for Tom's homecoming with full vigor. She and Rosalie baked and decorated a beautiful chocolate cake, blew balloons, picked fresh flowers and had a beef stew on the stove and fresh bread on the counter by the time Friday night arrived.

The little one sat by the window. "When they coming, Laura-mama?"

"They should be here any-"

"Here! Laura-mama! Joe Tom here!" Jumping and clapping her hands, the little one threw open the front door and ran outside.

"Rosalie!" Joe ran to her and hugged her tightly. Then she looked at Tom, a few paces back. Suddenly shy, she grabbed hold of his hand and led him to the door where his mother and Sam stood. Just then, Ben appeared, took Tom's hand in his, looked him in the eye with worry then hugged him, hard. "Am I glad to see you!" he whispered. Tom took a step backward, but then he brought his hands up and hugged Ben in return.

During their embrace, Laura got another look at her son. She had expected to feel full of warmth and love, but at the sight of him, standing there as if he hadn't put her through such pain, she began to steam. Once Ben and Tom broke apart and began to walk into the house, Laura walked in front of Tom and stopped him. "Look at me," she said. She had never used such a tone with him, not since he was a young child and only then when he had been very naughty. "Thomas Joseph McPherson, look me in the eyes, now."

Everyone seemed to sense a storm coming and went carefully around the two into the house.

"Mother," he began, looking at the ground.

"What on earth were you thinking? Disappearing for over two years. Why would you do this to me? To the whole family? Do you have any idea-"

Laura was on the verge of exploding when Rosalie who had been holding Sam's hand, turned back and went to the mother and son, looked at them a minute with her soulful brown eyes, and said, "Tom, I happy happy happy!"

Laura paused, tears clogging her throat. She was grateful to the little one for her timing, or perhaps her awareness of the overwhelming feelings Laura was combating. She smiled and ruffled Rosalie's hair. "Let's all just go inside and have supper," she said quietly.

That night, Laura slept badly and came downstairs just after dawn to the welcome sight of a steaming pot of tea. Tom was already up, dressed, his long hair combed back. "Mother," he started, tears already in his eyes. "It feels so good to be home."

Laura didn't say anything. She took up a cup and poured some tea. The cup trembled in her hand. She felt Tom approach her from behind and she turned. He touched her shoulder and she put down her cup and threw her arms around him. They held one another for a very long time. "If you weren't so big, I'd put you over my knee and give you a spanking," she said. They both laughed, tears still on their faces. "Just wait until you have to explain yourself to your aunt."

"She's coming?"

"As soon as the sun's completely up, I fully expect your aunt to be standing on the porch, hollering to see you."

Laura and Tom dumped out their now cold tea, poured new cups and sat at the table. "Now tell me why," she said.

After an uncomfortable lapse of time, Tom finally told his story, the same he had related to Joe.

"I raised you boys alike, so why did you choose that road? Was it the middle-child syndrome?"

"You've been reading fancy books again, haven't you?" he teased her.

"But there could be some truth to the theory; some say when you have three kids, the middle one is envious of the oldest and jealous of the youngest."

Tom tried to scoff. "Hardly." But he looked at her and said, "Well, maybe there's some truth to it. I admired Joe. He was my hero. And Ben, well, who doesn't like Ben?" He didn't say anything about the anger he carried around for his brother, the blame he'd put on him for his uncle's death. "What can I say; the booze was just convenient. I liked it too much and lost my way: drinking, bad company, no passion of my own…and, and Uncle George." He swallowed hard then took a deep breath and shook his head. "My brothers have always known who they were and what they wanted to do, and I still don't know anything. But I want to start again, on the right track this time." He looked down. "I'm sorry. I know I've caused you a lot of suffering."

Laura nodded, new tears adding to the old. "Why don't you stay here for a while, or take your old room with Aunt Peggy, live life with your family again, and see how it goes."

Tom smiled. "I'd like that."

Laura rose from her chair, "OK. That's settled."

"What's settled?" Peggy was in the doorway of the kitchen. She put down her basket and purse, looked at Tom and her face lit up like a star. Her shriek of joy woke the entire house.

Life back at home was hard at first as Tom suffered from withdrawal symptoms. Rosalie entertained him on her drums when he was feeling up to it and Aunt Peggy kept him busy doing odd jobs around the house, saying it was high time she had a man at her beck and call. Tom felt a sense of pride in being able to help her just as he always had. But the feelings of isolation and loneliness were still with him, especially with memories of his uncle confronting him in every moment and he wasn't able to just drink through them.

Then one day, Tom fell back into drinking. In the next few weeks, he was hiding bottles throughout the house, too drunk to collect them and take them out. One night he drank so much he vomited blood. Peggy found him slumped on the bathroom floor and Sam brought him to the hospital. He didn't know whether he was dreaming or it was real, but while he was there, he received a visit from his old friend Bill.

"Long time no see, buddy," Tom said from his hospital bed. "Got a beer on you?" he whispered.

"No, Tom. I'm clean."

"What?"

Bill talked about how his addiction had nearly destroyed him and his own growing family, not unlike his own father. He mentioned the same Alcoholic Anonymous program Joe had. "Give me a call, Tom, any time, night or day." Before Bill left, he laid a book on Tom's bedside table. "Something to help pass the time," he said simply.

When Tom was discharged, he tried to stay off alcohol. But his addiction was deeply rooted, and once he allowed that first drink, he was helpless to all that followed. He was admitted to the hospital several times after his initial visit. His mother and Aunt Peggy walked on eggshells for they never knew when a drinking episode would occur. Each time he was hospitalized, his friend Bill visited him and often brought others with him. They talked about their experiences, mentioned how religion and spirituality got them through. Tom wasn't sold; like his mother, since his dad had died, he'd always gone to church because it was part of his life, but only in gesture, not in faith. He'd had too many things taken away from him for him to put his trust in some almighty God.

Yet with each passing hospitalization, Tom grew sicker and recovered slower. The last time he'd drunk so much he'd poisoned his blood. The doctor not unkindly suggested Tom should either say goodbye to his family or get serious help because his body probably wouldn't tolerate another similar episode. That was a swift kick of realization, imagining what that would do to his mother and aunt, and his brothers, so he decided to hunt down Bill's number. Bill was very receptive and when Tom was released, he brought him to his first AA meeting.

Tom decided to get over his skepticism, and slowly he began to accept the program. He read his friend's book, referred to as the "Big Book". When he first cracked it open, he was stunned it was first published in the late 1930's. He'd imagined he was the only weak link in the world, the only one who drowned his troubles in such a way. That night, he read it cover to cover, not eating or sleeping. He saw the sense in it and the freedom and security in giving himself over to a Superior Power. He left his jealousy and self-pity behind, and from that night, began to recover from within.

Tom's health and sense of self continually improved, and soon he took a job at the Activity Centre as a caretaker. He realized how he'd missed the carefree laughter of the children and felt a new kind of happiness invade his body on his return. His pleasant disposition and good humour soon won the hearts of the students and his colleagues alike. It was obvious that he cared about his work and enjoyed sharing a joke or two with the people around him.

One day, as they were putting away the dinner dishes, Laura said simply, "I'm really proud of you, Tom."

Tom blushed. Pleased to be back home, he felt he belonged, once again. In his life and in his own skin.

* * * * * *

In June of 1965, Ben completed his Grade 11 and was accepted into the plant and science program at the Agricultural College in Truro. Just as Joe had been, he was as excited and as eager to begin this new adventure, yet it broke his heart to leave Rosalie and live some 100 miles away from her. Over the years, she had grown very attached to him, and the feeling was mutual. When they arrived at the train station, through tears and sniffles, Rosalie whimpered, "You not forget me...Ben the bug...my best friend."

Ben swallowed hard. After a last farewell to his mother, Aunt Peggy and Rosalie, he climbed aboard the train, barely hearing Peggy hollering with her hands cupped around her mouth, "Make sure you eat breakfast, don't drink and smoke..."

From the distance, he saw Sam trying to comfort a tearful Rosalie. Deep down he knew it was the right decision for him to go, yet leaving hurt. He suddenly realized how his brothers must have felt when their mother had to leave them behind not once but twice.

After he settled in his seat, he closed his eyes, thinking of Rosalie. His feelings for her had always been complicated; he loved her like a child, yet they had such a strong bond. At times he wondered whether he loved her more. But of course he knew that could never be, so he banished such thoughts. He wiped away a tear as he stared out the window.

As soon as he was settled, as per his mother's instructions, he called her collect to tell her about the trip. Laura could detect a note of excitement in his voice and she felt a twinge of sadness. Her boy, her youngest son, was now a grown man. Rosalie tugged at Laura's sleeve, as she demanded to speak to Ben. "Ben! Miss you."

"I know Rosalie, me too. Remember to play your drums, practise every day and-"

"Ok, Ben, bye!"

And off she went. Laura took the receiver and laughed. "Can you hear that noise in the background?"

"Yes, Mother," he quietly answered.

"Now, we'll be listening to drums all day long! How could you!" his mother giggled.

"Have to go, love you."

"Love you too, Ben. Good luck tomorrow."

As he hung up, he again felt the bittersweet feeling of loss and enthusiasm happening at once.

Ben's greenhouse adventures with his Grandpa O'Brien proved to be a definite asset to his schooling. His knowledge and enthusiasm quickly impressed his peers and professors alike. He was different, yet completely approachable and soon won everyone's respect. He had also grown to be a handsome young man. He hid his natural curls under a baseball cap, had a round face with dimpled cheeks, and an easy smile. These casual good looks and gentle spirit caught the eye of a pretty girl named Bella. The two of them were just getting to know one another when Ben travelled home for Thanksgiving.

Sam met him at the bus station. "Hello, Ben! Good trip?"

"Yes, but where's Rosalie?"

"I came from work," smiled Sam, chuckling. "How do you like your course?"

Ben raved about the work he was doing. He rattled on until the car turned into the driveway where Rosalie and his mother were waiting at the gate. As soon as he saw her, his heart almost stopped. After countless hugs and kisses, she announced proficiently as if rehearsed, "Laura-mama and I go see doctor...have sore ear!"

He swallowed hard. "I'm sorry to hear that. My, Rosalie, your speech has improved since I've been gone."

"Laura-mama teach me. Good teacher, Laura-mama!"

Ben hugged her again to hide his tears and replied, his voice trembling, "Yes, Laura-mama, good teacher."

Rosalie, then added in a nonchalant manner. "Let's go, Laura-mama. Can't keep doctor waiting!"

Off she went, pulling Laura's hand towards the car. When they reached the vehicle, Laura turned around to wave. Noticing Ben's sad expression, she wondered what was troubling him. "It's good to have you home, Ben. We won't be long. There's food in the fridge."

After the initial shock of seeing Rosalie since his absence, Ben grabbed his fishing pole and blindly ran to the nearby stream. She had Downs, yet he'd always found her just perfect. Her chocolate brown eyes with their little slant, her small hands, her compassion and joy for life, her round, gentle face. But now, it was as if he were seeing her as others did for the first time in his life, and it scared and saddened him. He felt a door close on who they'd always been to each other, or what he'd thought they'd been.

Nonetheless he suddenly felt warm all over. He was no longer caught in a confused space of his love for her. He understood his love, and it was pure for her as the beautiful little sister she was. Nothing more was realistic. Wiping his tears on his sleeves, he rose from his spot and slowly returned to the house where he tended to the flowers in the greenhouse and lost himself in the blooms and earthy scents.

* * * * * *

A few days after Ben's graduation in June 1967, Laura and Sam were showing Rosalie how to make the snapdragons sing by pinching the red and pink blooms, the three of them having a good laugh in the warm sun, when the phone rang. Laura went inside to answer it and was gone only a minute before she called out, "Rosalie, it's for you!"

Rosalie dashed into the house, her pigtails flying, but after only a few moments, she burst from the house crying, ran to where Sam was plucking out weeds from the flower bed, and threw herself onto the gravel in a rage. Laura came out of the house after Rosalie. "What on earth-" started Sam, bending down to try and help his daughter.

Laura made her way to Sam. She went onto her toes and leaned into his ear to speak above the screams, "Ben and Bella are getting married." When she lowered herself back down, she was smiling sympathetically. "It's wonderful news, but... it seems our girl isn't taking it so well."

"Ben my boyfriend...He told me! He said so! Not fair!" wept Rosalie.

Sam put his hands on her shoulders to try and calm her. "But Rosalie, Ben is your step-brother. You cannot marry him."

"Why?" she demanded, tears and dirt streaking her face.

"Well, when Laura and I got married, Joe, Tom and Ben became your step-brothers. Since he is your brother, you can love him very much, but you can't marry him. And he will always love you like a sister. That's very special."

Rosalie paused and Laura and Sam looked at each other. They couldn't tell if she was calming down or gearing up for another round of wailing. Her face was stone serious, but her storm had passed. "OK, Father and Laura-mama… no more married!"

"That's a good girl. Ben will always be your very best friend. And Bella is very nice. Did you know she plays the guitar? I bet she would like you to play the drums with her," said Laura.

"Drums? Bella plays guitar?" Rosalie finally smiled, and Laura and Sam sighed, relief on both their faces.

"And they're going to live here with us for a while."

"Here in big house with Rosalie?" Her eyes went very big.

"Yes," said Sam, smoothing her hair. "And tomorrow, it's the beginning of the Highland Games and our Majesty, the Queen Mother, is officially opening the annual ceremonies."

Laura said, "Oh, of course. It's the centennial year, I can imagine the excitement. Come Rosalie, let's see which pretty dress you can wear."

"Ok-Laura-mama…first, Rosalie play!" Suddenly her old happy self again, Rosalie ran to fetch her drums.

Laura asked, "Speaking of which, Sam, did you raise the new flag?"

"You bet I did."

"It is lovely, isn't it? I really like the single red maple leaf in the center."

"I agree; it's high time we had a flag of our own." Sam smiled but he was distracted by his thoughts. He watched Rosalie's pigtails bobbing as she disappeared into the house.

Laura watched him. "What's wrong, Sam?"

He was staring at nothing, thinking. Then he said, "Wouldn't it be something if Rosalie were normal? Your boys- they'll probably all get married like Ben, have children. A complete circle, but…" he trailed off into his thoughts again.

Laura hugged him, then pulled back to face him. She took his hands in hers. "The circle is complete, Sam. It's the way it should be.

It's the way it is." She broke into a smile. "We're fine. Just fine. And," Laura paused as Rosalie burst out of the house, her face alight with pure joy at the thought of playing her drums, "so is she. And," she laughed, "thankfully so is our front door from all this exercise."

Sam couldn't help but laugh. He had to admit, joy was a marvelous thing to have. As usual, Laura was right. Rosalie would be just fine. Probably better than most. "I know you're right. The little one is a blessing," he said. And in the saying of it, he felt it then to be quite true.

June of 1967 also saw Joe graduate from his program a full-fledged architect-in-waiting. He decided he'd stay in Halifax; it suited him, the fresh air, the people. He liked his life there. He'd already been offered positions at two different firms and was feeling ready for the next step of his life.

The news of his little brother's engagement came just a day before he received his diploma, and he marveled at how the three brothers were starting the next phases of their lives at the same time. He felt proud of them, like a father might, but mostly, he thought, like an older brother should.

When August 5th came, bells rang all over Truro, Bella's hometown, and could be heard far away as the invited guests gathered. It was a small wedding with Joe and Tom as groomsmen. When Laura walked inside the church and saw her three boys standing in front of the altar, she squeezed her sister's hand. She didn't dare look at Peggy for fear of bursting into tears. In his two-piece suit, Ben stood erect, a broad smile on his face and his new glasses resting on his nose. Bella wore a pretty wedding dress, a matching hat and clutched a most colourful bouquet Ben had handpicked that very morning.

After the ceremony, as the wedding party and guests lingered on the steps in front of the church, Laura happened to look across the street. She saw something that made her break into a sweat. An older woman with a warm, sad smile stood holding the hand of a little girl, maybe four or five, who looked exactly like Laura did at that age. The resemblance had to be more than coincidence, she thought, but then she scoffed at herself. She was being silly. Lots of people had brown curls. Just the same, Laura fanned her face and looked around quickly for Sam. "What in tarnation is wrong?" he whispered. "You look terrible. Are you ill?"

Laura could only shake her head and point across the street, but the lady and the little girl had disappeared. "I saw... it was so odd," she whispered.

"Alright, why don't we take a small walk down the street to calm you down. Maybe you'll see what bothered you so much and can show it to me."

Laura didn't know how to explain it, but she was not bothered at all; rather, she felt the possibility of something exciting in that simple looking woman and that familiar little girl. But of course, she scolded herself again, she was being ridiculous. She was just excited by the day.

* * * * * *

Ben couldn't explain how it came to be that Rosalie accepted Bella so fully, but he was truly thrilled by their relationship. Once they moved into the house, Bella took the girl beneath her wing as if they were sisters. Plus the fact that Bella was a music teacher was a strong selling point for Rosalie. Ben and Bella had already decided if ever came a time when Laura and Sam couldn't care for Rosalie anymore, they would take her into their own care.

Much to Ben's chagrin, though he was affable and witty in job interviews, and certainly possessed the skills employers were looking for, there simply weren't any jobs at the moment. Finally just to take something, he accepted a job in the town's furniture store. Moving and repairing old furniture wasn't new to him as he'd always helped his mother with her dump excursions, and he didn't mind the work itself, but all throughout that summer while he was working long hours and extra shifts to save up a nest egg for himself and his new wife, he began thinking up ways he and Tom could resurrect their business. It would take some work and money; his Grandpa Robert and Louise had been traveling so much between Canada and France, where Louise had many relatives, Robert hadn't been able to keep up the old greenhouse. And Ben was working so much, he would arrive home quite late full of ideas, but he was too tired to put any of them into action. He barely had enough energy to catch up with Bella at the end of the day.

In September, Bella began her teaching career at the village school. One evening just before Christmas, she revealed the reason for her special glow. Ben was very happy, yet as Bella fell asleep next to him, he wondered how he would manage a new baby with everything so unsettled. They needed a place of their own, which would cost more money. And he worried about Rosalie's reaction; she was used to being the baby of the family. He finally fell into a troubled sleep.

The family, not knowing of Ben's apprehension, was thrilled Bella was expecting. And once Bella began showing and Rosalie wanted to know why, to Ben's relief, even Rosalie seemed pleased. "New friend for me!" she cried.

Ben took an additional weekend shift at work, and Bella, despite this joyous time in her life, would retreat to their bedroom to be alone. As time progressed, she became increasingly withdrawn.

After a few months, the young couple found a small apartment in town. Ben made sure it had two bedrooms so Rosalie could spend weekends with them if ever Laura and Sam were away. Laura had to confess to herself she was glad when they moved out. Bella seemed to transfer her devotion from Ben, who was never there for her, to Rosalie. She didn't know whether it was genuine, though, and whether Bella could sustain that intimate a friendship with the little one once the baby was born. She felt it was best they strike out on their own.

* * * * * *

Ever since Peggy and Laura had begun making hats, Peggy had been slowly filling orders for people around town: large colourful hats for Easter time, smaller and unique ones for summer wear, and contemporary pillbox styles for fall and winter. One day she looked around her living room, more sewing workshop than resting place, and realized she'd unintentionally fallen into a business. She had a stack of orders stuck onto a long pin and was getting backlogged. Her neck and shoulders had also begun aching either from age or bending over the sewing machine, so she decided it was time to hire an assistant.

She and Tom had a conversation about how she needed the extra space in the house. "No kidding, Aunt Peggy. With all these hats and materials, I'm afraid I might roll over in bed on top of a pincushion," he joked. "I can move home if it means you'll be prettying up the local ladies. It's a noble service," he said, bowing deeply. Peggy whacked him in the bum with a pillow and it was settled.

Peggy was a tough customer in interviews, scaring away many an inexperienced young thing, until one day a young woman named Charlotte knocked at her door. Peggy liked her straight away; she had a confident smile and had brought samples of her own work. Peggy hired her on the spot, and Charlotte put on the kettle for a long day.

Instantly, as if the town intuited that Peggy now had help, the phone began to ring, and two women showed up for fittings at the same time. Measuring tape around her neck and a pincushion wrapped to her wrist, Peggy motioned that the girl should jump right in. And she did as if she'd been doing it for years, "Good afternoon, Peggy's Sewing Shop at your service! Charlotte speaking. How may I help you?"

A few weeks after Charlotte had been working with Peggy, Laura sent Tom over to pick up some curtains Peg had whipped together for the baby's room, a surprise gift for Ben and Bella. Tom was gone for hours and finally came home long after supper had been cleaned up. He whistled, kissed his mother on the forehead, and took the stairs two at a time, forgetting all about eating.

Tom started finding all kinds of reasons to visit his aunt's sewing shop. Initially Peggy worried things weren't working out with him living at home and perhaps this was his way of wanting to move back in with her, but when she saw how he looked at Charlotte, she realized with great affection how his coming around had nothing to do with her.

Finally he called up the nerve enough to ask Charlotte out on a date, and soon the two were a steady couple. She even helped him move Ben and Bella into their new apartment and wallpaper the baby's room. Around her he felt whole and right. She accepted him as he was, laughed at his jokes, and warmed his spirit. He told her about his past and his struggle to stay sober and she told him she would be there for him no matter what. He believed her.

In late spring of 1968, just before Bella's due date, the young family decided to move back to the house so they could have the support of the family around them as they learned how to live with a newborn. When Bella and Ben's son was born, Laura was touched by this baby- her first grandson- in a deeper way than she's imagined. She'd been so busy battling the elements when she had her own sons, whether it was their poverty, the falling apart home, her health, and then Johnny's death, she hadn't been able to dwell on the feelings of complete body and soul wholeness a baby could give. She would spend hours holding him, brushing back his little waves of blond hair, marveling at how he was the product of such different worlds: Scottish, Irish, and French Acadian.

As soon as Joe received the news of the birth, he wanted to drop everything and take the first train home, but his work needed him, so he had to wait until the Friday afternoon train. When he arrived, he bustled in with his arms out. Laura laughed, happy to let Joe hold him. She sat back and watched as the same deep feelings of love bloomed in him that she'd had when she first held the baby.

The next afternoon, when they were quietly drinking tea and holding the sleeping baby while Ben was at work and Bella rested, Joe spoke into the quiet. "Mother, when you married Father, how did you know?"

Laura suspected she knew the reason he was asking, but he hadn't mentioned a special girl in his life since Delores, so she didn't say anything. "How did I know what?"

"How did you know he was the one you wanted to spend the rest of your life with?"

"Why do you ask?"

"You and Sam seem to have such a strong connection. But I've seen some of my friends' parents, and they don't appear as happy as you."

Laura was filled with a sudden, crushing love for her son. He had been such a ladies' man before he became consumed with school and work, always charming and handsome, but here he was, somberly wanting to make sure his feelings were the right ones. "So many ingredients are needed to make a marriage work, Joe. Commitment, devotion, respect for one another, but most of all, there needs to be love. If you love a girl, love her like you're ready to walk to China and back for her, and if she loves you the same way, then the seed is planted. Together you can overcome any obstacles life throws your way. In the end, there's no guarantee. You just have to follow your heart," she softly added. She recalled her earlier misgivings with Sam and how lonely their road sometimes was, the nagging doubt that his feelings for her were tainted with his need to have her help him raise Rosalie, and it might have also been that she craved a certain security for her family she knew he'd provide, but she didn't talk about any of this. She focused on the deeper heart of their love, and spoke from that. Smiling, she continued, "When I talked to Aunt Peggy about marrying Sam, that's what she told me: listen to your heart."

Joe stretched and stood. Laura couldn't help herself. "Is there someone you have in mind?"

"Maybe," he paused and bit a fingernail. "The thing is, I haven't seen her in six years, but-"

"And you still think about her. Delores, was it?"

He nodded and frowned. "But how do I follow my heart?"

"You'll just know. When the time is right."

He kissed his mother, then the baby, and left to head back to Halifax. All the way, he was lost in thought about Delores.

When baby Timothy was a month old, the family held a christening. Even Louise and Grandpa Robert returned for the occasion. In her letter, Louise hinted that it would do Robert some good to see his family.

Laura saw what Louise meant; Robert seemed not at all himself. He had a wan smile and seemed distracted. Louise talked to him about restoring the greenhouse, which in their absence, had fallen into disrepair, but his eyes glazed over, and he just patted her hand.

Sam watched him and was worried too. "Maybe he's just tired and needs to rest for a while," he said quietly to Laura. But deep down, Sam knew something was amiss. His father could still recite the names of all the prime ministers in order up to Pierre Elliot Trudeau yet when he held the car keys in his hands, he looked baffled.

After Peggy and Charlotte left, and Sam, Laura and Rosalie went to bed, Bella went upstairs to put the baby down, and Joe and Tom sat with Ben in the living room. They opened some of the containers of food from supper and began snacking. "Imagine," Joe smiled, "The youngest of us is first to be a father."

Ben smiled and tilted his head towards his brother. "What are you waiting for, Joe? You haven't found the right one yet? You're not queer, are you?" he blurted out.

Joe sputtered out some potato salad and laughed. "Very funny. No, I just can't seem to get Delores off my mind."

Ben interrupted, "But that was five or six years ago, wasn't it?"

"I know, but I really liked her." He thought a moment. "I loved her. But I was so preoccupied with my work and courses that I neglected her. It's a little funny that I was working two jobs so I could afford a ring, but before I had enough money, she left."

"Did she know about the ring?"

Joe's face fell. "It was to be a surprise."

"Where is she now?"

He shrugged. "Haven't seen her. She could be anywhere." He turned abruptly to Tom. "What's going on with you and Charlotte?"

Tom smiled and said nothing.

"Any wedding bells in the near future?"

"Maybe," Tom paused. "Actually, I'm not sure if I want to keep on working at the Centre. I'm kind of considering finishing my Grade 11 and even get my Grade 12." He glanced over at Joe. "Joe, forget about me for a minute. You look like you lost your best friend. Why don't you look for her? You're a pretty good detective; you found me, after all."

Joe cracked a smile. "You might be on to something," he said. But he didn't know if that was such a good idea. If she'd married or had children with someone else, he didn't know if he could stomach that.

"OK, well, now it's my turn to feel down," said Ben. "I'm sitting here, a father, and I'm looking at you two, knowing you remember our father, but I don't have a single memory. How am I supposed to be a father myself if I can't remember my own?" He looked then quite like his younger self, his still-round face surrounded by curls, his eyes soft and vulnerable.

Joe smiled. "I don't recall a lot, but this much I know: he was kind and funny. Very charming. And he loved to take us fishing whenever he had the chance, especially on Sundays. One time, Mom packed a picnic basket and bundled you up and off we went to the brook behind the house. Do you remember, Tom?"

Tom nodded and smiled. "A bit. But what I remember most was his spit."

"What?!"

Tom gestured with his hands. "What can I tell you; I can see it clearly right there," he pointed to his forehead. "He had this way of spitting so it'd go into the air in an upward curve and land almost every time exactly where he intended."

Ben and Joe bent over with laughter. "I loved skipping rocks on the lake with him; we'd practice whole afternoons," said Joe. "Oh, and the time he was so busy fishing, he let Ben float out into the current in his basket. He joked to Mother that you looked like a little Moses."

Ben widened his eyes. "Come on, you're not serious." The boys all laughed.

Joe nodded. "I am quite serious," he said.

Ben whispered softly, "I wish I'd known him."

Tom sighed. He looked hard at Ben. He knew he loved his brother, loved him with his whole heart. The old anger was still inside him, brewing like a waiting disease. It wasn't doing him any good to hold on to that darkness. He took a deep breath, and decided he needed to let go of all those irrational residual feelings. He shut his eyes and tears came. "He rocked you in his arms every night, Ben," he said quietly, his voice quaking. "I know you don't remember, but he's a big part of you, just the same." It was actually a relief to let go of his anger, so very misplaced. He'd always admired his brother for the same reasons he admired his uncle: steadfastly sticking with what he loved, his solidity, his resourcefulness.

From upstairs, baby Timothy began crying for his feeding and they heard Bella shush him and hum a lullaby. "I should go up and check on them," said Ben. It was quite late, so he got some blankets and pillows for his brothers and they all camped out in the living room. It almost felt like old times.

The next day the three brothers awoke early with cricks in their necks: Ben from being up with Bella while Timothy nursed, Tom and Joe from sleeping on a too-small sofa and arm chair, but each had a new resolve in his heart, as if the reunion of the three of them brought together their best, most heartfelt selves. Ben resolved to be the kind of father he knew his own had been and that he'd always wanted to be: fun, lively, and respectful of his son as a person. He wanted his son to always feel loved, something he had felt himself, but with his father dead so young, this feeling existed for him only in theory and left a small hole in his security where the rest of him was bathed in the warmth of his family.

Tom felt like he'd just left behind a long winter and spring had begun. That same morning at the Centre, he'd huddled by the phone and made some calls to learn how he could finish school. He found that he could take the GED exam to complete his high school education and still keep his job during the day. This was exactly what he was looking for, and once he solidified all the details, he burst into the kitchen after work where Laura was sitting at the table with a cup of tea listening to the radio. "Good news, Mother!"

"Tom, you nearly gave me a heart attack. What is it?" she laughed.

"Joe and I are both going on a drinking spree for the next two weeks. Sam is coming with us!"

Laura stood and turned up the radio. She sat back down and took a sip looking everywhere but at him. "Oh, come on, Mother. Have a heart. I was only joking," he said. She clicked off the radio and sat down again. He took her hands and told her about the GED program.

Her eyes filled with tears. "I have always known how capable you were," she said. "I'm so proud of you, Tom."

Once Joe was back in his regular routine in the city, he decided, as he'd done with Tom, that Sundays would become his day when he would search for Delores. He figured if he found her and she was married or not interested, he'd at least be able to move on.

One fall day, walking to work, he finally spotted her. She was in the park, holding a little girl's hand. His heart fell, for even though he'd prepared himself for this eventuality, he was deep within so hoping she'd held on to him as he had her. He ducked his head and picked up his pace.

To his side he heard a gentle and breathless, "Joe?"

Joe turned around and they locked eyes. He opened his mouth to greet her but his heart was stealing the air from his words. He stared into her warm blue eyes then looked down at the little girl.

"My daughter, Caroline. Honey, this is an old friend. His name is Joe."

"Hi, Joe," came a little voice so beautiful it ached inside him.

"Why don't you go play on the swings? I won't be far."

The little girl turned and ran to join the other children. Joe was hot and cold and above all his head was throbbing with confusion and possible joy. "Why... why does Caroline look exactly like my mother, Delores? Her curls, her dimples, am I crazy?"

Delores shook her head and smiled sadly. "No, she's yours, Joe."

They sat down on a park bench together, her warm body close to his, tears pooling up in his eyes. He was trembling. "But why…why didn't you tell me? When? I don't understand."

"You were just too busy for me. We hardly saw each other. When I returned home for my break just before the fall session, I discovered I was pregnant. I couldn't tell you; you didn't have time for me let alone a baby. It was just easier to do it on my own. I left the city and stayed with my aunt and uncle in Truro for a few months."

The hot tears in Joe's eyes dropped down his face. He stood and began to pace in front of the bench, unable to contain himself. He was filled with questions but his throat was too tight for him to speak.

"But it's all working out just fine," she said reassuringly. "I'm a nurse now, got a day position. The hardest times are behind me," she said. "And who knows. Maybe the best are yet to come," she said, her face reddening.

He sat down, pressing his jaw over and over. "I had a right to know," he said so low and quietly it was almost inaudible. He looked away and wiped his nose on his sleeve. He put his head down and held it in his hands. "Did you marry?" he asked. His voice was muffled.

"No."

"No one was right?" he slowly turned towards her.

She looked him in the eyes as squarely and straight as a poker. "No one but one man has ever been the one, Joe."

Joe began to tremble harder. He'd dreamt of such a moment, never believing it could come true. Delores put her hand on his thigh. Her hand, her fingers, that warmth on his body. He remembered them as if they were his own. He looked down and took both her hands in his. She held him as tightly as he held her. "I haven't been able to stop thinking about you, even after all these years. What about this other guy? Are you serious about him?" He swallowed hard.

"Yes." she answered.

Joe's stomach fell, but after a moment, he realized she meant him. "Oh, Delores. I've missed you," he whispered. He held her hands tightly, afraid if he loosened his grip even a bit, she would float off again. Finally he couldn't hold himself back any longer. He leaned in and kissed her, and in that kiss, it was the homecoming he'd so desperately wanted.

They whispered and held hands until Delores said gently, "I really should go get Caroline. Come with me?"

He didn't let go of her hand the whole time they walked.

"Did you finish your studies?"

"Yes, after six long years, I'm an architect."

"That's wonderful. Do you like it?"

"I do, but with the right person, or persons, by my side, I would be the happiest man on earth."

She squeezed his hand. "How about if we take this slowly? See how it goes?"

In that moment of wishing he could shout his joy from the top of the tallest building, that was the last thing he wanted, but of course he understood. "Will you tell Caroline I'm her father?"

"In time."

Joe didn't leave Delores and Caroline's side until the girl was in bed and Delores walked him out onto her porch and gave him the sweetest goodnight kiss he'd ever known. He went home and though it was after midnight, he was too full of excitement to keep everything all to himself, so he called his brother. "Tom? You won't believe it!"

"What on earth, Joe? You woke the whole house!"

"Shoot, I forgot what time it was. I ran into Delores today. I have to talk to you. You're not planning on coming to the city soon, are you?"

"Well, actually Charlotte mentioned something about going. She wants to check out some material for the sewing shop. We could meet then. It's great you saw her, but what's going on?"

"I'll tell you when we meet!" Joe hung up knowing he wouldn't sleep for a minute that night, and not minding one bit.

Tom and Charlotte reached the city late on the following Friday night. As they drove in, his nose against the window of the bus,

Tom saw the bright lights, the busy streets and the hasty shoppers and began to feel ill.

"Tom, you're sweating," whispered Charlotte. "What's wrong?"

He kept his eyes to the window but held her hand. "I'll be OK." He then turned and looked at her face, full of worry. "I just wish I could introduce you to my shoeshine man, is all." He'd forgotten how it might feel to be back where he had been his sickest and most bereft. The task of making amends, part of the AA mandate, was also now feeling very real. They pulled into the station. He took a deep breath and they disembarked. Joe was standing there, looking like he'd won a million dollars.

They made idle chitchat on their way to a nearby diner, where over cokes, Joe leaned in and said, "Delores and I are getting back together."

Tom rolled his eyes. "That's old news already. What's the rest of it? You've got something."

Joe laughed. "She's five, she's beautiful, and she looks exactly like mother."

It took Tom and Charlotte a second before Tom let go of a whoop. Some nearby diners looked over. "You have a daughter! But, how–"

"Let's go," said Joe, throwing some bills on the table. "You can meet your niece."

"Joe, I hate to be the sensible one here, but it's coming up on 10:00 p.m.; she's not in bed?" laughed Charlotte.

"Yes, Come on!"

Joe was so excited the other two couldn't help but laugh along with him as they sprinted through the now driving rain toward the truck. Joe drove too quickly to the house, skidding the truck around every corner.

When she opened the door, Tom was happy to see that Delores was bright and alert, pretty and wholesome looking just like Joe had described. "Tom, Charlotte, I'm so glad to finally meet you. Come in, come in."

Joe paused. "I really want to show them–"

She laughed. "I know. Come into the bedroom. You won't wake her. She's sound asleep."

They all crept in and looked at the sleeping little girl. "It's amazing! She does look just like Mother!" whispered Tom. "Have you told her yet?"

Joe shook his head. Delores noticed this and worried that Joe was keeping this very important new person in his life a secret for fear his mother would disapprove.

The next morning Tom, a list of addresses in his hand, went to repair broken fences. He was gone until lunchtime, and in those few hours, he found most of the people he wished to see. To some, he apologized for his behaviour; to others, he repaid past debts. Not everyone was so gracious about the past, but Tom embraced the difficult feelings, accepted this as part of life, and carried on. When he arrived back at Delores' flat to meet the others for lunch, he felt stronger, fuller, much more himself than he had in a long time. He was happy to stay home with Joe and eat egg salad sandwiches with Caroline while the ladies went out to get Charlotte's supplies for the sewing shop.

At the table, little Caroline wearing an oversized apron and a cute bonnet, came to the men with her notebook. "Hello, sir. Would you like a menu or will it be the usual?"

Tom laughed and Joe explained. "Her aunt, actually, Delores' Aunt Florence, waits on tables in a little restaurant down the block...she's a special woman. I hope you get a chance to meet her before you and Charlotte return home."

"I look forward to it," said Tom. He turned to Caroline. "The usual, please," he said grandly. "And a Pepsi. I feel like celebrating."

Out in town doing their shopping, Delores felt an instant closeness with Charlotte and told her part of her story. How her mother had cast her out for becoming pregnant out of wedlock. "All I remember her saying, with this big sneer on her face," said Delores shaking her head, "was 'how could you do this to me, Delores?'" She sighed. "Over and over, she said it. Ultimately, that was what made my father leave her, not long after I had Caroline. He said he couldn't bear being married to a woman who cared more about what the neighbours thought than her own daughter." Delores paused then smiled. "But my aunt accepted me, cared for me, as if I were hers. Quite like the way Peggy did with Joe, Tom and Ben, actually. Maybe that's why I already feel like I know her," she said shyly.

Charlotte shook her head. "You're a brave woman, Delores. And lucky that you had your aunt to help you. But I don't think my parents would be much better; I'm sure they'd ship me to Japan if I had a child out of wedlock." She paused and knitted her fingers together. "Actually they're not very happy about my situation with Tom. You know he's a recovering alcoholic."

"Tom is taking such strides, Charlotte. They'll come to love him. Or, I certainly hope that's the case."

Charlotte looked at Delores and felt respect. She was so upbeat, but Charlotte could see all the hardship she'd experienced in her eyes.

"So what's Aunt Peggy like?" Delores giggled. "It's funny that I haven't even met her and already I call her Aunt Peggy."

"And she'd love it! She really does care about the boys as if they were her own. But she's had her share of pain; she lost her husband a few years ago in a fire. Sometimes even nowadays she peeks out the window as if she's hoping to see him around the barn." Charlotte was quiet a moment then smiled. "Tom stayed with her for a while after the accident. Aunt Peggy says she now knows why her whites turned grey overnight. He did the wash!" She turned to Delores. "You'll love her."

"I'm sure I will." Both young ladies fell into silence.

Delores wanted to ask about their mother, Laura, but she held back. It was troubling to her that Joe hadn't shared this new big news in his life with her, but she didn't know what to do about that.

Joe knew it bothered Delores that he hadn't mentioned bringing her and his daughter home to Antigonish to meet his mother and the family. He didn't think Laura would disapprove necessarily; she'd seen too much in her life to judge, but he wasn't quite sure how to tell her. He could see he was hurting Delores, though, so he gave it some serious thought and came to understand he was trying to present himself as perfect, a finished product for his mother to see and be proud of, rather than as a person with flaws and mistakes. Once he realized that, he phoned home and said he was coming in for a visit.

On a Sunday morning, he brought Delores and Caroline home to Antigonish. Laura opened the door, and when she saw Delores, and a little girl beside her, she gasped. "I've seen her before," she whispered. She looked at Joe, then back at the girl. "Is she…"

"Mother, you remember Delores." Then he put his hands on the little girl's shoulders. "And this is our daughter, Caroline. She's five years-old."

Before Laura could snap from her reverie, Rosalie thundered past her and into Joe's arms. She broke away and extended her hand to Delores then she did the same to the little girl. Caroline wrapped her arms around her mother's waist, but Rosalie looked at Joe. "She play with Rosalie?" She bent down to Caroline. "Hi, girl, I have drums, come play, come play!"

"That you, Joe?" called Sam from the kitchen. He came out wiping his hands on a towel and hugged Joe, then shook hands with Delores. "And who is this?" he bent down to see the little girl, pausing a moment when the clues of her appearance added up. "Joe?"

"You girls go play," Joe said, and Caroline took Rosalie's hand and they ran into the house.

Once everyone was over the initial shock and thrill of seeing Joe with his long lost love, and his new daughter, they phoned Peggy and told her to drop everything. "I've got work stacked up to my ears," she protested. "Tell him to come over here."

"Peggy, you really should just get here as soon as possible," said Laura cryptically. Sure enough, half an hour later and breathing heavily, Peggy arrived, still wearing her apron. She was gleeful enough for all of them, shrieking and laughing, every bit her old self. "Oh, I wish your uncle could see you now, Joe," she said, roughing up his hair. He laughed and let her.

Later, when dinner was over, Joe, Delores and Caroline packed back into their truck and returned to Halifax. When the evening was quiet again, everyone off in his bed, Laura sat down in her usual spot by the window to admire the moon and its faithful companion, a bright star floating low in the sky.

"It's been quite a day," said Sam, massaging her shoulders. He laughed, "Caroline is certainly pretty as a picture."

Laura smiled. She felt so contented seeing Joe so happy. "And what did you think of Peggy's reaction? She didn't seem surprised as much as happy."

Sam shook his head. "Peggy is hard to read. When you assume she's going to explode, she's often meek as a lamb. I think she's getting mellow in her old age."

"What were you two laughing about when Tom and Charlotte were ready to drive her home?"

Sam chuckled, "She winked at me and whispered, 'Esther is going to have a field day with this bit of news.'"

Laura laughed. "That Esther; do you know, I think she and Peggy are a perfect pair. They keep each other on her toes!"

Chapter Thirteen
Life Goes On

When Joe and Delores and Tom and Charlotte announced their engagements within days of each other and decided it would be a double wedding, the whole family was flooded with joy.

Months before the wedding date, Peggy sat the brides down and presented the whole event from start to finish on a sheet of butcher paper, complete with headers, categories and sub-categories. Laura would handle the food, invitations and decorations, and Peggy would naturally take on all the sewing. Charlotte was touched by Peggy's devotion but still knowing the limits of Peggy's hands, she delicately tried to suggest she share in the sewing of the outfits. But Peggy wouldn't hear of it. "Charlotte," she said, her eyes filling up. "You're the closest thing I'll ever have to a daughter. Please, let me do this for you?" At this, Charlotte began to choke up and soon everyone was laughing and crying at the same time. In the end, the brides found themselves so busy and so over the moon in love, they were glad to not have to worry over details much more than agreeing to centerpieces or bouquets.

When the wedding day arrived on August 2, 1969, Laura ducked out of the hot, humid day and entered the beautiful cathedral. It was cool inside and radiated a sense of peace. She then flushed; at her own engagement, she'd been so adamant that she not marry Sam in such a place. But the cathedral was serene and elegant with its tall windows and overall feel of calm and hope.

Soon, when the guests finished filing in and the organ music began, she glanced at her two eldest sons standing in front of the altar. She felt full, as if her heart had no more room for happiness, seeing their radiant, proud smiles. Joe by the grace of the Lord had found his long lost love and his own child, and Tom had found love and stability for himself in a good woman who loved him through it all. Laura swelled seeing him and his brother in their two piece suits and ties, shoes gleaming in the light, and was so grateful Tom had consented to cutting off his long hair, though she realized now it wouldn't have mattered, long hair, short hair, hair curlers, beautiful hair, hair dryer, as long as he was happy.

She paused her word game as Charlotte walked down the aisle with her father and everyone stood. She felt so grateful Charlotte and Peggy had forged such a close relationship; they worked well together and now Charlotte would be something like a real daughter to her. She glanced at Peggy and knew from her beaming face and wet cheeks that her sister felt it had been worth the wait.

Then came Carl, Delores' father, with Delores on his arm. Her smile was as bright and beaming as Charlotte's. Both brides wore identical white silk gowns, with transparent long sleeves, tight waists, and flared skirts with layers of crinoline underneath. After they reached the altar, Carl took his place beside his ex-wife, who didn't even look at him, and his granddaughter. Carl hugged the girl to his side and bent down to kiss her hair. He cleared his throat then turned to scan the faces of the congregation. A ripple ran over his forehead as he looked again, slower this time.

Delores turned as well, her face also taut with concern, before she looked back at her father and shrugged. Delores' mother was oblivious to her daughter and ex-husband's worries; she was busy trying to discretely fluff her hair and adjust her suit. Delores' lip turned at seeing this. She took Joe's hand and held it tight.

The sermon was lovely and both couples carried themselves with bright, honest purpose, as if they knew they were entering into their whole lives in this moment. The mass over, they began their walk out into the sunshine, and Delores greeted her father first. "She's still not here is she?" she whispered worriedly into his ear.

He held her shoulders. "I'm sure something happened. Florence would never miss this. Never."

Tears formed in Delores' eyes as she looked imploringly at her father.

"I'll make some calls, see if anyone at the restaurant knows anything." Carl quickly slipped away into the rectory, in search of a telephone. He got Florence's boss on the phone and learned that it wasn't serious, but Delores' aunt had slipped and fallen- they weren't sure what had caused it- and broken her ankle. Carl was relieved but at the same time knew it would affect Delores' joy; Florence was nearly a mother to her, had nurtured her and her child, loved and cared for her where her own mother had cast her out.

When he came back outside, he caught his daughter's eye and gave her a thumbs-up. Later in a quiet moment, he explained what happened. Delores' whole face and spirit seemed to cloud over. "What is it, honey?"

"I feel so relieved it's not more serious..." she paused, "but now, well, this sounds so trite in light of things, but she was going to watch Caroline while Joe and I were on our honeymoon." She dropped her shoulders and smiled. "I told you it was silly. At least she'll be alright eventually. I was so worried!"

Carl took his daughter's chin in his hand. "Delores, you deserve the best darn honeymoon there ever was. I'll make sure you get it. Leave it to me."

Delores threw her arms around her father and wept into his neck, not just out of gratitude, but also as a release. Her aunt would be alright. And she'd get to go away with her husband. She felt very lucky in all ways.

After Joe and Delores returned home to Caroline, who declared she wanted to live with her grandfather forever because "he let me have ice cream *and* lemonade!" Joe looked around their little apartment and decided it was time to make a change. It was a Saturday, and as they finished up their lunch sandwiches, Joe slapped his thighs and stood. "Well, what do you say we go look for a new home! Come on, girls. We're going house hunting. This old apartment has outgrown us three."

Delores couldn't help but smile. "A backyard and swings would be nice," she said.

They picked up the real estate listings and drove to several houses, but nothing was too appealing. Delores was quiet on the drive home. "Want to run by the hospital to see Aunt Florence?" Joe asked.

Delores squeezed Joe's arm in response. They had a good quick visit then left with promises to Caroline of an ice cream cone. On their way out, Delores' father was whistling up the main walkway, a bouquet of flowers in hand.

"Hello, Dad," laughed Delores, raising one eyebrow at the roses.

He knelt down and hugged Caroline. "How's my favourite grand-daughter? Not married yet?" He pulled back and said quietly, "I miss having you around, you know."

The little girl rolled her eyes and grinned. "Me too," she whispered. She looked down at the beautiful blooms and her eyes widened. "Are those flowers for Auntie Florence?"

Carl blushed and nodded. "So how is she?"

Delores looked at Joe and grinned. "She's coming home tomorrow! I wish she would stay with us for a while, but she insists on returning to her apartment, says we don't need an old bag like her around. She also insists on taking Caroline after school like she's always done, but Mrs. Grunderson down the street has offered to take Caroline. She already cares for another little girl, so Caroline can have a playmate. I think that will be a good situation. And she needs her rest."

Carl opened his mouth as if to offer his help again, but Delores stopped him. "Dad, I'm sure you used up all your vacation days, and frankly," she grinned, "I think Aunt Florence will be glad for some adult company." She'd seen how her father had developed feelings for Florence and she couldn't have been any happier for them both.

"Is it that obvious?" he asked, laughing.

Delores just grinned.

The next day, Delores came to help her aunt home. Before Florence limped into the car, she paused and smelled the air. "I can't tell you how nice it is to be outside." She looked at her niece. "Delores, I feel terrible about not being able to take Caroline while you went on your honeymoon." Her voice was soft and clear, which was such a contrast to her tall, heavy-boned physique that she gently tried to maneuver into the front seat without banging her leg.

Delores' eyes teared up, but she blinked hard. Her aunt had taken her in when her mother threw her out, pregnant and alone. Nastiness ran in Delores' mother's family; Florence had been married to Delores' mother's equally nasty brother and had had to leave him for his abusive ways. Despite knowing her sister-in-law would likely cast her aside as well, Florence not only offered Delores a home, but she gave the girl a heart when she needed it most. Her generosity and selflessness were extraordinary. Here she was injured and all she was worried about was Delores. "Don't you concern yourself about anything. It all worked out for the best. Caroline had a great time with Dad. But enough about that; we should get you home. Are you in any pain?"

"No, but the itch from this cast is driving me crazy," Florence laughed, her smile as warm as ever, her cheery disposition unflagging.

At the apartment building, Florence couldn't put too much weight on her foot so she crawled up the stairs. "Auntie, this is ridiculous. I can't leave you here."

"You can and you will, my dear. Now brew us some tea, sit down and drink it, and then go home to your husband and child. You've organized enough. I promise I won't trip on a thing."

After Delores left, Florence had no sooner settled in her chair to relax when a knock woke her from her reverie. She limped to the door. "Carl! What a nice surprise. Come right in."

Delores' father fumbled with the door, some flowers and a box of chocolates. "Hello, Florence," he said softly. He looked deeply into her eyes. His daughter's pregnancy and Florence's love for her had opened his eyes to the possibility of true love. He'd been falling in love with her from afar for years, but he'd decided. On this day, finally, from the moment he entered Florence's tiny apartment, without speaking the words, he entered her life as a permanent resident.

Some months after the wedding, Peggy presented an additional gift to Charlotte and Tom. A new seniors' residence had just opened downtown with every amenity one could ask for. It was within her pensioner's budget and she'd had enough of caring for the house and land herself. "Imagine," she said, "they even change my light bulbs if they burn out! Now that's service!" Since she knew the couple was tired of renting and wanted to put down roots, she insisted they buy her home from her, and at a significantly lower monthly rate than they'd been paying in rent.

Peggy could see from Tom's delighted expression at her suggestion that he would find the rootedness he needed from living where he'd grown up for half of his life. They agreed happily and moved in as soon as Peggy was settled at the residence.

In Halifax, Joe and Delores continued their search for a house where they could raise Caroline and put down their own roots. Finally, they found it: a bungalow overlooking the harbour.

The cool autumn air was settling in when moving day came. After all the boxes and furniture were unloaded from the truck, Joe and Tom returned the truck and went to fetch something for dinner. While waiting for their husbands, Delores and Charlotte brought Caroline to play in a pile of leaves across the street from the house so they could admire it from afar.

"I'm just sorry Laura and Sam couldn't be here today," said Charlotte. She looked at the ground. "Laura says Sam hasn't been feeling well these days. He's probably run down. Keeps the schedule of three people."

Delores was so wrapped up in the excitement of the day, she didn't notice her sister-in-law's worried tone of voice. She had her eyes trained on the street, and when she noticed her husband and Tom, her face relaxed. "Well, Joe will have to phone to check in as soon as the dust settles. It's a pity he can't get away to visit Antigonish more often."

Checking in was all Joe could manage. Between work, the new house and its attendant repairs, and come Christmas time of 1969, Delores' pregnancy, he was happy and contented, but stretched too thin for time to return home.

* * * * * *

Laura would've liked to talk more with Joe, consult with him, and hear his input about how things were developing back in Antigonish with their family. Ben had changed so radically into a different person, almost overnight, Laura didn't know how to relate to him. The few times she'd approached him, he'd nearly snarled at her like a tiger. She hoped it was a phase, work stress, anything that was fixable. Every time Laura saw Bella, bursting with their second child, she looked glum rather than glow in the way an expectant mother normally did. Even when she played with Timothy, who was growing into a curious, funny little toddler, she seemed a bit lost. Bella assured Laura her health was fine, her life was fine, but she didn't smile much and at night, Laura suspected she cried more than was healthy for someone in her condition. Particularly since she knew Ben was coming home late and leaving for work before sunup.

One evening when Laura was over helping make dinner while Bella rested in the bedroom, Ben did come home, but rather than overhear pleasant conversation between the pair, Laura heard them arguing and Bella crying. "You're never home, always so busy. We have a lovely little boy and another on the way. Don't you care anymore?" she said between tears.

Without answering, he barged out of the apartment, banging the door behind him. The sky was full of stars and the moon shone brightly, yet he stumbled out into the dark, oblivious to the world around him. Ben had gotten lost; no one knew of the prison he felt he was inside, locked away. One child, another on the way, a job that made him feel dead inside. For a moment he looked up and his eyes glazed. He thought about the greenhouse, how alive he'd felt when he was in among the plants and flowers.

When he finally returned to the apartment, he slept on the sofa, depleted in every way but without any solution as to how to fix his situation.

More weeks like this followed: Ben saying less and less, drinking more and more and Bella saying nothing out of fear of him leaving her. One evening in early January after putting Timothy to bed, she bent over to pick up some puzzle pieces, and her water broke, contractions beginning in earnest. She grabbed the phone. "Charlotte? Please come. I'm in labour, and I'm all alone with Timothy."

Charlotte and Tom arrived in no time; Charlotte plucked a sleepy Timothy from his bed and carried him wrapped in blankets to the car. Tom drove the women to the hospital and dropped them off, letting Charlotte accompany Bella up to the maternity ward then he brought Timothy to Laura's for the night. Once Timothy was snuggled in the spare bed, Tom drove back to the hospital to see if he could find Ben. When he got upstairs, Charlotte was pacing in the waiting room. She hadn't heard from Ben at all.

On instinct, Tom got back in the car and raced to Ben's work. He knew his brother had been slipping into a quiet despair for some time. He hated that he recognized the signs in his brother that he'd seen in himself, but at least he could then interrupt the pattern before it got so bad.

His hunch was right. In the back room, his eyes in deep shadows by the single bulb hanging from the ceiling, Ben sat at the desk reeking of whisky, a pen idly in his fingers. Tom felt afraid; his brother looked so lost he didn't know if he'd be able to reach him after all. "Ben," he said gently, "your wife is in the hospital. She's having the baby."

Ben looked up at Tom, but his eyes were vacant. "A baby?" he repeated quietly.

Tom couldn't help himself. He'd been there and had wasted years of his life in a daze. Here now Ben was wasting the best things in his life, and his life was graced far more than most people's. Tom exploded. "What the hell is wrong with you? Go to her. She needs you." Tom looked at his watch. "It's not even close to visiting hours yet but I'm sure they'll let you in, for twenty minutes or so after the baby is born." He shook Ben. "It's your baby."

Ben looked absent, his eyes somewhere else. "Do you remember when we used to run our flower business, you and I?"

"Ben! Don't you want to go to the hospital? Another son or a daughter! Isn't that wonderful? Aren't you proud! Have a cigar! Drink some coffee. Get it together."

But Ben didn't even seem to hear Tom. "I wish we could..." His voice cracked. He pushed his chair back and put his head in his hands. Outside the wind was picking up and snow swirled against the windowpane. Normally Tom would look out at the storm and want to get home, but tonight he was filled with the idea that anything was possible: it was January 1970, the start of a new era, a new decade, and for himself and his brother, a new life.

Yet he looked at his brother and loss filled his core where the joy had been. Tom felt tears start in his own eyes. His brother seemed so broken. "Ben, what's the matter, for Christ's sake?"

"I don't ... I don't ...I feel like I've gotten lost, lost from everything I used to love, things that made me feel alive." Ben was crying openly now, his nose running. "This, all this," he gestured angrily at the workshop, "it pays the bills, it's a living, but it's dead, it's... not for me."

"What do you really want? What's your dream?"

"I want... to take over the flower business on a full time basis... do you think we could make it work, you and I...a landscaping service, laying sod, planting trees and flower gardens, providing customers with fresh flowers...a flower shop...like we used to but on a larger scale... I realize it's a new thing...might take a while to kick in. People are not used to this kind of service...I'm sure Sam can drum up some business to get us going..." Ben was given over to his dreams now. "How does it sound...Ben and Tom's Landscaping and Nursery Enterprises?"

Ben stared at him, as alert and awake as he'd been in a very long time. Tom shook his head. Then, looking very serious, he slapped his brother on his thin shoulder. "No, that wouldn't work at all. It has to read 'Tom and Ben's Landscaping and Nursery Enterprises.'"

Ben's eyes lit up and he leapt into the air. "You mean it? It would be like old times." He paused. "But you can't do it just for me."

Tom nodded, "Ben, we weren't very old when we ran our little flower affair, but I have to say, those were the best times ever." He smiled. "I think it could work." The brothers jubilantly shook hands. "Now are you ready to go to the hospital?" Ben whooped and the boys ran to the car.

When they arrived, they found Charlotte sitting in the waiting room with a huge smile. "Any news yet?" asked Ben as they burst in.

Charlotte smiled even bigger. "A brother for Tim!"

Ben sighed. He lifted his head up and closed his eyes. A few moments later, when Ben quietly entered the room, Bella was asleep, her face at peace. Ben sat at her bedside and broke down and cried. After a minute, she opened her eyes and saw Ben leaning on the blanket, his hands knotted tightly together. Through runny eyes, he touched her cheek. "He's beautiful and so are you," Ben whispered. "I'm so sorry. Bella, I'm so sorry." He stood and kissed her then wiped both of their tears away with his palm.

In the waiting room, Tom sat beside his wife and told her what happened.

"Is that what you really want?"

"You know, I enjoy working at the Activity Centre, mowing the grass, tending to the flowers, changing the landscape, even all the repairing and fixing," smiling, he continued, "Sometimes I feel like the shoeshine man. I whistle while I work and enjoy talking with the people around me. But," he paused, "I think it's time to move on."

"But this is a big step. Remember, you and Ben worked together before and you felt like his shadow. You said it was his project, not yours."

Tom nodded. "That's true, but this time, it's different. It'll be our project together. I really think it can work. And it feels like the absolute right thing to do."

Charlotte took Tom's hand. "Your mother is going to be so happy for you two. A new baby and a new family business, all at the start of a new decade. So many births at once."

* * * * * *

That night, as Laura was looking out for the moon, her thoughts were on her three sons. She held the rosary between her fingers, absently rubbing each pearl, not making any headway reciting the Hail Marys. When Sam came in from brushing his teeth, he gently took her knitted fingers apart and held them. "What's to worry about; the moon isn't in a good mood tonight? We have a new grandson," he smiled. "We're the richest people in the world."

She stared at him. "I know I should feel elated, but instead I can only focus on how I feel like I've let them down so many times. They stepped into dark places when I wasn't there for them."

"Laura, I might have come into parenting quite late in the game, but I do suspect the point of being a good parent is to give your children the tools they need to figure out the world for themselves, mistakes and all."

She shook her head. "But that's just it, Sam! I wasn't there for them to give them those tools when they needed me most. I was away at the convent or the san!" Then more quietly, she continued. "And I was so busy feeding my own ego as the director of the Activity Centre, I didn't even know how in trouble Tom was. I could have helped him."

"And yet here we are: the boys have families of their own, they have jobs, they're well adjusted."

Laura thought about Ben, how suddenly that afternoon he seemed enlivened and caring toward his wife in a way she hadn't seen from him in a long time. She hoped with her whole heart that he and Bella were on their way toward repair, toward a new life with their new little family.

Sam held her hands tighter. "Space is healthy for a growing person. And you're here now, to reap the reward of their work. Grandchildren!"

Laura had once left everything up to God. He had failed her time and again, but she knew Sam was right. "We are but grains of sand," she murmured. She wound her fingers into Sam's and they sat in quiet, staring out at the moonlight together.

* * * * * *

With Bella and the baby safely at home, Ben and Tom got to work on their business plan. First and foremost was getting collateral. Ben wrote to their grandfather in France, where he and Louise had been living for the past few years, but beyond that they didn't know where else to turn. They'd promised each other not to say anything to their mother and Sam until they knew their upcoming business was a sure thing.

Weeks passed and Tom was feeling despondent that they weren't moving more quickly. Then one afternoon as he arrived home from work, he noticed a package sitting on his doorstep. Tom looked around, puzzled. He eyed Esther through her kitchen window; she was doing dishes and didn't look up. She must have missed the delivery of the package or else he knew she'd have come running right over when he got home to tell him all about it.

He stared down at the box in his hands then carefully undid the heavy brown paper. It was a wooden box, edged in carved leaves quite like the one the shoeshine man used to carry around. Feeling weak, he sat down on the steps with the box in his lap. Finally, he slowly lifted the lid, and the smell of pine instantly reached his nostrils. Inside was a note: "Look inside before looking outside for the prize." A riddle. The shoeshine man always had a riddle for Tom, greeted him with one each morning. Tom shook his head and held the box. "What does it mean, what does it mean?" he muttered. "Nothing; it means nothing. Just a nonsensical note in a box is all." He laughed at himself. "Nonsensical" was a word he'd learned in school. Mother would like it too. The apple never did fall far from the tree, he figured.

Handling the box carefully he brought it into the house and set it on the window sill. With each day that passed, he struggled to find the answer to the riddle, something the shoeshine man would do. Tom could almost hear him laughing his gentle laugh.

All throughout that winter, as Tom's spirit flagged from his inability to start up the new business, Charlotte worried her husband might get so discouraged he would start drinking again. But he was stalwart in his determination; he never missed his weekly AA meetings, even one night with a fever he went, and his faith in God kept him sober.

Then one day in that spring of 1970, as he was planting the vegetable garden at the Centre, suddenly he knew. 'Inside' didn't mean the inside of the box, but his own insides, his heart, his faith, like the shoeshine man's gruff exterior: a bit repellent, with the corners of his old coat trailing on the ground, but once he spoke, those who heard him quickly looked past the outside and craved the inner peace he had on the inside. But what about the outside, then? Tom shook his head; this riddle was driving him crazy. It had been several months, and now he decided he couldn't think about it anymore or it would drive him mad. He moved the wooden box to a shelf in the closet and forgot about it.

Months later, as Charlotte was rummaging around in the closet looking for a blouse, she knocked her elbow into the box and it fell to the floor. It opened and revealed a secret compartment. As she bent down to retrieve the box, a large amount of cash spilled out and she screamed. The riddle had showed itself: 'Look inside before looking outside for the prize.' Ecstatic, she phoned the Activity Centre. "Tom? You'd best come home, right now!"

Days later, coincidentally, Tom received a letter in the mail from the attorney assigned to the shoeshine man's case after his passing. Apparently, the old man had no family and had named Tom his sole heir. Many wonderful memories raced through Tom, and he felt humbled and grateful. He smiled and shook his head. Who would have thought?

The money was more than enough to satisfy the bank, and as soon as Ben and Tom finalized the financial arrangements and signed the legal papers, they went to Sam to ask whether he'd let them use the old greenhouse and his fields for cutting sod. He was very happy to give his blessing, and the boys felt like they had the world at their backs when they visited their mother to tell her the good news. She was working on a puzzle at the kitchen table with Rosalie. They explained the project in detail until Laura's eyes glazed over. "Mother, you're daydreaming."

She smiled, caught, and playfully slapped Ben's hand. "Now you know where you got it from!" Secretly she'd been trying to stave off tears of joy.

Tom chuckled. "How strange life is. The answer was in front of me all this time. My shoeshine man was right. I just realized it when Ben proposed this scheme to me."

"What did he say that was so right?" asked Laura gently.

Tom's face grew peaceful, as if he were transported. "He said one should look within before looking without. It's so simple, but so true."

Seeing her son so moved, and feeling the strength of those simple words, Laura silently thanked God for his blessings, and the tears she'd been trying to hold back fell with abandon down her face. Without warning, Tom grabbed his mother by the hands and pulled her to her feet. He started dancing to the sound of the song that was coming from the little blue radio on the table.

His mother happily joined him while Rosalie jumped into Ben's arms. At that exact moment, Sam entered the room a bit hunched over. At the happy scene, he sat in a chair and his grayish pallor warmed. Laura smiled at him and continued to spin in circles with her sons.

* * * * * *

As soon as Robert O'Brien read Ben's letter, he convinced Louise to return to Canada for good. They had had a good life in France, but in the last years, he'd missed his family terribly. He was becoming increasingly disoriented, often thinking he needed to tuck Rosalie in or check something in his library. He'd been trying to hide these episodes from his wife, but when he finally confessed, she was quite happy to relocate close to his family.

On October 1, 1970, after the plane landed in Halifax, the O'Brien couple hired a taxi to drive them home to Antigonish. Louise tried to chat with her husband about all the wonderful things they could do with the family, but over the two and a half hour drive, Robert just gazed out at the landscape and dozed. He was asleep when they neared the town. Louise figured he must have been quite tired from the trip. They detoured to go along Main Street so she could pick up a few things, and while she dashed in, she left him to sleep in the car.

Louise was inside the store paying for her purchases, when she heard a sickening squeal of tires over the asphalt. Despite the warm day, she felt instantly cold all over and ran outside. Robert was lying on the road, lifeless like a doll, dark blood spilling out into a pool beneath his white hair, the pages of a newspaper scattered around him.

She rushed to her husband. The driver who had hit him was standing nearby, waving his arms. "He...he just appeared from nowhere!" he cried.

That evening, before ever reconnecting with his family, Robert died in the hospital. His homecoming with Louise had turned into a terrible nightmare. Sam was mute all the while at the hospital, and later during the wake.

After the funeral, Louise sat in the living room surrounded by her adopted family. She spoke softly. "His spells of confusion began to happen more often. He did his best to keep them from me, but I knew. He talked about tending to the garden, looking after you all. He repeatedly said, 'I want to go home...I want to go home,' but then soon thereafter he'd reassure me he was happy in France and wanted to stay."

Laura wrapped her arm around Louise's shoulders. She was shaking. "What am I going to do?" she said numbly. "I loved him with all my heart and soul. I don't want to sleep alone."

Everyone rubbed their misty eyes as Laura guided Louise into the guest room where she remained for the rest of the day. Laura was devastated for her own loss, but it was made so much worse seeing her friend; she had finally found the love of her life only to have it snatched away in an instant. Laura's grief stretched to Louise and was almost too painful to bear.

Eventually, Louise settled down in the cottage by the big house. As was her way, she worked hard to remain positive and peaceful. Having been married to a wonderful man such as Robert O'Brien was the best thing that had ever happened to her, she liked to say. Although she missed him terribly, she cherished her memories and appreciated the support offered by his family. It also helped her to step in and assist Laura. Now that Rosalie was getting older, she preferred to stay home some days from the centre and play on her own or help out around the house. Laura found she tired more easily these days and needed an afternoon nap and Louise was glad to entertain the little one. She came to look forward to her afternoons with Rosalie, just the two of them.

One afternoon, watching Rosalie insist that she could bake muffins by herself, dropping batter all over the place, Louise whispered to Laura, "There's nothing or no one like Rosalie to keep you on the right track."

Laura paused and her face fell. "She is special, isn't she?"

Louise looked hard at Laura. "What is it? What's the matter?"

"Well, Sam and I are not getting any younger. I sometimes think about what will happen to her when we're gone."

Louise nodded. "True. It's not something we ever used to think about as young people, is it?"

* * * * * *

By late summer of 1971, Sam came home from work, pulled off his tie, and announced, "My trip to Chéticamp is scheduled for the middle of September, the last work trip I'll ever do." He tickled Laura under the chin. "It's a week after my retirement party." He grinned. "Only I would retire then turn around and go on a work trip, but it has to be done. My last time," he said.

Laura didn't care when they went, she only let her heart leap at the names of her home villages. "To Chéticamp, by way of Inverness?" she asked excitedly.

Sam nodded.

"How long will we be gone?"

"About a week, and if you're up to it, we can maybe tour the Cabot Trail on our way back, stop in Baddeck, visit the Bell museum–"

"Don't say anymore! Rosalie, start packing. We're going to Cape Breton!"

Sam laughed. "I think we've still got some time," he said. "Even though I have to work while we're there, we'll make sure this is a proper holiday." He shook his head and frowned. "I should have pushed this trip to earlier," he said. "I really do work too much."

Laura patted his shoulder. She didn't comment on how exhausted he seemed, how ashen his skin had become. "I'm happy when you're happy, and that's all there is to it," she said simply, kissed his cheek, and went to make tea for Sam and quietly celebrate their upcoming trip. Home, she'd be going home. There was habit in thinking it, but it sounded curious to her ears, almost like she was convincing herself of something not quite accurate.

* * * * * *

Retirement was in the air; Peggy had also decided to hang up her needles and take a back seat to the new owner of the "Sew Sew Terrific Sewing Shop", Charlotte, who had moved the store to Main Street downtown. Peggy had developed advanced arthritis in her hands, and since she herself had taught Charlotte to do the more intricate needlework, she knew the business would be in good care. Despite being newly retired, however, Peggy, who viewed retirement differently than most, still came in every day punctually at 9:00 a.m. to answer the phone and consult with clients. Charlotte liked to tease Peggy that she just liked to hang around to chat with her clients, most of whom had over the years become friends.

When Laura and Rosalie arrived this time, Peggy waved them in while she finished up a call, and Charlotte greeted them with hugs and guided them into the sewing room. She was wearing a measuring tape around her neck and a pincushion around her wrist just like Peggy always had.

"I love your accessories! Is it a new style?" teased Laura.

"It's your sister's invention," winked Charlotte.

"I've come to see about a new outfit for Sam's retirement party, and a matching one for Rosalie," Laura said as she squeezed the little one's hand and smiled.

"Is Sam retiring?" Charlotte seemed truly surprised.

"Even Sam knows when it's time to quit. Quite shocking, isn't it? The party is at the beginning of September. Will you have time to put something together?"

"I most certainly will make time. But in addition to that, I have a shipment of clothes coming in next week you might be interested in."

"Are you expanding?"

"You know, I thought it was time to sell some ready made things along with my own creations and alterations, just to branch out a bit. Anyway come back then and check it out; in the meantime, I'll make you and Rosalie matching dresses. How would you like some hot pants?" Charlotte winked.

Laura swatted at Charlotte playfully, just as Peggy walked into the sewing room, arms opened wide. "For you, my best sister, whatever you want will be ready yesterday. Hi, Rosalie! How is life for you girls these days?"

Laura laughed. "I'm your only sister!" She looked sorrowfully at Peggy, realizing how long it had been since they'd seen one another. "Is life so busy that we hardly have the time to visit anymore?"

Peggy wanted to hear every detail of what they'd been doing and the boys' upcoming business. It was wonderful to see her in such an enthusiastic mood. She had a permanent sorrow in her eyes, that much Laura could identify, but her sister had managed to find peace with God, moving on from George's death by keeping busy at the shop and participating in church projects. It seemed in between work and family, Peggy had found her calling in helping others in the name of the church.

"Laura, the parish council is training lectors for the mass and different committees are being set up. Why don't you sign up?"

"Me? Well, maybe. But what about you; are you still playing the organ, Peggy?"

"Yes, every week when we meet for prayers. Join us, Laura. Sam could drive you. I'm sure he wouldn't mind."

Laura didn't know why, but every time Peggy mentioned how Laura should become more involved in the church, she felt uncomfortable. Her complicated relationship with God, more habitual than heartfelt, was her private affair and hard to explain. "You pray enough for the both of us," Laura joked and ducked her head, before looking at her sister. "One of these days, I'll surprise you and join," she said seriously. "You'll see." Laura took a deep breath. "Now, how about that dress?"

On the morning of his retirement party, Laura woke up early and crept from the room to begin preparing. The fall chill was starting early, she noticed, shivering a bit in the morning air. She'd need to make sure to bring plenty of sweaters to Cape Breton. She brewed her tea and was folding some napkins enjoying the stillness when there was a horrible thud. She bolted to their bedroom. Sam was crumpled on the floor, unconscious. She ran to call Louise. When she hung up, a silence invaded her heart. When she returned to him, she held him in her arms and rocked him. She knew he was dead. She held him a long while before breaking into the morning stillness with a prayer. Then came the tears, coursing down her cheeks as if it were Johnny all over again. Sam hadn't been feeling well for weeks, yet he'd only worried over Laura, carrying on as usual with his steady, generous personality. Laura felt torn in two.

For the funeral, Peggy urged Laura to wear the outfit she'd commissioned for Sam's party. "It's a way of celebrating his life, Laura. You've been there, but under very different circumstances. At least now you're financially stable, your health is holding, you have your whole family flourishing around you."

Peggy's words were kind, but Laura barely heard them. All she could think was how she'd lost both her husbands, her soul mates, the same way. There would be no future of companionship, no support, no last trip to her home with the one she loved. She felt as though God was testing her now more than ever, though for what reason she couldn't begin to guess. It didn't matter anyway, she thought bitterly. There was no such thing as home. Everywhere you go, everywhere you make your life, the things that matter get ripped away, like storms tearing out trees by their roots.

Peggy saw Laura was lost to her grief. She stroked Laura's hand a few more minutes before quietly rising to get back to the kitchen where she was baking rack after rack of biscuits for after the funeral.

A few nights later, as Laura was tucking Rosalie in for bed, the girl asked, "Father...a flower?"

"What? What do you mean?"

Gesturing with her hands, she explained, "Small...grow big... and die. Everybody like a...flower?"

With tears in her eyes, Laura patted Rosalie's head. "Go to sleep now. Goodnight, little one."

Laura quietly walked out of the room but paused in the doorway. She turned around and looked at Rosalie. The little one was already fast asleep. She swallowed hard. Pain pierced her insides. She quickly shut the door and sank to the floor in the hallway. The walls felt cold, as if the house was no longer inhabited in the ways it was supposed to be.

Laura decided quickly that she didn't want to stay in the big white house without Sam. When she mentioned it, it was Rosalie who came up with a solution. "We move...in cottage... Grandma Louise...need friend!"

Rosalie never failed to surprise Laura, or inspire her with her generous feelings. Quite like her father in that way, Laura marveled. She packed and moved quickly without looking back, and soon it was all arranged with the family; she and Rosalie settled into the cottage, and Ben, Bella and the boys took over the big white house. Laura welcomed the distraction of watching the little boys play and run in the yard as winter came. And Rosalie was ecstatic.

Soon some of the hope and warmth Laura had lost slowly began to occupy the empty space inside her, and she was able to joke and laugh again with her grandchildren.

The following year in 1972, Ben was offered a job at the Cape Breton Highland National Park at the Chéticamp office. When Ben told Laura, her throat seized. It was as if Sam had been looking out for the family from above.

"What about your growing business with Tom?"

"I talked to him and he's willing to take it over. You know our part-time guy, Bob? He's keen to have more hours, and he's a really nice fellow, so now we'll, or rather Tom will, hire him full-time. He's got an incredible eye for landscape. We're lucky to have him."

Laura frowned. She'd been so preoccupied she hadn't considered what would happen if Ben did get the job. "Chéticamp is so far away. Rosalie will be lost without you." She knitted her fingers together over her slacks. How odd that her son would be the one going back and not her. It felt curious, unsettling. Like something was being stolen from her.

Ben took a deep breath. "I was thinking, Mama. She can move in with us. I've made some inquiries, and it seems they have a daily program in the village for someone like Rosalie."

Laura shook her head. "What are you saying, that you want to bring her with you, all the way to Chéticamp?"

Ben leaned over and touched his mother's hand. "You can visit anytime, you and Aunt Peggy. Wouldn't you enjoy that?"

"Does Bella know about this plan?" Laura felt suddenly desperate as if the world were slowly trying to take from her, piece by piece, all that mattered to her in life.

"We've discussed it at length, even when we first got married, that when the time came, we would take care of the little one. Mama, you deserve a holiday; why don't you go on a trip, you and Grandma Louise? You've spent all these years caring for Rosalie, not really able to go away. You deserve it. You could ask Aunt Peggy to join you. Wouldn't that be something?"

Laura smiled at her son's suggestions. He was trying very hard to make sure she felt happy. The furrows on his forehead touched her. "Peggy and I really have gone our separate ways in the last few years," she mused. "She did mention her charismatic group is going to Charlottetown for a five day tour. That might be fun." She rose from her chair, and then sat down again.

"What is it, Mama?"

Laura played with her fingers. "But are you sure you're ready to take full responsibility for Rosalie? She can be very stubborn, quite difficult."

"Don't worry, Mama, I know how to handle the little one," Ben assured her with utmost confidence.

Laura looked at his face. She believed him. "What about Bella?"

"What about me?" asked Bella as she walked in. She looked at the love and intensity passing between the mother and son and said, "Are you talking about Rosalie? We've been talking about this move and especially Rosalie's care for a long time, now." She sat beside Laura and smiled. "She will be fine."

Laura smiled back and tried not to feel like Bella was conspiring to take Rosalie away from her but rather that this plan was well meaning and filled with love and care. She missed Sam, then, terribly, wishing he could have a hand in deciding his daughter's fate. "Did you talk to Rosalie about this?"

Ben and Bella looked at each other. "No, not yet. We wanted to run it by you first."

Laura didn't say anything.

"We're leaving at the end of the month, so we shouldn't wait too long to decide."

"That soon?" Another loss, another door closing on her. But Laura realistically knew she couldn't continue to care for Rosalie alone much longer. Suddenly she needed to either laugh or cry or else she thought she might explode. Implode. Diode. Geode.

"The job begins in early April, a few months before the tourist season gets fully underway. You know I have Sam to thank for this. The superintendent told me he highly recommended me for the job."

Laura sighed. She didn't admit to having known all along that Sam's phone call a year before had gone very well and that the superintendent had agreed to hire Ben when the time came.

Ben gently urged Laura, "Go on, Mama, call Aunt Peggy about the trip. You'll be glad to get out of town for a spell."

The couple stayed in the living room talking quietly while Laura called her sister. When she returned, walking her lopsided gait back to her son and his wife, she felt a bit forlorn. She shrugged, "Peggy explained. It's a conference for Charismatic members only. I probably should have taken her advice and joined the group. They gather once a week to pray, but that's not such a cross to bear for the companionship, is it?" Laura chuckled mirthlessly.

"That's too bad." Ben looked at the ground then snapped his fingers. "I don't know why I didn't think of it before. I'm so dumb. Why don't you and Grandma Louise come with us to Chéticamp? You'll get a chance to see your home village again, and you two could keep an eye on Rosalie and the boys while we get settled in our new home."

Laura didn't have the heart to tell him it didn't matter to her anymore. It wasn't home, just a place, a spot on the map. Nonetheless, her body was feeling energized just from the idea of going, even if only to spend some time with the family and breathe in some new air. Perhaps she was just being petulant since Sam died before they had a chance to go back. She thought this time she could try a little harder to reconnect with some long-lost parts of herself. It might be just the thing she needed. She brightened. "I'll talk to Louise."

The next day, Laura helped Rosalie pack a few things, half hoping the little one would break down and refuse to go. "You … visit…me, Laura-mama?"

"You bet! Actually Grandma Louise and I are going for a few days, maybe a week or so, to help you move in to your new house. You can ride with us!"

"No…Rosalie ride…with…Ben."

"Oh. All right, then. We'll follow," said Laura. Rosalie was humming as she put her coloured pencils and folded up pages she'd torn from magazines in a pink pencil case. Laura looked at her adopted daughter, how mature she'd become and what strides she'd made from being so loved in such a family and suddenly felt less despondent than she'd thought she might. It was clear Rosalie would be fine.

At the end of April 1972, the youngest of the McPherson clan moved to Chéticamp with his family. Ben led the way in the pick-up, followed closely by Tom and Charlotte in the Bel Air, while Louise and Laura trailed behind. All three vehicles were packed solid. By the time they reached the Canso Causeway, Laura surprised herself by feeling excited. Each time she saw 'Welcome to Cape Breton', engraved in the steel arch beneath the larger trestle on the bridge, her heart sped up a bit. Even the deep rich green color of the sign seemed almost magical.

Louise looked over at Laura. "Are you feeling all right, Laura?"

"Yes, just a bit excited. Why do you ask?"

Louise laughed. "To be honest, I haven't seen you this alive in a long time. It's wonderful. We should have come to Cape Breton long before now."

The drive in was beautiful but just like the years before when Laura and Sam had come on their honeymoon, the landscape, the feel of the place, they were nice but didn't resonate in her heart. Late in the afternoon the three vehicles parked in front of Ben and Bella's future home. It was a single-story house with clapboard shingles and a deep front veranda.

"Well, Mama, what do you think?"

"Not bad, not bad at all. With a new coat of paint and curtains, it will be very cozy indeed. And it's close to the park, which is so nice for the boys. Oh, and Ben, did you notice the lobster boats in the harbor and beyond? Are the fishermen setting their traps?"

"Yes, and tomorrow, we'll treat ourselves to a big feast of lobster."

Tom clapped his hands like a five-year-old and grinned. "Shall we start unloading, Ben? The clouds are coming in."

"Good plan. Back the truck to the door."

Before he could start the motor, a gentleman approached them, extending his hand. "Allo! My name is Pierre. Looks like we're going to be neighbors!"

"Mighty fine to meet you, Pierre. I'm Ben McPherson. This is my brother Tom."

"Yes, yes, 'eard you were coming, Bella your wife and two little boys, Timot'y and...?"

"Yes, Timothy and Blaire," smiled Ben.

"You're new at the park? They come and go...trainees, I guess.... What exactly is your job?" He squinted at the piled up things in the car. "Need a 'and?"

"Kind of you, but I think we can manage."

"I'll say 'dat dere car is sure nice! Is it yours?"

"I wish," grinned Ben, looking at Tom.

Pierre carefully examined the car and let out a long whistle. "It's a beauty!"

"Yes! A '59 Chev Bel Air," proudly said Tom. "Was my stepfather's."

"What would I give to own a car like dis! Dey don't make them like dey used to, nowadays!"

Ben and Tom excused themselves to unload some boxes from the car. Tom whispered, "You better get mother to put up some curtains before she leaves. I wonder if he's related to Esther? Could've been separated at birth." Tom's laughter could be heard above the noise of the children.

Ben brought in a few chairs and Laura accepted one and a cup of tea from Bella who came in, brandishing the tea pot.

Thunder began rumbling around them, so the men unloaded as quickly as they could. Laura and Louise sipped their tea and finished their inspection of the house. In that time, the boys had packed the kitchen full of boxes. When they returned and saw how sleepy the children were, lolling around the boxes, Laura said, "I think we won't get in your way anymore today. We'll find a place in the village for the night." Laura took Louise's arm. "I know the exact spot. Just hope they're open." She motioned to her daughter. "Rosalie, let's go."

"It's OK, Laura. The little one can stay with us," said Bella as she combed through a box of supplies.

"Pardon?" Laura was caught off guard. "Are you sure?"

Bella smiled and nodded. The little one happily waved farewell.

They left and dodged the scattered raindrops on their way to the car. "Where shall we go?" asked Louise.

"A little past the church, across from the store, there's a motel," Laura pursed her forehead. "But I'd bet they aren't open for visitors just yet. Hmm, we can drive down and see if there's something. And there's a restaurant where they make the best fish and chips."

"I can't believe you remember all of that! I bet this place brings back so many memories. Did you bring your journal?"

"I did." Laura wanted to reveal to Louise that part of her enthusiasm was now for show, the residual feeling of hope she'd had that returning here, of knowing her son was to make his home here, would restore something in her. But it didn't. Only parts looked familiar; mostly she didn't remember much. It just didn't feel right. Maybe she would feel more at home in Inverness; after all, that's where she grew up. But in the end, Laura knew that wouldn't feel right either. She smiled. "There, see, another restaurant, and it's beside the fabric store. I'm sure they'll have something great for Peggy; we'll check it out tomorrow. But," she paused. "Would you mind if we took a small detour before supper? There's something I'd like to see."

Though she was reticent, she decided not to leave with regrets. And, after all, she'd saved that little hand drawn map all these years. A quick visit to the house where her mother grew up might give her one last chance to feel connected to her roots. If it didn't, at least she'd know she had done all she could to rekindle her feelings for this place.

Laura's maternal grandparents' property was located on the Chéticamp back road. When they arrived, Laura saw the glimmer of the brook that flowed through the property beside the old farmhouse. The overgrown trees waved gently, creating a deep green feel to the air. The mountains were close, looming to the southeast.

"Do you want to get out and have a look?" asked Louise gently.

Laura sat still a moment then shook her head. "No, it's alright." Something told her that this was enough. The farmhouse was dilapidated, half of its roof sunk in. But the swish of the trees, the light, these touched her slightly. And slightly would suffice. She would give Chéticamp over to Ben and his family, to Rosalie now. Let them have their lives there. That would be enough to rest on, she decided. Louise started up the car again and they drove back.

* * * * * *

Once Laura and Louise returned home to Antigonish, they joined the charismatic group and began participating in various community functions. The widows kept busy, but Laura was aware of the small hole that Ben, Bella and their children left in her days. Most of all, Laura was deeply touched by Rosalie's absence, and she had to remind herself often that letting her go was the right thing to do, for them both. Even the house, despite being empty, needed some attention that Laura was finding hard to get to. Peggy had been after Laura to sell Sam's house and move into the seniors' residence in town with her, but Laura knew Peggy was so busy, she wouldn't see her any more than she already did. Plus this home fed her soul in a way her sister couldn't understand. She'd grown her family here a second time, in a way, and unlike the old homestead which was full of beautiful memories but also hardship and pain, this house was pure of all that. It had always just been a loving home. As long as Louise wanted to stay, Laura was happy to live with her in the cottage. She had Tom who checked in on the greenhouse in addition to running the business they set up in town, and she'd already looked into hiring a hand to help out with the odd repairs and keep up the grounds. At night, she found her solace in gazing out at the big white house. This made her feel content. They'd be fine.

In the fall of `77, Louise discovered a lump on her breast. As a former nurse, she was quick to act, knowing denial meant death. Laura held her friend's hand on the way to the hospital, her mind racing, a lump on her breast, a lump of coal, a lump in your throat. Stop it! she yelled at herself. What an awful time to play word games.

After the operation, Louise reticently submitted herself to cobalt treatments that were meant to catch any remaining cancer cells. They were invasive and painful, and soon all the stress and grief from her illness slowly changed her from someone who was normally loving and gentle into someone bitter and nervous. Still Louise spoke of her faith in God, which Laura tried to share. But when she offered to wash her friend's back as Louise could no longer do it herself and saw how the treatments had burned her skin to a crisp, she bit down her nausea and tears and again wondered about this grand plan God had for his children and why inside of it there had to be so much suffering.

After four years, on April 25, 1981, the cancer won and Louise died with Laura and Peggy by her side. Peggy tried to maintain her good cheer and joked with Laura about how that was it: neither of them could pass away before the other, but even as Peggy was speaking, Laura let herself slip away as if beneath a ripple in a stream. She'd lost and lost and lost again and was feeling as though she herself were nearly gone as well.

After Louise's death, she stayed by herself in the cottage, close to the empty white house. Laura's days were long and lonely. Laura would be early to bed and late to rise. She had lost all interest in reading and writing and just spent her time staring at the television set. She always welcomed Tom and Charlotte's visit though she mostly kept quiet, not asking any questions about how they were doing. Charlotte would bring her groceries and sometimes Laura would complain that the tomatoes were not fresh or the bread was stale.

Her sons worried, but their Aunt Peggy reassured them she would eventually revert back to her old self. "She always does," said Peggy kindly. "She's been through the worst a person can go through, apart from losing one of you," she paused and smiled. "Let's just give her a bit of time."

Yet this time it didn't seem she would return. The family continued to visit Laura regularly, but each came away feeling like she was present only in body; her eyes had lost their shine and there was no life in them. It didn't seem she was cooking any of the food they brought her, and was subsisting on bread and molasses.

Peggy finally called Joe in Halifax and asked him to come. He arrived in the evening, and they sat over meat pie and fresh bread to brainstorm some solutions. "I think you should send Caroline to stay with Laura for the summer months," she suggested. Joe seemed skeptical, but they talked through the options for both the girl and her grandmother, and realized it was a plan that could actually work.

By now, Laura's oldest granddaughter was eighteen years old. When Joe told her about his idea, she was completely against it. She didn't want to leave her friends and her home for the two best months of the year, especially those before university started. Laura was in no better shape, having little interest in hosting the young girl whom she loved but didn't know very well. But the family decided and that was that.

The girl came and was sullen from the outset. Seeing her moping around while the sun was blazing and the flowers were swaying in the breeze stirred up something that had been lying dormant in Laura. Without knowing why, she began zealously cleaning and weeding until she realized she was angry. She was grieving for her loss, yet she was supposed to entertain the teenager, make her come around and act civil toward her? Once Laura's energy for annoyance kicked in, she decided she'd ignore the girl until she came around. She threw herself even more fully into housework, cleaning and cooking, planting and taking long walks alone.

Perhaps Caroline was lonely or she began to see her petulance wasn't doing her or her grandmother any good, but after a few days, she snapped out of her mood and joined Laura. They explored the countryside bursting with flowers, walked in the woods, even fished for trout, which Caroline was squeamish about initially but soon she cast her line with the flick of a pro. Laura took pride in showing Caroline her natural world, as if it were in fact hers, a secret to share with someone gently opening to it, learning to embrace it as if it were hers too. In return, Caroline showed Laura how to work her walkman and Laura loved listening to a tape of the soundtrack to *Love Story* that Caroline had bought her in town. One evening for dinner, Caroline surprised Laura by baking cinnamon rolls, thick, doughy things with heaps of icing, and they ate them instead of a proper dinner while playing cards. Laura came to see her granddaughter as smart, effusive, and full of love for life and she loved to listen to her stories about her friends at school and her great Aunt Florence, whom she adored.

"I see you two are getting along, then," said Joe over the phone one evening.

"Oh, we're getting by," said Laura, winking at Caroline.

Gradually, Laura felt the itch to get back to her journal. She bought Caroline her own journal and the two of them enjoyed writing side by side in the cool morning air. Laura didn't have the heart for reliving the sad memories, but she enjoyed noting things about the world around, birds and flowers, just like Sam's original suggestion. That in and of itself turned out to be a kind of healing.

One day Peggy visited in a new car. "Remember George's old aunt in the States who used to send barrels of clothing?" she said. "The dear left me some money when she passed, so I went for my license; Tom loaned me his car, wasn't that sweet? And Charlotte, bless her heart, she must have nerves of steel, because she sat with me in that front seat, time and time again until I could do what she said was the most perfect parallel parking she'd ever seen. So even though it took me four tries, I finally got the darn piece of paper. Which meant, of course, after all that effort, I had to get a decent car," she winked.

They piled in and she wound her way through the back roads, eventually ending up at Laura's old shack. Peggy knew Laura's grief from losing Sam was compounded by her loss of Johnny, and the fact that she never got closure from his sudden death. There was barely any white remaining from the time the boys and Sam had painted it over twenty years ago. The trees were now full grown; the tall grass and rose bushes had overtaken the yard. It was indeed the sight of a much neglected old farm.

"Oh, Peggy," Laura put her head in her hands and began to cry quietly.

"Grandma, what's wrong? Was this your house?"

Laura didn't speak but got quietly out of the car. She stood in the hot wind, letting memories wash over her. Caroline climbed out and put her arms around Laura's waist. "Daddy never told me about his childhood. Is this where he grew up? Is this where you lived with my grandfather?"

Laura wordlessly took Caroline's hand. She looked at Peggy, tears brimming in her eyes. She gave her a small smile and they linked arms on the other side. Slowly they made their way to the front steps, brushed away the cobwebs and tried the door. The wood had swollen but it opened. Laura headed straight to the sunroom but stopped short in the doorway. "What in the world?" she whispered. Small kegs and cigarette butts lay everywhere. Laura and Peggy looked at one another and muttered, "Tom."

"Uncle Tom?" Caroline was incredulous. "But he's so clean cut. He'd never do anything like this." Laura and Peggy were quiet a moment then they both burst out laughing. What time had done with their family!

Upon their return to the cottage, Peggy stayed a while to put some dinner on the stove, for she could see from Laura's slumped posture the visit had taken quite a toll on her. Then suddenly, an idea came to mind. "Laura, I'm thinking, what if we cleaned out the old place and made it into a retreat, a place to reunite with the kids, you know, on special occasions? It would be great for everyone especially for Joe and you, and Caroline, since you live in the city, it could give you a sense of freedom and whiffs of fresh air, a place to run with no worries. I'm quite sure the boys would help!"

Laura smiled at Peggy's enthusiasm. "After some of your cooking, I'll be in a much better frame of mind for planning. Let's eat."

When summer was nearly at its end and it was time for Caroline to go home, Peggy came around to see her off and it wasn't clear from either Laura or Caroline's faces, whom the parting would be harder on. The grandmother and granddaughter hugged a long time. "I'll miss you," said Caroline, her face buried in Laura's shoulder.

Laura murmured, "I will too. You won't know how much."

Peggy didn't trust that Laura would remain in such a solid place once she was on her own again, so she continued to ask her to move to the apartments in town. Laura refused her each time. Even though Laura led a less active life than she used to, gardening and strolling a bit less, she still felt very much at home in the cottage. Plus once the weather cooled down, she and Peggy immersed themselves in the shack project, painting, making new curtains, and bringing over utensils and useful items so it would be a fully functional home. Joe and Tom reconnected the running water and handled minor repairs.

By Thanksgiving weekend in October, Laura and Peggy were thrilled as the men organized yet another grand opening, similar to the one they had had for the cottage. Ben, Bella, Rosalie and the boys drove in and the boys were thrilled to be together again, and the cousins played as if they'd never been apart. Caroline was happy to be back with Laura and Peggy and stood with them in the kitchen coring apples and pears the others had picked from the orchards.

Laura wiped her brow off on her apron. "I thought the purpose of fixing our old home was to relax and have some fun. I've never worked so hard in my life: Apple jelly, apple pies, apple tarts..." she laughed, knowing this was a big understatement. She could recall, with tremendous clarity, the calluses she'd once had on her hands from carrying buckets, hoeing, sewing, milking and haying. She remembered well the nights of aching muscles.

Peggy grinned. "Life sure isn't what it used to be."

"Amen to that," said Laura. She cringed remembering the rough pages from the Eaton's catalogue they'd had to use in the outhouse and the buckets sprinkled over the floor to catch the rain. How poor and helpless and alone she was.

Laura spied Joe and Delores whispering on the porch and snuck up on them. "What are you two planning?" she asked, pretending to be stern. Joe broke into a huge smile. "Nothing yet. But maybe something soon."

"Well, if that doesn't kill me with curiosity, I don't know what will," said Laura returning to the kitchen. She tried to imagine what it could be, but her family was very good at surprising her and she knew she'd never guess.

* * * * * *

It took five years for Joe and Delores to make their plan of moving back home a reality. When they told Laura their idea that they wanted to tear down the old house and rebuild a modern house for their family, her heart fell inside her chest. She tried to tell herself she felt the loss mostly for Tom and Ben, who would be sentimental about it, especially after they'd spent the time and effort fixing it up. If one or the other were supportive of Joe and the other not, it could return them to the rift they'd had following George's death. She couldn't bear any further animosity between her boys. She was thrilled they wanted to move home, but this weighed heavily on her mind.

When Joe and Delores and the kids returned to Antigonish in 1986, while the construction took place, the family moved into the big white house. Laura tried not to think about how her son was bulldozing her history for his family and instead concentrated on having them close to her, which was truly rewarding. She loved seeing the house come to life again and looked forward to the grandchildren's visits, preparing their favorite foods and putting out games and books. Tom's daughter Mary was also vivacious and full of fun, and though Caroline had her hands full after graduating from university, marrying a young man who hailed from Halifax, and making their home in Antigonish, she enjoyed spending time with her grandmother and still came around quite often.

At 66-years-old, Laura wasn't old by most people's standards, but her life had taken its toll on her body. She continued cooking, visiting with the family and her daily walks, but she spent more and more time reading or in quiet reflection. Rather than mind the stillness, she came to embrace it. She realized if she reflected on her life in writing, the work lent her a sense of agency and authenticity, as if putting words to her memories and experiences and letting stories emerge made her and her life matter.

Of late, she'd developed a lingering chest cold and was often short of breath, her one lung tired of substituting for two. When Laura had an episode of being unable to catch her breath one afternoon following her walk, she finally listened to Caroline and Joe's suggestion that she move in with Joe and the family once the new house was completed. She felt uneasy, apprehensive about returning to her beginnings, even though the new house would be wiped clean of any of that. Beneath her surface anger about the new house, she was aware that her memories were more tenacious than a building; the plywood and brick might have been new, but her memories were built into the soil.

In the end, she conceded the move would be for the best. Her body had grown fairly weak and even the little efforts of cooking and cleaning were becoming harder. Laura didn't fear death, but she did fear the idea of emptiness. She might have come around in terms of her attitude for life, but her private soul was still quite empty from the grief of loss that accompanied her every moment of each day.

Once her health returned, she took in the day slowly through her pen. Her journal became her refuge, and in her thoughts and memories, she began to see the shape of a story happening: her life with Johnny and the journey of her family. Tears often poured down as she wrote, but she ploughed on. When her hand and mind tired, she would sit back and revel in the pages she'd created, the worlds she'd given a voice to. How many women in her situation would go on being voiceless from birth to death because they couldn't read or write, she wondered. She thought about Robert, dear, loving Robert, her Sam, and her Johnny, and felt a reinvigorated purpose. She was blessed with more gifts than any one person deserved. She would keep writing as a tribute, and as a record, to give shape and meaning to their lives. In her writing, she saw a kind of prayer. It centered her, gave her a feeling of wholeness that rooted her to the earth more deeply, more meaningfully, than she'd ever known before.

By Labour Day weekend in 1987, most of Laura's belongings were already in the new home. She was waiting outside the old place with Caroline and her great-grandson, Johnny, for Joe or Tom to bring her over with the car. The sky was pure blue and the air warm and fine. As Caroline ran after the two-year-old boy, who dashed about yanking up flowers and leaping from the front steps, she breathlessly asked, "How on earth did you manage to raise Uncle Tom, Uncle Ben and Dad by yourself, Grandma? I can hardly manage with one!" She scooped him up into her arms and cuddled him. He curled up and laid his head on her shoulder.

Laura chuckled and the two women sat on garden chairs listening to the gentle wind rustle the grass. "It wasn't easy." Her eyes took on a distant look. "You know, Caroline, I was only a few years older than you when I was widowed. It was 1950, I was thirty years old, no money, no way of earning a living. But I suppose it could have been worse." Laura smiled at little Johnny who was yawning. He nestled into Caroline's arms.

"How could it have been worse? That sounds pretty hard."

"I had three mouths to feed. That is a lot by today's standards, but back then at some places there might have been ten, twelve or even fifteen."

Caroline looked horrified. "Fifteen kids! How did they live? And the poor mother, giving birth to all of them." Caroline was overcome with the thought of such a life. She held little Johnny, who had just drifted off to sleep in her arms, tightly.

"Perhaps less during my youth, but during my mother's time, it was common for women to die during childbirth." Laura frowned. "Poverty was a way of life for most as well. No work, food was scarce. Children often went to bed hungry. Women toiled day in and day out, carrying pails and pails of water to cook and wash. They also worked the fields and milked the cows."

"Milked the cows? Did you?"

"I milked the cows on the farm in Inverness and later on our own farm. So did your dad."

"He never talks about that."

Laura shook her head. "Your father doesn't like to remember those days, especially the poor ones. He always had a drive, a mission towards financial security. But you know, there's such a thing as too much drive. He almost lost your mother, and you, because of it."

Caroline smiled. She laid the baby in his stroller and offered her grandma a glass of water, then made sure she was comfortable. After such a hectic life she'd been leading since the baby was born, it was reassuring to sit with her grandmother and learn about her past. The few times she'd tried to ask Laura stories about her younger days when she spent the summer with her, she supposed Laura hadn't been ready because she always managed to change the subject. "What about Aunt Peggy's husband? What was he like? Was he kind?"

"Ah, George was a kind man, yes. He took the boys in as if they were his own when I had to leave them behind." Laura's mouth deepened into a heavy frown. "A woman should never leave her children. Never." She reached a trembling hand out to the little boy's foot and touched it lightly, holding her hand to his pudgy ankle a moment.

Caroline knew she was referring to the time she spent at the convent and the sanitarium; her father had told her about those experiences. Laura went on. "Yes, George was a kind, patient man, and quite resourceful. He took time to teach the boys many handy skills. They primarily grew up without a father, so...oh, and he loved to play pranks." Laura shuddered. "The only problem with George was that he died too soon like Sam and Johnny."

"You miss them, don't you."

Laura smiled sadly and sighed. "Yes. But life goes on. The sadness passes with time yet just when you think you're doing fine, a sudden sharp pain pinches your insides. Then it passes, until the next time. It can be something so small; an odor or a simple gesture will often throw me off."

"How did you get to be so wise?"

Laura giggled. "I'm not wise, just old."

Caroline laughed. "Hardly! 67, right?"

Laura nodded.

"And Grandpa Johnny; what was he like?"

Laura shifted her position and in an instant, seemed to be magically transported into another world. "He was the love of my life, a mixture of your father, Tom and Ben. He was full of life and mischief. He made me laugh. He was lucky; he could read a bit. He'd often help your father and Tom with their schoolwork."

"Wait," Caroline put up her hand. "You couldn't read?"

"Not until I began working for Sam. It was not unusual for young ones to stay home to help out, some as young as eight or nine-years-old."

"That would be Grade 3?" Caroline asked flabbergasted.

"I was one of those kids, and so was Johnny. His father took sick so he stayed home. Lord knows what he might have become if he had been allowed to continue his studies. He was a smart man even if he had but his Grade 5. When his father felt better, Johnny continued working on the farm. For some reason, he never returned to school. His father had a horse and wagon and he would peddle his farm supplies: eggs, vegetables, mittens his mother knitted, but most women knitted, so it was mostly eggs. That's how he earned a living. They would leave very early in the morning and return late at night and would only have travelled a few miles. Sometimes if they went farther, they would stay overnight at a stranger's house."

Laura put her hand on Caroline's knee and leaned in. "You'll like this: one time, they started their journey home too late and had to stop for the night. Most people were quite friendly, happy to receive visitors. But they tended to go to bed quite early." Laura winked. "Could be the reason for such large families," she chuckled then sighed, "but people were also quite poor back then. They slept over at the home of a very kind husband and wife. In the morning, the woman asked them if they wanted a cuppa tea. She took the pee pot, went outside to empty its contents, then returned to the house and scalded the pot with hot water. His father was scared that she was going to make tea in the same pot so they quickly made their excuses and headed home."

"You mean to say she would have made tea in the same pot?"

"It looked that way. It might have been that she didn't have any other pot." Laura shook her head. "I'm glad times are more prosperous now."

Caroline shuddered and laughed. "Ick. Me too. When was this?"

"Johnny would've been about twelve years old, so this was probably in the early 1930's, during the depression."

At that moment, little Johnny yawned and lifted his eyes to his mother. "Hi, Mama," he said, breaking into a toothy grin. He held his arms to her and was content to nestle there for a while.

"When is William coming home?" asked Laura. She tickled Johnny under the chin; he giggled and wriggled his short legs.

Caroline smiled. "Tonight, thankfully. He loves the job and he likes Halifax and says we should move there so we're not apart all week, but it's hard for me to imagine..." she trailed off and took Laura's hand.

Laura looked solidly at her granddaughter. She knew how important her family was to her. What a long way she'd come from that surly teenager who showed up on her doorstep. She squeezed Caroline's hand in return. "I love having you close by; the whole family cherishes having you here, but..." she paused, "your place is with your husband. You should go with him. You never know what the future will hold."

She closed her eyes. "When I was small, Mama often took Peggy and me to the beach for a swim, especially in the evenings. The Inverness beach was lovely. She used to say it was one of God's most magnificent creations, and nothing filled her with the same tranquility and peace it did. Meanwhile all Peggy and I cared about was having lots of loud fun. We loved building sandcastles and worked hard to make huge, exotic ones but then, the tide would come in unexpectedly and, like that," she snapped her fingers, "they'd be gone."

Laura paused and stared sadly into space. "Peggy and I cried a bit but we quickly resumed our good spirits, for Mama assured us that we could always build another one. And we were driven; we ignored the magnificent sunsets, didn't taste our snacks, just went back to building, this time higher up on the dune so the tide wouldn't reach us, with 'a bit more wisdom in our hearts and souls', those were Mama's exact words." She laughed. "I can't believe I remember that."

Laura continued as if in a trance. "Peggy and I were always excited to start a new sandcastle. Sometimes, miraculously, it would still be standing upon our return, but more often than not, its shape would have changed or it would've completely disappeared. Before going home, Mama would make us sit on the sand and face the ocean and tell us to smell the salty air, feel the setting sun and the soft breeze on our skin and to breathe deeply. At first Peggy and I just giggled because it was so difficult to sit still. But with Mama's coaxing, it became a ritual. Soon, we were the ones who sat first. Later on, I always thought she made us do that so we would calm down after the evening's excitement, but maybe she had other things on her mind."

"Like what?"

"Instilling a sense of appreciation for the beauty of nature, maybe."

"Gee, Grandma, that's intense! You could write a book!"

Laura smiled. Her granddaughter didn't know it; in fact, no one knew it, but in effect, she already had. She wondered what would happen when the boys found her journals, what they would think. She wished she had the energy to organize them herself, but she knew that Tom, ever the wordsmith just like her, would know exactly what to do.

She looked at Caroline. "Caroline, remember when you first came to stay with me and I bought you a journal?"

"Of course I do! I still keep one, though I write less than I used to, now that my hands are always so busy." She laughed.

Laura felt a sense of peace pervade her body. All these years she'd kept the journal the Englishman's children had given her. She'd kept it, but had never written in it, the blank pages always a reminder to her of how far she'd come. Every so often, she'd bring it out of its tissue paper she kept it wrapped in, its pages a little more brittle, a bit more yellowed, and would marvel at how much progress there could be in a single life.

"Will you go get something for me? It's in my bedroom in the closet in a flat white box beneath my sweaters."

Caroline looked puzzled but scooped up the baby and went into the house. Laura let her eyes flutter closed for a moment. When Caroline came back with the box, Laura opened her eyes. "Open it, child," she said gently.

"Grandma, what is this?" she said, turning the old book over in her hands.

"Let's just say it's a very old book that's full of memories even though it's blank. It's yours now. I want you to fill it with your own story. Will you do that?"

Caroline felt her nose grow hot and she blinked away tears. "I will. Thank you." She walked over to the garden with Johnny to let her grandmother rest. A lithe grey spider was picking its gentle way over the gravel in the lane. She marveled at it a moment; such tenacity life had. She looked down the lane for her Uncle Tom. Her Grandma Laura was such a pioneer, such a brave woman. And what a zest she had for life. She thought about her maternal grandmother and tried to imagine her dancing with bare feet in the sand, singing childish melodies or tickling her daughter's toes, triumphing over poor and difficult times, but all she could see was her sitting like a statue in an overbearing chair in a stylish restaurant, sipping tea from a china cup with her pinkie in the air. She had shunned her only family, her own daughter, and as a result, she was utterly, painfully alone. Caroline shook her head. Her Grandpa Carl and Aunt Florence seemed so happy together. They had found peace in the other.

Just then, there was a scuffle of noise coming down the lane. Laura woke up instantly. "What is that noise? Sounds like a horse. That can't be..." The three of them squinted to look into the distance. Sure enough, as they watched, a horse and buggy came into view and pulled up right in front of them. Tom was sitting in the front seat dressed as a porter with a top hat and his daughter Mary sat by his side in a colorful, frilly costume holding a parasol. Laura whispered, "Jésus, Marie, Joseph," and looked delighted. She leaned on Caroline for support. "Did you know about this?" she asked.

Caroline only grinned and shrugged, putting her hands up in feigned innocence.

Mary caught her grandmother's reaction on camera while her father hopped off his seat. "You like?" Tom asked, imitating Rosalie's sweet voice.

With tears in her eyes, Laura nodded.

"Our gift to you, Mother, on your homecoming, from the whole family!"

"Where did you get the outfits?"

"Ben brought them up from Chéticamp. They have an annual tradition in the middle of Lent where people disguise themselves and go from house to house hoping they won't be recognized. He says it's a lot of fun."

"I'd bet it is. We should go next year!"

"Will do, Mother!"

"Rosalie?"

Tom nodded. "She's waiting!"

Laura beamed. She had missed Rosalie terribly. This was truly a wonderful reunion. Tom grabbed little Johnny and let him pet the horse before safely installing him in the back seat. Then Tom helped his mother into the carriage while Caroline and Mary climbed in. "Are you all set...Laura-ella?" His mother quickly glanced at him then opened her mouth in surprise. She hadn't heard that name in a while. It brought on a flood of happy memories. Or mostly happy memories, Laura had to laugh. Tom winked, turned around, laughed wholeheartedly and off they rode.

It was indeed a beautiful late summer day with a dry crisp breeze brushing against their faces. As the horse navigated its way down the narrow path, the beauty of the early fall foliage soon captivated the group. Tom slowed the carriage to a halt and climbed down to pick up a bouquet of green and gold flowers. "One for you, Mother, and another for the kitchen table."

Laura sighed but didn't trust her voice to speak. It had been a long time since she had been this happy. As the horse trotted down the once familiar path to her little shack, she linked arms with Caroline and remained peacefully quiet and relished every moment. Little Johnny had settled into his mother's arms and seemed to be in a trance as Caroline pointed out the different trees and colors.

As they slowly approached the house, Laura thought she would burst as a new surge of energy engulfed her. She was spellbound by the work her sons had done. The new house was painted a pure white. It looked the same, yet it was far more spacious with two large gables. They got out of the carriage and went inside. The highlight of her surprise was the sunroom and her own bedroom, which Joe had recreated down to the faded rug and her old rocking chair. It felt indeed as if she were coming back home. Laura smiled. "Full circle," she thought. Full of fullness. So very full.

As she took her seat in her familiar rocking chair, her family gathered around. "I can't thank you all enough for this wonderful adventure. For my life." She looked at Peggy. "Did you know about this scheme?"

Her sister nodded. "Thought the whole thing up myself," she said proudly then burst out laughing as her nephews launched their protests.

In the days that followed, Laura kept at her journal, trying to write faster to keep up with the flood of memory. One late morning, she paused to look out the window and laid down her pen. The yard looked so sculpted, filled with flowers of all kinds, velvety petals swaying in the warm breeze. She was aware of a coolness that had crept in where it had not been a few hours before. Fall was coming. And with it, frost, then snow, and this whole yard would be skeletal and dead. She marveled ruefully that she'd never been one to think so darkly about nature. But surviving one death after another, loved ones leaving her, she wasn't so innocent any more. She didn't

351

mind. It was the circle of life just doing as it should. She felt the chill in the air herself. She knew it would come. Yet this time, there was peace in such thoughts that she hadn't felt before.

Laura came down with a serious influenza a few weeks later. Her one lung struggled and her breath was labored. Joe and Delores begged her to let them take her to the hospital, but she refused. "I've spent enough time in hospitals for three people, thank you."

Then during the night of the fall's first frost, she suffered a stroke. In the morning, when Delores discovered her, she expected the worst but was shocked when Laura began speaking in rapid-fire French. At once, Delores called the doctor then her husband. Before Joe left work, he contacted Tom. By the time they arrived at the house, Laura was sitting up in bed, asking over and over for Marie Margaret-Anne. They tried to comfort her as best as they could but she repeatedly asked for this unknown woman.

"Mother, please speak in English so we can understand what you want."

Laura looked vaguely at her sons and continued rattling on in French. Then Joe suggested, "Call Aunt Peggy, maybe she'll know whom Mother is referring to."

When Peggy arrived, without bothering to remove her coat and gloves, she barged into the bedroom. "Laura, what in tarnation is going on?"

"Ah! Marie Margaret-Anne!"

Laura reached for her sister's hands and held tight. Peggy sat on the bed and both sisters slowly, then picking up speed, conversed in the rich Acadian French language that was their mother tongue. Though the women had certainly come around to love one another, freed of the earlier emotional burdens of their younger years, this rapport was pure, like that of two delighted children. It was all just love. If the situation hadn't been so tense, the boys would have sat back and enjoyed the show.

"What's going on, Aunt Peggy? Are you Marie Margaret-Anne?"

Peggy nodded and smiled.

"But how? Why? We don't understand."

"Give us a minute, boys. Delores, would you please make some fresh tea?"

The boys and Delores lingered in the sunroom, waiting for their aunt to shed some light on the situation. The mood was tense but at the same time joyous; after all, Laura seemed delighted to have such a return to a self long since forgotten. After what seemed like forever, Peggy finally appeared in the sunroom. "She's sleeping now."

The boys settled into various chairs and waited for their aunt's explanation. When they heard the story, they were fascinated. Joe was particularly quiet, his forehead pursed. "Something wrong, Joe?" asked Peggy.

"I feel like I don't know Mother at all. We used to beg her to tell us stories about her past, but most of them seemed to pain her, her time in the convent, the years she lived at the san, her childhood. Those are holes in her history, our history, and now we may never get to know them." He looked down at his hands. "When we got older, we just assumed Mother didn't want to talk about her past; she liked just to keep her eyes forward."

Peggy nodded. "She might have wanted only to spare you from the pain she endured. She's had her share of it, that's for sure." She sat back in her chair. "You know, your mother actually is one of the most reflective people I've ever known. I'll bet you anything that if you check her notebooks, she's detailed quite a bit about her life there."

The boys looked at each other tentatively, all of a sudden realizing that their mother, the loving, wholesome, caring whole of her, had a rich past that they could get to know. Much of it for the first time.

Eventually, to everyone's relief, Laura's speech returned to normal, but whenever Peggy dropped by, both giggled and chatted in French. The boys found it quite amusing.

When Ben came for his next bi-weekly visit, he gathered his brothers and aunt around his mother's bedside. "What's the big surprise?" asked Tom.

Ben smiled and held out a photograph of a house. His mother looked a moment then turned her eyes to him, confused. Ben murmured to her, "Mama, this is your grandparents' house. Your mother's parents' home. Well, it's mine now, or ours. We bought it."

Laura blinked back tears and smiled proudly. "You bought my grandparents' property? Back in Chéticamp, this is where my mother was born," she turned to her family holding out the picture. She looked at the photos and soon seemed lost in her thoughts. "You returned," she whispered. "You returned." Calm fell over her face. "My home is here with you. But no tree lives without its roots. Sam said that, differently, but he did. Such a good man..." she drifted away again.

Ben took his mother's thin hand in his and held it tightly. "Chéticamp is where I feel like I belong, Mama. It was the right move. I like my work, Bella still substitutes at the school now and then and volunteers at the workshop; the boys keep us busy especially in winter with hockey. The people are friendly. And look," he went to his satchel, "I brought some fresh potatoes, turnips and carrots, straight from my own garden."

Laura looked around at her boys, heard the children playing and laughing in the yard. There were late season birds and the warm glow of the afternoon sun made squares through the window on her coverlet. She was overcome with a feeling she'd always known was inside her, a connection to God, a connection to her life, all of it at once. She'd felt this before in more fleeting moments, recalling vaguely a light coming on in her when Tom told her his dear shoeshine man's words, but that was just the start; now it was a wave, one that washed over her and wrapped itself around her heart, then her body. She fell into sleep, knowing her world was exactly as it should be.

The boys quietly wandered into the sunroom and sank into chairs. They were men now, each with families of their own, stories of their own to pass down to their children. Joe, now 44-years-old, had creases around his eyes but less from worry and more from laughter. Though he was still lean and strong, he had thickened in the middle from Delores' cooking and looked more solid than the willowy young man he'd once been. He'd learned life could be fun if he leaned back and enjoyed it, stopped trying to swim upstream against the current, especially since the birth of his son, David. He wanted to experience the joy of seeing the world through a child's eyes, something he'd missed with Caroline and didn't want to miss a single second of this time around.

Tom had found his purpose in love, having always had so much of it in his heart: for his family, for life, for finding the humour in a moment. His thick brown hair framed a face that was vivacious and alert despite his eyes occasionally revealing a bit of loss for those whom he'd loved and had leaned on so much and whose souls were a part of him despite their being gone from this earth. Mary made him realize how precious life was, and his wife never failed to inspire him with her tenacity and solidness.

And Ben, his curls as thick as ever, his eyes still round and bright, had gone through innocence and into experience. Now, sobered by his past frailties and strengthened by the things that rooted him to the earth: his love of nature, his children, and his wife who had stuck through the hard times steadfast as a rock herself, he liked to think of the line, "I have promises to keep," from Robert Frost, a poet he'd come to see as a kind of soul mate and companion.

Without a word, Joe suddenly leapt up and climbed the stairs to the attic. There was thumping and scraping for a moment, then he came back down with two boxes in his arms, returning for more. "There's stacks more, absolute stacks," said Joe with pride and incredulity. "When did she write so much?"

He placed the boxes in the centre of the sunroom, and the boys, all men now, sat around them as if they were at a campfire, letting them warm them with their sheer volume, all their potential between their pages.

Delores poured tea for everyone then quietly excused herself so the men could spend some time alone. "You know, I think Mother had it right," said Joe. "Here we are, living our lives, going through the days, not thinking about them, just making mistakes, having little successes, children, wives, homes, moving, working..." he paused. "But until you slow down and reflect on any of it, it doesn't mean anything, does it?"

They were silent a moment. Then Ben said, "She didn't just learn to write; she learned to live. Look at this," he said, riffling through the top box of journals. "And this is only the first box." He looked at them stacked atop each other. "She wrote all of this to make sure it was real, to make it part of the record of history. Mother's life was extraordinary to us, but think of all the stories we didn't hear, that she held secret all these years. They'll end with her. But," he smiled softly, "I'd bet that in her letters and stories, for anyone who reads them, he feels a part of them. They become part of that history. They carry her legacy for her."

"I suppose that was her point, wasn't it," said Tom. He looked at the others, and they looked at him, each seeing the other as he had always been and as he had become, a reality made up of that history. "I suppose that was exactly the point." He smiled.